W9-BJZ-108

THE CROSS COUNTRY RUNNER

COLLECTED SHORT STORIES & NOVELLAS   VOLUME 3

BY ANDRE DUBUS

The Lieutenant

Separate Flights

Adultery & Other Choices

Finding a Girl in America

The Times Are Never So Bad

Voices from the Moon

The Last Worthless Evening

Selected Stories

Broken Vessels

Dancing After Hours

Meditations from a Moveable Chair

We Don't Live Here Anymore

The Winter Father

CHARLESTON COUNTY LIBRARY

ANDRE DUBUS

The Cross Country Runner

COLLECTED SHORT STORIES & NOVELLAS   VOLUME 3

Introduction by TOBIAS WOLFF

Series Editor JOSHUA BODWELL

DAVID R. GODINE · *Publisher*

Boston

This edition published in 2018 by
DAVID R. GODINE · *Publisher*
Post Office Box 450
Jaffrey, New Hampshire 03452
www.godine.com

The Last Worthless Evening Copyright © 1986 by Andre Dubus
Voices from the Moon Copyright © 1984 by Andre Dubus
Introduction Copyright © 2018 by Tobias Wolff
Editor's Note & Acknowledgements Copyright © 2018 by Joshua Bodwell

All rights reserved. No part of this book may be used or reproduced
in any manner whatsoever without written permission from the publisher,
except in the case of brief excerpts embodied in critical articles and reviews.
For information contact Permissions, David R. Godine, Publisher,
Fifteen Court Square, Boston, Massachusetts 02108

LIBRARY OF CONGRESS CATALOGING-IN-PUBLICATION DATA

Names: Dubus, Andre, 1936–1999 author. | Bodwell, Joshua editor.
Title: Collected short stories and novellas / Andre Dubus ;
edited by Joshua Bodwell.
Description: Jaffrey, New Hampshire : David R. Godine, Publisher, 2018. |
Includes bibliographical references and index.
Identifiers: LCCN 2018003815| ISBN 9781567926279 (v. 1 : softcover :
alk. paper) | ISBN 9781567926170 (v. 2 : softcover : alk. paper)
Classification: LCC PS3554.U265 A6 2018 | DDC 813/.54—dc23
LC record available at https://lccn.loc.gov/2018003815

ACKNOWLEDGMENTS

The Last Worthless Evening
"Deaths at Sea" first appeared in *Quarterly West*; "After the Game" in *Fiction
Network*; "Dressed Like Summer Leaves" in *The Sewanee Review*; "Land
Where My Fathers Died" in *Antaeus* and as a limited edition published by
Palaemon Press; "Molly" in *Crazyhorse* ; and "Rose" in *Ploughshares*. Dubus
extended his gratitude to the National Endowment of the Arts and the Creative
Writing Program and the Department of English at the University of Alabama.

Uncollected Stories
"The Cross Country Runner" first published in *Midwestern University Quarterly*;
"Love is the Sky" in *Midwestern University Quarterly*; "The Blackberry Patch"
in *Southern Writing in the Sixties, Fiction,* John William Corrington and Miller
Williams, eds. (Louisiana State University Press); "Madeline Sheppard" in
Midwestern University Quarterly; "They Now Live in Texas" in *Indiana Review*;
"The Curse" in *Playboy*; "Riding North" in *Oxford Magazine*; "Corporal Lewis"
in *Epoch*; and "Sisters" in *Book Magazine*.
Printed in Canada

DEDICATED TO ANDRE'S CHILDREN

Suzanne, 16 August 1958

Andre, 11 September 1959

Jeb, 29 November 1960

Nicole, 3 February 1963

Cadence, 11 June 1982

Madeleine, 10 January 1987

CONTENTS

Writers and Friends by Tobias Wolff   ix

VOICES FROM THE MOON   1

THE LAST WORTHLESS EVENING

Deaths at Sea   91

After the Game   148

Dressed Like Summer Leaves   156

Land Where My Fathers Died   170

Molly   211

Rose   276

PREVIOUSLY UNCOLLECTED STORIES
BY ANDRE DUBUS

The Cross Country Runner   319

Love is the Sky   336

The Blackberry Patch   355

Madeline Sheppard   363

They Now Live in Texas   379

The Curse   384

Riding North   391

Corporal Lewis   428

Sisters   430

Editor's Note & Acknowledgments   455

Author's Biography   467

WRITERS AND FRIENDS

TOBIAS WOLFF

I FIRST MET Andre Dubus in 1981, at a dinner in the home of his publisher and friend David Godine. Andre had written me some months earlier to say he'd liked a story of mine and that he hoped we could get together sometime. I had been reading his stories for years, and teaching them in my classes, as did writer friends of mine, so I was grateful to David when he arranged this dinner, grateful and anxious in a puppyish sort of way. Andre was the last to arrive. I was having a drink with the other guests when he made his entrance—an expression I use deliberately, because, as I came to learn, that man could never simply walk into a room, he had to take it by storm. His raucous voice preceded him like a fanfare, there was some crashing about in the hallway, then he came bustling in, laughing, loud, teeth flashing in his beard, short and bullish in his dense, muscular physicality, advancing directly on us as if to plunge a horn between our ribs.

Advancing on me, I should say. He must have recognized my face from the photo on my book, because he came straight up to me and grabbed my ears and pulled my face down to his and gave me a smacking wet kiss on the lips. Then he stepped back and burst out laughing at my evident shock and horror.

It wasn't the introduction I'd imagined, but it certainly worked as an ice-breaker. He had, among his other gifts, a talent for keeping me off-balance, a talent he honed to perfection through the nearly two decades of the close friendship that followed this peculiar beginning.

Of our friendship I will speak more later. But I should say again that I had been his attentive reader long before I met Andre. I'd first encountered his work in a back issue of *Plough-shares*, a story called "Corporal of Artillery." Having spent four years in the military, I was struck by his faithful rendering of that life, and the way the story identified the potential for significant experience in peacetime rather than implying, as most fiction with a military setting does, that important things happen to men only when they are at war.

From that story I moved on to his collection *Adultery & Other Choices,* of which "Corporal of Artillery" is a part, and was struck by the emotional honesty of Dubus's voice, its seriousness, richness, intimacy, and—over a range of subjects, through different characters and settings—his signature braiding of moral concern with compassion for those caught in spiritually challenging situations.

My own first brush with his fiction was to some degree misleading—Dubus is not a "military" writer, important as that experience, that subject, was to him. A relatively small part of his work concerns the uniformed life, and though we can sense his keen interest and sometime affection for a community at least nominally devoted to values of brotherhood, loyalty, and courage, his work is also critical of that life, dealing as it does with the evil of men being frozen in a vision of manhood that discourages tenderness, enthusiasm, the admission of need for encouragement and love—that teaches them to spurn the warmest springs of their humanity.

We see that complex, illusionless sense of the limitations of military life in the first short story of this volume, "Deaths at Sea." Here the brotherhood of the uniform is exposed as an ideal always subject to conditions, in this case the condition of race. Several sailors are waiting on a pier in Japan for a launch to return them to their ship after a night on the town. A white sailor calls a black sailor the inevitable incendiary name; they fight, tumble into the water, and the white sailor drowns. Left there, we would have a familiar story of backward, working class resentments finding their usual scapegoat, but in fact we see the same divisive conditions played out among the officers on board the ship, where a white fighter pilot from Georgia is happy to lecture a young black officer about the liberal, Northern misunderstanding of ante-bellum Southern culture, especially the pernicious myth that slaves were mistreated: "Why in hell would a man whip or starve the people that kept him rich? Hell, those old boys sent their sons to the War Between the States, but not their slaves. No sir. The slave was a valuable piece of *prop*erty. You see what I mean?"

The black officer sees exactly what he means. He has seen it all his life, and now must confront the fact that he will continue to see it and live with it in this community, for all its lofty professions of equality in the service of country. The story is further complicated by the reactions of the white narrator, himself a young Southern officer and the roommate of the black officer, to the challenges created by the recent integration of this once monolithically white officer corps. He strives to be open-minded and just in his actions, but cannot shake the discomfort he feels in proximity to his roommate, which expresses itself in an effortful, at times mawkish attempt to offer friendship, and to show his right-mindedness and freedom from prejudice. In other words, he exerts himself in ways he would not think to do with a white roommate, and we see in his striving, awkward, but good-willed attempts at solidarity the narrator's guilt-tinged struggle with his own conditioning, the history and culture that has shaped him. This gives the man, and the story, a prophetic authenticity. For all our egalitarian dreams, as individuals and as a society, we are fated always to contend with the demons of our history. Contend we must, and contend we will, but it has not become easier, and probably will never be easier, than it is for this narrator and his roommate.

Despite its military setting and implicit social commentary, "Deaths at Sea" is essentially a personal story, in the sense that it locates the real drama of the narrative not in the attempts of its protagonist to overcome some external threat or evil, like racism, but in his own internal struggles, his attempts to overcome himself. We see that pattern throughout Dubus's work, and markedly in the stories found here. In "Love is the Sky," Curtis Boudreaux is invited by his college-student son Jack to a football game on Dad's Day. Curtis drives to the campus and discovers that his son is living not with a girl, as he happily imagined, but with a man. Jack is gay, and finally, under pressure, reveals this to his father. Nothing in Curtis's life has prepared him for this. His vision of being father to a son was entirely shaped by the conventions of his society, and Boudreaux family tradition: fathers and sons hunt and fish together; work together, with the son to inherit the firm; sons marry and give grandchildren—preferably grandsons—to their fathers, and thus the cycle is renewed. They do not love and cohabit with other men.

Curtis's shock at this revelation causes him to renounce his son. He tells Jack not to come home again. From this dismal scene he goes on to the football game with a doctor friend of his, but he is not at peace with himself. He cannot make sense of what has happened, and what he has done. He knows he was wrong, and that he must make amends, but he doesn't know how. He is lost, and overwhelmed by a sense of his own mortality. Here we see a man who with some moral shorthand might be cartooned as a brutish homophobe, a mere bigot, but even as we are made witness to his earlier hopes for his son, the cultural and familial limitations he has inherited and unreflectively assumed, we see him begin to resist those bonds, and to imagine scenes of reconciliation and acceptance. But he cannot imagine them all the way through. He doesn't know how. Though he wants to love his son without conditions, knows he should love him without conditions, he is unable to break through the hard shell his personal and cultural history have formed around him. The story does not allow us to despise him. Finally, he is a touching and even tragic figure, a decent, well-meaning man defeated by assumptions "natural" to his place and time and tribe, that have taken deep root in his spirit without his ever being aware of their malignance.

Dubus's recognition of the disabling power of inherited convictions and social constraints does not necessarily doom his people to play tragic roles. Indeed, it also offers them the possibility of braving social cost and asserting their freedom—as in his masterful novella "Voices from the Moon"—and even acting heroically, as in his story "Rose."

Rose is married to a man she once "hoped to love," a construction worker who has turned hard and bitter with disappointment and drink. He begins to abuse their three young children, two girls and a boy, at first with shouts and hisses, then with his large hands. The boy, only five, suffers particularly from his father's moods. Rose does not want to irritate him further by protesting or arguing. She tries to placate him, to get her family through these moments, for the sake of her marriage and what she understands to be her duty to her husband. She is Catholic, and lazily, unreflectively assumes that she is somehow doing what is expected of her by playing the part of a loyal wife and tolerating this increasingly brutal, dangerous situation. Thus, she becomes a partner to evil, of the worst kind—a silent partner.

But finally her husband goes too far, and breaks through Rose's passivity and fear. In rousing herself at last, and acting from the fierce, protective love she feels for her children, she discovers that she is not the meek, powerless creature she has imagined herself to be, and allowed herself to be. She rises to meet the evil in her home, and heroically overcomes it, though tardily, and not without penalty.

"Voices from the Moon" is my favorite of all Andre Dubus's stories and novellas. It concerns itself unabashedly and unsentimentally with love—the love of parents for their children, of men for women and women for women, of a boy's love for God, and a teenage girl's love for cigarettes. The story is too rich to paraphrase, but in brief, a divorced man has fallen in

love with his son's ex-wife, and she with him. They mean to
live together. The family is shaken to its roots by the apparent
betrayals involved, and not least by the social impropriety of
such an arrangement—its radical flouting of convention. Yet
as the story proceeds we see its people react not with the sort
of virtuous outrage we might expect, but with hard-won understanding, generosity, forgiveness, and love. In essence, the
family declares its independence from submissive concern or
embarrassment about how things might look to others, finding freedom in their refusal to let their lives be shaped by the
expectations and decorums of social custom. Sensational as
the premise of the story may be—it was inspired by a newspaper
article Dubus happened upon—he illuminates his people's
lives not by heating up the drama inherent in their situation,
but by allowing each of them quiet, ordinary moments in
which to reveal themselves, to profound, extraordinary effect.
It is altogether Dubus's strangest, most moving, beautiful
piece of work.

Reading his stories again in anticipation of this celebratory
reissue, I find myself missing Andre acutely. I miss his growly
voice. I miss his constant needling, conducted over the phone
when he couldn't do it in person. Though I had told him truly
and repeatedly that my service in Vietnam had not been
heroic or even competent, he insisted on calling me "Silent
Death," affecting to believe that my disavowals were mere
self-deprecation, and a sort of proof that I had single-hand-
edly waged terrible war against the enemy.

I miss the pleasures our families shared—angling for blue-
fish off the coast, watching a movie, listening to Sinatra, sending out for pizza, talking about books we loved, telling stories,
always telling stories. My young sons, loving his swagger and
bluster, called him "Yosemite Sam."

I miss the meetings of a support group Andre and I
founded, Sissies Anonymous. We were the core members and
usually the only members in attendance, though we welcomed
drop-ins. S.A. was open to former Marines, SEALS, paratroop-
ers like me, and all those fellows we knew who had chosen

tough military duty or manly civilian work to prove they weren't sissies, though in their hearts they knew they were, yes, and always would be. We gave tearful testimonials of recovery and backsliding, though neither of us could sustain recovery long enough to earn a chip—he would cry at the first words of a grandchild, I would cry at the death of an animal in a movie. Hopeless.

How grateful I am for those days, that friendship, the stories Andre told, the stories he wrote. Well, here they are, some of the very best, a feast. Dig in.

VOICES FROM THE MOON

to my sisters, Kathryn and Beth

A Good Excuse

It is snowing again.
A fine snow is sifting
Over the broken fields.

There is nothing more
That you can do.
You need not think

Again of moonlight
Or of the several voices
Which have called to you

Like voices from the moon.
Where would they have you go
That is not the same

Blank field? No, there is
Nothing left for you
But to stand here

Full of your own silence
Which is itself a whiteness
And all the light you need.

Michael van Walleghen

1

IT'S DIVORCE THAT DID IT, his father had said last night. Those were the first words Richie Stowe remembered when he woke in the summer morning, ten minutes before the six-forty-five that his clock-radio was set for; but the words did not come to him as in memory, as something spoken even in the past of one night, but like other words that so often, in his twelve years, had seemed to wait above his sleeping face so that when he first opened his eyes he would see them like a banner predicting his day: *Today is the math test*; *Howie is going to get you after school.... It's divorce that did it*, and he turned off the switch so the radio wouldn't start, and lay in the breeze of the oscillating fan, a lean suntanned boy in under-pants, neither tall nor short, and felt the opening of wounds he had believed were healed, felt again the deep and helpless sorrow, and the anger too because he was twelve and too young for it and had done nothing at all to cause it.

Then he got up, dressed in jeans and tee shirt and running shoes, went to his bathroom where a poster of Jim Rice hung behind the toilet, gazed at it while he urinated, studying the strong thighs and arms (in the poster Rice had swung his bat, and was looking up and toward left field), and Richie saw again that moment when Rice had broken his bat without hitting the ball: had checked his swing, and the bat had continued its forward motion, flown out toward first base, leaving

5

Rice holding the handle. This was on television, and Richie had not believed what he had seen until he saw it again, the replay in slow motion.

His bicycle was in his room. He pushed it down the hall, at whose end, opposite his room, was the closed door leading to his father's bathroom and bedroom. He went out the front door and off the slab of concrete in front of it, mounted, and rode down the blacktop street under a long arch of the green branches of trees. As he pedaled and shifted gears he prayed for his anger to leave him, and for his brother Larry, and Brenda, and his father, but as he prayed he saw them: Larry and Brenda when they were married, sitting at the kitchen table with him and his father, Brenda's dark skin darker still from summer, her black hair separating at her shoulders, so that some of it rested on the bare flesh above her breasts. The men were watching her: slender and graceful Larry, who acted and danced, his taut face of angles and edges at the jaw and cheekbones, and a point at the nose; and Richie's father, with Larry's body twenty-two years older, wiry and quick, the face not rounded but softened over the bones.

Then he was at the church, and he locked his bicycle to a utility pole in front of it and went in, early for the seven o'clock Mass, genuflected then kneeled in an empty pew, and gazed at the crucifix, at the suffering head of Christ, but could not stop seeing what he had not seen last night but imagined as he lay in bed while his father and Larry sat and stood and paced on his ceiling, the floor of the living room. He shut his eyes, saw Larry's blanched face looking at his father, and saying *Marry her? Marry her?* and saw his father and Brenda naked in her bed in the apartment she had lived in since the divorce, saw them as he had seen lovemaking in movies, his father on top and Brenda's dark face, her moans, her cries, seeming more in pain than pleasure. As two altar boys and young Father Oberti entered from the left of the altar, Richie stood, praying Please Jesus Christ Our Lord help me, then said to Him: It will be very hard to be a Catholic in our house.

Knowing it would be hard not only in the today and

tomorrow of twelve years old, but even harder as he grew older and had to face the temptations that everyone in the family had succumbed to. Even his mother, living a bicycle ride away in her apartment in Amesbury. Though he had never seen her with a man since his father, or heard her mention the name of one. Everyone in the family living in apartments now: his mother, Larry, Brenda, his sister Carol, older than Larry by a year, in her apartment in Boston, never married so not divorced, but at twenty-six had three times broken up with or lost men who lived with her. So only he and his father lived in the large house that to him was three stories, though his father said it was a split-level, the bedrooms and bathrooms on the first floor, then up a short flight of five steps to the kitchen and dining room and the west sundeck, up five more to the undivided one long room they used as two: at one end his father's den with a desk, and at the other the living room with the television; outside that long room, past the glass door, was the east sundeck where they kept the hammock and lawn chairs and grill. Now Brenda would move in, and he must keep receiving the Eucharist daily, must move alone and with the strength of the saints through his high school years, past girls, toward the seminary. Hard enough to stay a Catholic, he prayed; even harder to be a good enough one to be a priest.

He was in bed and near sleep last night when he heard the front door open and knew it was Larry, because he had a key still, then he listened to footsteps: Larry's going up to the kitchen, his father's overhead, coming from the right, from the den. Richie flung back the top sheet, but did not move his feet to the floor. He was sleepy, already it was past ten o'clock, and five times this summer he had turned off the radio when it woke him, gone back to sleep and missed the weekday Mass and waked at nine or later, a failure for the day that had only begun. He pulled the sheet over his chest, settled into the pillow, and listened to their voices in the kitchen, the popping open of beer cans, and their going upstairs to the living room over his bed. He again pushed the sheet away and this time got up; sleepy or no, he would at least go see him, touch him, at least that. He opened his door and was going up the short flight to the kitchen when he heard Larry: "I don't be*lieve* this."

Richie stood, his hand on the flat banister. His father's voice was low, and neither angry nor sad, but tired: "It's divorce that did it."

"Whose?"

"Yours. Mine. Fucking divorce. You think I chose her?"

"What am I supposed to think?"

"It just happened. It always just happens."

"Beautiful. What happened to will?"

"Don't talk to me about will. Did you will your marriage to end? Did your mother and me? Will is for those bullshit guys to write books about. Out here it's—"

"—Survival of the quickest, right. Woops, sorry son, out of the way, boy, I'm grabbing your ex-wife."

"Out here it's balls and hanging on. I need her, Larry."

Richie imagined them, facing each other in the room, in the blown air from the window fan, as he had seen them all his life, facing each other in quarrels, their arms bent at their sides, fists clenched, save when they gestured and their arms came up with open hands; they never struck the blow that, always, they seemed prepared for; not even his father, when Larry was a boy. Even as Richie stood in dread on the stairs, his fingers and palm pressing down on the banister as if to achieve even more silence from his rigid body, he knew there would be no hitting tonight. His father was not like any other father he knew: at forty-seven, he was still quick of temper, and fought in bars. Yet he had never struck anyone in the family, not even a spanking: *for your kids,* he said, *the tongue is plenty.* Richie backed down the stairs, turned and crept into his room, and softly closed the door.

He stood beneath them and listened for a while, then lay in bed and heard the rest of what came to him through his ceiling when their voices rose, less in anger, it seemed, than in excitement, and his heart beat with it too, and in that beat he recognized another feeling that usually he associated with temptation, with sin, with turning away from Christ: something in him that was aroused, that took pleasure in what he knew, and knew with sadness, to be yet another end of their family.

He prayed against it, incantations of *Lord, have mercy*, as he prayed now in Mass to overcome his anger, his sorrowful loss, and to both endure and help his family. Father Oberti was approaching the Consecration and Richie waited for the miracle, then watched it, nearly breathless, and prayed My Lord and my God to the white Host elevated in Father Oberti's hands, and softly struck his breast. Beneath the Host, Father Oberti's face was upturned and transformed. It was a look Richie noticed only on young priests, and only when they consecrated the bread and wine. In movies he had seen faces like it, men or women gazing at a lover, their lips and eyes seeming near both tears and a murmur of love, but they only resembled what he saw in Father Oberti's face, and were not at all the same. Now Father Oberti lifted the chalice and Richie imagined being inside of him, feeling what he felt as the wine he held became the Blood of Christ. My Lord and my God, Richie prayed, striking his breast, immersing himself in the longing he felt there in his heart: a longing to consume Christ, to be consumed through Him into the priesthood, to stand some morning purified and adoring in white vestments, and to watch his hands holding bread, then God. His eyes followed the descent of the chalice.

From there the Mass moved quickly forward, and he was able to concentrate on it, to keep memory and imagination from returning to last night and tomorrow, or at least from distracting him. Images of his father and Larry and Brenda collided with his prayers, but they did not penetrate him as they had before the Consecration. Even when he was a boy of seven and eight, nothing distracted him from the Consecration and the time afterward, until the Mass ended, and he had believed he was better than the other children. Now, at twelve, he knew he had received a gift, with his First Communion or even before, and that he had done nothing to earn it, and he must be ever grateful and humble about it, or risk losing it.

He rose to approach the altar. With clasped hands resting on his stomach, his head bowed, he walked up the aisle behind three white-haired old women. When it was his turn, he stepped to Father Oberti at the head of the aisle, turned his left palm up, with his right under it, as Father Oberti took a Host from the chalice, raised it, said *Body of Christ*, and Richie said *Amen*. Father Oberti placed the Host on his palm. He looked at it as he turned to go down the aisle. Then with his right thumb and forefinger he put it in his mouth, let it rest on his tongue, then softly chewed as he walked to the pew. He felt that he embraced the universe, and was in the arms of God.

When the Mass ended he kneeled until everyone had left the church. Then he went up to the altar, genuflected, looked up at Christ on the cross, and went around the altar and into the sacristy. The altar boys were leaving, and Father Oberti was in his white shirt and black pants.

"Richie."

"Can I talk to you, Father?"

They watched the altar boys go out the door, onto the lawn.

"What is it?"

"My father and Brenda. My brother's ex-wife? They're getting married."

"Oh my. Oh my, Richie, you poor boy."

Father Oberti sat in a chair and motioned to another, but Richie stood, his eyes moving about the room, sometimes settling on Father Oberti's, but then he nearly cried, so he looked again at walls and windows and floor, telling it as he both heard and imagined last night.

"And, see, Father, the whole family is living outside the Church. In sin. And now Dad and Brenda will be in the house."

"Don't think of it as sin."

He looked at Father Oberti.

"It's even against the law," Richie said. "Massachusetts

law. They're going to get married in another state, but Dad's talking to somebody in the—legislature?"

"That's right."

"To try to change the law."

"It's probably a very old law, Richie." Father Oberti did not look shocked, or even surprised, but calm and gentle. "The Church had them too. It was to prevent murder, or the temptation to it."

"Murder?"

"Sure. So that hundreds of years ago your father wouldn't be tempted to kill Larry. To get his wife, and all her land and so forth. It's just an old law, Richie. Don't think of your father and Brenda as sin."

"I'm afraid I'll lose my faith." Heat rose to his face, tears to his eyes, and he looked at the dark blue carpet and Father Oberti's shining black shoes.

"No. This should strengthen it. You must live like the Lord, with His kindness. Don't think of them as sinful. Don't just think of sex. People don't marry for that. Think of love. They are two people who love each other, and as painful as it is for others, and even if it *is* wrong, it's still love, and that is always near the grace of God. Has he been a bad father?"

Richie shook his head.

"Look at me. Don't mind crying. I'm not scolding you."

He wiped away his tears and raised his face and looked into Father Oberti's brown eyes.

"It is very hard to live like Christ. For most of us, it's impossible. The best we can do is try. And two of the hardest virtues for a Christian are forgiveness and compassion. Not judging people. But they are essential parts of love." His hands rose from his lap, and he clasped them in front of his chest, the fingers squeezing. "We can't love without those two. And the message of Christ is love. For everyone. Certainly you will love your father. And his wife. Try to imagine what they feel like, how they comfort each other, how much they love each other, to risk so much to be together. It's not evil. It may be weak, or less strong than the Church wants people to be; than *you* want people to be. And of course you're right. It would be far better if they had fought their love before it grew. But there are much worse things than loving. Much worse, Richie. Be kind, and pray for them, and I will too. I'll pray for you too. And I hope you'll pray for me. People don't think of priests as sinners. Or if they do, they think of sex or drinking. That's very simple-minded. There are sins that are far more complicated, that a priest can commit: pride, neglect, others. He can be guilty of these while ministering sacraments, saying the Mass." His hands parted, reached out, and took Richie's shoulders. "You'll love your father and his wife, and you'll grow up to be a good priest. If it's what you want, and if it's God's will. Don't leave God out of this. Your father and the young lady are in His hands, not yours. You will have some embarrassment. Even some pain. What is that, for a strong boy like you? A devout boy, a daily communicant."

His right hand left Richie's shoulder, and he moved it in a cross between them, then placed his palm on Richie's forehead.

"Thank you, Father."

"We can keep talking."

"No. Thank you, Father."

Father Oberti stood and held out his hand, and Richie shook it.

"I'll see you tomorrow," Father Oberti said.

"Yes."

"Or sooner, if you want."

"No. Tomorrow."

"Good. Go play baseball, and live your life."

Richie lifted his hand in a wave, then turned and left the sacristy, entered the church near the altar, genuflected, looked up at Christ, and went down the aisle. At the door he turned back to the altar, looked at Christ on the cross, then pushed open the heavy brown wooden door, and stepped into warm sunlight and cool air.

On the street near his house, in the shadows under the

arch of maples, he saw Melissa Donnelly and her golden retriever. She was two blocks ahead, walking away from him in the middle of the empty street. He pedaled harder three times before he was aware of it, then he slowed but did not touch the brake, and the bicycle kept its quiet speed on the blacktop. Melissa was wearing faded cut-off jeans and sandals, and a blue denim shirt with its sleeves rolled up to her elbows. The dog was named Conroy, and was not on a leash; he zig-zagged, nose to ground, in the grass beside the street. When Richie was close, he braked and Melissa looked over her shoulder, then smiled and said: Richie. He said hi and stopped, and walked the bicycle beside her. She was thirteen, three months older than Richie, and he liked her green eyes. Her hair was curls of very light brown, and hung above her shoulders. She wore lipstick.

"Where you going?" she said.

"Home. You walking Conroy?"

"To the field. So I can smoke."

"How did he get his name?"

"He's named for an old friend of my dad's. From the war."

"Which one?"

"Korea."

"Did he die?"

"No. My dad just never saw him again."

Her shirttails were knotted above her waist, showing a suntanned oblong of her stomach. Her legs were smooth and brown. He was looking past the handlebar at her sandaled feet, when the blacktop ended at a weed-grown, deeply rutted trail beside a stand of trees. Beyond the trees was the athletic field.

"Come on," she said, and he followed her through the trees, while Conroy darted ahead and onto the field. On open ground at the edge of the trees they stopped, and Richie stood his bicycle with its stand. Melissa leaned against an oak, looked over each shoulder, then drew a pack of Marlboros from between her breasts and offered it to him. He shook his head.

"Afraid of cancer?"

"I just don't want to smoke."

She shrugged, and he watched her eyes and the cigarette in the middle of her lips as she took a lighter from her pocket. She inhaled and blew smoke and said: "Ah. First since last night."

He imagined her, while he lay in bed before Larry came, or maybe as he stood on the steps or later as he listened in his room, saw her out here under the stars, the glow of her cigarette in the shadows of these trees as Conroy ran in the field.

"Did you walk him last night?"

"Yeah. You'd think they'd catch on. They used to have to tell me to, and now I'm always walking the dog."

"What time were you out here?"

"About ten, I guess. Why?"

"I was wondering what I was doing then."

"You should have been out here. It was beautiful, really. Cool and quiet, and all the stars."

She half-turned toward him. If he moved a hand outward, it would touch her. He folded his arms, then leaned with his side against the tree. He was so close to her now that he could only see her face and throat and shoulders, unless he moved his eyes.

"Where have you been?" she said.

He said to her eyes: "I went to Mass." Then he said to her mouth: "I go every day."

"You do? Why?"

"I want to be a priest."

"Wow."

"It's not just that. I'd go even if I didn't want to be one. Do you receive on Sundays?"

"On Sundays, sure."

"So you believe in it. So do I. That's why I go. Because it's too big not to."

"Too big?"

"You believe it's God? The bread and wine?"

"Yes."

"That's what I mean. It's God, so how can I stay home? When He's there every day."

"I never thought of it like that." The cigarette rose into his vision, and she turned in profile to draw from it. "You feel like you have to go?"

"No. I like it. I love it. It's better than anything. The feeling. Do you think I'm dumb?"

"No. I wish I felt that way."

"Why?"

She shrugged. "The things I do, everybody does them."

He unfolded his arms, and touched her cheek.

"You're so pretty," he said.

"So are you."

His face warmed. "Pretty?"

"Well. You know. Good-looking."

She looked out at the field, finished the cigarette, then called Conroy. He was at the other side of it, near the woods where Richie cross-country skied. Conroy stood still and looked at Melissa's voice. Then he ran toward it.

"Are you going to play softball this morning?" she said.

"Probably. Are you?"

"I don't know."

Conroy stopped on the infield of the softball diamond, sniffed the earth, then moved, with his nose down, to short right field. He straightened, circled three times in the same spot, as though he were drilling himself into it, then squatted, with his four paws close to each other, his tail curled upward, and shat. He cocked his head and watched them, and Melissa said: "Remember that, if you play right field. Are you in a hurry to get home?"

"Not me."

"I'll have another cigarette."

She withdrew her cigarettes from her blouse, and he watched her suntanned hand going down between her breasts, watched as she returned the pack, and imagined her small white breasts, and the brown from the sun ending just above and below them.

"Aren't you playing softball?" he said.

"Late. I have to do housework first."

"Last night—"

When he stopped, she had been frowning about house-work, but her face softened and she looked at his eyes, and said: "What?"

"Nothing."

"What's wrong?"

"Maybe I'll tell you sometime."

"Tell me."

"Sometime."

"Promise?"

"Yes. I just wish I had been here."

"Was that it?"

"No."

"You'll tell me?"

"Yes."

He unfolded his arms, lowered them to his sides, where they made him feel as though he were stiffly posing for a pic-ture. Slowly he let them rise, let each hand rest on her shoul-ders, then move down and lightly hold her biceps. She watched him. Then he swallowed and patted her lean hard arms, and turned away from her, letting his hands slide down to her elbows and away, and he folded his arms on his breast and looked out at the field. Conroy was lying down, chewing a short piece of a branch.

"You've never smoked?" she said.

"No."

"Here. Try."

He looked at her, and she held her cigarette to his lips; he drew on it and inhaled bitter heat and waited to cough as he quickly blew out the smoke, but he did not. Then a dizzying nausea moved through him, and was gone. He shook his head.

"Did you get a kick?"

"Too much of one."

"You have to get used to it. Want another?"

"Woo. Not today."

She smiled at him and ground out the cigarette with her foot, and he watched her toes arch in the sandal. She called

Conroy. He came with his head high, holding the stick in his jaws, and Richie walked his bicycle behind Melissa, into the trees, and onto the road. As they walked, the bicycle was between them, and she rested a hand on the seat. In front of his house he stopped.

"So maybe I'll see you later," he said.

"Yes. Maybe tonight too. Father Stowe."

His cheeks were warm again, but he was smiling.

"I feel like a bad girl."

"Why?"

"I gave you your first drag on a cigarette." Then she leaned over the bicycle and with closed lips quickly kissed his mouth, that was open, his lips stilled by surprise, by fear, by excitement. She walked down the road, calling for Conroy, and a block away the dog turned and sprinted toward her, ears back, the stick in his jaws. Richie stood breathing her scents of smoke and lipstick and something else sweet—a cologne or cosmetic—or perhaps he only smelled memory, for it did not fade from the air. He watched her stoop to pet Conroy and nuzzle his ear, then straighten and walk with him, on the side of the road, in the shade of the arching trees.

When she turned into her lawn, he pushed his bicycle up the walk and onto the concrete slab at the front door. He crouched to lock the rear wheel and was very hungry and hoped his father was making pancakes.

2

He was. Greg Stowe had waked when he heard the front door shut behind Richie, and now Richie was nearly an hour late and Greg stood on the narrow east sundeck, which they rarely used because it was shaded by maples and pines and was sunlit only in the middle of the day. But he drank coffee there in the morning, all during the warm months, and often in the colder ones too, in late fall and winter, on windless sunny mornings when the temperature was over twenty. And at night when he knew or believed he was not the same man he was in the morning, he drank beer out there long past midnight, because it was darker, the trees that blocked the sun forming a good black wall between him and the streetlights nearly a hundred yards behind the house. He had bought both lots, so that no one could ever build behind him, and his lawn would always end at streets, not another man's property, and he had left the trees on the back lot, so he had a small woods. Children played there, and teenagers hid and left behind them beer cans and bottles and cigarette butts. But the teenagers always gathered at the same spot, and their trash was contained. He thought it was funny that teenagers, except when they were in a car, did not seem comfortable unless they were stationary in a familiar spot, like an old person, or a dog, in a house.

The front sundeck was good for drinking with friends before dinner, but there was a streetlight, and the lights of other houses, and he could not feel alone there. He liked drinking alone in a place so dark he had to remember the color of his clothes, or wait until his eyes adjusted to discern at least their hue. On those nights, and last night was one of them, time stopped, while his sense of place expanded, so there were moments when the sudden awareness of the dial of his wrist-watch, and of where he actually stood, beer in hand, came to him with the startling sense of being wakened by an alarm clock. In the morning, drinking coffee and standing where he had stood the night before, he simply planned his day.

Not this morning, though, for today was a continuation of last night with Larry, interrupted only by his grieving beer-drinking on the deck and a short sleep, and it would resume with Richie as soon as he came home, and end with Carol. So his day was not only already prepared for him, like a road he had to follow (or, more accurately, he thought, an obstacle course), but in truth it could not be planned, for he had no idea—or too many of them—of how, and even when, it would be finished. Nor did he know what he meant by *finished*. What he hoped for was Carol and Larry and Richie and Brenda sitting in his kitchen while he cooked.

But he knew he had as much hope for that as for the traveling he did on the deck at night; he called them his Michelob voyages. He did not have the money for all of them, but he had the money for any one of them, even each of them in turn, if he spaced them by ten or so months and lived out a normal life. He would like to buy a boat with galley and sleeping quarters, learn to repair and maintain it, to navigate, and then go on the Intracoastal Waterway, the fifteen hundred and fifty miles from Boston to Florida Bay, then the eleven hundred and sixteen to Brownsville, Texas. His image was of Brenda on the boat, and maybe Richie, and himself on the bridge, simply steering and looking at America. But he did not want to do it as a vacation, something you had to come home from, and at a certain time. Take a year off, Brenda said.

But he could not. He was the sole owner of two ice cream stores; fifteen years ago he had bought them with a partner, and seven years ago he had bought out the partner, who retired and went to Florida and, according to postcards, did nothing but fish. These stores, one of them in an inland town and open all year, with a soda fountain and sandwiches too, and one at Seabrook Beach in New Hampshire, open from Memorial Day weekend till Labor Day, sold homemade ice cream, or as close to it as people could get without doing the work to make it in their own kitchens. Greg had learned that Russians and Americans ate more ice cream than the people of any other countries in the world, and some nights on the deck he amused himself by thinking about opening a store on the Black Sea, at Odessa or Sevastopol.

But he could not leave for a year, or even half of one, not for the Intracoastal Waterway or for any other place—Kenya, Morocco, Greece, Italy, Spain, France, places where he wanted to walk and look, to eat and drink what the natives did— because as well as owning his stores he ran them too. It was something his partner had not had the heart, the drive, to do; and that was Greg's reason for borrowing to buy him out, figuring finally that debt and being alone responsible for everything was better than trying week after week to joke with, tease, and implore a man in an effort to get him to work; when all the time, although Greg liked him, and enjoyed drinking and playing poker with him, and going into Boston to watch games with him, he wanted every workday to kick his ass. So he bought him out, freed him to fish in Florida, a life that sounded to Greg right for the lazy old fart who liked money but not the getting of it, while he himself liked getting it but had little to spend it on, and was not free to spend it on what he would like to.

At night on the east deck, when time relinquished its function in his life, and space lost its distances and limits, he completed his travel on the Intracoastal Waterway by sending his boat from Brownsville to the mouth of the Amazon, in the hands of a trustworthy sailor for hire, then flying with Brenda to Rio de Janeiro where they would live the hotel life of sleep and swimming and drinking and eating (and daytime fucking: yes, that) until he was ready for the rigorous part that excluded Richie from the day-dream. He would go with Brenda to the mouth of the Amazon, by car or train, however they traveled there. He would rendezvous with his boat and sailor at one of the towns he had looked at as a dot on the globe on his desk. Then he and Brenda would walk west along the river. They would take only canteens, and he would carry a light pack with food for the day. They would wear heavy boots against snakes, and he would wear his .45 at his waist, and carry a machete. They would see anacondas and strange aqua birds and crocodiles. At the day's end the boat would be waiting, and they would board it, and fish, and sip drinks and cook and eat, then lie together gently rocking in the forward cabin with the double bed. Sometimes he imagined the river's bank stripped of trees, and an asphalt road alongside it, with rest areas and Howard Johnson's. But no: it must be jungle, thick living jungle, where each step was a new one, on new earth, so that you could not remember how you felt retracing your steps through the days of your life at home. He went there at night on this deck, and always with the focused excitement, the near-quietude, of love. Only in the mornings with his coffee, or driving from the inland to the beach store, or at other moments during his days, did he ever feel the sadness that he forced to be brief: the knowledge that he would never do it.

If you weren't there, on the job, they either stole from you, at the least by giving away your ice cream to their friends and taking some home as well, or they screwed up in other ways, and the operation went lax, and you had two stores selling ice cream but something was wrong. So he was at both stores every day, and he sometimes worked the counters there too, and washed dishes, and swept floors, all of this to keep things going, Goddamnit, and because he could not be idle while others worked, and every night he was there to close out the register; he took the money with him for night deposit, the .45 in his belt till he was in the car, then on the seat beside him. He carried the pistol in his hand when, at the bank, he walked from the car to the night depository. He had a permit. When he told the police chief, who approved the permit, how much money he carried to the bank each night, the chief asked if he had ever thought of buying a safe. Greg shrugged. He said he liked doing it this way, but that each store did have a safe he used only on nights when he couldn't get there, but anybody could get money from a safe if they wanted to so badly that they'd take the whole damn thing. He alternated the stores, taking the money from the inland one on one night, the beach store on the next, so his manager at one store would not always be last to be relieved of the money, and so last to go home. But most nights, when he reached the second store, his people were still cleaning up anyway, and he helped them with that. Some nights he thought he did not use a safe because he hoped some bastard, or bastards, would try to take his money. His pattern was easy enough to learn, if anyone were interested.

Larry was the only man he knew whom he could trust to do everything, and Larry had never wanted to give himself fully to the stores. During college he had needed his days free, and after college he needed his nights for dance or play rehearsals. This was not a disappointment for Greg; when he felt anything at all about Larry's lack of involvement with the stores, it was relief, for he wanted Larry to be his own man and not spend his life following his father. He believed the business of fatherhood was to love your children, take care of them, let them grow, and hope they did; and to keep your nose out of their lives. He did not know, and could not remember if he had ever known, whether Larry hoped to be a professional actor or dancer, perhaps even an established one with all the money and its concomitant bullshit, or if he was content to work with the amateur theater and dance companies in the Merrimack Valley. As far as he knew, Larry had never said, and he had never asked, and Larry's face had always been hard for him to read.

But before Brenda, when with no woman or a faceless one for his daydream he rode the Waterway and walked the Amazon on his dark sundeck at night, he had hoped that a time would come when Larry would want or need a break from performing, and would want to work the stores for a few months, and earn much more money, perhaps for an adventure of his own, a shot at New York or Hollywood or wherever else the unlucky bastards born with talent had to go to sell themselves. But not after last night. Probably, after last night, he would not ever show up at the store again, unless it was to collect his final paycheck. As difficult as it was for Greg to believe, as much as his heart and his body refused to accept it, both of them—the heart surrounded by cool fluttering, and the body weary as though it had wrestled through the night while he slept—threatening to quit on him if Larry simply vanished, that was what Larry had said he would do.

Greg had phoned him to come and have a nightcap, at ten at the earliest, saying he had work to do till then. He had no work, unless waiting for Richie to go to bed was work, and finally he supposed it was. Greg had phoned his two managers and told them to put the money in the safes. He did not know what he expected from Larry. An unpredictable conversation or event was so rare in his life that, as well as shyness, guilt, and shame, he felt a thrill that both excited him and deepened his guilt. He brought Larry up to the living room and tried to begin chronologically. He saw his mistake at once, for early in Greg's account Larry saw what was coming and, leaning forward in his chair, said: "Are you going to tell me you've been seeing Brenda?"

"Yes."

"I don't be*lieve* this."

Greg looked at the floor.

"It's divorce that did it," he said.

"Whose?"

"Yours. Mine." He looked at Larry. "Fucking divorce. You think I chose her?"

"What am I supposed to think?" Larry said, and was out of the chair: he never seemed to stand up from one, there was no visible effort, no pushing against the chair arms, or even a forward thrust of his torso; he rose as a snake uncoils, against no resistance at all, and Greg fixed on that detail, finding in it his son of twenty-five years, holding that vision while the room and Larry and Greg himself faded in a blur of confusion and unpredictability.

"It just happened," Greg said. "It always just happens."

"Beautiful. What happened to will?"

Greg stood and stepped toward him.

"Don't talk to me about will." And they were lost, both of them, in anger, in pride, facing each other, sometimes even circling like fighters, then one would spin away, stride to a window, and stare out at the dark trees of the back lawn; and it was at one of those times when Larry was at the window, smoking, silent, that Greg watched his back and shoulders for a moment, then took their long-emptied and tepid beer cans down to the kitchen, returned with beer and opened and placed one, over Larry's shoulder, onto the windowsill, then opened his own and, standing halfway across the room from Larry, spoke softly to the back of his head.

"You have to know how it started, you have to know the accident. The women, you know: when there's a divorce, they get dropped. You know what I mean. They lose the friends they had through the marriage. The husband's friends. God-damn if I know why. Doesn't matter if the husband was the asshole. Still it happens. And they're out of his family too. So I'd have her over for dinner. After you guys split up. Her and Richie and me. Shit, I—" Now he did not know, and in a glimpse of his future knew that he never would know, why he had invited her, not even once a week and not only to dinner, but ice-skating and cross-country skiing, always with Richie, and finally canoeing and swimming in lakes, and by June when the ocean was warm enough Richie still went with them, but he and Brenda were lovers. "I just didn't want her to be alone. To feel like the family blamed her."

"The family?" Larry said to the window screen. "You and Richie?"

"Well, Carol's not here. And Mom's—"

"—Come on, Pop."

"Will you let me explain?"

"Go on. Explain." He spoke to the window still, to the dark outside, and Greg was about to tell him to turn around, but did not.

"That's how it started. Or why it started. I'll leave all that analyzing to you. All it does is make your tires spin deeper in the hole."

"That might be good, depending on the hole."

"Jesus. What happened is, sometime in the spring there, I started loving her."

"Great." Now he turned, swallowed from his beer, looked at Greg. "I knew you and Richie were doing things with her. He told me."

"What did you think about it?"

"I tried not to think anything about it. So I thought it was good for Richie. He likes her a lot. I even thought it was good for her."

"But not for me."

"Like I said, I tried not to think anything about it. It looks like one of us should have. Mostly you. What do you mean, you started loving her? Are we talking about fucking?"

"Come on, Larry."

"Well, are we?"

"What do you think?"

"I'm staying on the surface: my little brother and my father have been taking care of my ex-wife."

"You want to hear me say it. Is that it?"

"Isn't that why you called me here?"

Greg pinched his beer can, pressing it together in its middle, and said: "I called you here to say I'm going to marry her."

Like wings, Larry's arms went out from his body, his beer in one hand.

"*Mar*ry her? *Mar*ry her?"

"Larry, look; wait, Larry, just stand there. I'll get us a beer. You want something different? I got everything—"

"—You sure the fuck do."

"Come on, Larry. Scotch, rum, tequila, vodka, gin, bourbon, brandy, some liqueurs—"

"—I'll take mescal."

"You'll take tequila."

"And everything else, it seems."

Greg left him standing with his empty can, and carrying his own bent one descended the short staircase, got the tequila from one cabinet, a plate from another, took a lime from the refrigerator and quartered it on the cutting board, put the lime and salt shaker and shot glass and bottle on the plate, then opened himself a beer. Upstairs he walked past Larry and laid the plate on top of the television set near where Larry stood. Greg sat in an armchair across the room.

"Let me talk to you about love," he said.

"Paternal?"

"*Love*, Goddamnit. I don't believe I feel it the way you do."

"Looks like you do. You even chose the same woman."

"I didn't *choose*. Now let me talk. Please. You get to be forty-seven, you love differently. I remember twenty-five. Jesus, you can hardly work, or do anything else; you wake up in the morning and your heart's already full of it. You want to be with her all the time. She can be a liar, a thief, a slut—you don't see it. All you see is her, or what you think is her, and you can walk off a roof with a shingle and hammer in your hands, just thinking about her. But at forty-seven, see, it's different. There's not all that breathlessness. Maybe by then a man's got too many holes in him: I don't know. It's different, but it's deeper. Maybe because it's late, and so much time has been pissed away, and what's left is—Is precious. And love—Brenda, for me—is like a completion of who you are. It's got to do with what I've never had, and what I'll never do. Do you understand any of that?"

"All of it," Larry said, and stepped to the television set, and, with his back to Greg, poured a shot of tequila, sprinkled salt onto his thumb, licked it off, drank with one swallow, then put a wedge of lime in his mouth and turned, chewing, to Greg. "But it sounds like you could have had that with anybody."

"No. Those feelings came from her. I didn't feel them before."

"All right. All right, then. But why *marry*, for Christ's sake?"

"I need it. She needs it. It's against the law, in Massachusetts. We'll have to do it some other place. But I'm going to see Brady. See if he can work on changing the law."

"You're bringing this shit to the fucking legislature?"

"Yes."

"God *damn*. Why don't you just fuck her?"

"Larry. Hold on, Larry."

"I *am* holding on, Goddamnit."

Larry's face was reddened, his breath quick; he half-turned toward the television set, picked up the bottle and shot glass, then replaced them without pouring. He looked at Greg, and breathed deeply now, his fists opening and closing at his sides, in front of his pelvis, at his sides. Then, at the peak of a deep breath, he said quietly: "You have to marry her," and exhaled, and in the sound of his expelled breath Greg heard defeat and resignation, and they struck his heart a blow that nearly broke him, nearly forced him to lower his face into his hands and weep.

"Yes," he said. So many times in his life, perhaps all of his life, or so his memory told him, he had stood his ground against opponents: most of them in the flesh, men or women whose intent was to walk right through him, as if he were not there, as if the man he was did not even occupy the space that stood in their way; there had been the other opponents too, without bodies, the most threatening of all: self-pity, surrender to whatever urged him to sloth or indifference or anomie or despair. Always he had mustered strength. But now he felt the ground he held was as vague as a principle that he had sworn to uphold, and he could not remember feeling anything at all about it, yet was defending it anyway because he had said he would. The word *marry* was as empty of emotion for him as, right now, was the image of Brenda's face. And it struck him that perhaps she too, like so much else, like Goddamn near everything else, would become a duty. Because when you fought so much and so hard, against pain like this as well as the knee-deep bullshit of the world, so you could be free to lie in the shade of contentment and love, the great risk was that you would be left without joy or passion, and in the long evenings of respite and solitude would turn to the woman you loved with only the distracted touch, the distant murmurs of tired responsibility. Again he said: "Yes."

"She'll want children, you know," Larry said.

Greg shrugged.

"You'll give them to her?"

"There's always a trade-off."

"What the fuck does that mean?"

"You can't marry a young woman, then turn around and refuse to have kids."

Larry turned to the television, poured tequila, and, ignoring both salt and lime, drank it, and Greg watched the abrupt upward toss of his head. Larry put the glass on the plate, his downward motion with it hard, just hard enough so it did not crack the plate; but the striking of the thick-bottomed glass on china created in the room a sudden and taut silence, as though Larry had cocked a gun they both knew he would not actually use.

"You do that, Pop," he said, facing the corner behind the television. "I'm going."

Then he was walking past Greg and out of the room, and Greg moved in front of him, and when Larry sidestepped, Greg did too; Larry stopped.

"Where?" Greg said.

Larry started to go around him but Greg stepped in front of him, looked at his eyes that were sorrowful and already gone from the room, as if they looked at a road in headlights, or a bed somewhere in a stripped and womanless room, or simply at pain itself and the enduring of it, and Greg thought: *Why they must have looked that way with Brenda, around the end, they must—*

"Where are you going?"

"Away. And I don't want your blessing. I've already got your curse."

Then, very fast, and with no touch at all, not even a brush of arm, of sleeve, he was around Greg and across the short distance to the stairs, where Greg watched his entire body, then torso and arms and head, then the head, the hair alone, vanish downward. He stood listening to Larry's feet going down the second flight. He listened to the first door, to the entryway and, as it closed, to the front door open and close, not loudly as with the glass and plate, but a click that seemed in the still summer night more final than a slamming of wood into wood.

3

Richie prayed *Please Jesus Christ Our Lord help us* as he went up the stairs into the kitchen; then he saw his father standing on the east sundeck. His back was to Richie, and a coffee mug rested on the wall, near his hip. Then he turned, smiled, raised the mug to his lips, blew on the coffee, and drank. Beyond him were the maples that grew near the house, at the edge of the woods.

"Pancake batter's ready," he said. "Bacon's in the skillet. You want eggs too?"

"Sure."

His father stepped into the kitchen, and slid the screen shut behind him; at the stove he turned on the electric burner under the old black iron skillet where strips of bacon lay. From the refrigerator behind him he took a carton of eggs and a half-gallon jar of orange juice, poured a glass of it, and gave it to Richie, who stood a few paces from his father, drinking, waiting, as his father placed a larger iron skillet beside the first one, where grease was spreading from the bacon. His father poured a cup of coffee, lit a cigarette, and Richie knew now it was coming: what he wanted neither to hear, nor his father to be forced to tell. So when his father began, looking from the bacon to Richie, stepping to the counter opposite the stove to stir the batter, back to the stove to look at the bacon and turn on the burner under the second skillet, all the while glancing at Richie, meeting his eyes, and talking about love and living alone, or at least without a wife, and how Richie living here made him happy, very happy, but a man needed a wife too, it was nature's way, and a man wasn't complete without one, and that he, Richie, should also have a woman in the house, that was natural too, and come to think of it natural must come from the word nature, and the needs that Mother Nature put in people; or God, of course, God, Richie stopped him. He said: "I heard you and Larry last night."

For a moment his father stood absolutely still, the spatula in one hand, the cigarette in the other halted in its ascent to his lips. Then he moved again: drew on the cigarette, flicked its ash into the garbage disposal in the sink beside the stove, turned the bacon, leaned the spatula on the rim of the skillet, then faced Richie.

"What do you think?" he said.

"I want you to be happy."

Blushing, his father said: "Well—" He looked at the floor. "Well, son, that's—" He raised his eyes to Richie's. "Thank you," he said. He looked over his shoulder at the bacon, then back at Richie. "You like Brenda?"

"Yes."

"You don't mind her moving in with us? After we're married?"

"No. I like her."

"There must be something."

"Larry."

"Yes."

"Am I going to visit him, like I do Mom?"

His father had not thought about that, Richie saw it in his face, the way it changed as abruptly as when he had stood so still with the spatula and half-raised cigarette, but more completely, deeply: the color rushed out of it, and the lips opened, and he stood staring at Richie's eyes, his mouth, his eyes. Then in two strides his father came to him, was hugging him, so his right cheek and eye were pressed against his father's hard round stomach, his arms held against his ribs by the biceps squeezing his own, the forearms pulling his back toward his father.

"You poor kid," his father said. "Jesus Christ, you poor, poor kid."

Still his father held him, and vaguely he wondered if the cigarette were burning toward the fingers that caressed his back, and he understood that his father had not yet thought about him seeing Larry because there had been so much else, and he would have got around to that too, he always got around, finally, to everything; but there had not been time yet (then he understood too it was not time but relief, peace; there had not been those yet); then against his cheek his father's stomach moved: a soft yet jerking motion, and he knew that above him his father was crying. He had never seen his father cry. Nor did he now. In a while, in his father's embrace, the motion ceased and his father said, in almost his voice, but Richie could hear in it the octave of spent tears:

"He's got to come through. Larry. You pray for that, hear? He will. He'll come through, he'll come see us."

Richie nodded against the shirt, the taut flesh; then with a final hug his father squeezed breath out of him and turned back to the stove. Richie waited for him to wipe his tears, but his hands were lifting out bacon and holding a plate covered with paper towel. When he took the batter from the counter, his cheeks and eyes were dry, so maybe as he held Richie he had somehow wiped them; but Richie, already forming the embrace and tears into a memory he knew he would have always, had no memory of his father's hands leaving his back where they petted and pulled. He slid open the screen, stepped onto the sundeck, leaned against its low wall, and watched a gray squirrel climb a maple. The tree was so close that Richie could see the squirrel's eyes and claws as it spiraled up the trunk, in and out of his vision. Near the top it ran outward on a long thick limb, then sat among green leaves, while Richie imagined the tears in his father's eyes, and going down his cheeks, then stopping; then disappearing as though drawn back up his face, into his eyes, lest they be seen.

Saint Peter cried after the cock crowed three times (and still was not under the cross; only Saint John and the women were there, and many times Richie wondered if he would have had the courage to go to the cross), and Christ cried, looking down at Jerusalem, and there must have been other times in the Gospels but he could not remember them now. Four summers ago when he was eight he had come home from the athletic field, bleeding and crying, unable to stop the tears and not caring to anyway, for the boys who had hurt him were teenagers, and the salt taste of blood dripped from his nose to his mouth. It was a Sunday, the family was home, and his father picked him up, listened to his story, blurted, and broken by breaths and sobs, then handed him to Carol and his mother, one holding his torso, the other his legs, and Brenda in front of him, touching a wet cloth to his nose, his lips, and his father and Larry ran out of the house. He twisted out of the arms holding him, away from the three faces he loved and their sweet voices that made him surrender utterly to his pain and humiliation and cry harder; he struck the floor in motion, out of the house, onto his bicycle. His father and Larry were faster than he imagined, but he reached the field in time to see them: each held a bully by the shirt and slapped his face, back and forth, with the palm, the back of the hand, the palm, and the cracks of flesh were so loud that he was frightened yet exultant, standing beside his bicycle, on the periphery of watching children. Then his father and Larry stopped slapping, pushed the boys backward, and they fell and crawled away in the dirt, crying, then stood, holding their bowed heads, and walked away. His father and Larry came toward him, out of the small boys and girls standing still and silent. With a bandanna his father wiped blood from Richie's nose and lips, and with a hand under Richie's chin turned his face upward, studied his nose, touched its bone. Then his father and Larry stood on either side of him, their hands on his shoulders, and he walked his bicycle between them, back to the house.

Watching the squirrel (he could see only the bush of its tail, and a spot of gray between green leaves) he could connect none of this with the mystery of his father's tears: not the actual shedding of them, but the fact that they had to be gone before his father faced him, and gone so absolutely that there was no trace of them, no reddened eyes, or limp mouth, as he had seen on the faces of Carol and his mother. All his instinct told him was that seeing your father cry was somehow like seeing your mother naked, and he had done that once years ago when he had to piss so badly that his legs and back were shivering, and without knocking he had flung open the bathroom door as she stepped out of the shower; as though drawn by it, his eyes had moved to her black-haired vagina, then up to her breasts, and then to her face as she exclaimed his name and grabbed a towel from a rack. He felt the same now as he had felt then: not guilt, as when he had committed an actual sin (using God's name in vain, or impure talk with his friends, yet frightening for him because he knew that soon it would be not words but the flesh that tempted him, and already his penis had urges that made him struggle); so not guilt, but a fearful sense that he had crossed an unexplained and invisible boundary, and whatever lay beyond that boundary was forbidden to him, not by God, but by the breath and blood of being alive.

When his father called him in, he ate heartily, and with relief, and saw that his father did too. And that relief was in his voice, and his father's, when they did speak: of the Red Sox, of Richie's plans for the day—softball in the morning, riding in the afternoon—and what they'd like for dinner. Their voices sounded like happiness. His father asked him if he were jumping or riding on the flat; he said jump, and his father said that'll be ten then, and peeled a bill from a folded stack he drew from his pocket, and Richie, bringing a fork of balanced egg and speared pancake to his mouth, took it with his left hand, and nodded his thanks, then mumbled it through his food. While his father smoked, he cleared the table; his father said I'll wash today, but he said he would, and his father said No, you go on and play ball. By then he had cleaned both iron skillets, the way his father had taught him, without soap, only water and a sponge, and they were drying on the heating burners. He sponged the egg yolk and syrup from the two plates, put them and the flatware in the dishwasher, told his father it wasn't full yet and he'd turn it on tonight when the dinner dishes were in it. He poured the last of the coffee into his father's cup, brought him the cream, and said he was going. He was at the door to his room when his father called: "Brush your teeth, son."

The taste of toothpaste was fading, and he could taste the bacon and syrup again as he rode onto the athletic field and realized that among the faces he scanned, he was looking only for Melissa. She was not there. For the rest of the morning, playing soft-ball with nineteen girls and boys, he watched the trees, where he had stood with her after Mass, watched for her, in the next moment, to emerge in her cut-offs and blue denim shirt. And he watched the road that began at the field and went back to his house and then hers. He watched secretly, while waiting to bat, talking to friends behind the backstop; or standing in left field (because it was Jim Rice's position), he watched between pitches and after plays. When he looked from the outfield to the road, most of it hidden by trees along its sides, or looked at the stand of trees behind the first base line, the grass and earth he stood on seemed never touched before, in this way, by anyone; and that earth seemed part of him, or him part of it, and its cover of soft grass.

He remembered her scents and the taste of her mouth; he no longer tasted the syrup and bacon, save once in the third inning when he belched. He tried to taste her, and inhale her, and he smelled grass and his leather glove, the sweat dripping down his naked chest and sides, the summer air that was somehow redolent of freedom: a warm stillness, a green and blue smell of leaves and grass and pines and the sky itself, though he knew that was not truly part of it, but he did believe he could faintly smell something alive: squirrels that moved in the brush and climbed trunks, and the crows and black-birds and sparrows that surrounded the softball game in trees, and left it on wings, flying across the outfield to the woods where he cross-country skied, or beyond it to the fields where now the corn was tall.

By the eighth inning, and nearing lunchtime, Melissa had not come. He imagined her pausing with vacuum cleaner, or sponge mop, or dust cloth, to wipe her brow with the back of her sun-browned forearm. He tried to imagine her mind: whether in it she saw him, or softball, or lunch and something cold to drink, and it struck him, and the sole-shaped spots of earth and grass beneath him, that he did not know what she liked to eat and drink. He thought of chili-dogs, hamburgers, grilled cheese with tomato, Coca-Cola, chocolate milk, then realized he was thinking of his own lunches, so he thought of Brenda, of tunafish salad, egg salad, and iced tea; but he could not put those into Melissa's mind. Then, picking up a bat and moving to the on-deck circle (there was no circle, and no one kneeled, waiting to hit; but to him there was a white circle around him), he saw what her mind saw. The image made him smile, yet what he felt was more loving and sorrowful than amused: she wanted a Marlboro. Her mother was in the house, working with her, and more than anything in her life now, Melissa wanted to smoke a cigarette.

4

It was fitting, Larry thought, that he should be seeing Brenda in daylight, whose hours had so often haunted him with remorse. As he drove slowly on Main Street, the hands of the old clock outside the clothing store joined at noon, and the whistle at the box factory blew. It blew at seven in the morning, at noon, at twelve-thirty and one, and at five in the afternoon; and sometimes he wondered, with sorrow and anger whose colliding left him finally weary and embittered—a static emotion he believed he should never feel, at twenty-five—whether the timing of the whistle had once ordered every worker in town to factories, and to two shifts for lunch, and then to their homes. That was long ago, when people called the town the Queen Slipper City because the workers made women's shoes; but that market was lost now, to Italian shoes, and the few remaining factories did not need a whistle you could hear wherever you stood inside the town. If you wanted to see factory workers, you had to be parked on one of the old brick streets, outside the old brick factory, when the men and women entered in the morning, left in the afternoon. He imagined those streets in the old days: thousands of men and women carrying lunchboxes, speaking to each other in English, Italian and Greek, Armenian and French, Polish and Lithuanian, walking toward the factories, disappearing into them at seven o'clock, as if the whistle roared at their backs.

Yet he was the son of an entrepreneur, and worked for him too. His father had worked at a shoe factory as a young boy, long enough to vow that someday he would never again work for another man. Now he made a lot of money selling a frozen tantalizer of people's craving for sweets. It was good ice cream, made by another man who owned and worked his own business in the Merrimack Valley, and Larry's father, by charming him and paying him well, was his only distributor. Ice cream. It seemed to Larry the only delightful food of childhood that adults so loved: they never spoke of, or indulged in, candy and cookies and popsicles, even malts and milkshakes, as they did ice cream. The faces of both men and women became delighted, even mischievous, as they said: Let's go get some *ice* cream. So his father sold it. He was good to his workers, he did not keep them working so few hours a week that he could pay them under the minimum wage, and the young people who worked his counters started at minimum wage, no matter how few their hours were, and his father raised their salaries as soon as he approved of their work. Since he was at the stores every day, working with them, they were soon either gone or making more money. Now his father was planning a way for all workers, above their salaries, to share in the profits, and was working on a four-day week for his daily and nightly managers, because he believed they should be with their young families, and he said there ought to be a way of allowing that and still selling fucking ice cream. This was as deeply as Larry had talked with his father about the philosophy of work in society; but Larry thought of him, a man who seldom read a book, as a good-spirited, moneymaking, gun-carrying anarchist. And a man now who had violated the lines and distances between them: lines they had drawn and distances created through the years, so they could sit in the same room, in the comfort of acknowledged respect and love.

He crossed the bridge on Main Street, turned right and followed the Merrimack River, glimpsed a sparkle of sun on its moving surface, this river that law and people were allowing to live again as a river ought to, so that now instead of receiving waste along its upriver banks, it was hosting salmon at its mouth. He turned left, passing an old cemetery where once he had walked, reading gravestones, but there were too many dead children and babies there, and he left, his head lowered by images of what were now nuisance illnesses or

complications of birth taking the suffering breath from children, and breaking forever the hearts of mothers and fathers.
His car climbed under trees and past large old houses and
he reached the one where Brenda lived, in an apartment at
the rear, on the first floor, and in the lawn behind her kitchen
was a birdbath in the middle of a fountain that looked as old
as the eighteenth-century tombstones in the cemetery. But
he drove on.

Just for a while, up the hill, and around the reservoir where
the purple loose-strife was growing now, purple-flowered stalks
standing in the marshy ground near the bank; Canada geese
were on the water, and across it were tall woods. A long steep
hill was there, but you could only see it in winter when the
leaves had fallen, and now it was marked by the rising green
curve of trees. He turned onto Route 495, three lanes going
east to the sea, cutting through wooded hills. Just for a while,
so he could breathe against the quickness of breath and coolness beneath his heart that were stage fright before a performance, when he needed it; but, going to see Brenda, it felt too
much like the fear and shame he believed he deserved.

He did not know how it started: somewhere in his mind,
his spirit, as though on what he called now—and then too,
sometimes, then too—those Faustian nights of their marriage,
he swayed in feigned drunkenness to a melody he had
dreamed. Rose from the couch in pantomime of a tired and
drunken husband, waved and sighed goodnight to Brenda
and the man they had brought home with them from one of a
succession of bars in neighboring towns. In these bars there
was music, usually one man or woman with a guitar, and the
bar stools had arms and were leather-cushioned, the bar had
a padding of leather at its front, and a long mirror behind it,
and men and women alone came to drink and hope, but few
of them to both hope and believe they would get what he and
Brenda trapped them into receiving. Ah, teamwork: he and
Brenda, and Mephistopheles. Start talking to a man alone,
Brenda sitting between him and Larry, the man at first cordial,
guardedly friendly, drawn to Brenda (Larry could see that,

over the rim of his glass, in the mirror), but for the first drink or two the man's eyes still moved up and down the mirror, and to the door, for it was Friday night and time was running out and he was wasting it with a married couple. *Run slowly, slowly, horses of the night*. That was Marlowe's Faustus speaking to time, as Mephistopheles approached on it. Yes. The line itself was from Ovid's *Amores*. Yes.

The highway rose to his right while curving to his left and he was going up and around too fast, and he stopped breathing as he shifted down, into the curving descent, and headed north. He breathed again, and slowed for the exit to the New Hampshire beaches. Easy enough, those nights. Lovely enough, was Brenda, so at the bar she had to say very little by way of promise; her eyes spoke to the man, and when Larry went so often to the men's room, she touched the man's hand, murmured to him, and always afterward she told Larry what she said, and always it was nothing, really, or almost nothing: something gentle, something flirtatious, that any woman might say to a man; because, Larry knew, she could no more say *Come home and fuck me* than she could sing an aria. She could dance one, though. Larry also knew, and she admitted it, that she feared risking the man's startled *No way, lady*, and that, equally, or perhaps above all, she delighted in mystery, so long as she was the source of it. The men followed them home for a nightcap.

Only one refused her: a young businessman from Tennessee, on one of those trips to another state, to visit another company, to observe, to comment, to learn, to advise, and the way they spoke of it, you expected to see them wearing field uniforms of some sort, military or civilian, green and new and creased, and to have binoculars hanging from their necks, pistols from their belts. In their living room, the man from Tennessee had passionately kissed her—or returned her kiss—but said *Back home a man can get shot doing this*, and fled to his motel. But the others stayed. Larry had a drink, sitting beside Brenda on the couch; then pleading sudden drunkenness or fatigue or both, he would leave them, shutting the hall door behind him, going the few paces into the bathroom where he would shut that door too, loudly, and stand at the toilet, even at times sway there, because his performance did not stop the moment he left the living room. Whether he used it or not, he flushed the toilet so they would hear that further sound of his drunken decline of consciousness. At the lavatory he stood before the fluorescent-lighted mirror and ran the tap full force, then shut it off and brushed his hair and tossed the brush clattering to the counter that held what he called Brenda's spices: save for his shaving cream and aftershave lotion and deodorant and razor and hairbrush, the surface was nearly covered with bottles and jars, their glass or plastic or perhaps their contents aqua and gold and amber and lilac and white, creams and fluids whose labels he had never read, nor contents sniffed in their containers, because he did not want to alter their effect when he breathed them from her flesh. In the first year of their marriage he had worked hard at cooking something more than broiled chops or fish and steamed vegetables, and had learned too much, so that now he enjoyed meals both a little more and a little less, because after a few bites he could name their seasonings.

Leaving the bathroom, he looked always at the closed door to the living room; beyond it, their voices were lower than the music, so he could hear only Brenda's soft tones, and the man's deeper ones, but no words amid Weather Report or Joni Mitchell or Bonnie Raitt. He walked heavily down the hall, to the bedroom, and shut that door too with force, enough for them to hear if indeed they still listened. Then the music was faint, and he had to concentrate to hear a melody as, at the opposite side of the apartment, he undressed anyway with the sounds of a drunk: sitting in a chair he took off his boots and threw them toward the closet. He left his clothes on the chair, brought cigarettes and lighter to the bedside table, and lay on his back in the dark, naked, warming under blanket and quilt in winter, or a light blanket in fall and spring, and summer was best when he lay under nothing at all, and waited.

He imagined the living room, drew it into the bedroom

with him, so he did not see dark walls and light curtains and pale ceiling, the silhouettes of chairs and chest and dressing table with its mirror, but black-haired Brenda on the couch, and the man across the coffee table from her. Some nights they would dance, and that was how she let them know, though most nights she did not have to: her face alone was enough, and they crossed the room to sit beside her on the couch Larry had left. Always she knew how much passion a man could bear before he would risk discovery by the husband. Except with the exploring businessman from Tennessee, haunted by shootings in the hills, or perhaps something else: the Old Testament, or Jesus. *He won't wake till noon*, she would say, her tongue moving on an ear, a throat.

Sometimes his hand slid under the covers, where his erection pushed them into a peak, or on warm nights his hand rose to it, standing in the dark air, and he touched it, held it, but nothing more. Though some nights he did more, and still waited unslaked for Brenda, listening to the faint music, seeing their dance slowing to an embrace, a kiss, their feet still now, only their bodies swaying to the rhythm. Or he listened for the man's feet crossing the floor, the weight of two bodies on the couch. He never heard any sound but music, then a long silence when the cassette ended. He wanted Brenda to put a tape recorder in her purse, leave the purse in the kitchen when they brought someone home, and he would turn on the recorder before he left them and went to the bedroom, and she would bring the purse to the floor by the couch. But she was afraid of the clicking sound when it stopped. He wanted to go out the bedroom window, and around the apartment to the living room; Brenda wanted that too, but they were both afraid a neighbor would see him looking in the window, and call the police. And he was afraid to creep down the hall, and listen at the living room door; each time he wanted to, but was overwhelmed by imagining the man suddenly leaving Brenda to piss, opening the door to find him crouched and erect in the hall.

So he heard and saw her in his mind where, in the third

and final year of their marriage, he so often and so passionately saw her with a lover that one night, set free by liquor
and Brenda's flesh in his arms, he frightened himself by telling her. She increased both his fear and elation when, without
questions or reflection, she said she would do it, and her legs
encircled his waist. They were in a dance company then, were
performing a dance together, and within the week they were
going after rehearsals to bars where no one knew them. On
the third night they brought home a young bachelor, a manager of a branch bank, and Larry stayed with them nearly too
long, so when he left for the bedroom he pretended drunkenness that was real, and when he lay on the bed the room
moved, so he stood and sat and stood, until he heard her light
feet in the hall, and he lay on the bed and watched her enter
the room and cross it in the dark, and it was worth the fear.

His fear was not of anything concrete; certainly it was
not rooted in jealousy, for he shared and possessed those dark
recesses of Brenda's spirit, so her apparent infidelity was in
truth a deeper fidelity. Also, the fear burned to white ash in
what he felt as he waited on those nights. The minutes passed
slowly, their seconds piercing him with a thrill like that of a
trapezist who, swinging back and forth, lives in those moments
of his hands on the bar, his body gaining speed and arc, while
also living the two and a half somersaults he will perform, and
the moment his hands will meet and grip the empty trapeze
swinging toward him, and, if an inch or instant off, his fall to
earth. Then she was in the hall, then at the bedroom door, and
it swung in and she was framed in it, a cigarette glowing at
her side, then she crossed the room. Lying on the bed, he
opened his arms. She lay on top of him, her tongue darting and
fluttering in his mouth as he unzipped and unbuttoned her
clothing, then pushed her up until she was sitting; he lifted
his legs around her and off the bed, and stood. He took the
cigarette from her and, before putting it out, held it to her lips,
then his own, tasting lipstick. He lifted her to her feet and
took off her clothes and let them fall to the floor as she began
telling him, in the voice she either saved for or only had on

these nights, in her throat, but soft, a breathy contralto, and he kneeled and pulled her pants down her smooth hard legs: *kissed me for a long time, and touching my breasts, and I started rubbing his thigh and he put his hand inside my pants—*

Sometimes he believed that first he remarked that part of her, saw in her brown eyes and open lips bridled yet promiscuous lust, and then his visions of her and a lover began. Then he also wondered if he were truly the one who changed the velocity and trajectory of their marriage, sending or leading them to that terrible midnight. *Run slowly, slowly, horses of the night.* And he recalled a teacher in college, talking about the mystery of life in general, of plants in the specific, saying that perhaps it was not man's idea to drink and smoke, that rather we were lured by the desire of the tobacco leaf and grape: *smoke me*, they whispered; *drink me.*

Yet it was she who said finally: *There's something dark in us, something evil, and it has to be removed,* and he told her *We can just stop then; we won't even talk about it again, not ever, it'll be something we did one year.* He kept insisting in the face of her gaze that lasted, it seemed, for days and nights: those unblinking eyes, sorrowful yet firm, looking at him as though they saw not his face but his demons; saw them with pity for both him and herself; and seeing his demons reflected in her eyes, he shrank from them, and from her, and from himself. Then he blamed himself for all of it, and pleaded for forgiveness, and the chance to live with her in peace as man and wife, and her eyes and her closed lips told him he understood too little about how far they had gone. Then she told him: *You take too much credit. Or blame. I liked it. I like it. I could do it right now, with you standing there watching.* Her eyes left his and he watched them move about the living room and settle on the couch before they looked at him again. *This isn't our home anymore,* she said. *It isn't anybody's. Or it's too many people's.* Then he grieved and so could not think, not for weeks, then months, as he lived alone and worked for his father and at night rehearsed dances or plays and then went home and wondered, with fear and pain and nothing else, what she was doing that moment, and with whom.

They had lived apart for over a year and were amicably divorced (he did not even have to go to court) and still all he knew, or thought, was that somehow it had to do with his youth: that had he been older (*as my father is*, he thought, driving now past a salt marsh, nearing the sea; *as my father is*) he would not have been so awed and enslaved by her passion, and his too; but without hers his own was ordinary, as it had been before her, as it was since he lost her. So her passion. Older, he believed, he would not have explored it; he would have left it in her depths, like a buried, undetonated bomb. That was all he knew now, and perhaps that had been the source of his fear on those nights, as he lay waiting.

Ahead of him was a bridge over a tidal stream, beyond it was the junction with the road that paralleled the sea; then he saw a farm stand on his side of the bridge, and he slowed and signaled and turned onto the dirt and gravel in front of the stand, a simple place: a rectangular roof resting on four posts and only one wall, at the rear, and in its shade were the boxes of fruit and vegetables, and an old woman behind a counter whose surface was just wide enough to hold a scale and cash register. She spoke to him as he chose tomatoes; she told him they were good, and the corn was picked fresh this morning. He praised the tomatoes and they talked about the long dry spell, and how so much of last summer was cool and rainy, and last fall was more like summer than summer was. He took three large tomatoes that Brenda could eat today and tomor-row, then nine more with graduated near-ripeness that she could place in the kitchen window, to ripen in the sun, and he imagined each of them red on a new day. In his heart he sang: *My true love brought to me three red tomatoes, nine tomatoes ripening*, then he remembered as a boy hunting grouse, which some natives here called partridges, with his father; and see-ing him and his father walking armed into woods made him pause, holding the last tomato above the crisp paper bag.

Then he started talking to the woman again, asked how her stand was doing, and she said Pretty well, and weighed the tomatoes and punched the register and said You know how it is, and he said he did, and paid her, and left.

So he did not go to the sea, but back to 495, and to Brenda's, sadly now, the stage fright gone at some time he did not remember. She came to the door barefoot and wearing white shorts and a red tee shirt, and he could not speak. He wanted to hold her very tightly, in silence, then move her backward, with the grace of a dance, to the couch, pull her shirt up past her shoulders and hair and above her head and raised arms, and fumble at her shorts. The couch was a new one; that is, it was a year old. They had sold all the furniture in their apartment, and left it like a box that had contained their marriage.

"I brought you some tomatoes," he said, and handed her the bag; she took it at its top, and the weight lowered her hand.

"Come in the kitchen," she said, and her voice was all right, not impenetrable like her eyes, like her lips had been. They had shown neither surprise nor guilt, nor pity, nor dislike—none of the emotions he had imagined as he drove to the house, walked around it to her door at the back. She had finished lunch, and he recognized its traces: jellied madrilène had been in a bowl, cottage cheese and lettuce on a plate, and a small wooden bowl held dressing from her salad. A tall glass was half-filled with tea and melting ice. She offered him some, and he said Yes, that would be good, and at the counter, with her back to him, she squeezed a wedge of lime over a glass, dropped in the wedge, went to the freezer for ice, then set the glass in front of him and poured the tea. She turned her back to him, and exclaimed over the tomatoes as she took them out of the bag, and put the nine in the window and the three in the refrigerator. He said to her body bent at the vegetable bin: "Are you dancing?"

"Only alone."

She straightened, shut the door, then sat opposite him and lit a cigarette from her pack on the table.

"Here?" he said.

"Yes. I'll get back with a company soon. When things are settled."

"Right."

"Are you?"

"We have a performance next week."

"What are you doing?"

"One I choreographed. To Ravel's Piano Concerto in G Major."

"That's ambitious. The whole thing?"

"Second movement. *Adagio Assai*. It's nine and a half minutes."

"It's beautiful. I'd like to see it."

"Would you?"

"Yes."

"Will you?"

"Yes."

He reached to his shirt pocket for a cigarette, but stopped and his hand went to her Benson and Hedges, and holding the gold pack, and shaking out a cigarette, he felt for a moment married to her again, in this apartment, all the darkness left behind them in the other place, as if their only trouble had been renting an apartment that was cursed, evil, that had to be fled or exorcised. Then the illusion ended, and he felt his eyes brimming, and he could not remember what he had come to say. Last night he had wanted to come to her in rage, but he was in too much pain then to drive here, to knock and enter, let alone yell at her what was in his mind. She looked up from tapping ash into the ashtray (it was new too; or a year old) and saw the tears in his eyes, then her hand covered his and she sat rubbing the back of his palm. He could say nothing at all. With the back of his other hand he wiped his eyes. Then he knew why he had come: in love, and simply to look at her, to sit like this, for a few minutes resurrected from their time together before they destroyed their capacity or perhaps their right to share it till one of them died. She was silent. But those dark brown eyes were not: they were wet, and then tears distinct as silver beads went down her dark cheeks. Her full lips, too, were those of a woman whose heart was keening, and he was certain he would never again see her face like this, for him, and he committed it to memory.

"Please don't ever tell him," he said.

She shook her head.

"I know no one can ask that," he said. "Of a lover. A wife."

"You can."

He stood and skirted the small table, and was on his knees, with both arms turning her chair, her body, to face him, and his face was in her lap, her hands moving in his hair; her lap was cotton shorts and the tight flesh of her large strong thighs, and pressing his face to it, he said: "Please, Brenda. Please."

"Never," she said, and as he started to rise, he held her against his chest, and her arms went around him, released him as he stood and looked down at her upturned face. He bent to it, not touching her, and kissed her lips. Then he went out of the kitchen and through the living room and out the door, holding still her unlit cigarette, glimpsed through a blur the birdbath and fountain, turned the corner of the house into the direct light of the sun, and walked fast to his car.

5

In late afternoon Brenda lay on the couch in the living room, barefoot and wearing a leotard, drinking iced tea while her sweat dried and her body cooled. Across the room were two windows facing the back lawn, and at their sides pale blue curtains moved back and forth with the breeze, as though someone stood behind each of them and gently, rhythmically, pushed. She was looking at the curtains and the windows and nothing in particular beyond when she saw Greg: he walked into her vision from the right of the window, where the driveway was. He walked slowly on the grass, profile to her, his hands in the pockets of his khakis, his hard stomach pushing against his blue shirt and protruding over his belt. Her only movement on the couch was to reach for a cigarette on the coffee table and light it, as she looked at his dark muscular arm—the left one—beneath the short sleeve of his shirt, and at the side of his clean-shaven dark face, slightly bowed, as if with thought or fatigue. She did not know why his arms were so well-muscled; nor why, at forty-seven, his biceps had not begun to flatten, his triceps to sag. He did not know either. She had asked him, had jokingly accused him of clandestine push-ups or isometrics or some other exercise that no one did anymore. Or no one she knew. Nearly all her friends, women and men, had rituals of aerobic exercise, and many now had joined clubs where they used a Nautilus machine. She meant to join one tomorrow. But Greg told her he did nothing at all, had not done a push-up since the Army, and would never do one again on purpose, unless it was to raise himself from a barroom floor out of his own vomit. His vanity about not being vain was endearing. Also, she knew that, at times, the refusal of his arms and legs to age normally gave her confidence in the longevity of his body.

Now, at the fountain and birdbath, he turned from her, and stood looking down at the water that trickled over the sides of the bath, into the stone fountain, watching it as if he saw ideas in its motion. About what, though? Larry and Richie and Carol? His walk along the Amazon? Sometimes when he was tired and a little drunk and bitter, and certain he would never see, much less walk in, that jungle on that river, he said: *Surely by now some sons of bitches have laid a highway*; while Brenda imagined the riverbanks so thick with trees and brush and vines that, after hacking with machetes for the first mile, they would give it up, then travel the river by boat. Still, she would go with him. She would go with him because he wanted to, she would go with him there before Venice and Athens and the Greek islands and Spain, the places where she wanted to walk with him on city and village streets and eat long and leisurely dinners and sleep till lunchtime and make love in the afternoons that only hotels, and especially hotels in a for-eign country, could give you. She had done that in Mexico City on her December honeymoon with Larry, and in the

afternoons there she never felt that she was distorting daylight by performing a nocturnal act in defiance of schedules
and telephones, commitments and errands and chores. In
Mexico City, she and Larry knew no one, and did not speak
the language anyway. It was odd, she thought, perhaps even
sinister, that the world had contrived to give lovers only the
night; and the world wanted those nights to be earned, too, by
what used to be the sweat of the brow, but was now too often
foolish work in rooms with temperatures so regulated that
they did not seem to exist on the earth, with her seasons. Then,
on the purchased bed, surrounded by the dwelling and the
acquisitions that filled it, you could have the night. Yet afternoon was the time she felt most erotic, and before dancing
today, she had masturbated on this couch. She would go with
Greg first to insects and discomfort because she loved the boy
she had found in his older man's body, beneath his man's style.
She called it Peter Pan, to herself, and she called him that when
he was tired, and a little drunk, and bitter; and on nights when,
making love, she sensed it in his body: a tender and humble
and grateful presence that seemed to swoon in her arms.

She saw the boy when he took her to his bars. He had two
favorites, near his stores, where he drank with men he called
his friends, but they could not be, not really. In her life, a
friend was a woman you spoke to on the telephone four or
five times a week, and bought gifts for, something inexpen-
sive that reminded you of her when you saw it in a shop, and
you visited each other and drank coffee or tea or, if at night, a
little wine; and you tried to make time at least twice a month
for dinner together in a restaurant, or lunch and shopping in
Boston, though it was usually once and sometimes not even
that because you both had men in your lives, and some of the
women had children too. And with your friend you talked,
you did not banter; and you knew as much and probably more
about her than her husband or lover did, and she knew as
much about you. Though no woman knew, or ever would know,
about that year with Larry when she learned how heedlessly
she could draw someone's life into her own, into the lustful

pleasure and wicked dreams of her marriage, when she had
learned that the state of being married, which had opened that
life to her, was the very state that kept her from being a slut. So
she had to take herself, and her slut with her, and go away
from the marriage, and Larry; and she had to hold down that
part of her being she had, she supposed now, always known
was there, but in the nether reaches of her soul, where it was
supposed to be, far from the light of sun and moon, to live only
in the solitude of masturbation. She had to push it down again,
into an oubliette, and keep it covered with the weight of a new
life, and then with the solidity of a man who, by chance, or the
circumstance of their being in-laws, turned out to be Greg.

So that, by trying to save herself, she had become again a
woman she could not have, even two years ago, predicted herself to be. Now she had broken promises so implicit that you
never spoke them: *I will not make love with your father, take
him from you and you from him, and your home, and Richie,
and—* So she was still a scandal to her self, the self who
believed in honor, in trying one's best to be a decent human
being whose life did not spread harm. Sometimes, for no
immediate reason save that her mood suddenly changed, she
saw her vagina and its hair as a treacherous web, and with
luxurious despair she imagined the faces of women, wives
and lovers of men whom she had drawn to her from their
places at the bar until they sat across the coffee table from her
and Larry on the couch, and when Larry left she drew them
across the room and into her body, where she spent them and
then expelled them forever from her life. Because she and
Larry never brought the same one home twice, even if they
saw him again in a bar, even if he came to sit with them, for
they were afraid that no man could believe his second night
with Brenda was anything but collusion between wife and
husband, and so perversion. And once she walked them to the
door, she took their lovemaking into her bed, and lived it
again with Larry, and as his passion crested hers did too, again,
and she embraced both him and the lover, and they grew up
and around her, like wisteria.

She did not believe any of these men ever felt used; but she knew they ought to, and most of them would not have gone home with her and Larry, would not have accepted the gambit nightcap, had they known the truth beyond her body, her face. So in those moods she punished herself, whether or not the men knew she deserved it; she punished herself by sustaining and deepening the mood with memories of her lies to the men (how many times had she pretended to be seduced? and how many times had she murmured: *I've never done this before*?) and with imagining the faces of the women who loved them, carvings of betrayal that hung like masks before her eyes.

No: she would never tell that shame to one of her friends but she told everything else and she knew they did too, and that was the friendship. It was as deep as her own feelings about herself, and she could not feel in harmony with the world unless she had that friendship with at least one woman. She was, she thought, more fortunate than most: she had three women she loved. While the men Greg called friends were carpenters and electricians and cops and men who made telephone parts at Western Electric, and Greg only knew them because he liked drinking in the same places they did, stand-up bars where nearly everyone drank beer, and there was no blender and a bartender could work months without using a cocktail shaker, and only kept lemons and limes in the fruit bin, and not many of them, or they would soften and turn brown. Bartenders called them shot-and-a-beer bars. Brenda liked the ones Greg brought her to; she liked standing at the bar, and watching the men; and she liked the ceiling fans, and not having a jukebox or electronic games, and having the television on only for ballgames or hockey or boxing. She liked the men Greg called his friends too; they were in their forties and fifties and sixties, were near-courtly toward her, lit her cigarettes and were not profane unless Greg was, and then only moderately, never the words she had been hearing from her friends, and saying with them, since her teens. She did not feel superior to them because they worked with their hands. Her father had been a house-painting contractor, but he and one man had done all the work, and they also laid hot top on driveways.

What she did feel was baffled: when she walked into a bar with Greg, and he saw his friends, he called their names, he waved, their faces brightened and they beckoned him and Brenda to the bar, made room for them, bought them drinks, and Greg and the men touched each other. Always. Handshakes and pats on the back and squeezes of biceps, squeezes and rockings of shoulders. Then their strange talk began, or seemed in some mysterious way to continue from the patting and squeezing, and she listened to them, intently because she was baffled, but amused too, because she could listen for two hours or more, and still learn almost nothing about their lives. They talked about their lives, but not the way she and her friends did. She could not tell whether they were married badly or well; and, with some of them, whether they were married at all. She could not tell how they felt about their work, nor most of the time what it even was. She learned these from Greg, in the car going home to her apartment. But they talked about their lives: they told stories about themselves, about mutual friends, or a man they worked with, and when she first went to the bars with Greg she told him she knew now why he called talking to his drinking friends shooting the shit. His drinking friends: he called them that. There were others she had never met, and they were his hunting friends or his fishing friends and some of them were both; but it seemed that, when she was able to keep track of the names in his hunting and fishing stories, there was one man he went with for trout fishing, and two or three for deer hunting, but one of those went deep-sea fishing too, and another may have been his trout fishing friend.

When she became a regular with Greg at the bars, she began to see what was beneath the men's stories, and their teasing each other about their mortality defined by their enlarged stomachs, and their hair graying or vanishing or both; and their other talk that was rarely serious, yet somehow was not dull either. They were trying to be entertaining, and hoping to be entertained. It was the reason they gathered to drink. And she began to think about Richie, as she stood at the bar, and during the days too, when she mused about this difference between men and women she had not remarked so clearly in Larry; for, like her, Larry had three close friends, and they talked seriously about acting and dancing, and death and love, and books they had read and movies they had seen. But in Richie and his friends she saw no difference at all, except alcohol and tobacco, from Greg and his friends. The essence of the friendships was sharing a game or sport or beer-drinking, and she could no more imagine Greg talking soberly and deeply with one of his friends than she could imagine Richie sitting in a living room and talking quietly with one of his about what he wanted and loved and feared.

My God, there was something about boys that domestic life and even civilization itself could not touch, and often they were infuriating and foolish, and yet when they lost that element, as boys or men, they became dull. So as a woman you were left having to choose between a grown boy and a flat American male, and either was liable to drive you mad, but at least with the boy your madness was more homicidal than suicidal, as it was with the other. No wonder the men at the bar, and on the hunting and fishing trips, called themselves *the boys*. They said: *I'm going to have a beer with the boys; I'm going fishing with the boys*, and in their eyes there was a different light, of distance, of reverie, and of fondness, as if they were unfolding a flag they had served when they were young.

And Greg still fought. His friends did not; and after the one fight she saw, they had patted him, squeezed him, and laughed and told him he'd better leave that stuff to the kids, or get himself a younger heart. He had won. He told Brenda once that his ex-wife Joan had said to him, many times: *The trouble with you is nobody's ever beaten you*. Brenda said: Is that true? and he told her he thought it probably was, because he could remember getting the shit kicked out of him, but never losing. She was surprised by the fight she saw, in the bar near the beach store, because she was neither frightened nor scornful nor compassionate. She watched with excitement yet from an odd distance, as though watching two strangers have an equally-matched marital quarrel. The reason for the fight was as shallow as the other exchanges in that bar, and later she knew the true reason was simply a need they had not outgrown. The other man, in his late twenties or early thirties, said to the bartender that she—and he looked down the bar at Brenda—was too young and pretty to have all them old turkeys around her. He said it loudly, and he meant to say it loudly, and Greg was gone from her, was up the bar and turning the man to face him, then they were like two male dogs. They did all but sniff asses and scratch the earth: they growled and snapped and pushed, and she watched, and Greg's friends watched, and everyone else watched, save the bartender who talked too, tried from across the bar to at least try to stop what he knew he could not. Then Greg swung and the other did and they punched and grappled and fell holding each other to the floor, and by then she knew, without knowing how she knew, that also like dogs they would not hurt each other. That was when she understood why they were fighting. They rose from the floor punching, then the young man went backward and down, got up quickly, and men grabbed him from behind, Greg's friends held him, and the two yelled at each other till the bartender, still at his post, yelled louder and told them both to shut the fuck up. Then he told the young man to leave and come back another night when he didn't want trouble. The bartender was not young either. That's probably why he told him to leave, Greg said later, and because anyway the guy had started it and he wasn't a regular. The young man took his change from the bar and left without looking at anyone, and Brenda watched his face as he walked, the blood over one eye and at his mouth. Greg was not bleeding, and he was laughing and buying a round for her and his friends, then he said make it a round for the house, and he overtipped the bartender, as he always did. Once she had told him he tipped too much, from sixty to a hundred percent, and he had said he had the money and the bartenders needed it and worked for it, and if he wanted to save money he'd buy a six-pack or two and drink them at home.

She watched his back; he still looked down at the water in the fountain, and it occurred to her that she had never watched him when he was oblivious of her. She had watched him when he pretended not to know she was, while he worked in his stores. But always she knew he felt her eyes on him. Perhaps he did now too. Though she did not think so, for he was a tired-looking man of forty-seven (forty-eight soon, in November) whose back and shoulders and lowered head showed weariness as a face does. Had he known she was watching, he would be standing tall now, and he would have crossed the lawn minutes earlier with quickened movements, for he was proud that she loved him. He had sculpted a style for himself, until he became that style, or most of him did, so he could take money from the world and hold onto enough of it to allow him to walk its streets with at least freedom from want and debt and servitude. On some nights, in her bed, when he had drunk enough, that style fell away like so much dust and he spoke softly to her, his eyes hiding from hers, and told her how happy he was that she loved him, how he woke each morning happy and incredulous that this lovely young woman loved him; told her that when he first saw it lighting her eyes, when he and Richie and she were eating dinners after the marriage, all of his thinking told him what he saw in her eyes could not be there, not for him; and his heart nearly broke in its insistence that he did see what he saw, and that he loved her too. And he said he would not blame her if she woke up one morning knowing it was all a mistake, that he was just someone she had needed for a while, and left him. *Never*, she said to him. *Never*.

Nor did she know why. He was good to her, and he made her laugh. He liked to watch her dance. He had watched Larry, as a father will watch a son perform anything from elocution to baseball to spinning a top. But that was not why he liked to watch her. Nor was it the reason he understood what she was trying to do with her body, and the music, on a stage or here in her living room. His senses told him that. And he knew why she danced, and why she had to keep dancing, while other people—her parents in Buffalo, and her two older sisters whose marriages had taken one to Houston, and the other to Albuquerque, and some of her friends too, though not the close ones—did not understand why she worked so hard at something and was content to remain an amateur. But Greg did. He was neither surprised nor amused when she told him she taught dance to make a living, but she could not remember ever wanting to be a professional dancer, though she had to dance every day, whether she was working with a company or not. She had seen recognition in his eyes. He listened, and nodded his head, and stroked his cheek, then said: *Some people have things like that, and they don't have to make money at it. It's something they have to do, or they're not themselves anymore. If you take it away from them, they'll still walk around, and you can touch them and talk to them. They'll even answer. But they're not there anymore.* She said: *Are you talking about yourself?* His eyes shifted abruptly, toward hers, as if returning from a memory. *Me? No. I was thinking what Richie would be like, if they shut down the stables, and Catholic churches, and banned cross-country skiing.* He had been sitting on this couch, and she had been standing in front of him. Then she sat beside him. *What's yours?* she said. *I don't have one,* he said. *My father did. He was a carpenter.* She said: *I thought he worked for the railroad.* He smiled and touched her cheek. *He did,* he said. *He was a carpenter at home. At night, and on the weekends. God, you should have seen that house grow.*

Now he turned from the fountain, and with her heart she urged him to straighten and stride with energy, but he did not, and he seemed to fade past the window and out of her view. She stood and went to the refrigerator and got two bottles of beer, opened them, went back through the living room, and reached the door before he did. He smiled at her through the screen, and came in, and she kissed him over the bottles, felt his hold on the beer in her left hand, and released it to him;

kissing him and feeling the cold bottle leave her fingers, she was struck by a sadness that was sudden yet so familiar now that she did not even have to call it death anymore. She looked up at him.

"I've been watching you," she said.

"And?"

She smiled.

"I was trying to figure out why I love you."

"And?"

"I just do. Come hold me, and tell me about your terrible day."

"How do you know it was terrible?"

"I've been watching you. Come on."

She put her arm about his waist and they went to the couch and sat, and she rested her head on his shoulder.

"Richie this morning," he said, above her head.

"How was he?"

"He's tough."

"That's good."

"I wish to fuck he didn't have to be."

She nodded and nestled against him.

"He'll be all right," he said.

"Larry was here."

"Was it bad?"

"He wasn't. It was."

"Jesus. Tonight I see Carol. After dinner."

She looked at the moving curtains and the bird-bath and fountain. Then she said: "I'm lucky. Wickedly lucky."

"How's that?"

"I'm going to enjoy telling my family."

"On the phone."

"No. I'll write letters."

"You'll enjoy that?"

"They never have known me. They might as well keep on, or start trying."

"Do you love them?"

"Sure I do. But I love them better by mail. I need a shower."

"I need another beer. At least."

He went to the kitchen; in the bedroom she pulled the leotard down over her breasts and hips, and stepped out of it as he came in. He arranged two of her four pillows, then lay on the bed, his shoulders propped up so he could drink.

"I've seen worse," he said.

"You've probably fucked worse."

"I have," he said, as she walked away from him, the sadness gone as she felt, because he watched her, the grace of her flesh, and its colors from the sun and her bikini. He had showered here last night, so she lowered the nozzle to keep her hair dry, and waited outside the tub till the water was hot. She stepped in and turned her breasts to the spray and closed her eyes, as she always did, not to keep water from them, but because she shut them to nearly all sensuous pleasures: lying in the sun and dancing alone in her living room and masturbating and making love. Only smoking and drinking and eating were better with your eyes open, and sometimes when she first inhaled or sipped or chewed, she closed her eyes then too. She turned her back to the water and soaped herself, and turned again and rinsed, and stayed, contained by the shower curtain and the hot water, until it began to cool. Then she turned the handle and lifted her arms as cold water struck her breasts and stomach, and she circled in it, her arms above her head, till the cold drew from her an exhaled sound, soft yet shrill, like a bird's. She turned off the water and stepped out, rubbed her cool skin with a thick dark blue towel, then wrapped it around her body, from the tops of her breasts to her thighs, and went to the bedroom.

He had brought her a beer, set on the table at her side of the bed, and the other two pillows were waiting. She lay beside him, leaned against the pillows, and drank. He lit one of her cigarettes and gave it to her, then slid his leg toward hers so they touched. She said: "Maybe next summer I'll be pregnant."

"It's better in winter, when it's not so hot."

"Then maybe next summer I'll have a baby."

"Why not."

"Damned if I know," she said. "So why not."

The ashtray rested on his chest, and moved with his breathing. They lay quietly, as she felt the evening cool coming now to the lawn, and through the window behind the bed. She listened to the silence of the room, and their smoking and swallowing and quiet breath, and she felt held by tranquility and shared solitude, as the hands of her parents had held her on the surface of water when she was a child. She wanted to tell him that, but she did not want to speak. Then she knew that he sensed it anyway, and she lay, her bare leg touching his trousered one, her eyes closed, in the cool silence until he said he had to go now, he had to cook dinner for Richie.

6

Between Richie's squeezing thighs and knees, the sorrel mare Jenny turned with the track, and he saw the red barn, then she was cantering straight toward the jump, and over her head he saw Mr. Ripley's white house and a flash of green trees and blue sky beyond its dark gray roof. He fixed his eyes at a point on Mr. Ripley's back wall, directly in line with the middle of the upright posts. He held the reins with both hands, his leather riding crop clutched with his right, angling down and backward over his thigh, and with the kinetic exhilaration that years ago he had mistaken for fear, he glimpsed at the bottom of his vision Jenny's ears and the horizontal rail. Then he was off the earth, flying with her between the uprights, his eyes still on that white point on the wall, his body above the saddle as though he sat on the air they jumped through. When her front feet hit he rocked forward and to the left but only for an instant, then he was in position again, his knees and thighs holding, and he leaned forward and patted her neck as she entered the curve of the oval track, and spoke to her: Good girl, Jenny. Good girl. Then she was around the curve and approaching the other jump; beyond it were the meadow and woods, and he found the top of the pine rising above clumped crowns of deciduous trees, and held his eyes on its cone of green. He listened to Jenny's hooves as their striking vibrated through him like drumbeats, listened to her breathing as he felt it against his legs, and listened to his own quick breath too, and the soft motion of air past his ears: a breeze that was not a breeze, for he and Jenny were its sources, speeding through air so still that no dust stirred from the track before them. Then he was in it, in the air, the pine blurring in the distance, and down now, a smooth forward plunge that pulled his body with it, but this time he held, and when Jenny hit, his body did not jerk forward but flowed with hers, in horizontal cantering speed down the track, as he patted her neck, and spoke his praise. He did not take her into the leftward curve. He was still looking at the pine, and with his left knee he guided her straight on the track, then off it, past the curve and toward the woods. Because Mr. Ripley had said it was awfully hot for both him and Jenny, and if he wanted to, he could jump her for fifteen minutes and then take her on the trail to cool down, and pay only eight dollars instead of the ten for an hour's jumping.

He veered right, away from the pine, and angled her across the meadow, then slowed her to a trot and posted, his body moving up and down in the rhythm of her strides. He looked at the sky above the woods, then around him at the weeds and short grazed-over grass of the meadow. For a quarter of an hour he had smelled Jenny and leather, and now that they were moving slowly, he could smell the grass too. The two-thirty sun (though one-thirty, really: daylight savings time) warmed his velvet-covered helmet, and shone directly on his shoulders and back, like the hot breath or stare of God. For he felt always in God's eye, even when he heard sirens, and knew from their sounds whether it was a fire truck or ambulance or police car, and he imagined houses burning, and bleeding people in crumpled and broken cars, and he knew God saw and loved those who suffered, yet still saw and loved him, and heard his silent prayer for the people at the end of the sirens' long and fading sound. Sister Catherine had taught them that, in the fourth grade: whenever they heard a siren, she told them to bow in prayer at their desks, to pray for those who were suffering now. He reached the entrance to the trail cut into the woods, and Jenny went on her own between the trees, turned left, and slowed to a walk, into the deep cool shade. He settled into the saddle, and shifted his weight to his hips.

He knew that God watched him now, had watched him all day, and last night as he listened on the stairs, then in his room; had watched him on this day from the beginning of time, in the eternal moment that was God's. As soon as He made Adam or started the evolution that would end with people who stood and talked—*and loved*, he thought, *loved*—He had known this day, and also had known what Richie did not: what he would do about it, how he would live with it. Richie himself did not know how he would live with it. Everyone had to bear a cross as Christ did, and he lived to prepare himself for his, but he saw now that he had believed he had already borne the one for his childhood. Nobody had ever said you got one as a child and one or even two when you grew up, but there it was: he had felt spared for a few more years. Two years ago his mother moved out and then they were divorced and he carried that one, got himself nailed to it, hung there in pain and the final despair and then released himself, commended his will and spirit to God, and something in him died—he did not know what—but afterward, like Christ on Easter, he rose again, could love his days again, and the people in them, and he forgave his parents, and himself too for having despaired of them, for believing they could never love anyone and so were unworthy of love, of his love too, and unworthy even of the earth, and its life. Had forgiven himself through confession to Father Oberti one winter morning before the weekday Mass, while snow fell outside, so he had to walk to the church, and snow melted on his boots in the confessional, and he whispered to Father Oberti what he had felt about his mother and father, and how he had also committed the sin of despair, had believed that God had turned from him, that he could never again be happy on this earth, and had wished for his own death, and his parents' grief; had imagined many times his funeral, and his parents, standing at opposite sides of the grave, crying. Father Oberti had said it was a very good confession, and a very mature one for a young boy. Behind the veil between them, Father Oberti looked straight ahead, his cheek resting on his hand, and did not know who Richie was, but Richie had said, at the beginning, *Bless me, Father, for I have sinned; I'm ten years old.*

Now he had a second cross, its weight pressing down on his shoulder here on the trail beneath the trees, pressing on his heart, really, so he thought: *That's it: being sad is the cross.* And he knew that somehow he must not be sad, even though he was, and he thought of Larry standing at the fence around the indoor ring in winter, Sunday after Sunday, and the outdoor ring in warm seasons, all those Sundays Larry driving him to Ripley Farm and waiting. Yet he did not have to wait. Most of the children who rode with Richie were driven to the stables and then picked up, but always Larry waited, and he did that until Richie was old enough to ride his bicycle to his lesson, and still in winter or rain Larry drove him. He had been grateful but had never said so, and he had been grateful to Larry for teaching him to cross-country ski, and he saw Larry now skiing beside him, stopping to help him up when he fell on his back in the snow, his ankles turned with the skis he partly lay on, and he had never told Larry that either: how Larry had given him the two sports he most loved. He played softball and touch football, basketball and hockey with his friends in the neighborhood, and he played well enough to like these games, but he did not like the games enough to enjoy them unless he was playing with friends. This was what he loved: big strong Jenny under him, and the woods around and above him; and cross-country skiing over the athletic field and into the woods on the trail marked with orange circles painted on trees. A small college was near his house, and the college owned the athletic field and woods, and the trails were marked for the students; so he saw them sometimes, skiied around them or waited while they skiied around him, but they did not disturb him any more than chipmunks running across the trail did here, or the male cardinal he saw leaving its perch, or the blue jay, or the two doves. In riding and skiing he had found an answer to one of his deepest needs, without even knowing he had the need, and so without even seeking an answer. He had learned to make his spiritual solitude physical and, through his flesh, to do this in communion with the snow and evergreens, and the naked trees that showed him the bright sky of winter; and with the body of a horse, and the earth its hooves pounded, the air it breasted, and this woods and his glimpses through leaves of the hot blue sky.

So he wondered what he had ever given Larry, and what he could give him now, what he could do without hurting Brenda, or his father. He patted Jenny's neck, looked between her ears at the winding trail, and looked about him at the woods, with its air that was close and still, yet cool, and he saw the world as a tangle of men and women and boys and girls, thick and wildly growing as this woods; some embraced and some struggled, while all of them reached upward for air and rain and sun. He must somehow move through it, untouched by it, but in it too, toward God. He knew he could do that on a horse, and on cross-country skis, and at Mass when the Consecration sharpened his focus so that he was only aware of himself as a breathing heart, and two knees on the padded kneeler, and two arms resting on the wooden back of the pew in front of him; and then when he took the Body and Blood of Christ from the priest, and placed it on his tongue, and softly chewed as he walked back to his pew. At all those times, he was so free of the world and his life in it that he could have been in another country, in another century; or not even on the earth, and not mortal.

So it was people. They were the cross, and the sadness they brought you, and he could not spend the next five years, till he entered the seminary, on a horse or on skis or at Mass. From Christ he had to receive the strength or goodness or charity or whatever it was to give his father and Brenda more than forgiveness and acceptance. He had to love their days in the house with him, and they had to know he did. And he had to be with Larry outside of the house, as he saw his mother now. Saint Paul had written that all the works were nothing without love. He had to love them all, and he could do that only with Christ, and to receive Christ he could not love Melissa. He knew that from her scents this morning, and her voice, and her kiss.

7

When Carol was a girl, and her father had spoken to her like this, his face and voice so serious, his speech slow and distinct, as though he studied each word before speaking, she had thought he was stern, and she was frightened. But now she was smiling. She knew she ought not to be, and when she was conscious that again her lips were spread, she drew them in, and tried to return his gaze whose parts were greater than mere seriousness: he was contrite, supplicatory, and he looked trapped too, as if he were lying to her. At twenty-six, she loved him from the distance of a grown daughter, and so more easily, warmly, perhaps more deeply. Yet she felt nostalgia too, a tangible sigh of it in her heart, for the love she had for him when she was a girl: when she believed he was the best father anyone could have, and the most handsome, and that he could do anything on earth she would ever need him to; and she believed that, more than Larry, more even than her mother, she possessed him. When she had outgrown those feelings she had outgrown her fear of him too, and if she had had a choice, she would have chosen the way she loved him now.

She had cleaned her apartment for his visit, and put on a dress, but that was pride, not fear. She had even picked up two blouses and a pair of jeans that had fallen to the closet floor some time ago, and placed them on hangers, and she had slid the closet door shut, which she would have done anyway, but she knew she was doing it to hide two of René's shirts hanging among her clothes, the shirts touching a blouse on one side and a dress on the other, a charade of their owners. All of this was so foolish and, besides, even if he did peer into her closet like some prying detective of a father, which he was not, René's shirts were small enough to be a woman's. So maybe there was still fear, a trace of it, but more likely it was the habitual defense through privacy that one maintained against parents. She had been anxious, though, because of his voice on the phone that morning, and his refusal to tell her why he was coming, save to assure her that the family was in good health, there was nothing to worry about, nothing terrible had happened. Still, when she cleaned her dressing table, she opened the drawer and looked at the vial of cocaine and packet of marijuana. She sat, trying to decide which to employ, before she remembered she had begun by trying to decide whether to use any drug at all. She closed the drawer, stood and glanced about her bedroom whose windows looked out at treetops and down at Beacon Street. She worked for a travel agency and could not afford the apartment but it was worth it and she thought no more about that. She went to the living room, saw on the mantel a Gauloise pack René had forgotten, and brought it to the bedroom and put it in the drawer with the cocaine and marijuana. As she had all her life, she saw this recurrence as a sign: it was meant for her to reach for either the marijuana or the cocaine. But she shut the drawer and sat in the living room, in a wing-backed chair, and waited. Now she was drinking her second Stolichnaya; so was her father, and she watched the level in his glass. She did not want to finish first, and she wished he would hurry.

It was not the vodka that gave her mouth control of itself, so that it smiled when it should not. At times she even laughed, and brought her hand to her mouth, and cleared her throat, and he looked relieved, though puzzled. She felt herself blush too, when she laughed, but there he sat in the old leather-cushioned rocker she had bought from Diana, last year's roommate who had left to live with her boyfriend in Brookline; they had believed they would remain close friends, but Carol had not seen her since winter, and that once was by chance. So the rocking chair often reminded her of Diana, and of the death of friendship that lovers so often caused, and he sat in that chair and talked about Larry and Richie and his friend Brady the state representative, and she not only felt mirthful but could not keep from showing it. Finally his face became more quizzical than anything else, and he stopped talking, looked at her for a moment, then with two swallows finished his drink while she held in her mouth and savored the last of hers.

"You taught me to dance on your toes," she said, and took his glass and went to the kitchen. At the sink she ate his onions and tossed out the ice, put in new cubes, poured vodka from the bottle in the freezer, and forked onions from a jar into the glasses, ground pepper over the ice, then in the doorway she stopped and let the smile come and stay.

"You stood on my feet," he said. "How old were you?"

"Eight. No, nine."

She brought him the drink and sat looking at him.

"That was good," he said.

"It was. Remember, we'd do it late into the night? Even after Mom went to bed. And I thought Mom was jealous. I thought I could see it in her face at breakfast."

"You probably did."

"Was she?"

"I didn't ask."

"Did you ever?"

"Ask if she was jealous? No."

"Ask her anything."

He lit a cigarette, and she knew it was to shift his eyes and his face, and to use his hands, but she quietly waited. How confused they became, these men. For so long she had not known it, even when she first had lovers (not lovers, boys: high school boys), but in college or in her early twenties, she could not recall precisely when, or even what man she had learned it from, she knew with the sudden certainty of one who wakes with the answer to last night's enigma. No matter how old they were, there was something in them that stopped aging at nineteen and, if they loved her, she could summon it from them at will.

"I didn't mean it that way," she said.

"Which way?"

"Trying to blame you. It was affectionate. You see, it's so *funny*. That's why I keep laughing like an idiot. You've always been—you know what you've been. I don't know about you and Mom. But I'm sure of one thing. If you ever asked her how she felt about something, whatever she said wouldn't stop you."

His face reddened and he smiled and looked down at his drink, pinched an onion out of it and put it in his mouth.

"So I'm a selfish bastard," he said, and chewed and watched her. But she knew he did not mean it, for she had seen in his lowered face, and his smile, that look men wore when they knew they were bad boys yet were loved by a woman anyway. At once she saw him in bed with Brenda, and she glanced at his crotch, then looked at her cigarette, drew from it, seeing him as he must be in Brenda, an aging and grateful bear.

"I always thought of you as a bear," she said.

"A bear?"

"A wiry bear. Just wandering through the woods like it's all his. Eating berries. Catching fish. But don't fuck with him."

"Sounds like a grizzly."

"That's when I was a little girl."

"And now?"

"Tonight? A puppy."

"Not even a bear cub?"

"Maybe a cub. Ah, Daddy, you crazy wonderful old thing. Let's dance."

"Dance?"

"Come on."

"I wouldn't know how. Not to your music."

"What if I've got something you can dance to?"

"Jesus. After today— Don't you have anything you want to say?"

"Sure. But I've got Sinatra too."

"No."

"I do. Think you can handle it?"

"I was dancing to Sinatra when—"

"—I know, I know," she said, standing, "when I just wore pants to the beach."

She finished her drink and put out her cigarette, and near the fireplace she kneeled on the carpet and opened the leather cassette box Dennis had given her. He was last fall's lover. Her cassettes were arranged alphabetically, and she took Sinatra and put it in the cassette player on the mantel, and turned to her father. He stood, and said: "Want to roll back the carpet?"

"Take off your shoes," and she reached down to a bent leg and pulled off her sandal, then the other one, watching him sitting to untie and remove his shoes. She crossed the room to him, her arms held out, and he took her hand and waist, and together they turned and swayed and side-stepped between her four chairs, then past them to the rectangular space at one end of the room, near her bedroom door. The song was "My Funny Valentine" and he sang it with Sinatra, softly in her ear; and he was her father, yes, but not of a girl anymore, and as a woman she saw him more clearly, as if her own erotic life had given her an equality or superiority that years alone could not have.

So she saw him as a man too, apart from her mother for two years, alone too much (at least without a woman too much), and he had fallen in love with a very lovable young woman. That was all. And her simple feelings about it made her think she ought to feel more but could not, because the love she had given others and taken from them had left her unable or unwilling to look at the complexity of love; had left her knowing only the tight circle that surrounded the lovers themselves, so she could feel little more than recognition of pain touching Larry or Richie. He sang in her ear, and she rested her head on his chest, and thought that no, it was not some jaded selfishness; it was being a woman and having the courage to admit that when you loved, you changed your life, if that was what it took, and you changed other people's lives, and you could not let even your own children stop you. Because lovers had always to be selfish, turned to each other, their backs to the world, if they wanted to keep their love. As much as she had wanted Diana to stay, for their friendship and to share the rent, she had known Diana was right when she moved the few miles to Brookline, dropped her old life and went to a new one, with the hope that this time this love would be the one that lived and grew like a tree. When you had loved several times, there was a great urge to give up and say it did not exist and had never existed, had always been a trick of nature to keep itself going, and at those times you wanted only to take lovers to help you make it through the nights, as Kristofferson sang. But you had to fight that, even if you did take the lovers, had to keep alive that part of yourself that still hoped, believed, so if love did come you would be ready enough, and strong enough, and then no one could stop you, not even yourself.

Sinatra started "I Get a Kick Out of You" and her father gently moved her backward, and danced a slow jitterbug, his hand on her waist guiding her into a turn, and she circled under their clasped and shifting hands, faced him, her right hand in his left, their free arms waving with the beat, his fingers snapping.

"So you fell in love," she said. "So what."

"I'm not sure that's what it is."

"What is it then?"

His eyes were closed now, his head moving from side to side with the music.

"I don't know. Maybe I never will."

He raised his arm, and she turned toward him and past him, under his arm, and behind her he turned so when she completed hers they were facing.

"Why not call it falling in love?" she said.

He pulled her to him, into a slow dance, but faster and

with circles like a waltz, and said: "Because at a certain age you don't fall. You just sort of gradually sink."

"Lordy."

"That doesn't mean it's bad."

"What do you call it then?"

"Different. You don't leap anymore. It's solid, though."

"So you sink."

"Something like that. And you know what? I don't care what's wrong with her."

"What's wrong with her?"

"It doesn't matter. I don't care. Comes from age."

They moved apart, holding both hands, then raised their arms and turned from each other, back-to-back, their twisting hands touching, then he took her right with his left, and they danced sideways, back and forth in their rectangle, to the faster beat. At the song's end he swirled with her, then dipped, his left arm supporting her back as beside her he bent his forward knee and leaned with it, as though to kneel. He pulled her up, and held her, and they danced slowly, silently, to "Little Girl Blue." She remembered lunch once with René at a French restaurant that he said was good. He was some sort of chemist and was working in Boston now and all she understood about it was that he might go back to France, and he might not. They were eating paté and she was talking about her father and he said he would like someday to meet him. *No you wouldn't,* she said. He paused, his downturned fork in his left hand, his bread in the right. *Why is that?* She said she had gone to Paris three years ago and when she got back she told her father the Parisians were rude and did not like Americans, and he had said: *If it wasn't for us, they'd be talking German now.* René smiled and said: *Perhaps we would not talk about history.* And she said: *Besides, I don't think he likes men who are fucking his daughter.* He chewed, watching her, then drank wine, and said: *And has he met many of these men? Not if I could help it,* she said, and moving on the carpet with her father's body she knew she would not tell him about René, even if he asked if she were seeing anyone, and for the same reason she had hidden the tracks of René's life into hers: for too long her lovers had seemed from the start ephemeral, no one to arouse his paternal interest; so she had said nothing about any of them, as an adolescent dilettante might decide to stop drawing her parents' enthusiasm toward each new avocation.

"Do you go to Mass at all?" he said.

"Not for years."

"Why?"

"Do you?"

"No," he said. "Why don't you?"

"I don't feel anything there anymore. Is that why you don't go?"

"No. I know it's there. I just can't fit it in."

"Time, you mean?"

"No. My life."

Gracefully he turned and she followed him, on the balls of her feet, her left hand on the back of his neck, her right hand in his left, rising and swinging outward from their circle.

"Richie does, though," he said. "Fits it in."

"Still wants to be a priest?"

"Yes."

"That would be funny. In this family."

"I hope he does it. I tell you, some days I think he ought to go for one of those monasteries. Where nobody talks."

"Trappists."

"That's the one. They make good preserves."

"Great preserves. Daddy?"

"What?"

"Be happy."

"Okay."

"And bring Brenda here for dinner."

"Okay."

"A lot."

"That's very nice."

"No it's not. It's not nice at all. I love you, Daddy. That's all it is."

He hugged her then, and they stood in the music in the room, holding each other, and she felt the life in his chest and hoped it would be long, and happy with love, and she wished more than she had wished for anything, in a very long time, that she could give him those, that they would flow from her heart to his as they stood embraced to a song.

8

Joan's love had died of premature old age. She lived in a small apartment in the town of Amesbury on the Merrimack River. The apartment was on the second floor of a wooden building that years ago had housed a family. She had chosen the place because the other tenants were quiet, retired, and old (at forty-seven she was the youngest) and because her apartment had room for no one but herself to sleep. She had bought a double bed not to share but because she was accustomed to one, and she liked to roll toward its middle and spread out when she was nearing sleep. The closet would not hold all her clothes, but she was as tired of giving them attention as she was of love, and she gave clothes for all seasons to Goodwill. She placed small rugs at either side of the bed, and the rest of the floor was bare. It was old dark wood with slight undulations, and she liked it. There were two windows at the side of the room, and two at the front, and she pushed the dressing table and chest of drawers against walls, clear of the windows. Since she was on the second floor she rarely had to close the Venetian blinds, or even lower them, and nearly always she kept them raised. She liked waking to the blue or gray coming through the windows to her right, and at her feet; and going to sleep looking at their dark, and a gleam from the streetlight half a block away. Three recent and large photographs of her children, in color, hung on the wall above her bed. The other three walls were bare, their flat surfaces interrupted only by a door in one, and two windows in each of the other two. The closet was beside her bed. The two front windows were opposite the foot of the bed, above the short, slanted, blue-shingled roof of the front porch, and past that she could look down on the lawn with its two maples and one oak, and the quiet street.

A chair at the window would clutter the room, so on some nights when she could not sleep for an hour or so past her usual time, she brought a straight-backed chair from the kitchen, and sat at the window, and with the blinds raised she smoked and gazed out at the night, and opened her mind to whatever images came, casting away the ones that brought sorrow or anger or remorse, as deftly as, when snapping beans, she tossed out the ones that were wrinkled. In truth, she could have kept a chair at the window, grown used to its jutting into the little space she had, but she planned to live out her life in this quiet place, alone, and she was cautious about patterns, like becoming the old woman sitting at the window. Old age meant nothing to her; she did not care whether she attained it or not. But she did not want to look like she was living out the last days of a long life, when she was only resting from twenty-seven years of marriage. She meant to keep resting too, until someday a neighbor found her (not too long after death, she hoped), lying on her bed, open-mouthed in final peace (given her with suddenness and without pain, she hoped).

The bedroom was adjacent to the living room, whose door opened to the corridor above the stairs. The living room was small enough too, and she did not have in it a couch anyone could sleep on; she had one armchair with a hassock and floor lamp for reading, a small antique roll-top desk for paying bills and writing an occasional note to Carol, whom she saw less than the other children, and twice a year or so a letter to her brother in Monterey. There were three other chairs in a semicircle facing her armchair, and outside their circle, against the walls, were her bookshelves, filled with fiction written from 1850 to 1950, and of these her favorites were Zola, Kate Chopin's *The Awakening*, and Jean Rhys, de Maupassant, and Colette. There was a television set she rarely watched and a radio and phonograph she played every day, and at night when she came home, with the volume low both day and night, for she always felt she could hear her old neighbors, most of them living alone, either sleeping at night or napping in the afternoon or simply being quiet. She played classical music in daylight, mostly symphonies by Schubert and Mozart and Beethoven and Tchaikovsky, whose sounds changed the very look of the apartment, as tangibly as a fresh coat of paint on the walls. So did Bach's cantatas, and Horowitz playing Scarlatti and Schumann, Chopin and Debussy. Larry and Brenda knew this music, yet when they talked with her about it, they might as well have tried explaining a philosophical abstraction. All she knew was that its deep beauty changed the walls and ceilings and floors of her home. Late at night she liked Billie Holiday and Ella Fitzgerald, Brubeck and Ellington and Charlie Parker, John Coltrane and Sarah Vaughan, and these, as she sat at the window, or leaned back in the armchair in the dark, sculpted her sadness into something strong and lovely.

On her living room wall were framed, glass-covered prints by Monet and Manet and Cézanne, and a Renoir print hung in the kitchen. Where there was room—on windowsills, the tops of bookshelves, and hanging from the kitchen ceiling—she had put potted plants. The kitchen, with its small working space, and small refrigerator and gas stove, was made for one person, and she ate there, at a table she constantly bumped as she cooked and cleaned. She had bought two chairs for the table, and only Richie or Larry sat in the extra one with any regularity, and once every month or six weeks Carol sat in it, and ate what Joan cooked and was garrulous (and honest, Joan believed) about its flavor.

The sadness that stayed with her was less an emotion than a presence, like the Guardian Angel she had believed in as a child. You never felt the Angel, as you felt shyness or confidence or affection; but often, when you had forgotten about it, you felt it standing beside you, so close that its airy body touched your side, and one large wing enfolded your back. These might be times of danger, to your body or to the self that in childhood you worried most about, the heart and soul that were your name. Or they might be times when you were flirting with the forbidden, pretending to yourself that you would only look but not touch, while knowing that the closer you approached, the more certain was your fall. Now, though, her sadness did not manifest itself only on certain occasions that were connected to it, either directly or by association. Its wing did not wait to touch her when Richie phoned, or when she phoned him, or waited in the car for him to come out of the house and go with her to her apartment; or when she saw a mother with a young son on the sidewalks of the town, or a family with a young son at the restaurant where she worked. No: the wing remained on her back, the body at her side, even when she was in good spirits, alone in her rooms or drinking after work with the other waitresses; her peaceful solitude or talk and laughter were not destroyed, but they were distracted, and so diminished.

She would rather endure carrying Richie in her womb, and the bursting pain of bearing him, than what she had suffered the day she told him and, that same day, left him, and what she had to keep enduring, it seemed, for the rest of her life. She should have left before she conceived him, but she could not wish that, because then he was not alive, and she could not imagine that, nor wish for it, nor survive with her sanity one day in a world he had either left or, because of her, had never joined. Yet a time had come when, still married, and living every day with Richie, she had believed if the phone rang once more, if she drove across the Merrimack to the supermarket one more time, if she cooked one more meal, or if Greg did or said or only started to do or say one of the fifty to one hundred things she could not witness without a boredom that was plummeting toward revulsion, she would go mad. But it was none of these that had defeated her. Nor was it Greg. She could make a list of his parts she disliked, even despised; but any wife could make the same sort of list, any wife who loved; or any husband, for that matter. It was that she had outlived love. A century ago she might have died in childbirth or from the flu, while she was young. Nutrition and medicine had preserved her life, yet without the resilience to love so long. Then each phone call or errand or chore, each grating part of Greg, was love's passing bell.

The restaurant where she worked was owned by Hungarians, the chef had come from an expensive Hungarian restaurant in Boston, and Joan was proud of the good food and low prices that drew from the Merrimack Valley customers who dressed casually and worked for salaries that did not allow luxuries. The restaurant was a white wooden building with two dining rooms and an eight-stool bar, and it was in the shade of trees beside Route 110, a two-lane country road. She could have sat forever at her bedroom window with what Greg sent her twice a month, though she had asked for nothing—at least nothing material—but she worked five nights a week to be with people. She had never been a waitress, and now she was a good one, and she liked the work: liked learning the names and some of the lives of the regular customers, and knowing their drinks before they ordered, so as she turned to each one she could name the drink with a question in her voice. They would nod and praise her memory, and she knew their smiles came from a deeper source: she made them happy by making them feel welcome, by giving them what at least felt like affection, and usually was, beneath the simple exchange of money for food. While she served their tables they talked to her, and often people calling for reservations asked for her station, and always people gave her good tips. She did not need the money, but its meaning gratified her.

The kitchen closed at ten and the bar closed between twelve and one, so when she had cleared all her tables she sat with the other waitresses, at a table near the bar, and drank till closing time. She had always had a little to drink before dinner, when Greg came home, but only as a break from cooking and a greeting to her husband, and the drinks themselves were not important. But now, for the first time in her life, she knew the pleasure of finishing an intense period of fast hard work, and sitting down to drinks with the other workers; their talk was never serious, but gay and laughing, the sounds of release, and each cold drink, each cigarette, soothed her, from her tired feet and legs to her brain, till she felt as if she were talking and laughing from a hammock.

At ten-thirty that night, she was at a table with three women when she glanced down the length of the long dining room, her eyes drawn to its door that opened to the front parking lot, and she saw Larry standing at it, watching her, and knew that was why she had looked and that whatever it was, it was bad. How many times had she felt the tingling heat of lactation in her breasts when he was a boy and no longer nursed but was crying in pain? She stood, and the women stopped talking and looked at her.

"It's my son," she said. "I'll see what he wants."

"Call him over," one said, and Joan saw another motioning her to silence, and so she knew that what was in her heart had reached her face too. *Richie. It's Richie*, seeing him dead under a bent bicycle. She was walking toward Larry and he came to her and they stood between the wall and the room of tables covered for tomorrow.

"Is anything wrong?"

"Yes. I need to talk."

"Is anything *wrong. With* somebody."

"No. No, everybody's fine."

"Thank God. I thought something had happened."

"Something did. But everybody's well."

"Good. Then let's hear about it."

She saw Richie in his bed, with whatever he dreamed; now she knew the trouble was love and she felt the hammock again, lifting her, and she sank into its idle swing. She could hear about love from there, without a sigh or the tensing of a muscle. She led him to an empty table opposite the end of the bar, near the television turned to a Red Sox game but without sound, and two empty tables away from her friends, and she seated him with his back to the women, to protect his face.

"Dad called me to the house last night."

"Don't you want a drink?"

"Yes. What's that?"

"Vodka and tonic."

"I'll have one."

She stood, and he reached out a hand that fell short of hers, and said: "Wait. Let me—"

"—Relax, and have a drink. I thought you'd come from the morgue."

She got the drinks from young handsome black-bearded Lee at the bar, and he shook his head at her money. Larry was smoking and staring at the silent ballgame. She sat and he lit her cigarette and said: "Dad and Brenda have been seeing each other. Now they're getting married."

She leaned back in her chair, and studied his face.

"Well," she said, and she saw Greg, foolish and wild, and angry and sweet, both too much and not enough of him to live in the world, let alone with one woman; at least by the time he burned out Brenda he would be nearly dead. "What about you?"

"I'm going fucking nuts. Excuse me. I'm going nuts."

"Don't. At least he didn't take her from you."

"Thanks, Mom."

"You left her or you lost her. That's all. Nothing else matters."

"My father marrying her matters."

"Of course it does. It stinks."

"It's even against the law," he said, and he looked down at his drink, as though ducking his petulance.

"What law?"

"Massachusetts."

"That doesn't surprise me. But it doesn't have anything to do with you. Listen: your father has always been a son of a bitch. That's one reason I loved him for so long."

"Why?"

"Because he never wants to be one. It was exciting, watching him struggle."

"How long would you have stayed? If it weren't for Richie. The accident."

"Richie was no accident."

"Really? You were—" He closed his eyes, his lips quietly counting. "Thirty-five."

"Your father thought it would save us."

"Did you?"

"He could always talk me into things."

"I told him last night I wasn't coming home again. Or to work either."

She nodded, watching him. You knew so much about your children; too much. They changed so little from infancy that, if you dared, you could come very near predicting their lives by the time they started school. At least the important parts: Richie had always been solitary and at peace with it; Carol had wanted happiness whose source was being loved, and she had looked for it with each new friend, had changed her child's play and dress and even speech with these friends, and had never looked for it by doing something she loved, or even doing nothing at all, in her own solitude; and Larry, the one with talents, with real gifts, had always waited for some-one—a friend, his family, a teacher—to see those gifts and encourage him. He could no more leave his father now than he could have twenty years ago.

"What do you think?" he said.

"I understand. But I don't think you will."

"Why not?"

"It'll only break your heart, and Richie's, and your father's."

"Not yours?"

"I live here now. You can't work at the stores? Really?"

"No."

"But you don't hate him."

"No."

"You're just hurt."

"Just."

"Want another?"

"All right."

Lee refused her money again, and she thanked him with the freedom she had earned: very early, on this job, she had let men know that she did not want a lover. She had done it with subtlety and, if that wasn't clear, with kindness; and she accepted free drinks because she was a worker there, and a good one.

"I love this time of night," she said to Larry. "You should come in more often, about now."

"Maybe I will."

"We have fun. What about you? Do you have fun?"

"When I'm working."

"At the stores? Or performing?"

"Dancing. Acting. Are you coming next week?"

"Yes. Somebody's working for me. Listen: can I tell you something?"

"After last night, anybody can tell me anything."

"You're a good dancer, a good actor. I've seen you, and I know. I don't have the training to judge like a professional. But I feel it. But you only *want* to be a performer. Then you wait for it to happen. You don't go after it. You let too much get taken from you. You wait too much for things to happen. You think too Goddamn much."

"Jesus."

"You know it's true. I'm not trying to hurt you. I want to tell you something."

"What's that got to do with Dad marrying my Goddamn ex-wife?"

"Look at you. You can't even sound angry when you say that. I think some artists would be set free by all this. No more father, no more job, no ex-wife in the same town. They'd use this like a train to take them away. New York; wherever. Just throw themselves at the world: here I am. What makes me feel so—what gives me pain about you is that you won't. So sometimes I think you got just enough of a gift to be a curse, and not enough to be a blessing. You share that with your father."

"What's his gift?"

"The second part: here I am, world. And the world always sees him. But there's no talent to see. Only the energy, the drive."

"You're sure I won't leave?"

"Yes."

"Me too. I guess that's why I came to see my mommy."

Then he pushed back his chair, started to rise, but she reached across the table and held his wrist till he eased into the chair and slid it forward.

"Stay a while," she said. "Let's talk."

"All right."

"I'm going to keep you here till you smile."

"What time do they close?"

"Time enough. I'll tell you something you don't have to believe tonight, or for a long time. You'll keep working for your father and, after a while, it'll be all right. You'll see him at the store, and you won't think of him with Brenda. There might be a twitch, like some old injury that reminds you it was there. But you won't see the pictures. You probably feel that twitch whenever you see your father anyway, because you've always fought, you two, and you've always loved each other." He nodded, and she saw, so joyfully that she had to force her words to be slow and calm, that he was listening, truly listening, and how many times had she ever been able to tell one of her children something she knew, and to help the child? So much of motherhood was casting lines to children beyond reach, that she could count with less than two digits the times their hands had clutched the rope and pulled. "Finally, at the store, it'll be the same. You'll go get Richie the way I do, sitting in the car, tooting the horn, and you'll bring him to my place for dinner. I'll get a third chair for the table. Then one evening your father will come out to the car while Richie's still inside. He'll look sinful as a scolded boy, and he'll ask you in for a beer. You'll want to curse or cry, but you'll go have the beer instead, and Brenda won't be in the house. Because he will be planning this, because he loves you. You'll just pass the time of day over your beer, and you'll have a second, and when you leave with Richie he'll offer you his hand. You'll shake it. One day after work he'll take you out for drinks and dinner. He'll show up at a play or a dance concert, just him and Richie, and afterward they'll take you someplace for a beer. He'll invite you to Sunday dinner, and you'll go, and everyone will have tense stomachs and be very polite, and Brenda won't kiss or touch your father, but she'll kiss you hello and goodbye. Soon you'll be dropping in and someday it won't even hurt anymore. You and your father will be able to laugh and fight again. Everyone will survive. I told you I'd make you smile."

"Was I?"

"You have tears in your eyes. But there was a smile."

"You know why?"

"No."

"Because I knew all that. When I heard it, I knew I had known it since I woke up this morning."

"Good. You know why I like my waitress friends so much? And what I learned from them? They don't have delusions. So when I'm alone at night—and I love it, Larry—I look out my window, and it comes to me: we don't have to live great lives, we just have to understand and survive the ones we've got. You're smiling again."

"Tears too."

"Wipe them fast, before my friends think something terrible is happening."

9

At ten o'clock Richie's father phoned to say he was still at Carol's and would be home around midnight.

"Are you all right?" his father said.

"Sure."

"Are you going to bed now?"

"After a while."

He put the phone back on the receiver on the kitchen wall and looked at it, then at the clock on the stove. He went down the stairs to his room and took his key ring with the keys to his bicycle lock and the front door and back door; he was passing the open bathroom when he stopped and looked at Jim Rice over the toilet with its raised seat. He went in and brushed his teeth, and his rump tightened against the danger of the bristles and the flavor in his mouth, and his careful brushing of his hair, and tucking in and smoothing of his shirt. He started to pray *Lead us not into temptation* but stopped at *Lead* and hurried out of the house, leaving on lights for his coming back.

Houses were lighted, and leaves of trees near the street-light, but beneath him the grass was dark and he walked care-fully, like a stranger on his lawn. Then he was on the road under the trees, and he could see objects now, distinct in the darkness: shrubs and flowers, and mailboxes near doors, and above him the limbs of trees. He watched the trees where that morning they had talked; then the blacktop ended, and clum-sily he stepped through weeds and in and out of ruts, and started to sweat in the warm, close air whose density made him feel he moved through smoke he could neither see nor smell nor taste. He did not risk stumbling loudly through the trees, approaching her like someone frightening or, worse, an awkward boy. He looked up at the treetops against the stars and sky, then left the trail, and went around the trees and stood beside them, in their shadows, and looked at the infield through the backstop screen, and scanned the outfield.

First he saw Conroy, the dog, a blond motion, then a halted silhouette in left center field. He looked to both of Conroy's sides, saw only the expanse of dark grass and the woods past the outfield. Then he stepped out of the shadows, stood in the open, and peered down the edge of the trees. He saw the brightening glow of her cigarette, then it moved down and away from the small figure that was Melissa, profiled, sit-ting on the ground. Above her, cicadas sang in the trees. At once he moved and spoke her name. Her face jerked toward him, and he said: It's Richie; then he was there, standing above her, looking down at her forehead and her eyes. He could not see their green. He sat beside her, crossed his legs like hers.

"I didn't think you'd still be here," he said.

"Is that why you came late?"

"No. I had to wait for my Dad to call."

"Where is he?"

"Visiting my sister in Boston."

"Can you see Conroy?"

He looked at left field.

"Yes."

"Where?"

"Straight that way."

He pointed his right arm and she touched it with her cheek, sighting down it. Slowly he tightened his bicep so her face would feel its muscles.

"I don't want him in those woods. Once he went in there and wouldn't come out for an hour."

"Look where my finger is."

"Okay, I see him."

"I think he's coming this way."

"He is."

She drew on her cigarette, then tossed it arcing in front of them, and he watched it burn in the grass. He could see its thin smoke, but he could still not see the color of her eyes. She wore the cut-off jeans from this morning and the blue denim shirt with its sleeves rolled up, and the shirttails knotted in front; her skin looked darker. He had not noticed her shifting, but she had, when she looked down his arm, and now her knee still touched his, and her left arm his right, till one of them moved; and her shoulder rubbed his or rested against it. Beneath the sound of cicadas, his breath was too quick, audible; he tried to slow it, held it for moments after inhaling, and breathed through his nose.

"Why did you have to wait for your father to call?"

"He wanted me to. So I'd know when he'd be home."

"Oh. I thought maybe she was sick or something. Your sister."

"No."

"He sounds nice."

"My dad?"

"Yes."

"I hope so."

"That's a funny thing to say."

He nodded. In her eyes now was a shade of green. Except for tobacco smoke and lipstick, her scents had faded since morning: the cologne or cosmetic was gone. Her clothes and skin too, morning-fresh when she had kissed him, held the smells of the day: its long hot sunlit air, and the restful and pleasant odor of female sweat.

"Why did you say it?"

"Because I want him to be."

"Are you going to tell me?"

"Tell you what?"

He was watching her mouth, and he swallowed, and knew he was lost. If only he could be lost without fear. If only his heart could keep growing larger and larger until he had to hold her, else it would burst through his ribs, if only he could look to the stars—and he did: abruptly lifted his face to the sky—and find in them release from what he felt now, or release to feel it. He looked at her eyes, her nose, her lips.

"You know," she said. "What you told me this morning. That you'd tell me sometime."

"Last night—"

"Go on," she said. "Last night."

"My brother came over, to see my dad. He's twenty-five, and I was in bed. But I got up to tell him hello. I was on the stairs going up to the kitchen, but then I heard what they were saying. So I just stayed and listened. After a while I went back to my room. It's under the living room, and they were right over me, so I heard it all."

He lay on his back. Then she was beside him, her arm touching his, and he slid his hand under her palm. Slowly and gently he squeezed, and her fingers pressed. When he found that he was trembling, he did not care. He watched the stars, and talked. When he paused after telling her of that morning, of his father's tears he never saw, she said: "You poor guy."

He did not correct her. But he did not feel that way at all. He did not even have to control his voice, for there were no tears in it, nor in his breast. What he felt was the night air starting to cool, and the dew on the grass under his hand holding Melissa's, and under his arms and head and shirt, and only its coolness touching his thick jeans, and the heels of his shoes. He felt Melissa's hand in his, and the beating of his heart she both quickened and soothed, and he smelled the length of her beside him, and heard in the trees the song of cicadas like the distant ringing of a thousand tambourines. He saw in the stars the eyes of God too, and was grateful for them, as he was for the night and the girl he loved. He lay on the grass and the soft summer earth, holding Melissa's hand, and talking to the stars.

THE LAST WORTHLESS EVENING

to Cadence

... that whole hopeful continent dedicated as a refuge and sanctuary of liberty and freedom from what you called the old world's worthless evening ... and He could have repudiated them since they were his creation now and forever throughout all their generations until not only that old world from which He had rescued them but this new one too which He had revealed and led them to as a sanctuary and refuge were become the same worthless tideless rock cooling in the last crimson evening ...

WILLIAM FAULKNER
The Bear

DEATHS AT SEA

for William B. Goodman

2 July 1961
At sea

Hello Camille:

I suppose we fled the South. I still don't know. Maybe it was just time for us to leave, and be together away from Lafayette, where so many people have known us since we were babies. We've talked about this for four years, so why do I mention it again? Because of Willie Brooks.

And I think of you, alone in a quonset hut in Alameda, California, with officers' wives and not a Negro among them. And I'm on an aircraft carrier in the Western Pacific, and Filipino stewards are the Navy's Negroes. They do the cooking and serving in the officers' wardroom, and they clean the officers' staterooms. It's like the life you and I, thank God, never had at home: those affluent people who had Negroes doing everything for them. Now, after my first months aboard the *Ranger*, I believe my count is accurate: there are three Negro officers. Out of a ship's crew of thirty-five hundred men, and I don't know how many people in the Air Group we have aboard. Ah: I see you reading this, saying Wait a minute. And

91

you're right. I did tell you there were only two, and both were with the squadrons, and were not part of the ship's company; and one is a flight surgeon, the other a personnel officer. No Negro pilot. But now we have a lieutenant junior grade of our own. He is in public relations. (He wants to work in radio or television when he gets out.) He is from Philadelphia. His name is Wilson Jason Brooks. And, Camille, he is my roommate.

Fate? God? Bill was transferred to a destroyer. That left a bunk in my room. Then Willie came aboard. So my flight from the South, if that's what it was, has indeed brought me further away. At first, when he knocked on the door and I opened it and saw his black face, hesitant but smiling, I believed I had come back full circle. But very soon, by the time I had shown him his desk next to mine, pointed out that we had our own lavatory and shaving mirror—which of course he could see, but I was talking talking *talk*ing, in my shyness, my excitement, and yes: my fear—and by the time I had told him I slept in the upper bunk, but it didn't matter to me and he could sleep in whichever was more comfortable for him, I knew I had not come full circle. Because I was as far now from the South as I could imagine: I had a Negro roommate. Then I knew he would also be my friend, when he said: "I'll take the lower. You may have problems enough, without giving up your bed."

"Problems?"

"You didn't get that accent in New Jersey."

"I'm Catholic," I said.

He looked at me as if I had said I'm married, or I'm five-eleven, or I'm twenty-six years old. Then he laughed, a short one, but not forced: it came up from his chest, and he was smiling.

"Is that why you offered me your bed? Pope told you to?"

"I meant I was from south Louisiana. Cajuns and Creoles. French Catholics. I thought I talked like one."

"Well, you don't sound like a cracker. But there *is* a trace, Gerry. Must've been some mean *Bap*tists hanging out in your neighborhood."

"Are we going to shake hands?" I said. "Or stand here try-ing to guess how bad it could be?"

He extended his hand, a large one, and we squeezed each other, the way men do. *Never shake hands like a dead fish,* Mother told me. Why her, and not Daddy?

"Did I just get a cherry?" he said.

"Nope. Integrated college for my last three years. And in summer I worked construction with Negroes. And there was a man when I was a boy. Leonard. He mowed the lawn once a week. I liked him. And there *were* some mean Southern Bap-tists around. Mean Catholics too."

"Calm down, man. It'll be all right. I'm scared shitless too."

"Have you had trouble?"

"Who, me?"

Probably this sounds to you, reading a letter, more like a confrontation than a meeting. But it wasn't. You see—and you've told me that my face always shows what I'm feeling—he *knew* how I felt. He could see it; almost smell it, he told me later. He said there was guilt in the very air of the room, and he knew from my eyes that I had not earned it but had simply grown up with it. Or, as he said later, in a bar in Yokosuka, I was like a man who had seen a lynching once and tried to stop it and got beat up and didn't get killed only because he was white and they already had a Negro to hang; and I blamed myself still, and could not stop blaming myself for throwing rocks at a wheatfield and not breaking one stalk.

We were at sea when Willie arrived. They flew him to the ship, and we stayed out for another week before going to Yokosuka. During the day, except Saturday afternoons and Sundays, we rarely saw each other. We woke together. We wake to his alarm now, because its ringing is softer than mine. That's almost a metaphor, isn't it? For—Oh, God, Camille; damn this distance and these letters. I want to hold you, let you hear me and feel me while I tell you this: I've told him all of it: about you, and me, and the two of us and Emmett Till and the night in the bar when I held my knife against that ignorant bastard's throat. Willie liked that. I mean, he was moved. But he covered it up quickly by saying: "And with a knife. I thought only my people carried blades."

And I was relieved. For there was too much emotion between us that night, his fourth or fifth in our stateroom. Or too much of mine, as I told him of our sorrow and anger as witnesses, told this to a victim, but without guilt, as though we were talking about a disease he had survived, and I was telling of others suffering with it and dying, and I could do nothing for them but watch. That's it: we could have been talking of the flu epidemic in 1918. We were sitting in our desk chairs, the chairs turned so we faced each other. Then he said: "I'm glad you didn't kill him."

He laid his hand on mine, resting on my desk. Then he lifted my hand and turned it, my palm to his, and squeezed.

"The old ten percent," he said.

"What?"

"People like you. When will it be ninety? And ninety of me, for that matter. We had no money, but my parents got us through college. I'm a Naval officer. You can't know what that means to them. They'll never have to put up new wallpaper. Not in my old bedroom, anyway. Unless they take down all those pictures of their boy Willie. In khakis. Blues. Whites. That's the funny one."

"I understand."

"I know you do."

"But not about the ten percent like you."

"That was bitterness. Sometimes you get so angry at the ones keeping you down, you get angry at your people who stay down. No. It's not ten percent. We're not Indians yet. They kept us alive."

We wake together, and take turns shaving. He's a tall, broad man and, no, I haven't seen him naked yet, so forget that myth for a while. My devout Catholic and concupiscent Cajun wife. We have breakfast in the wardroom. Then I go to the Gunnery Department and he goes to the Public Relations Office and we meet again for lunch. I proposed this for the first few days, as I would to any new roommate, and at noon we wait for each other in the passageway outside the wardroom.

On the second or third day, as I waited for him, I realized that my excitement did not come only from finally having a chance to do more for Negroes than pray; I felt that redemption was at hand, for I could finally show my feelings, and the history of my feelings, to a Negro at close quarters. As close as his body is to mine. With only a smile, a greeting, a shared lunch. After work we get to the stateroom at four-thirty or so, and talk or read, then go to dinner at six. Since Bill left, I'm the senior lieutenant junior grade in the junior officers' wardroom; so, after the ringing of four bells, I must start the meal with the blessing. I say the only one I know, the Catholic one, and Willie enjoys this, sitting to my left or right—I sit at the head of the center table—and says he likes the prayer's brevity. And that I look like an aging altar boy when I say it.

26 July 1961
At sea

… and after eight days of it, two of those spent dry aboard ship because I was on duty, I do believe I'm still hung over. It's strange what being at sea does to you. Sometimes at sea, for even two weeks, I *think* of a beer once in a while. But I don't need one. Then we hit port and I go mad, drink as though I'm preparing for hibernation. Wonderful Japanese beer: Asahi, Kirin. Saki. Or Willie and I bring a fifth of Gordon's gin—for a dollar and a quarter—from the base to a bar where they sell us set-ups. Every time I go to sea I write you this, but I can't stop: like the need for booze, my loneliness is worse when I'm in port. Of course, because in every bar there are Japanese bar girls, and it is not their faces and bodies and their kimonos and obis, lovely as all of those are, that make my loneliness so deep that it approaches grief. It's their voices, whether in faltering and comic English, or chattering (or so it seems) in that rapid falling and rising like surf—if surf sang like a bird. I can read French and Spanish and Latin and can even converse, slowly, in all three, but even now, on my fourth Pacific tour, I cannot distinguish Japanese syllables, detect the end of a sentence or the start of one. Still, it is their voices. And, as I told you on my very first deployment out here, I do not feel lust. Lust would be easier to deal with. My hand. And I no longer confess it; I do not believe God concerns Himself with the built-up semen of sailors. I did *not* mean that as a pun. No, not lust: loneliness. And no hand can assuage it; nor could the body of another woman. I want to be home, and I wonder whether I can actually stay for twenty or twenty-five years in the Navy. But how else can I work on the sea? There must be a way. If there isn't, I'm afraid I'll become landlocked; or maybe I can teach history near at least a coast. Soon now I'll be a full lieutenant.

I think booze and loneliness are paradoxically much less of a problem at sea than in port because I change when I board the ship, knowing we'll be out for a week, ten days, two weeks. It's like taking a minor vow, like the senior retreat in high school, when for three days we could not speak, except to pray and to confess. Then we return to port and most of us drink too much and many husbands are unfaithful, and perhaps their wives or other wives are too in Alameda, and I cannot find blame in any of them. Willie is married, and they have a year-old son, and he and I do what my (faithful) married friends and I have always done: we don't drink with the women. Willie's wife is Louisa, and she's still in San Diego, his last port before coming to the *Ranger*, and she won't move up to Alameda till we return from sea in January. I wish she would move there now. So you could meet her. Their son is Jimmy.

In Yokosuka Willie eased my loneliness. Not as my other friends do, by sharing it, by talking of their wives and children. (When will we have a child? We're the only practicing Catholics we know who don't even use rhythm and are still childless, while the others have babies year after year and are in despair and moving closer to a time when they will leave the Church. Everything is mysterious. Perhaps that is why I love the sea.) No, Willie eased my loneliness by being a Negro, giving me the blessing of drinking and talking with him, giving me a reprieve from my childhood when I could only watch them and listen. A reprieve too from our last three years in college when, finally integrated, there was too much history for us and the Negro students to overcome; we were overwhelmed by it, and we softly crept over its surface, by speaking politely to each other, by nodding and smiling in the halls and on the campus grounds. The Japanese girls want Willie: they are childlike, gleeful, and shy with him; and some want to press their small palms against his. He allows this, and courteously tells them he is married and a *papa-san* and no butterfly boy. Too bad, they say, and tell him their names. Maybe next time *Lanegah* come Yokosuka you change mind. Then Willie and I drink.

All his life he has had white friends, so I think it is only my discomfort that makes his eyes shift from mine; a difficult evasion, for him, since mine are shifting too. But discomfort is of course not the right word for what I bring to our booths, our chairs at the bars, our room aboard ship. And he knows it, and understands my need to tell him all I can remember— with you, and before you: those horrors I saw and heard as a child, an adolescent, and whatever I was in college. I told him of imagining Christ in the electric chair, as I said the rosary on the night they electrocuted Sonny Broussard; then, with the terror and grief of the boy I was, seeing myself, through Christ and so through Sonny, strapped into the chair. Willie is not religious. Or, more precisely, he does not belong to a religion. But I am able to talk with him about saying a rosary for Sonny, trying to meditate on the Agony in the Garden, the Scourging at the Pillar, the Crowning with Thorns, the Carrying of the Cross, and the Crucifixion and Death. As I am able to tell him that I grew up with hardly any bigotry at all, because of the Christian Brothers' school and my parents— I think especially Daddy, with his contained and quiet sorrow about Negroes, while as a Southern man (Daddy would even say gentleman, since in the South money isn't a prerequisite for that) he followed the old ways, the traditions, the rules, but with an uneasiness I could sense even as a boy.

Almost no bigotry at all, save what I acquired simply by being there, by listening to—and telling—the jokes; by watching and hearing Negroes from that great distance between us, whether at their rear section of the bus or standing before me: Leonard taking the plate of food I gave him at the back door so he could eat under the sycamore's shade in the noon sun, while I watched (sometimes) from our dining-room window, and the oscillating floor fan blew on me and my family. Willie listens to all of this: from Christ, to Sonny Broussard's terror and final pain for raping a white girl, to Emmett Till, to Leonard, and the Negro section of town whose smells I rode through on my bicycle, going that hot summer afternoon with my friend on his paper route. And the Negro boys and girls going up to the balcony to watch from above us, as my friends and I sat downstairs for the Saturday serial and western movie. So he understands my need to—I was going to write "unburden myself." But I shall use the real word: Willie understands my need to confess.

And like Christ, Willie's yoke is easy, his burden is light, and he gives me rest. On the second or third or whatever night in a booth in a bar in Yokosuka, I nearly cried when I told him about Daddy going outside, alone with his bourbon and water, when news came that Emmett Till was dead. So I muttered the male exorcism of tears.

"Fuck it," I said, and completed the ritual: I swallowed some beer, and lit a cigarette. Then I looked at Willie, and he smiled.

"Did you tell your Daddy you almost stuck a knife in that guy?"

"No."

"Pretty decent family, for crackers."

"I'm not a cracker. I'm a Cajun. We're known to be tolerant, cheerful—let the *bon temps roulé*—and hot-tempered."

"Carry blades too, I hear. You talk French to the slaves down there?"

"Always. Called them *bête noires*."

"I hear we have a distinct smell. Maybe just to the cracker nose."

"They did."

"Did it smell a little bit like poverty?"

"Their part of town did. And neglect."

"They do seem to go hand in hand. Smell like fear maybe too? Like a dog at the vet's?"

"I don't know. Sweat, maybe."

"Ah: a little of both, then. Because they was workin' theah black asses off fo' the *cuh*nel, choppin' his cotton and wet-nuhsin' his chillun an' fetchin' him mint *joo*leps own the ve*ran*dah. White people smell like milk. We get nauseated in a theater full of white people."

"They didn't have that problem at home."

"Oh I *reck*on not. Smell *gun* powdah if dey go to a movie wif de white folks."

"Do I smell like milk?"

"Right now you smell like Asahi. At sea you smell like wet dreams."

"You too."

"But dreams that stimulate a huge cock." He held his hands apart, as though showing the length of a fish that fought him for thirty minutes and then threw the hook. "Actually I'm an insult to my people. Louisa thinks I've got a cracker in my woodpile."

"You can dance, though."

"Sing too. Want to hear something from *Porgy and Bess*? Or *Show-boat*?"

"Want to hear a Southern joke?"

"They have those?"

"It's sociological."

"It ought to be."

"Maybe it's even philosophical. Maybe Eleanor Roosevelt started it. Sent a chain letter to Negroes."

"I didn't know they could get mail down there. Can't read enough to vote, how can they get mail?"

"It's very complex. There are heroic deliveries."

"Night riders?"

"Of the New Frontier."

So I told him those two jokes. There in the booth, which was small like everything, it seems, in Japan; our feet and legs bumped and drew back and shifted beneath the low table. In that bar lit by softened red lights, much like the passageways aboard ship, to protect the pilots' night vision. But the lights were softer, and came from behind the bar and perhaps a couple of dim ceiling lights. Faces at nearby tables were shapes with vague features. Cigarettes rose to them, glowed, descended. My eyes burned. At the tables and in booths and sitting at the bar were officers in civilian suits and ties (Willie and I had taken off our coats, unbuttoned our collars, loosened our ties), and sailors and Marines in uniform, some with women, some waiting their chance, a few oblivious. The waitresses carried trays among the tables as if they did not need to see. They were slender shapes in kimonos, wide sleeves moving like shadows with substance, their hair darker than the darkness of the room, their faces in the light a pale glow, with brightly darkened lips and eyes. While men stumbled and bumped their way to the toilet, these women glided, like the figures a child is afraid he will wake to see entering his bedroom and, without a sound of breath or feet, crossing its floor.

"There's this boy living on a cotton plantation, and he goes off to college, and after a while he writes to his daddy and says everybody in the fraternity has a monkey and will his daddy buy him one too. So the man buys his son a monkey, and the boy brings him home on vacations, and when he's finished college he asks his daddy if he can leave the monkey at home, because he's going out into the world. So his daddy says sure, son, that'll be fine. So the boy leaves and the monkey stays, and one day the man goes outside and sees the monkey out in the cotton field. He's carrying a gunny sack and going down the rows, picking cotton and putting it in the sack, and the man watches him for a while, going down the rows and filling sacks, and then he says to himself, Now if I had me a hunnerd monkies like that, I wouldn't have to pay nobody to pick my cotton. So he goes to the pet store and orders a hundred monkies, and the owner of the pet store wants to know what he's going to do with one hundred monkies. So the man tells him, and the owner says: Nossir, I ain't goin' to order you them monkies, and I'll tell you why. The next fellow down the road'll see them monkies in your field, and he'll get to thinking, and he's goin' to order him two hunnerd. Then some old boy with a bigger plantation he's goin' to order three hunnerd, and pretty soon the South'll be overrun with monkies, and some damn Yankee lawyer's goin' to come down here and turn 'em loose and they'll go to school with my chilren."

Willie laughed. He laughed till his eyes watered, while so many of my white friends, from the Northeast and West and Midwest, had never given it more than a courteous sound resembling laughter, and some had frowned and said: Bad, Gerry, bad. But Willie understood the true butt of the joke.

"It's economic," he said. "So I guess that makes it socio-logical. Even philosophical. Course it generally is economic."

"Sure. It was an agrarian society. An aristocracy even, with—"

"Not just Negroes and whites. It's generally economic when somebody's shitting on somebody else."

"I suppose it is."

"Northern mills went South after the Civil War. You think it was for the climate?"

"Cheap labor."

"Cheap white labor. That's how Shoeless Joe Jackson got started playing ball. Played for a mill. Baseball was good for the m*orale*. Fat cats always have ideas about how to keep poor folks happy without signing a check. You think those mills have unions yet?"

"Nope. But I have another joke."

"From down home?"

"Again."

"Sounds to me like you hung out with some liberals. I

thought the good old boys kicked their asses on Saturday nights, till they all went North."

"I seem to be in Yokosuka myself."

"Indeed you do, my friend, indeed you do. You going to retire down there? If you can stand this Navy bullshit for twenty years?"

"Never," I said. Then: "I don't think so, anyway."

Because we haven't even talked about it, you and I, and until Willie asked me I had not known I had thought about it at all. But something in me had. Or had at least made a decision without telling the rest of me about it, through the process we call thinking. (Maybe all murders are premeditated but the killer never knows it.) Because I said *never* at once, with firmness and certainty and, in my heart, the awakening of an old dread that had slept, but lightly, on the edge of insomnia. As though Willie had asked me whether I would sleep with a coral snake.

"Some of my people miss it," he said. "They go down at Christmas. My grandparents went back to Alabama last year, to stay."

"I didn't know you were from Alabama."

"I'm not. My parents were born in Philadelphia."

"Why did they go back?"

His shoulders tightened, and just as quickly his eyes were angry. He said: "Social Security buys more down there." Then his eyes softened, and his shoulders relaxed—no: slumped toward the table that was so low I could see his belt—and he said: "To see their people. To die at home. They left it to have my father and aunts and uncles in the North. But Alabama was always home. Isn't it strange? Home? How it can shield you from all the shit out there? The evening meal of the poor— beans and greens and cornbread and rice—and the old bed and the tarpaper roof."

"You've been down there?"

"No. I wouldn't be able to stand it. I couldn't get leave anyway. My father wrote to me, after they went down last Christmas."

"Did he say it was bad?"

"Hell, no. It was a happy letter. He said compared to the sixth floor of a tenement, it was a Goddamn resort. A little house with a little yard with flowers, and they have a vegetable garden, and two oak trees, and a dirt road, and a front porch with a swing where they can sit. And friends. Old people. They gather on the porch at night and drink coffee and talk. No gangs of punks. No junkies. No dealers. Sometimes there's a fight at the bar."

"That's the best kind."

"Of fight?"

"Of bar."

"I forgot. You don't like the officers' club. Mean-ass Cajun carries a knife. Holds it at a redneck. Poor guy's celebrating. Just being happy because they found what the fish and the river left of Emmett Till."

"A pocket knife. For fishing and hunting. And in general."

"In general."

"I've always had one. Since Daddy gave me my first one—"

"When you were two."

"Eight. To go with my first long pants."

"No button on it? Makes the blade come out smelling blood?"

"Here."

I twisted in the seat and tried to put my hand in my pocket, but he said: "Shit no, man. Don't pull that thing in here. This is your kind of place, not mine. I like quiet plastic bars. I don't need some drunk Marine charging over with a bayonet. Just happens to be taped to his leg. Tell your joke."

"You're not kidding, are you?"

"About what?"

"Violence."

"Not at all, friend. If it weren't for the draft, I wouldn't even be a public relations man in a fucking uniform."

"I think—"

Then I stopped, and looked away, at the reddened darkness and the moving shapes of people.

"You think what?"

I looked at him.

"That if I were a Negro I'd be dead now."

"Or you would have learned how to stay alive. The joke, Mr. Fontenot. And I hope it's not as complex as you are."

"I'm not complex."

"No," he said. "You're not." He finished his beer, looked at my near-empty glass, and raised his hand without looking at the bar, or at the waitress when she somehow and at once noticed him and came and he ordered Asahis. He was looking at me, at my eyes. "My Cajun shipmate," he said.

"There's a monkey walking down the road. In the South, a gravel road, a country road, and he's walking on the side of it. He hears a pickup coming behind him, and he looks around, and there's a white man at the wheel, speeding up and aiming at the monkey, and the monkey jumps off the road just in time and lands in a deep ditch. Truck goes on and the monkey climbs out and brushes himself off and shakes his head. Then he starts walking down the road again. After about a mile he sees a car coming toward him, on the other side of the road. There's a Negro driving, and when he sees the monkey he comes across the road at him, and the monkey jumps in the ditch and the car misses him and goes on by. Monkey climbs out of the ditch again. He brushes off the dust and watches the car driving away, and shakes his head and says: My people, my people ..."

Again Willie laughed, even as the waitress appeared suddenly out of the dark and noise, and he reached back for his wallet, doubling forward with that motion and his laughter too, and gave her some yen and shook his head and held his hand up to refuse the change and she thanked him in Japanese—I can't spell the word; its sound is *arrigato*—then he stopped laughing and drew on his cigarette but he laughed again as he inhaled, then he coughed. I was laughing and he waved a hand at me to stop so he could clear his throat and breathe, but I couldn't stop, for still I was seeing that Darwinian monkey on the dusty gravel road, in the hot afternoon of summer, shaking his head, bewildered and sad. Willie coughed again, breathed clearly a couple of times, swallowed some beer; and then, as though he saw too what I did—that puzzled and doleful monkey—he was laughing.

There is something about true laughter. Or at least about laughter whose source is not really comic. Like yesterday at sea—I was going to get to this but I can't stop writing about being ashore with Willie—when we were firing live rounds with VT fuses from the five-inch fifty-four gun mount, and during the firing exercise the magazine jammed and the sailors in my gun crew had to unload it by hand, carrying one shell at a time, cradled in their arms and held against their chests, having to carry the round to the turret's hatch and hand it to a sailor waiting at the top of the gun mount's ladder, then that sailor had to back down the short but vertical ladder and carry the round across the small deck, then down and down the series of angled ladders going below decks, where he could at last hand it to someone else to store. The danger of this is dropping it. The VT fuse at the head of the round is a variable time fuse, meaning once the round is fired from the gun the fuse is activated and will explode not on contact but when it approaches something—fifty feet away, thirty feet, whatever, depending on the fuse's setting. I was of course frightened, as the sailors were, and I stayed with them, so if a sailor dropped a round and set the fuse into action and it exploded he'd at least know his officer's meat and bones would join his on the bulkheads of the turret, which had always seemed comfortably large, with enough space for men to move about in, but as each sailor removed a round and carried it to the man on the ladder, our place seemed smaller and smaller, just enough to contain all the force of an explosion and what was left of the two men who before the sound and flash had been standing, breathing, speaking.

Do not think of me as brave. It was simply required. Besides, there was a detachment about my fear. I was watching myself doing my work as it ought to be done, and I concentrated more on that than on images of my body in flung pieces, and never seeing you again, or the sea and the sun, and all else that I love. Then a sailor, a seaman by rank, a lanky and gentle man from Idaho named Mattingly, dropped a round. He had just removed it from the gun's magazine, had turned toward me to pass me and hand it to the sailor on the ladder. It simply fell, as though his arms decided to uncurl from its weight. It struck the steel deck and slid perhaps a foot between us, then stopped. Its fuse was bent at nearly a forty-five-degree angle. It had hit the deck loudly, and there was the sound of its slide, then Mattingly and I looked at each other in a moment of new and absolute silence, though outside the turret, now that the firing exercise was over, planes were catapulting from the flight deck. Mattingly's face was pale, like that of a man who without warning is about to vomit. Probably mine was too. I know my mouth had opened, as Mattingly's had. Then he bent for the round, and I spoke before I knew that I could.

"Don't touch it," I said.

We watched it. Then I turned to the sailor on the ladder, only his head and shoulders appearing above the hatch. The sun was on his face, but his flesh was pale too, as though he had been in the engine room for months.

"Get off the ladder," I said. "Take the other men off the deck. Then lock the hatch behind you. Don't let anyone out here. Wait. Except Ensign Stark. You know him? The EOD officer?" The sailor nodded. "And his chief. He'll probably bring his chief. But nobody else. Do you understand? Mattingly's going with you too."

"Mr. Fontenot," Mattingly said.

"Go on."

"I'm the one dropped it."

"Go on, Mattingly."

"Yes sir."

There was not relief in his voice; or fear either; or any tone that implied hurry. He spoke like a man obeying someone at a funeral. Then he was gone, and on the phone at the bulkhead I dialed Stark's number and told him.

"You said VT?"

"Yes."

"And it's bent? The fuse? Where are you?"

"Standing here looking at it."

"We're on the way. And you get out of there."

"I want to make sure it doesn't move."

"On this big fucking ship? A grocery cart wouldn't move. I'm there," and he hung up.

He and his chief came with a manual. Stark was first up the ladder, the color still in his face (and I hoped mine was restored, if in fact it had left), and in one hand he was holding the book. His starched khakis were crumpled. He stood looking at our companion on the deck, at its bent fuse. He pushed up the visor of his cap, and blond curls showed at his forehead. Everett Stark is twenty-two years old, married just before we sailed, and he is my drinking friend. He is a cheerful drinker and is the ship's explosive ordinance disposal officer and also our diver, scuba and deep-sea. His chief stood beside him, a dark wiry man nearing forty. He had a tool kit with him; he nodded at me once, and looked at the round. We could have been standing over a corpse, not of a friend, but of a man we had all known. Stark said: "Did you call the OOD?"

"Yes."

"What did he say?"

"To keep him informed."

"Should have told him just to keep his ears open. He'd be the first to know."

The chief took off his khaki cap, tossed it to the deck, and said: "The fourth." Then he kneeled beside the round and, with one finger, touched it. "At least it ain't a fucking misfire," he said. "Fucker's cold as my old lady."

Stark grinned and kneeled beside him.

"Good thing it's not as hot as mine."

"Mr. Stark's a bridegroom," the chief said, looking at the fuse while Stark read the table of contents of his manual.

"I know," I said.

"You can go," Stark said. "In case you need to call the OOD."

"In case he can't hear a big bang," the chief said.

"So you can write the report."

"In triplicate," the chief said.

"I'll stay."

Stark shrugged. "What the fuck. It won't be the first last call we've had."

"Mr. Stark," the chief said. "Is that book talking to you yet?"

"Not yet."

I did move toward the hatch, close enough to be blown up, far enough to feel that at least I wasn't as close as they were, at least I wasn't touching it.

"Here it is," Stark said. "Want to hear it?"

"I can't understand that shit. Just read it to yourself and tell me what it says. If you don't mind."

Stark read, then talked to the chief, his voice low until he finished; then he laughed and slapped the chief on the shoulder.

"I think it says be careful," he said.

"Seems to be the message. Maybe Mr. Fontenot could call the OOD, inform him we're being careful. In accordance with the manual."

I wanted to. Because it had become bizarre. Only a few feet outside the hatch was the sea, and I wanted to pick up the round and go down the ladder and to the rail and drop it into the Pacific. But Stark and the chief had to know whether the fuse had been activated and was ready to explode as soon as it looked at something, and for some reason had simply chosen not to yet, but might at any time: as it was carried past a bulkhead, or through a hatch. They worked quietly. They murmured to each other, passed and received screwdrivers and pliers, finally spoke hardly at all: *Okay*, they said, or *That's that*, and once Stark picked up the open manual and looked at a diagram and showed it to the chief who nodded and leaned over again with his screwdriver. There was such concentration in their faces that it seemed their bodies existed only to keep their faces alive. And their hands, their fingers. Then the fuse was off, resting bent in the chief's hand, looking as lethal still as it had on the round. Then at once Stark and the chief started laughing. I watched them. Then I smiled.

"Gerry," Stark said, between his laughter. "Call the OOD."

"Tell him," the chief said, one hand on Stark's shoulder, the other rubbing the fuse, as a gold prospector might hold and fondle a nugget, "tell him we got him a paperweight."

"To put under his cap," Stark said.

"Inside his skull," the chief said. "Give him something to roll around in there."

Together they stood, arms about each other's shoulders, laughing as though indeed they had drunk that lethal and lovely last call that would send them singing into the streets, howling at the moon, ready for fighting, lovemaking, or a bottle to share sitting on a curb. They even moved drunkenly to the hatch, and the chief leaned out of it and, sidearm, threw the fuse over the rail, into the sea. Then he released Stark and went backward down the ladder, smiling, shaking his head, then laughing again as he stopped midway and reached his hands through the hatch.

"Here you go, Mr. Stark."

Stark brought the round to the hatch and lowered it into the chief's hands. He backed down the ladder, went to the rail, looked at the water, then up at us standing at the hatch.

"You gentlemen want a forward pass or a drop kick?"

"Sissy stuff," Stark said. "See if you can throw it off the starboard side."

The chief looked up at the edge of the flight deck above the gun mount.

"I don't know. I'd have to clear the flight deck. And miss the bridge or go over it. Fuck it."

His back was to the sea. He bent his knees, then straightened them, and with both arms threw the round over his head, his straining face, and spun to watch it splash and sink.

"Beautiful," Stark said.

"Mr. Stark? Would you bring my cap down with you?" He

put a cigarette between his lips, patted the pockets of his khaki shirt. "And your lighter. And that funny little manual. What's this gun? Mount eight?"

I nodded.

"Mr. Stark, don't accept no more calls from this mount."

"Hazardous duty pay, Chief."

"They never said you had to *be* hazardous. And read a fucking manual that *tells* you you're hazardous."

Stark turned from the hatch and picked up the chief's cap and the manual. He was grinning again, and he called out to the chief: "Don't you want the tools?"

"Shit," the chief said. "Might's well leave them. We'll probably be back."

Stark took the tool kit and at the hatch he patted my shoulder with the cap and manual.

"Great guy," he said, "the chief. You can inform the OOD that the motherfucker is defused and at the bottom. See you at chow."

He stepped onto the ladder, and the chief came and took the kit and cap and manual from him so Stark could use both hands going down. I phoned the OOD, watching Stark and the chief smoking at the rail, the chief holding the manual before them, and they were looking at it and smiling, talking, sometimes laughing again, like two men looking at a photograph someone had taken of them in an instant of drunken foolishness.

That was going to be a separate letter, but Willie and I laughing so long at the joke, the monkey on the road, reminded me of it. For our laughter did not spring from the recognition of anything funny. No more than Stark's and his chief's did, as they laughed at the manual and their having to use it not only to do their jobs, but to save their lives. And mine too, but I was excluded from their mirth because I had merely chosen to watch, while they had done the work they had learned to do but probably had forgotten, because neither of them expected ever to handle a VT fuse that might be activated, because an activated VT fuse was supposed to be the nose of a round

already propelled high into the air, well beyond their respon-
sibilities, their lives.

Willie and I laughed at another death: not one that comes
in an explosion's instant, but a minute-by-minute, day-by-
day-for-centuries death of health, justice, and hope for an
entire race of Americans, and the lesser—because the suffering is less, even imperceptible—death of the white race as
well. If one believes, as you and I do and as Willie does, that
you cannot perpetrate or even tolerate or even close your eyes
to evil without paying a price.

Later, as we drank what we called our last beer, he said:
"When I get out of the Navy, I'm going to be Jason."

"Won't it feel strange? After—what, twenty-five years?"

"It's my middle name."

"I know. But most of the time I don't even remember
I have one."

"What is it?"

"Francis. For Francis of Assisi. My mother's favorite saint."

"Was he the rich guy who gave it all up?"

"That's him."

"Want to give up some yen for a beer? I've run out."

"Might as well. We'll be fucked up tomorrow anyway."

I raised my hand into the noises of louder, drunker voices,
and the dark and smoke that seemed to hover over our booth
like something my fingers could touch and penetrate.

"I'm tired of being Willie," he said.

I waited for words. Then she was there, so small that her
throat and chin were level with my vision. I ordered the Asahis; and in that pause, that turning away from Willie, I was
relieved, grateful, for suddenly I knew the words that I had
nearly spoken, and would have spoken had I drunk gin instead
of beer, or perhaps even three more beers. I had nearly said to
him: There's always Willie Mays. I had beer left in my glass,
and I drank it before looking at him. Then I said: "I like it.
Jason Brooks. Has style. Goes better with your boy's name too,
Jimmy. Jason and James and Louisa."

"You really like it?"

"It's a strong name."

"That's what I've been thinking."

"Jason, Louisa, and Jimmy Brooks. Shit. I got to have a kid."

"A boy?"

The waitress came and I gave her all my yen but the taxi fare, a *beau geste* of a tip. I didn't count it; her eyes and smile and repeated *arrigatos* told me.

"Boy, girl," I said. "Doesn't matter. Hell, two or three of each."

In the taxi, one of those blurred rides when you're drunk and know the motion of the car will get you there, but that's all you know, sitting in that speeding and slowing forward movement over streets and past lighted bars you don't see and would not recognize anyway, Willie said: "Okay, let me see it."

"See what?"

"That knife."

"Oh." I lifted and turned my hips and pulled the knife from my pocket. "Here."

He held it in front of his face, in the light from cars and the street, and looked at its brown wooden handle and dark gray folded blade.

"It's not even long."

"Legal size. I told you it's—"

"Yes, I know. How did it feel?"

He was still looking at the knife, holding it in two hands now, a thumb and forefinger at either end.

"I had the point at his artery. I pressed it a little, not enough to even draw blood."

"Was he bigger than you?"

"I don't know. All I saw was his eyes. And how still he was. He wasn't looking at me. His eyes went down and to his left. Toward the knife. Course he couldn't see it."

"I guess that's where a man would look."

"It was pure. My feelings. Like everything was in harmony, for the first time in my life. Everything I'd ever seen or heard of done to Negroes. Right there in that fucker's face. In his throat."

He lowered the knife to his lap, and held it in one open hand in the dark beneath the car window.

"And it was like it was just him and me. Finally it was all concrete, all defined in one man. And I had him. For an end to all of it. It was a fucking catharsis, is what it was."

He looked down at the knife, and unfolded the blade.

"It's just a plain old knife," he said. "Carbon steel." He moved his thumb across the edge of the blade. "Sharp, too."

"It needs some work. But I haven't been fishing in—God-dammit, how can you live on a ship and never get a chance to fish?"

We had to hold the rails of the brow as we climbed it to the waiting sober Officer of the Deck, and next morning was …

> 16 August 1961
> Iwakuni, at anchor

Hello Camille:

Last night was the ship's officers' party for the Air Group. I'm alone now in our stateroom, waiting for dinner. I don't know where Willie is. This morning when the alarm rang he turned it off and went back to sleep, and I shaved and dressed and went to work. He either skipped lunch or was on liberty today and went ashore to walk around Iwakuni.

It was a formal party. No civilian jackets and ties like they make us wear off the base so communists won't know we're officers and kidnap us and torture all manner of information from us. I have no information, except that we're not sup-posed to bring nuclear weapons into a Japanese port, but that's what our planes carry and I assume when officers of the Japanese National Defense Force come aboard as guests they know our planes carry nuclear bombs, and I further assume that only the Japanese people don't know this, and if there are any communists waiting in alleys they're not going to grab one Cajun lieutenant (j.g.) and interrogate his young ass about what they already know. Only a few senior officers are supposed to know what our next Japanese port will be, but the bar girls do: the ones in Yokosuka will say, "You go Sasebo now," and in Sasebo they say, "*Lanegah* go Kobe," and so on. No: the Navy doesn't allow us to wear uniforms in town because what they're really afraid of is an identifiable Naval officer becoming disgracefully drunk in public. Last night's party was confined to the base: at the Officers' Club, and we wore our whites.

Willie and I dressed together, fastened each other's high stiff collars, then with his cap under his arm Willie stood before the mirror above the lavatory. In the glass were his face, the collar that stiffened his neck, his broad shoulders in white and the navy-blue shoulder boards with the gold stripe and a half, and his deep white chest with the brass buttons going down it to his narrow waist and hips, which did not show in the mirror. I stood to his side, looking from him to his reflection, back to him. An expression was forming on his face, and I waited. Then he grinned.

"I look like a chocolate sundae," he said, and laughed, shortly, and in his throat.

"May as well put on the cap and gloves," I said. "Go all the way."

"Gloves?"

"I think we have to carry the fuckers."

"Shit. I forgot to wash them."

I was about to say it, but he looked away from the mirror, at me, as though he could read the words across my brow.

"I know," he said. "No one will notice."

"They won't be *on* your hands. Just *in* one of them."

"Maybe I should have joined the Air Force."

"Maybe they have whites too."

"We still talking uniforms?"

"I think we're talking gin. Let's do it to it."

He put on his cap, adjusting it in the mirror, and took a nearly immaculate pair of white gloves from the shelf of his wall locker, and we left the room and climbed ladders and walked passageways and climbed ladders to the quarterdeck, where a lucky ensign was the OOD, though he probably thought he was missing festivities rather than being spared them, and we smartly saluted and as smartly requested permission to leave the ship, then faced the stern and saluted the flag, and went down the accommodation ladder and joined the others sitting in the officers' launch, gently rolling in the *Ranger*'s shadow. When the coxswain got underway we all took off our caps and held them, and Willie and I turned our faces to the sunlit breeze. Japanese taxis waited at the pier and took us to the club. Willie and I stayed outside for a cigarette in the setting sun. Then we went in, to the long wide room reserved for the party. So already you can see it: hundreds of white uniforms and Caucasian faces, though few truly white but pink, florid, olive, tan, all colored by duty at sea or in the air or booze or ancestral blood, and the three black faces: the flight surgeon and the personnel officer from the Air Group, and Willie: faces which in truth looked better than all of ours, the black skin richer, somehow stronger, juxtaposed with the length and breadth and depth of the uniforms as white as altar cloths.

Late in the party Willie talked to the wrong man; or the lieutenant-commander, a pilot, saw him, stalked him, cornered him. By the time I joined them, and stayed for the rest of it, then went outside with Willie, then sat beside him in the taxi and then on the launch going out to the lights and silhouette of the ship, there was no longer reason to ask who had, as the saying goes, struck up the conversation. *Struck* is the right word, and I suspect it was the lieutenant-commander who, compelled by booze and the undeniable voices in his blood, saw Willie for the twelfth or twentieth time of the evening, and went to him. During the entire party, pilots talked to each other in groups, and often a hand was in the air, moving like a jet turning, diving, climbing. We of the ship's company stayed with each other too, except the Captain and Executive Officer, who talked with the Air Group Commander and his squadron commanders; and the Admiral, who moved about, patting people's backs, always with that smile of authority, confident of welcome, confident that no one will say or do anything to alter the spreading lips, the mellow voice. I imagine the lieutenant-commander standing at the bar, talking with pilots, glancing to his side and seeing Willie again, and this time he had to make his congee from the gold-winged brethren and follow or be drawn by his history. I see his walk across the room as a series of geometric angles and half-circles around men standing unnaturally erect while talking shop. Yet his true azimuth, that of his heart, was as straight as a carpenter's chalk line.

Willie and I had started drinking together, but the hors d'œuvres table, the bar, and other friends separated us for a drink, for two, until gradually we were together only for a few minutes at a time, and I had forgotten him for perhaps a half-hour when I saw them. They were some seventy feet away, a young forest of white uniforms between us. They were of equal height, Willie standing straight, the lieutenant-commander leaning toward him, his sunburned face close to Willie's, his hands moving: the one with the drink swinging back and forth as he spoke, or his free hand rising and falling. Willie's left arm was at his side; he held a drink in his right hand, his arm at a forty-five-degree angle, near-motionless, as though he were assuming some military stance. Twice, as I watched, he raised the glass and sipped; then he lowered the drink and his elbow stopped his forearm and held it level, stationary. I left the people I was with and went to him, my route as angled and skirting as I have imagined the lieutenant-commander's was, and my true course as straight as I have imagined his, and also following or being drawn by history.

Beneath the lieutenant-commander's gold pilot's wings were ribbons from Korea; he stopped talking to turn, hear my name from Willie, shake my hand as Willie said: "And this is Lieutenant-Commander Percy." His eyes were brown and had that wet brightness, that intensity, of alcohol and vocal excitement. He said: "Pleased to meet you, Gerry." My concern for Willie dissolved in adrenaline. Percy was from the South. Then I knew I had already known it, from his lips: they were thin and shaped by his pronunciation into a near-pout, as if they slouched toward his chin, and their corners drooped. They would have been sensual, were it not for a lethargic certainty about them, making him look pampered. They also grinned widely. And when he was intent, as he listened to my name and looked me up and down without appearing to, weighing my character, my worth as an officer, and later as he listened to me, or to Willie the one time he spoke, his lips were straight and grim, a mouth you would expect beneath eyes looking at you over a pistol barrel. I was trying to place his drawl when Willie said: "The Lieutenant-Commander is from Georgia."

"Atlanta?" I said.

"Oh hell no. Place called Rome. Little place. You're a Southern boy yourself."

"Yes sir. Louisiana. Sorry I said Atlanta. I'm from Lafayette—a little place—but people always think I'm from New Orleans. I mean even after I've told them."

"That's because they don't know us. Atlanta. New Orleans. Memphis. Words to them. Cities. They don't know our culture."

"Little Rock," I said.

He missed the expression on my face (or the one I felt there) and the tone of my voice (or the one I heard there); I believed I was cold and challenging.

"Right," Percy said. "Little Rock. They saw it on *T*-V. Saw the 82nd Airborne following the orders of their Commander-in-Chief." He looked at Willie. "Which I would have done too. Like that." He snapped his thumb and a finger damp from stirring his bourbon and ice, then with his cocktail napkin wiped the drops from his palm. (Yes: I am not adding that as a prop; I could smell his drink, probably sour mash.) He wore a gold wedding ring. "Same as if Kennedy sends me to Russia. People up North didn't see Little Rock. They saw a dumb governor and some dumb high-school kids and God knows what all, come to look at the soldiers. But they didn't see our culture, that's what they don't know anything about. Little places like Rome and Lafayette. In the bayou country, weren't you?"

"Yes sir."

"How long you been in now?"

"Four years and a couple of months."

His eyebrows raised and he cocked his head, looking at me with something like warmth. Hair in his eyebrows was bleached by the sun, but they were mostly brown, like his short hair.

"Almost a lieutenant. You staying in, then?"

"Yes sir."

"You two are roommates."

"Willie puts up with me."

"See?" He looked at Willie, then back to me. "You two boys're shipmates. Liberty buddies. Go ashore and get drunk together. Right?"

I told him yes, sir, we did some of that.

"That's what I been telling Willie here." He looked at Willie; then he shifted his feet to face him, leaving me as a point in the triangle, watching them. "The real Southerner is like Gerry. Not some poor ignorant son of a bitch that can't get along with Jesus Christ Himself, and's never learned you judge a man by what he is. Not by what he looks like. Or what he's called. Course I worked with more colored people growing up back home than I have in the Navy. But that'll change. Among the officers, I mean. We got plenty enlisted colored people."

"Negroes," I said.

He looked at me, with those shining eyes. Then his lips changed. They were open, perhaps on the last syllable of *people*. But they closed, straightened, and for a moment I could sense his absolute command over the demons in his soul. Then he grinned and with a turn of the head brought the grin to Willie. I watched Willie.

"Fine with me," Percy said. "I don't care what a man wants to be called. Long as he does his work, and does it the best he can. 'Sailor' is what I call them, whether they're black or purple or green. Or a pale scrawny white boy grew up in New York City. *But—*" he raised his glass so it was level with Willie's face, his nose and eyes, and pointed the forefinger. Willie looked at it. "*But*. If they fuck up, I come down. And I mean I come down hard. We got planes to fly, Willie. Them's not laying hens on that flight deck. And there's pilots in them. And two other men aboard the big ones. And we know what all those planes are for: one purpose, and one purpose alone. Get the fuck on that catapult and up in the air and drop the loads. There won't be a ship left to come home to. You know that. Gerry knows that. You boys'll get nuked up the ass by the big fish. About thirty minutes after the whistle blows. At *most*. And we'll run out of fuel. But *after* Moscow. We all know that. So when a sailor fucks up I call him a bunch of things. But I'll tell you this: if that man is a Negrah, Walt Percy don't call him a nigger. I might call him a worthless dumb son of a bitch. But not nigger. If you'll pardon the word. Because I'm trying to make a point."

Willie wanted to hit him. Or his body did; but he does not believe in it, so what Willie wanted to do, wanted to be allowed to do, was tell Percy, loudly and articulately and for a long time, that he was full of shit. Willie wanted to be a civilian, wanted Percy to be one too. Even if, as civilians, Percy were Willie's boss. Willie could tell him what he had to say, and quit his job. Yet there in the club, and aboard ship, or *any*where, in or out of uniform, Percy was not Willie's boss, only a senior officer, and still he constricted Willie as surely as a straitjacket; and Willie had to yield to the constriction, even help it with his own will. He was breathing deeply and his tight blouse showed each breath; the skin of his face was taut over his cheekbones and jaw, and his nostrils widened with his breathing. For his mouth was closed and I knew from his jaw and the muscle in front of his ear that his teeth were tightly pressed together, his tongue heavy and strong behind them, a wild animal he wanted to set free.

"Willie, we weren't allowed to say that word in our home. My big brother did. Just once. Name's Boyd. He was maybe fifteen, sixteen. Big old country boy. My daddy didn't scold him. No sir. And Boyd was a bit too big, too old, for a spanking. My daddy didn't slap him either. Or shake him till his head wanted to come loose, like he did to me once when he thought I lied to him. I did lie, but not as much as he thought. Had to do with some car trouble and getting home late from being out with a girl. No sir, Willie. My daddy didn't say a word to Boyd. We were at supper. He put down his fork and got up from where he was sitting, at the head of the table, there in the kitchen. He went to Boyd's chair. Boyd was sitting at one side of the table, next to me. We had a big family, three boys on one side of the table, I was the youngest, and three girls on the other side. I saw it coming. Boyd didn't. He was working on his supper and maybe thought Daddy was going to piss or something. Daddy took hold of Boyd's chair and pulled it straight back—with one hand—and turned it, so he was looking down at Boyd. All I could see was Boyd's back and Daddy's face and shoulders, but I could feel it in Boyd's spine, coming at me like a radio signal: let me tell you, he knew now. Daddy pulled him up from the chair with his left hand and turned him so his back was to the wall. I guess so Boyd wouldn't fall on me and my plate, waste all that food. Maybe break my nose. Then he hit him. With his fist, Willie. Coming up from way down. Sounded like a bat hitting a softball. Not quite a baseball, but a new hard softball. Old Boyd hit the wall and went down on the floor. He could still see and hear, but not much, and he sure as hell wasn't about to move. 'Boyd,' Daddy said, 'we don't say that word in this house. You want to talk like poor white trash, you know where you can find them. Maybe they'll even take you in.' Then he went back to his chair and finished his supper. Old Boyd got up and went on to bed. And that man—my daddy—went to school for seven years. That's it. Seventh-grade education. After that he stayed home and worked with his daddy on the farm."

Then Percy smiled and, oblivious of Willie's glare, his taut face, held Willie's bicep.

"Willie, I bet anytime old Boyd starts to say that word his jaw shuts him up, it starts hurting so bad." Maybe then he noticed Willie's face. He withdrew his hand, and looked at me, a friendly look, and at Willie again. "Hell, you know what I'm trying to say. A Southerner—a *real* one, mind you, not one of them no-counts doesn't have a pot to piss in or a window to throw it out of, and doesn't respect anybody or anything because he doesn't even respect himself, but a *real* Southerner—respects the South. Loves the South. And that means"—he looked at me—"Atlanta, New Orleans, Memphis, *Mobile*—" Then he winked at me, smiled, lightly punched my rigid arm, and said: "We don't count Mi*ami*."

His right hand with the drink swept away from me, past Willie's chest, as though turning Percy's head to face Willie. Willie gazed into his eyes. Gazed, not glared, and I believed (and still do) that Willie was seeing sharply every detail of Percy's face, hearing every inflection of his voice, and was also seeing and feeling too the years he had been carried and shoulder-pushed, then crawled and then walked as a Negro in America, and seeing as well the years beyond these minutes with Percy, the long years ahead of him and Louisa and Jimmy and his children still to come.

"And Rome and Lafayette," Percy said. "All the little towns Yankees like to poke fun at, little towns with decent people making do. And the farms and hills and swamps and, by God, mountains. But Willie—" Again he raised his glass, pointed the forefinger at Willie's nose or mouth or between his eyes. "What the Southerner respects most, and that's why we took on the Yankees in a war, is the individual. The individual as part of a whole way of life. We respect a man's right to work for his family, put a roof over their heads, whether it's a God-damn mansion or a little old shotgun house on a patch of ground wouldn't make a decent-size parking lot. And to raise his kids as he sees fit. Believe it or not, and by God I hope I'm helping you believe it, the Southerner most of all wants to leave people alone. And be left alone. Hell, that's why my family and everybody I know down there's always voted Republican. Tell you something else too, since we've gone this far. Slavery was a bad thing. Everybody knows that. But there's something not many Yankees know. Your slave was not mistreated. Why in hell would a man whip or starve the people that kept him rich? Hell, those old boys sent their sons to the War Between the States, but not their slaves. No sir. The slave was a valuable piece of *prop*erty. You see what I mean?"

"Yes sir," Willie said. He had not spoken in so long that I was surprised, and expectant, and I watched his mouth and waited. His voice was soft and respectful, and still was when he said: "We Americans have always placed a high value on property."

Percy was confused. The words themselves were sarcastic, and Percy's lips straightened and were tight and thin. But Willie's voice must have changed the meaning of the words in Percy's sour-mashed brain. His lips eased into their drooping pucker, then spread to a smile.

"There you go," he said. "Then they were free and that was an awful mess. *Aw*ful. Lynchings, *bully*ing. I'll tolerate the opinion of nearly any man, and even the action he takes to back it up. Depending on the action. But I can't stand a man who has to join with others, get help with his dirty work. I would personally shoot any KKK son of a bitch showed up with his gang of walking bedsheets. Shoot him dead center in his Goddamn hood and not even read the newspaper next day to see who the son of a bitch was. But we got past Black Reconstruction. And into a new century. Now we're over halfway through it. And it'll be good in the South. For your people. I can promise you that. Make bet on it. Because people like me and Gerry here *know* the Negrahs. You can't send them up North—I know, I know, they had damn good reason to leave home. But it doesn't work. Negrahs in a Northern urban environment. It hasn't worked, and it won't. What did they get? No money, and raising their children in Goddamn ghettos. Bad as it still is down home, a Negrah man can work for a little house to live in, have him a little yard for his children. And how many times, Gerry"—he only glanced at me—"you seen a Negrah daddy taking his boy down a country road, going fishing? Bamboo poles. Or going hunting? I don't think a Negrah man can walk down a city street up North, him and his boy carrying shotguns. It's going to work, Goddammit. Gradual integration. Starting with the little kids, the first-graders. Because those little white kids' daddies, like me and Gerry, and *our* daddies, we *know* the Negrahs. We've worked with them, we've *played* with them—"

He paused. He had not finished the sentence. It hung there in the middle of our triangle, its pitch still raised for more words, but they did not come; we stood suspended in silence, in a sense of incompletion, as though none of us could speak or even move until Percy finished the sentence, lowered his pitch to lead to the period that would allow us to do more than simply breathe. I did not know where to look. My eyes settled on Percy's ribbons: he had a Distinguished Flying Cross. I looked at the two and a half gold bars on his shoulder boards. We all lit cigarettes, Percy holding his Zippo for us, an old one with raised flier's wings on its worn surface, the color of a dime from the first march of them.

"Well," he said. His smile to Willie was tentative. He held the smile, looking at Willie's face; but his eyes now were like those of a man studying a statue, trying to know from the bronze eyes and mouth and nose and jaw what sort of man the artist had sculpted: to know if he was wise, courageous in battle, a lover of women; to know whether or not he would be a good man to drink with; to know what voices were most constant in his mind.

"Well, gentlemen. Willie—" He nodded to Willie. "Gerry—" He turned his face and nodded to me. "I'm confronted with a glass has more ice than Jack Daniel's in it. I've enjoyed our talk. Now I'll go see the real highest-ranking man at the party. That portly bartender."

He put his glass in his left hand and extended the right to Willie. Who took it. I watched Willie's knuckles and fingers. He firmly shook Percy's hand. Then the hand came to me and I did too.

"I hope we'll chat again," Percy said. "All it takes. More talks like this one."

Then he was gone. And you know what? Not only had he drunk enough to be forgiven his babble, but it didn't matter anyway. Not to Percy. For he would have no remorse next morning. *This* morning, ten hours ago. I know he did not wake, as I have so many times, as you have a few times, and lie in his bunk while the party's sounds and images were first blurred, then distinct, chronological even, until he remembered Willie and thought: *Oh my God I can't believe I—* No. He woke and remembered Willie and he was glad, even grateful to himself or God, that finally he had talked to Willie. He had been an officer and a (Southern) gentleman. He had given much of his evening to a young Negro officer from the ship's company. (Had the flight surgeon and the personnel officer in the Air Group had their share of him too, on other, earlier evenings?) He was a Navy pilot. He had distinguished himself in the air over Korea. He was proudly ready at any moment to climb into his cockpit and be catapulted into his final flight to Moscow. Last night he had left his jet-pilot friends, their unity so true and deep that, to an observer, it resembles love. He had left them to talk to the colored officer, the Negro, the Negrah, and to say that Willie was not as singular as he appeared, among the Caucasian faces and white uniforms. To say that he, Percy, with his Georgian speech, was not an enemy. That no Southerner, simply because he was a Southerner, was convicted. That all the evidence was not in; that the color of a man's flesh did not touch Percy's heart; and the place of a man's birth and childhood should not touch Willie's. He had done his best. Perhaps he woke this morning with a headache, and phlegm from too many Camels.

Willie woke to his alarm and turned it off. I imagine its ringing shot through his brain and blood and heart, and returned him to the last hours of the night. So he shut his eyes and, only because he was blessed with a hangover, he was able within minutes to return to the unconscious state those last hours earned for him; to retreat into the morning of sleep he deserved.

When Percy left us, I said to Willie: "Let's get a fucking drink."

He did not look at me. I stood at the point of the triangle

Percy's leaving had abolished, and Willie stared at the space where, seconds ago, Percy's flesh and voice had been.

"I'm going outside," he said. Still he looked at that air in front of him, as though it held Percy's shape. Then he walked through it.

"I'll bring them out," I said to his back.

I could not see his face. His back was erect, his shoulders squared, his strides long, purposeful, like a man on his way to settle a score, to confront someone who may badly hurt him, or take away his livelihood, even kill him, but the risk was nothing to him now, for he could no longer tolerate or even bear himself until he faced with the purity and freedom of just anger that man whose presence on the earth fouled his every breath. I hurried around people toward the bar, but watching Willie, so I grazed some men and bumped others and begged their pardons and continued on, guided by peripheral vision and a strange instinct that warned me of men in my path, and saw Willie taking his cap and gloves from the hat-check girl and, without looking back at the party, or to his left or right, walking to the door, pushing the crash bar, and going out. The door was slowly closing behind him when I reached the bar and waved to the bartender (probably a chief, a man in his late thirties; he was large but I would not have called him portly), and I nodded and even answered when friends spoke to me. I ordered two double gin-and-tonics. Watching the door, watching the bartender pouring gin on ice in the large glasses, I replied to people and saw Percy at the right end of the bar, standing with other pilots, grinning at a laughing lieutenant whose hand climbed at a low angle, as though from a flight deck, and sharply rose into the air. Then the bartender was in front of me, sweating, working fast, and I told him to keep the change from my five, not generosity but hurry (the bill was two dollars), and, sweating, he smiled and thumped the bar with his knuckles.

At the coat-check booth I overtipped for the same reason, gave to the young kimonoed Japanese girl two dollars that came out of my pocket in my plunging and grabbing hand, broke the club rules by putting on my cap indoors, then held my gloves between my left arm and ribs and, with a glass in each hand, pushed the crash bar and door with my side, turned through the opening, and was out before the door could close on my right hand holding Willie's drink that seemed so precious. Willie had not gone far. He was to my left, walking parallel to the long room whose walls and windows gave a muted immediacy to the loud and unharnessed voices of men drinking together. He walked slowly now, his steps short, his posture settling toward the pull of the earth, his white-capped head lowered. I could see the gloves in his left hand. I called his name. He nearly stopped: he was about thirty yards away, and I could see his back hesitate, an instant's motion as though not his ears but his back heard me, and it almost straightened, almost halted his legs. But he did not stop, and he did not turn to look over his shoulder, and he did not lift his face from its gaze at the ground, or whatever he saw there.

So I went to him, as quickly as I could, holding level the cold glasses, while gin and tonic dripped down their sides onto my hands, and I kept my gloves pressed between my bicep and ribs. I could not hear my feet on the grass and earth. I heard beyond the wall laughter and voices without words, sounds that had been merry until Percy, but were mocking now. *So*, I said to myself. *This is what it is. To be outside.* I could hear our drinks too: their soft fizz and the dull clicking of ice in liquid. Willie knew I was coming. I don't believe he could hear me, but he knew. When I drew within five or six paces of him, walking on his right so I could step beside him and put a drink into his hand free of gloves, I saw that, while his bent neck and head were nearly still, his shoulders and his arms at his sides were moving up and down, not jerking, but with the involuntary and rhythmless motion of resisted weeping. Then I was beside him. I did not want to violate him by looking at his face, but my eyes moved to it and quickly away from the tears on his cheeks, and I looked down at his hand. I lowered the drink in my right hand, touched the knuckles and back of his hand with it. We were still walking. He took the drink and brought it to his lips, sniffing deeply and spitting before his first swallow. I took my gloves from under my arm, then could drink. He stopped and said: "I'm out of cigarettes."

Still he looked ahead. I shifted my drink to the hand with the gloves and pulled a flattened pack from my trouser pocket and shook it till a cigarette pointed at Willie. He turned to me and took it. But as with my lips I pulled another from the pack, he faced again the direction he had walked. I held my lighter to his cigarette, then to mine, and drank with my gloves wrapped around my glass, as Willie did. I faced his side, watching now his wet eyes and cheeks, his open mouth breathing against the tears he still held back.

"I *hate* white people," he said, and they came then, loudly, his waist bending, straightening, bending, his upper arms pressed tightly against his sides, while his hands with drink and cigarette trembled beneath his face. Now I could not look away from that face. Nor could I touch him. All my life I have seen girls and boys and women cry, but until last night the only man I had seen cry—really cry, not damp eyes at a movie's end or when a man is talking with love about one of his children—was Daddy the night his brother died. I was fourteen then, and all I could do was sit across the room and watch him convulse in his chair, trying to keep his palms over his face, but his neck writhed away from them, his arms fell to his heart, his belly, and pressed them. Yet I have seen my mother and aunts and sisters and you crying at some pain of the heart, even keening, and still able to walk, to move from one room to another, even to the kitchen to boil water and make coffee or tea, even to speak with coherence—broken by sobs, yes, but still coherence. Yet I've never seen a man do that. Willie's face was both younger and older than he was. His control of it while listening to Percy was gone, and with that control something else was gone too, as if the flow of tears and the wet moaning—*oh oh aah*—as he both fought and surrendered to crying, were taking from him all the strength he had developed in his twenty-five years on earth: not only the strength to be resilient, but to be humorous too, and gentle.

He had the face of a brokenhearted child. Yet at the same time he looked old: old as the infirm look, finished, done in by something as inexorable as nature.

Then I was touching him, and it was my flesh that closed the short space between us while my mind held back, bound by its inertia, by its wish that none of this from the seventeenth century until 1961 had ever happened in America, by its sad desire to be no part of it, to have seen and heard none of it since my birth in 1936, and by its conviction that the pigmentation I was born with was, against my strongest will, responsible for every tear falling from his face, every moan he could not contain, every quick and terrible motion of his arms and head and stomach and chest, so that he looked like a man fighting for his life against an enemy neither visible nor large: some preternatural opponent clawing and biting the skin and bone that covered Willie's heart. But my flesh ignored my mind. It dropped my cigarette, and my left hand and arm slid across Willie's back, drawing my body to his, my hand pushing itself between his left arm and side, and though I did not weep but only watched his face, my body moved as though it wept with him, for I held him so tightly, and my torso rocked back and forth, and my waist bent and straightened, and pulled my face down and up.

"All of you," he said. His eyes were closed. I watched their lids, and his open mouth that still held tears, but his voice was more dry now. Then abruptly he looked at me. I was startled out of the silence our bodies had given my mind, and I could feel it gathering itself again to pull me away from Willie, to make again that space between our shoulders and sides and arms so I would stand alone and become under the night sky of Japan the apotheosis of slave traders and owners and the Klan and murderers and Negro-beaters and those who inflict their torment economically, or with the tongue, or with silence, and eyes that look at a Negro as if he were not even a tree or rain but only air. So I held him more tightly. My squeeze made him gasp, and with his sound my brain emptied, was pure, clean, primordial, and Willie's eyes changed: their bright anguish softened, and they focused on my face, and I felt, I *knew*, Camille, that suddenly he saw not a white man but me.

"I have to tell Jimmy," he said. He stopped to breathe: a deep breath, then another. If all his tears had not been spent, he would have cried again. But only his voice did: soft, nearly a whisper. "Someday I have to tell my son he's a nigger." Again he breathed. Then his right arm pushed backward between us, and I lightened my grip on him so it could move around my waist, and then I tightly held him as his hand holding his drink pressed into my right side, and his arm pulled me to him. "One year old. I have to tell him, Gerry. Soon. Too soon. But before he finds out."

Our free arms rose together as we turned to face each other and embraced with both arms and I could not hear the party inside, only our breathing and the faint scraping of our whiskered cheeks. We stood for a minute, perhaps less. Then we stepped back and drank, our glasses lacking at least a swallow spilled, and I drew out my cigarettes, more flattened now, and we shaped them round, and smoked and drank in silence as we walked toward the entrance of the club. Walked slowly, I looking at my watch—the taxis for those who were leaving the party early would arrive at ten-thirty, only eight minutes away—and Willie wiping his face with his gloves.

We got the first taxi that came and quietly finished our drinks in the back seat, tossed ice and limes out the windows, and left the glasses to roll on the floor. At the pier we waited for the others, the small taxis of officers who wanted the eleven-o'clock launch. We heard it coming, its engine low out on the water. We stood at the edge of the pier, on the opposite side from where the launch would tie up, and looked down at the dark water that always seems fathoms deep at night, and we looked out to sea at the lights of the *Ranger*. I had one cigarette left, a Pall Mall, and I broke it in half and handed Willie his. Taxis came in a fast column, their headlights shining for an instant on our faces. Willie's face now was the one I had known until tonight: an expression of repose, though now I saw clearly what I must have seen on the night he first entered our room, though I had not remarked it then, for my life, my past, had taught me to expect it. Now his face reminded me of a painting I saw long ago of an American Indian, a Cheyenne or Sioux, an old chief: he wore his war bonnet, and in the set of his jaw and lips, the years in his eyes, even in the wrinkles on his face, was the dignity of a man, sorrowful yet without self-pity, who has endured a defeat that will be part of him, in his heart, until he dies.

Officers climbed loudly out of taxis, slammed doors, called to friends standing on the pier or sliding and twisting out of other cabs. The launch's engine had grown louder, and now it slowed as the coxswain approached the pier. Behind Willie and me the officers clustered. The launch drew alongside, and Willie and I turned together and followed the others into the boat, and took off our caps. Men talked above the wind. For a while I looked at the *Ranger*; then I looked away from it, high above the faces across from me, at the stars and the silent sky, and the wind blew on my face and dried the sweat in my hair. Willie and I were last to leave the launch. I walked behind him up the accommodation ladder. On the quarterdeck he saluted aft, then the OOD, and spoke for the first time since we stood outside the club. He requested permission to come aboard.

We went quietly to our room, abreast in the passageways, Willie going first down the ladders, and the ship itself quiet, its steel having absorbed and separated the others returning from the party. He entered the room first too, and we quietly undressed, as we had on other nights when we came back to the ship so drunk and tired that merely undressing was a bother, and hanging the clothes in our lockers a task. He got into his bunk and I turned off the light and walked from the door in the dark toward the bunks, then saw them, and climbed the ladder near Willie's feet and crawled onto the mattress and pushed my legs under the blanket and between the crisp sheets a Filipino had tucked with a hospital fold during the day. I shut my eyes and saw and heard Percy, saw Willie's face as Percy talked, and his face later, outside the club, and I opened my eyes to the gray overhead in the dark.

"Gerry." It was his voice again, the one I had known. "I'm sorry I said that."

"Fuck sorry."

"The man got to me."

"You don't need to tell me that."

"Yes I do."

"Okay. But just once, Jason."

I closed my eyes and remembered the wind on my face in the launch coming back, tried to feel it moving over my skin in the closed and air-conditioned room, and I saw the stars again, in the sky larger than the sea. They began to disappear, as though rising from the sea and the earth and my vision, and I saw the black of sleep coming, when below me Willie made a sound like laughter, a humorous grunt, and said: "My people, my people ..."

He shifted, rolled to his side, and I lay on my back and for moments with closed eyes saw the stars again and focused on them until I knew from his breathing that Willie was asleep, then I let go of their tiny silver lights and received the dark.

11 September 1961
Okinawa, at anchor

Hello Camille:

There is not only a mystery in night itself, but it is intensified at sea. I am standing the eight-to-midnight watch, not the OOD on the quarterdeck, but the Duty Officer at the accommodation ladder for enlisted men. I drink coffee and smoke (not allowed on the quarterdeck, or here either, but not seen on this deck, at least not by officers). My assistant is a seaman second class, and he is also quiet. Our duties are simple enough. Every hour the enlisted men's liberty boat comes alongside from Okinawa, and we stand at the top of the ladder and as each sailor steps aboard he salutes aft, then salutes me and requests permission etc., and I grant it and he goes below. Our only important duty is to make sure a friend or, lacking that, one of the Masters-at-Arms takes below and puts to bed a sailor who is dangerously drunk: helps him down the steep ladders, and lies him in his bunk, on his side, so he won't drown if he vomits while asleep. Some of them have been drinking ashore since liberty call at noon.

And there is an interesting instruction left with the log for the oncoming Duty Officer: we are told to watch for sea snakes, which have been seen near the ladder. So Gantner (the seaman second class) and I peer down at the water as the liberty boat approaches. We are unarmed. Instructions like these make me wonder why they are not accompanied by a shotgun. The Navy seems to trust only the ship's Marines to handle any firearm smaller than a five-inch fifty-four. Ha: they don't know that tonight's Duty Officer, shepherd of the young and drunk and recently laid, is a slayer of many cotton-mouths and copperheads with his cheap but accurate Hi-Standard .22 revolver. I'm not only at sea and can't fish, I can't even shoot a sea-going cottonmouth. A very lethal one at that. So Gantner and I watch the water beneath the ladder that angles out from the ship, so we can yell to some poor bastard stepping from the boat to the ladder that he is about to be struck by a terrible snake, and before he even hears us he will have in his blood a poison that, as far as I know, does not have an antidote. But it adds excitement, or at least alertness, to our hourly stand at the head of the ladder. And at times makes me nostalgic for my snake-infested boyhood: a sure sign that the night and sea are at work on me, for in truth I have little nostalgia for that boyhood, and none at all for the sudden appearance of a poisonous snake in my path or, worse, beside or behind the spot where I have just stepped. What quick—no: startled—draws from the holster, what terrified fusillades with the .22. Remember? How many times did we picnic on a bluff over a bayou, or row a skiff on one, without coming as close to a cottonmouth as city people do to pigeons?

At night I feel more deeply. And my loneliness now is also like the feeling I sometimes have at Mass, at the Consecration or while singing or receiving the Host; and sometimes watching the sun set; or sometimes taking the hook from a fish's mouth; and always picking up a dove I have shot and holding its warm body and stroking its soft gray feathers; or listening to jazz, a female vocalist, in a dark club with people at every table but quiet and listening too. So it is not true loneliness, like Ernie's when I was on the *St. Paul* and for the seven months of our deployment his wife did not write to him and when we got home to the band playing on the pier and you waiting in your red dress and all the wives and children and lovers waiting she was not there, and he stayed on the pier till he was alone on it, then took a taxi to the apartment he knew had not been his home for months; he only did not know precisely why; and the key was under the mat and the apartment was empty save for his things in cartons on the bare living-room floor, and taped to one of the boxes a letter saying she had left him for a doctor she met and fell in love with at the hospital where she was a pretty twenty-two-year-old nurse coming home alone at night for seven months out of every twelve, to letters from the Western Pacific, silk from Hong Kong, pearls from Kobe, colored photographs of ports as the ship approached them, a kimono and happy shirts from Japanese markets, and the stereo he had brought home the year before. I remember the day he rode the train from Yokosuka to Tokyo and back and carried the stereo aboard.

So mine is not true loneliness, but closer to the love that saints feel for God: a sad and joyful longing. Like St. Teresa of Avila, whose heart held so much love of God that, in harmony with the earth, she transcended it too, was beyond it, reaching for union with Him. If Teresa imagined ascending through the sky I stand under tonight, then wife-lover that I am, abiding companion of Camille, my strong and wise and gentle woman, I traverse the sky to sit with you at breakfast. For about now you are in that cramped kitchen, and I can see you, smell your morning flesh and hair, and your first coffee and cigarette, and the bacon slowly frying and the biscuits in the oven as you read the *Chronicle* and enter your day.

I believe at night the world leaves us. We do not see it. It is gone. We are left with what little of it we can see, and without those distractions lit by day, our focus does more than simply narrow: it sharpens on what for most of us is the world—our selves. So the malaise that is held at bay by the visible motion and stillness under sunlight—people and cars and buildings and highways and woods and fields and water— can in the enclosing dark of night become despair. What does Ernie do now, at watch on the bridge at night, or in Japanese cities? Could bars stay in business if we all worked from midnight till eight, going to whatever home in the morning sun rising with promise, instead of the setting sun, harbinger of twilight and dusk, then night?

So now, seeing little more than the small deck I stand on, and its rail, and hearing only the water gently washing at the ship's hull, I receive the world less through my senses than through my spirit. But with the lovely smell of the sea. And I look at it too, unable to see anything that is not a prominent silhouette on its surface: another ship, a small boat; I cannot see the myriad waves, only a softly swelling darkness and a swath of moon-shimmer. Far beyond my vision of it, the Pacific ends at the sky, a horizon I see only because of the stars. They are low in the sky at the dark line of the ocean. I am writing on the podium that holds the log, and I stop for minutes between sentences, even words, to look up at the sky covering you like a soft sheet, though it is mid-morning in Alameda, and you are awake, you are in motion. I am on the starboard side, facing east, but I may be looking toward Oregon or Mazatlan. But these stars in their sheet cover you. As I cover you: in the ocean that touches the earth where you sit in the kitchen, and under the sky that is above you and east of you too, I am with you. My spirit, my love, move in the water, and through the air beneath the stars. Perhaps St. Teresa felt this about God during the day, praying, eating, talking to a nun about whether it would rain before noon or the clouds would blow.

I wrote all that, or got to the last sentence of it, at about ten-fifteen. Now it's eleven-forty-five. Romantic, spiritual, whatever the mood was, it's gone now, as distant as last month. I stopped writing because the OOD phoned and told me to watch for a sailor on the liberty boat that left the pier at ten o'clock. A Negro sailor, in a wet uniform. The Shore Patrol had radioed the OOD, told him there had been a fight on the pier, between a white sailor and a Negro sailor, and they had fallen into the water. The Negro had come out and climbed onto the pier and then into the liberty boat. The white sailor was still underwater, and divers were looking for him. The OOD told me to arrest the Negro, get his statement, and have the original delivered to him. He said there was no need to send the Negro to the brig.

The phone is on the podium with the log. I went to the hatch of the compartment where Gantner sat in one of two chairs: a small place with a gray wall locker, a coffee percolator, white mugs from the mess hall, a desk with strewn memorandums, ashtrays made from coffee cans, a typewriter. Gantner looked up at me standing at the hatch. He is a tall, lean man, probably my age. For moments we looked at each other. Then he stood and swallowed coffee without lowering his eyes from mine. Then I told him and he drained the cup and wiped his lips with the back of his hand and said: "Shit."

He put on his cap and followed me to the top of the ladder and we stood at the rail, looking east at the sea, listening for the liberty boat. Soon we heard its engine, distant, to our left, beyond the bow. We lit cigarettes.

"You know those Goddamn piers," he said. He was not nervous, or expectant, or, as many men would be, excited. His voice was bitter, and I looked at his face and then back at the sea, wondering where he had been, what he had seen in his life. "A lot of drunk guys. A lot of guys just worked up about being ashore, just a little drunk. Everybody crowded together. Just guys. You ever notice that, how it's different when it's just guys?" I looked at him but he was listening to the engine, steady and louder, and staring over the water, perhaps at the horizon. I looked at the sky above it. "Somebody bumps some-body. That's all. And it flares up like a gasoline fire. Shit." He drew on his cigarette, then threw it down at the water, threw it with enough force to break something, if it had not been a cigarette, and if the sea could break. "Some poor fucking drunk kid."

I leaned over the rail and dropped my cigarette and watched its glow falling, watched it instantly darken, and twice the cigarette washed against the hull, then disintegrated, and I could not see the last inch of paper. I knew from the engine that the boat was making its turn, and there it was, a long boat coming widely around our bow, and I felt Gantner watching it with me as it came out of its port turn and was broadside to us, then turned starboard and came with slowing engine toward us from the stern, and I watched its red and green running lights and listened to the engine slowing, then it was idling with its port side at our ladder, and I stepped away from Gant-ner and stood at my post. I heard him step behind me, felt his weary sadness, like that of a young man who has been to war, or who as a child lived too much for too long with cruelty or poverty or death, and I felt that he was not in his twenties, but older than the Ship's Captain, older than the Admiral, half at least as old as the sky and sea.

They walked up one at a time, performed their protocol, men ranging in age from eighteen to forty, and all of them to some degree drunk. But tonight they did not even have to try to disguise it. They were men whose bodies were still drunk, yet their faces were sober, some marked with that exaggerated and suddenly aging solemnity of a drunken man who has just heard bad news. Not one, even the youngest, spoke to me with the alcoholic warmth that, like an old friendship, is heedless of rank. Not one smiled. They saluted aft where in daylight the flag would fly, they turned and saluted me and said,

"Request permission to come aboard, sir," and I said "Permission granted," and they walked quickly off the deck, through the hatch, and down into the huge ship that sat as still as a building on land. The Negro was one of the last to come aboard. His white uniform clung to his skin, and he was shivering with cold, and I could feel him forcing his arms to his sides, away from his chest that wanted their hug and its semblance of warmth. His cap, tilted cockily forward over his right brow, was dry, except for its sides that had soaked water from his hair. It must have fallen off on the pier, before he went into the water. He turned his back to me and saluted the darkness, then faced me and saluted and before he spoke I said: "Just step behind me, sailor. Until the others have come aboard."

Two more sailors stepped on deck before I realized I could do something for the man whose shivering behind me I either heard or believed I did. I looked over my shoulder at Gantner, standing beside the Negro, watching me, looking as if he did not know whether he was a policeman or bystander or even a paraclete.

"Take him inside," I said. "Give him some coffee. And see if there's a foul-weather jacket in that locker."

He did not answer. I heard their steps on the steel deck, both of them slow, but I could detect the firmness of Gantner's, his feet coming down hard like those of an angry man, but one resigned to destiny; and the other's, soft, wet, and cold, wanting not motion but to be dry and prone between sheets and under blankets, his knees for a while drawn toward his belly, then, as he warmed, straightening until he lay at full length, even the memory of cold gone from his flesh. Soon the last sailor, a seaman first class who gave me the only sign I received from any of them—an abrupt and frowning shake of his head as his arm rose from his side to salute—disappeared through the hatch and left me alone on the deck. I stood at the railing and watched the liberty boat pull away from the ship.

Then I went through the other hatch, into the compartment: the Negro sat huddled in a chair, wearing a foul-weather jacket that was too large but not by much, its front closed above his wet trousers. His cap was on the desk beside his mug of coffee, and he was smoking one of Gantner's cigarettes and his other hand was wrapped around the mug. For warmth, I suppose. Gantner sat beside him, almost in the same pose, dry and warm but looking cold, looking near-huddled, and I thought of a blanket for him and fleetingly of the sky I saw as a starlit sheet covering you, then the Negro looked up and started to rise but with my hand I motioned him to sit, my palm pushing in his direction as though it touched his chest, not air. Then as Gantner's feet shifted to stand I pushed again at him, and he settled back. I asked him if he could type and he nodded and said yes sir and I told him to get carbon paper for an original and two.

Then the Negro moved. He was quick—motions of efficiency, not fear: he stood and carried his chair away from the desk, and Gantner, still sitting, pulled his chair to the type-writer and got paper and carbons from the desk drawer; I watched him roll them onto the carriage. The Negro stood behind Gantner and to his right, stood behind the chair, holding its back. He was directly in front of me, looking at me, his face more quizzical than afraid; but he was frightened too, and I knew then that Gantner had not spoken to him; then I knew, though I treated it as a guess, that he did not know the other sailor was dead. I told him to sit down, to have coffee, to smoke, and he pushed the chair closer to the desk and reached for his mug, but Gantner picked it up first and, twisting to his left, filled it at the percolator and placed it back on the desk, in the circle it had made before. The Negro took it. Gantner raised my mug toward me. I shook my head. He put his cigarettes and lighter and an ashtray on the edge of the desk near the Negro, then filled his coffee mug and lit a cigarette, and the Negro did too, then Gantner rested his on the ashtray, and his hands settled on the typewriter keys, so softly that not one key moved. Then I looked at the Negro, at his waiting eyes.

"I'm placing you under arrest," I said. "That does not mean the brig. You will simply go to your bunk. Tomorrow an investigating officer will talk to you." He was no longer quiz-

zical, and he wasn't more frightened yet either: he was alert
and he was thinking, with the look of a man trying to remember something crucial, and I imagined the pictures in his
mind and then the last one, the one that changed his face: a
sudden slackening, and now he was afraid, and more: in his
eyes was a new knowledge, a recognition that his entire life,
in this very moment, was finished; that is, his life as it had
been, as he had known it. "You're free to make a statement,"
I said. "Gantner will type it and you can sign it. And you must
understand this perfectly: anything you say can be used against
you in a court-martial." Gantner began to type; I paused, then
understood he was typing the beginning of such statements:
Having been informed of my rights and so forth *I do hereby
make the following voluntary statement . . .* "You can also remain
silent. You can say nothing at all. Just get up and go below and
get out of that wet uniform and take a hot shower. And go to
bed. That won't be held against you either."

"Mister—"

"Fontenot."

"Mister Fontenot? What am I charged with?"

He was from the North.

"The other sailor. The one you fought with. He didn't
come up."

"He didn't come up?" Now the knowledge, the recognition, was deeper, it was all of him, and I felt he was sitting in
an electric chair watching me at the switch. "How come?
How come he didn't just swim on up?"

"They don't know. They're looking for him."

"Wasn't *sharks* in the water. They sure he never swam to
the pier? I mean, I never looked for him. I just made it to the
liberty boat. I didn't even know the man. Just a white boy on
the pier. I looked around the boat, once we was underway, but
I didn't look real good. I was cold. I just tried to stay warm."

"Nobody said anything to you? On the boat?"

"No, Mister—"

"Fontenot."

"Mister Fontenot. No, sir."

"I think they knew."

"I don't know." He shook his head once, looked again as though he were trying to remember. "I just wanted to get to the ship, and do like you said."

"Like I said?"

"Yes sir. A hot shower and—"

"Oh."

He started to rise, but not to stand: his arms straightened and pressed down on the sides of the chair, so his weight shifted up and toward me.

"They *sure* that white boy didn't come up?"

"Nobody saw him. The Shore Patrol was there. They didn't see him. What's your name?"

He eased down on the chair.

"Seaman apprentice Ellis. Kenneth Ellis."

"Middle initial?"

"D. It's for Dalton."

"Where are you from, Ellis?"

"Detroit. Mr. Fontenot."

"Do you want to make a statement?"

"Yes sir. Yessir, I'll make a statement." He reached for his mug and cigarette, almost burned down now, and his fingers trembled. He looked at Gantner. "Want me to go slow?"

Gantner did not look up from the page in the typewriter.

"I'm fast," he said. "Don't worry about me. Take a cigarette when you want one. I got a carton in my locker and there's enough here to get me through this fucking watch."

He quickly looked up at me, apologetic, then defiant as his face lowered to the page.

"We was on the pier," Ellis said, and Gantner was typing. "I was by myself. I mean I left my buddies in the bar. I was tired. I was going broke too. I mean, they'd pay for me, but you know how it is. So I was standing on the pier, watching the boat coming. It was crowded, you know." He had been looking directly at me, and he still did but now his eyes were not really seeing mine, and his voice softened, as memory drew him back to the pier, and the man he was there, with the life he had there. "People close up against one another." I saw a motion to my right and looked at it: Gantner's face rising from the words under the keys, his eyes looking at mine. "There was some loud ones behind me. Southern boys. But they wasn't saying nothing. To me, I mean. Or doing nothing. After a while I forgot they was even there. They was loud, but I didn't hear it no more. I was just watching them running lights and thinking about sleeping and tomorrow." Gantner was very fast; it seemed that Ellis's words themselves struck the keys. "I got liberty tomorrow too. I had liberty tomorrow. I was thinking about where to go, and how much money I ought to bring. When was the next payday, and would it be before the next port. I must have stepped back. I guess I did. No reason. I was just thinking and I stepped back. I bumped one of the white boys. One of the Southern boys. He said— He called me nigger. Something about 'Watch what you doing, nigger.' Something like that. So I turned on him. Mister —" His eyes came back from memory, focused on mine. "Fontenot. Nobody's called me that since I was too little to do nothing. When I got my size maybe two, maybe three guys, they called me that. But they didn't come out so good." His size was not height, or in his shoulders and chest; he was a normal young man, five-nine or so, a hundred and sixty, but I knew he was telling the truth about the two or maybe three. It was in his eyes. He'd hang on like they say a snapping turtle does, and even if you finally beat him on strength alone, you'd end up wishing you had never seen him, and you'd make certain you didn't see him again. He lowered his head, looked at the space of deck between his thighs. Then slowly he shook his head. Twice, three times, more. He did not raise it when he spoke again. "But that white boy. On the pier. I wish— We didn't even hit one another. I grabbed him and got him in a head-lock. He was a heavy boy. We was kind of turning. Like spinning round, and I was holding onto his head. Then we went off the side. The water's deep there. We went down a ways before he let go my body. He had me around here." Still looking between his thighs, he pointed at his waist. Then he said it: "Around my waist." Under Gantner's quick fingers the keys clicked to a ring, and he slid the carriage back and the keys clicked again, dulled by the three pages and two sheets of carbon paper. "Soon as he let go I did. I swam right up. I was scared too. I mean, I didn't take a big breath to go under-water. I didn't know I was going under no water. I didn't have any air left. I started getting scared I was swimming to the bottom 'stead of the top. Then I was at the top and breathing. I mean that's all I could do, was breathe. And swim to the pier and grab the ladder. I wasn't even thinking about that white boy. I climbed up and—" Still he looked at the deck, but his head twitched upward, his neck tightened; then he let them ease down again. "Mister Fontenot's right. They must have known, on the boat. There was people on the pier. Sailors looking down at the water. When I come up the ladder. I just didn't think nothing then. I just wanted to keep sucking air, and get out of the water. Get on the liberty boat. And then the Shore Patrol come behind everybody and was yelling every-body get on the boat. So that's what we did. When I got on I checked for my wallet and I still had it. My watch was still ticking too. Then I just sat low as I could, keep out of the wind. I guess that's it."

Still he looked down. Gantner typed three more lines, and there was no ringing when he finished the last one. Then he spaced twice and typed faster than I could count but I knew the letters before they came, so I heard with each click the spelling of Kenneth D. Ellis. Then the room was silent. Gantner lit a cigarette, and Ellis looked up at me.

"Do you want to sign this?" I said.

"Sure, I'll sign it. Mister Fontenot, sir."

"Ellis."

"Sir?"

"Nothing will happen."

"Looks like a lot is happening. And a lot going to happen."

"Listen to me, Ellis. If they thought you were a man who goes around killing people, they'd have told me to put you in the brig. They didn't, did they?"

"No sir."

"So being under arrest is just a formality. I'm charging you with disorderly conduct. They'll appoint an investigating officer. Tomorrow, to get it done with. When he's talked to you, you'll be free. To go on liberty. You can do whatever you want till he sees you. You just have to stay aboard."

"What about that boy?"

"You didn't drown him."

"We went into the—"

"Ellis. Somebody provoked you. You wrestled with him. You both fell in the water. You swam out. He didn't. It's not like you held him under till he was dead."

"But—" Then all fear and confusion and his resignation to whatever fate he had imagined left his eyes, and they showed sadness, not of grief but remorse.

"You didn't kill him, Ellis. They won't even charge you with assault and battery. I'm sure of it."

"That's not it."

"I know it's not."

We looked at each other, his eyes imploring mine for forgiveness I could not grant, because I was not his friend; and imploring me too for some cleansing, some blessing short of removing him from the pier and restoring him with both energy and money to the bar with his friends, where he would drink with them and catch a later boat, long after the white boy who called him nigger was asleep in his bunk.

"Why don't you read that and sign it," I said. "Then get that shower. And some warm sleep."

As though rising after a long illness, he slowly pushed himself up from the chair, straightened his back, and was standing. Gantner pulled the sheets of paper from the typewriter and handed them to Ellis; then he stood and put on his cap and stepped toward the hatch, and I moved aside for him. He crossed the deck and stood at the rail. I looked at Ellis reading. Then I went out too and stood beside Gantner; we did not speak. After a while, and at the same time, we bent our waists and leaned on the rail, looking down at the sea, and I remembered as a boy loving to stand on those old wooden bridges over bayous, standing for an hour or more, watching the current.

Stark and his chief were on the eleven-o'clock liberty boat. I looked down into it and saw Stark, in his sport jacket and loosened tie. They came up last, Stark first up the ladder, then the chief, who was in uniform but did not salute either aft or me; and Stark, in civilian clothes and bareheaded that forbade saluting, did not go through the performance of standing at attention to face aft, then me, either. Nor did they request permission to board the ship.

"We got him," Stark said. "Where's your coffee?"

We followed Gantner into the compartment and he got two clean mugs and filled them. The chief took off his cap and tossed it on the desk.

"They put us to work," the chief said. "We were shitfaced."

"We started at noon. Lunch. Saki, and then everything."

"It was vodka. Nothing but vodka after the saki. We're sitting on the pier. Waiting for the first boat going to the ship. We'll stow away on the Captain's gig, if that's first. We don't give a shit: we're going home, set the eyelid integrity watch before we drop dead. Here comes the Shore Patrol. And Mr. Stark, he's eager, he volunteers."

"Bullshit, volunteered."

"Mr. Stark, when you say, 'Over here,' that's volunteering."

"He's right. I volunteered."

"I was about to myself," the chief said. "See, at first we thought the kid was alive. Shore Patrol guys running around, armbands, duty belts, nightsticks. Hollering. 'Is there a qualified diver on the pier?' Mr. Fontenot, try sometime hollering, 'Is there a qualified diver on the pier.' That is very official cop-like hollering. So Mr. Stark says, 'Over here.' He raises his hand too. So do I. Trouble was standing up."

"That's when I told them maybe we were not in the proper condition for underwater work."

"His exact words. Swear to God. Then they tell us the poor son of a bitch's been under there fifteen or twenty minutes.

So Mr. Stark says our gear's aboard our ship. This don't work with the fucking Shore Patrol. Guy says, 'We have gear in the shed.' Leads us off to his little shack, opens some lockers, out comes all this fucking scuba gear. Even knives. So we drop our clothes and put on the suits and the guy hands me a knife. I say what am I going to do with it? He says he don't know, it's part of the gear. So I say, 'Think of some place to stick it.' He just looks at me. Mr. Stark puts his on the desk in here. I say, 'Think hard.' He don't get it. He's looking at a drunk old chief dressed up like a reptile. I think they're soft, those Shore Patrol guys."

I looked at Gantner sitting on the desk; he had pushed the typewriter against the bulkhead, and his buttocks touched it. He looked at the chief and said: "So who was he?"

"The poor son of a bitch at the bottom? Kid named Andrew Taylor. Eighteen fucking years old. Mr. Stark found him. Mr. Stark has all the luck: he is a happy man with his wife, and thank the good Lord he is also the one to find the guy. Holy shit, Mr. Stark."

"What."

"Every time we fall into shit, your friend Mr. Fontenot, he's right there with us."

I said: "Where was he from?"

"Mississippi," Stark said.

"It was a Negro," I said. "The white kid—"

"I know," Stark said. "They told us. They got witnesses up the ass. Guys from some other ship, waiting for their boat. Let me tell you, man. I'm still fucked up. I've never seen a dead man outside of a coffin. And at the bottom of the water, and at night. There was a barge tied up at the pier. So apparently— apparently, shit: it's the only way—Taylor came up under the Goddamn barge. Probably he panicked then."

"They didn't go in holding their breath," I said.

"There you go," he said, and looked at the chief, who nod-ded and drank some coffee, then looked at his cap on the desk.

"We went under the barge first," Stark said to me. "Chief went one way, I went the other. I've got fucking vodka and rice wine in my blood and I'm scared I'll find him. I went down, it's muddy around the pier, and all I can see is what the light hits. And I can see the chief's light down at the other end. I keep moving and shining the light on the bottom. Then, Jesus, I see his hands. They're at the end of my light. That's all I can see. These white hands. Reaching up, and moving back and forth with the tide. Like this." He put his coffee on the desk and extended both arms straight at me, his hands vertical, the upturned palms toward my face; when he slowly moved them from side to side, his body swayed. Then he dropped his arms and expelled breath, and picked up his mug and drank. "I turned my light to the chief and waved it up and down till I saw his light coming. Then we brought him up."

The chief was looking out the hatch, his eyes focused above the deck and past the bulkhead, on the night above the sea.

It's past midnight now, and I'm sitting at my desk. Willie left its fluorescent light on so I could find my way. I crept into the stateroom and took off my uniform and I'm sitting here wearing that silk kimono and trying not to hate Andrew Taylor's father, or his mother, or whoever first said in front of him or allowed him to use out of habit the word that killed him. I can even say out of habit, though its source is greed for money or hatred or arrogance or some need to have inferiors, but all of these sound too simple, so perhaps I shall remain with the awful complexity of habit. And with fate too, though maybe after all fate is the conclusion of the patterns of history, and not a toss of cubes by the dark dicemen. But whatever it is, comprehensible or without meaning, it not only placed Kenneth Ellis and Andrew Taylor on the same pier at the same time and gave them long enough together on that pier for Ellis to step backward and bump or only touch Taylor, and for Taylor to say something, one hardly provocative sentence that ended with the word *nigger*; but it also put them both on an aircraft carrier that, simply because of its size, can only moor at the pier at Yokosuka, and must anchor off the other ports, and so forced Ellis and Taylor to return to it in a boat. Had

they been stationed on the same destroyer they would have
gone to it tonight, walked separately on the pier where their
ship was tied, and separately boarded it, for the deep long
sleep of boys.

In the darkness of our bunks Willie sleeps, and I cannot.
I write, and listen to his soft breathing. He is on his left side
now, facing the bulkhead, his back to me and my shaded light.
It is his final position when he sleeps, though later I shall hear
him shift a leg or move an arm, or turn his body once or twice,
while I lie above him. I had hoped he would be awake when I
came to our room. But I was relieved when I saw his shape
under the blanket and sheet, and the back of his neck and
head on the pillow. Yet I also wanted to tell him, and before
writing to you I sat here watching him, and wondering
whether he would want me to wake him and tell him now, or
wait till morning. And having written this I wish he had been
writing to Louisa, or reading in his bunk when I opened our
door. But he sleeps. So I will turn off this light and quietly
climb to my bunk above him, and quietly get under the covers,
and take care to move lightly on the mattress while I lie awake
and smoke and see Ellis in the chair looking at me but seeing
himself standing on the pier, thinking of sleep and tomorrow's liberty and money, and while I see Taylor's hands, their
palms turned upward to the surface of the sea, to air, to the
dark bottom of the barge, and moving in Stark's light as gently
as petals of a gardenia, floating with the ebb and flow of the
tide. I shall let Willie sleep until the alarm wakes him.

AFTER THE GAME

I WASN'T IN THE CLUBHOUSE when Joaquin Quintana went crazy. At least I wasn't there for the start of it, because I pitched that night and went nine innings and won, and the color man interviewed me after the game. He is Duke Simpson, and last year he was our first baseman. He came down from the broadcasting booth, and while the guys were going into the clubhouse, and cops and ushers were standing like soldiers in a V from first to third, facing the crowd leaving the park, I stood in front of the dugout with my jacket on, and Duke and I looked at the camera, and he said: "I'm here with Billy Wells."

This was August and we were still in it, four games back, one and a half out of second. It was the time of year when everybody is tired and a lot are hurt and playing anyway. I wanted a shower and a beer, and to go to my apartment for one more beer and then sleep. I sleep very well after I've pitched a good game, not so well after a bad one, and I sleep very badly the night before I pitch, and the day of the game I force myself to eat. It's one of the things that makes the game exciting, but a lot of times, especially in late season, I long for the time when I'll have a job I can predict, can wake up on the ranch knowing what I'm going to do and that I'm not going to fail. I know most jobs are like that, and the people who have them don't look like they've had a rush of adrenaline since the time somebody ran a stop sign and just missed colliding broadside with them, but there's always a trade-off and, on some days in late season, their lives seem worth it. Duke and I talked about pitching, and our catcher Jesse Wade and what a good game he called behind the plate, so later that night I thought it was strange, that Joaquin was going crazy while Duke and I were talking about Jesse, because during the winter the club had traded Manuel Fernandez, a good relief pitcher, to the Yankees for Jesse. Manuel had been Joaquin's roommate, and they always sat together on the plane and the bus, and ate together. Neither one could speak much English. From shortstop, Joaquin used to call to Manuel out on the mound: *Baja y rapido*.

We ended the interview shaking hands and patting each other on the back, then I went between the cops and ushers but there were some fans waiting for autographs at one end of the dugout, so I went over there and signed three baseballs and a dozen score-cards and said thank you twenty or thirty times, and shook it seemed more hands than there were people, then went into the dugout and down the tunnel to the clubhouse. I knew something was wrong, but I wasn't alert to it, wanting a beer, and I was thinking maybe I'd put my arm in ice for a while, so I saw as if out of the corner of my eye, though I was looking right at it, that nobody was at the food table. There was pizza. Then I heard them and looked that way, down between two rows of lockers. They were bunched down there, the ones on the outside standing on benches or on tiptoes on the floor, stretching and looking, and the ones on the inside talking, not to each other but to whoever was in the middle, and I could hear the manager Bobby Drew, and Terry Morgan the trainer. The guys' voices were low, so I couldn't make out the words, and urgent, so I wondered who had been fighting and why now, with things going well for us, and we hadn't had trouble on the club since Duke retired; he was a good ballplayer, but often a pain in the ass. I went to the back of the crowd but couldn't see, so took off my spikes and stepped behind Bruce Green on a bench. Bruce is the only black on the club, and plays right field. I held his waist for balance as I brought my other foot from the floor. I stay in good running shape all year round, and I am overly careful about accidents, like falling off a bench onto my pitching elbow.

I kept my hands on Bruce's waist and looked over his shoulder and there was Joaquin Quintana, our shortstop, standing in front of his locker, naked except for his sweat socks and jockstrap and his gold Catholic medal, breathing through his mouth like he was in the middle of a sentence he didn't finish. He was as black as Bruce, so people who didn't know him took him for a black man, but Manuel told us he was from the Dominican Republic and did not think of himself as a black, and was pissed off when people did; though it seemed to me he was a black from down there, as Bruce was a black from Newark. His left arm was at his side, and his right forearm was out in front of him like he was reaching for something, or to shake hands, and in that hand he held his spikes. It was the right shoe.

Bruce looked at me over his shoulder.

"They can't move him," he said. Bruce was wearing his uniform pants and no shirt. I came to Boston in 1955, as a minor-league player to be named later in a trade with Detroit, when I was in that organization, and I have played all my seven years of major-league ball with the Red Sox; I grew up in San Antonio, so Bruce is the only black I've ever really known. People were talking to Joaquin. Or the people in front were trying to, and others farther back called to him to have some pizza, a beer, a shower, telling him it was all right, everything was all right, telling him settle down, be cool, take it easy, the girls are waiting at the parking lot. Nobody was wet or wrapped in a towel. Some still wore the uniform and some, like Bruce, wore parts of it, and a few had taken off as much as Joaquin. Most of the lockers were open. So was Joaquin's, and he stood staring at Bobby Drew and Terry Morgan, both of them talking, and Bobby doing most of it, being the manager. He was talking softly and telling Joaquin to give him the shoe and come in his office and lie down on the couch in there. He kept talking about the shoe, as if it was a weapon, though Joaquin held it with his hand under it, and not gripped for swinging, but like he was holding it out to give to someone. But I knew why Bobby wanted him to put it down. I felt the same: if he would just drop that shoe, things would get better. Looking at the scuffed toe and the soft dusty leather and the laces untied and pulled wider across the tongue folded up and over, and the spikes, silver down at their edges, resting on his palm, I wanted to talk that shoe out of his hand too, and I started talking with the others below me, and on the bench across the aisle from me and Bruce, and the benches on the other side of the group around Joaquin.

That is when I saw what he was staring at, when I told him to come on and put down that shoe and let's go get some dinner, it was on me, and all the drinks too, for turning that double-play in the seventh; and Bruce said And the bunt, and Jesse said Perfect fucking bunt, and I saw that Joaquin was not staring at Bobby or Terry, but at nothing at all, as if he saw something we couldn't, but it was as clear to him as a picture hanging in the air right in front of his face.

I lowered myself off the bench and worked my way through the guys, most of them growing quiet while some still tried to break Joaquin out of it. A few were saying their favorite curse, to themselves, shaking their heads or looking at the floor. Everyone I touched was standing tense and solid, but they were easy to part from each other, like pushing aside branches that smelled of sweat. I stepped between Bobby and Terry. They were still dressed, Bobby in his uniform and cap, Terry in his red slacks and white tee shirt.

"Quintana," I said. "Joaquin: it's me, old buddy. It's Billy."

I stared into his eyes but they were not looking back at me; they were looking at something, and they chilled the backs of my knees. I had to stop my hands from going up and feeling the air between us, grabbing for it, pushing it away.

There is something about being naked. Duke Simpson and Tommy Lutring got in a fight last year, in front of Duke's locker, when they had just got out of the shower, and it was not like seeing a fight on the field when the guys are dressed and rolling in the dirt. It seemed worse. Once in a hotel in Chicago a girl and I started fighting in bed and quick enough we were out of bed and putting on our underpants; the madder we got the more clothes we put on, and when she ended the fight by walking out, I was wearing everything but my socks and shoes. I wished Joaquin was dressed.

"Joaquin," I said. "Joaquin, I'm going to take the shoe."

Some of the guys told him to give Billy the shoe. I put my hand on it and he didn't move; then I tried to lift it, and his arm swung a few degrees, but that was all. His bicep was swollen and showing veins.

"Come on, Joaquin. Let it go now. That's a boy."

I put my other hand on it and jerked, and his arm swung and his body swayed and my hands slipped off the shoe. He was staring. I looked at Bobby and Terry, then at the guys on both sides; my eyes met Bruce's, so I said to him: "He doesn't even know I'm here."

"Poor bastard," Bobby said.

Somebody said we ought to carry him to Bobby's couch, and Terry said we couldn't because he was stiff as iron, and lightly, with his fingertips, he jabbed Joaquin's thighs and belly and arms and shoulders, and put his palms on Joaquin's cheeks. Terry said we had to wait for Doc Segura, and Bobby told old Will Hammersley, the clubhouse man, to go tell the press he was sorry but they couldn't come in tonight.

Then we stood waiting. I smelled Joaquin's sweat and listened to his breathing, and looked up and down his good body, and at the medal hanging from his neck, and past his eyes, into his locker: the shaving kit and underwear and socks on the top shelf, with his wallet and gold-banded wristwatch and box of cigars. A couple of his silk shirts hung in the locker, one aqua and one maroon, and a sport coat that was pale yellow, near the color of cream; under it some black pants were folded over the hanger. I wondered what it was like being him all the time. I don't know where the Dominican Republic is. I know it's in the Caribbean, but not where. Over the voices around me, Tommy Lutring said: "Why the *fuck* did we trade Ma*nuel*?" Then he said: "Sorry, Jesse."

"I wish he was here," Jesse said.

The guys near Jesse patted him on the shoulders and back. Lutring is the second baseman and he loves working with Joaquin. They are something to see, and I like watching them take infield practice. In a game it happens very fast, and you feel the excitement in the moments it takes Joaquin and Tommy to turn a double-play, and before you can absorb it, the pitcher's ready to throw again. In practice you get to antic-ipate, and watch them poised for the groundball, then they're moving, one to the bag, one to the ball, and they always know where the other guy is and where his glove is too, because who-ever's taking the throw knows it's coming at his chest, leading him across the bag. It's like the movies I used to watch in San Antonio, with one of those dances that start with a chorus of pretty girls, then they move back for the man and woman: he is in a tuxedo and she wears a long white dress that rises from her legs when she whirls. The lights go down on the chorus, and one light moves with the man and woman dancing together and apart but always together. Light sparkles on her dress, and their shadows dance on the polished floor. I was a kid sitting in the dark, and I wanted to dance like that, and felt if I could just step into the music like into a river, the drums and horns would take me, and I would know how to move.

That is why Tommy said what he did. And Jesse said he wished Manuel was here too, which he probably did but not really, not at the price of him being back with the Yankees where he was the back-up catcher, while here he is the regu-lar and also has our short left field wall to pull for. Because we couldn't do anything and we started to feel like Spanish was the answer, or the problem, and if just somebody could speak it to Joaquin he'd be all right and he'd put down that shoe and use his eyes again, and take off his jockstrap and socks, and head for the showers, so if only Manuel was with us or one of us had learned Spanish in school.

But the truth is the president or dictator of the Dominican

Republic couldn't have talked Joaquin into the showers. Doc Segura gave him three shots before his muscles went limp and he dropped the shoe and collapsed like pants you step out of. We caught him before he hit the floor. The two guys with the ambulance got there after the first shot, and stood on either side of him, behind him so they were out of Doc's way; around the end, before the last shot, they held Joaquin's arms, and when he fell Bobby and I grabbed him too. His eyes were closed. We put him on the stretcher and they covered him up and carried him out and we haven't seen him since, though we get reports on how he's doing in the hospital. He sleeps and they feed him. That was three weeks ago.

Doc Segura had to wait thirty minutes between shots, so the smokers had their cigarettes and cigars going, and guys were passing beers and pizza up from the back, where I had stood with Bruce. He was still on the bench, drinking a beer, with smoke rising past him to the ceiling. I didn't feel right, drinking a beer in front of Joaquin, and I don't think Bobby did either. Terry is an alcoholic who doesn't drink anymore and goes to meetings, so he didn't count. Finally when someone held a can toward Bobby he didn't shake his head, but got it to his mouth fast while he watched Doc getting the second needle ready, so I reached for one too. Doc swabbed the vein inside Joaquin's left elbow. This time I looked at Joaquin's eyes instead of the needle: he didn't feel it. All my sweat was long since dried, and I had my jacket off except the right sleeve on my arm.

I know Manuel couldn't have helped Joaquin. The guys keep saying it was because he was lonesome. But I think they say that because Joaquin was black and spoke Spanish. And maybe for the same reason an alcoholic who doesn't drink anymore may blame other people's troubles on booze: he's got scary memories of blackouts and sick hangovers and d.t.'s, and he always knows he's just a barstool away from it. I lost a wife in my first year in professional ball, when I was eighteen years old and as dumb about women as I am now. Her name was Leslie. She left me for a married dentist, a guy with kids, in Lafayette, Louisiana, where I was playing my rookie year in the Evangeline League, an old class C league that isn't there anymore. She is back in San Antonio, married to the manager of a department store; she has four kids, and I hardly ever see her, but when I do there are no hard feelings. Leslie said she felt like she was chasing the team bus all season long, down there in Louisiana. I have had girlfriends since, but not the kind you marry.

By the time Joaquin fell I'd had a few beers and some pizza gone cold, and I was very tired. It was after one in the morning and I did not feel like I had pitched a game, and won it too. I felt like I had been working all day on the beef-cattle ranch my daddy is building up for us with the money I send him every payday. That's where I'm going when my arm gives out. He has built a house on it, and I'll live there with him and my mom. In the showers people were quiet. They talked, but you know what I mean. I dressed then told Hammersley I wanted to go into the park for a minute. He said Sure, Billy, and opened the door.

I went up the tunnel to the dugout and stepped onto the grass. It was already damp. I had never seen the park empty at night, and with no lights, and all those empty seats and shadows under the roof over the grandstand, and under the sky the dark seats out in the bleachers in right and centerfield. Boston lit the sky over the screen in left and beyond the bleachers, but it was a dull light, and above the playing field there was no light at all, so I could see stars. For a long time, until I figured everybody was dressed and gone or leaving and Hammersley was waiting to lock up, I stood on the grass by the batting circle and looked up at the stars, thinking of drums and cymbals and horns, and a man and woman dancing.

DRESSED LIKE SUMMER LEAVES

Mɪᴄᴋᴇʏ ᴅᴏʟᴀɴ ᴡᴀѕ eleven years old, walking up Main Street on a spring afternoon, wearing green camouflage-colored trousers and tee shirt with a military web belt. The trousers had large pleated pockets at the front of his thighs; they closed with flaps, and his legs touched the spiral notebook in the left one, and the pen and pencil in the right one, where his coins shifted as he walked. He wore athletic socks and running shoes his mother bought him a week ago, after ten days of warm April, when she believed the winter was finally gone. He carried schoolbooks and a looseleaf binder in his left hand, their weight swinging with his steps. He passed a fish market, a discount shoe store that sold new shoes with nearly invisible defects, a flower shop, then an alley, and he was abreast of Timmy's, a red-painted wooden bar, when the door opened and a man came out. The man was in mid-stride but he turned his face and torso to look at Mickey, so that his lead foot came to the sidewalk pointing ahead, leaving him twisted to the right from the waist up. He shifted his foot toward Mickey, brought the other one near it, pulled the door shut, bent at the waist, and then straightened and lifted his arms in the air, his wrists limp, his palms toward the sidewalk.

"Charlie," he said. "Long time no see." Quickly his hands descended and held Mickey's biceps. "Motherfuckers were no bigger than you. Some of them." His hands squeezed, and

156

Mickey tightened his muscles. "Stronger, though. Doesn't matter though, right? If you can creep like a baby. Crawl like a snake. Be a tree; a vine. Quiet as fucking air. Then *zap:* body bags. Short tour. Marine home for Christmas. Nothing but rice too."

The man wore cut-off jeans and old sneakers, white gone gray in streaks and smears, and a yellow tank shirt with nothing written on it. A box of Marlboros rested in his jeans pocket, two-thirds of it showing, and on his belt at his right hip he wore a Buck folding knife in a sheath; he wore it upside down so the flap pointed to the earth. Behind the knife a chain that looked like chrome hung from his belt and circled his hip to the rear, and Mickey knew it was attached to a wallet. The man was red from a new sunburn, and the hair on his arms and legs and above the shirt's low neck was blond, while the hair under his arms was light brown. He had a beard with a thick mustache that showed little of his upper lip: his beard was brown and slowly becoming sun-bleached, like the hair on his head, around a circle of bald red scalp; the hair was thick on the sides and back of his head, and grew close to his ears and beneath them. A pair of reflecting sunglasses with silver frames rested in the hair in front of the bald spot. On his right bicep was a tattoo, and his eyes were blue, a blue that seemed to glare into focus on Mickey, and Mickey knew the source of the glare was the sour odor the man breathed into the warm exhaust-tinged air between them.

"What's up, anyways? No more school?" The man spread his arms, his eyes left Mickey's and moved skyward, then swept the street to Mickey's right and the buildings on its opposite side, then returned, sharper now, as though Mickey were a blurred television picture becoming clear, distinct. "Did July get here?"

"It's April."

"Ah: AWOL. Your old man'll kick your ass, right?"

"I just got out."

"Just got out." The man looked above Mickey again, his blue eyes roving, as though waiting for something to appear in the sky beyond low buildings, in the air above lines of slow cars. For the first time Mickey knew that the man was not tall; he had only seemed to be. His shoulders were broad and sloping, his chest wide and deep so the yellow tank shirt stretched across it, and his biceps swelled when he bent his arms, and sprang tautly when he straightened them; his belly was wide too, and protruded, but his chest was much wider and thicker. Yet he was not as tall as he had appeared stepping from the bar, turning as he strode, and bowing, then standing upright and raising his arms. Mickey's eyes were level with the soft area just beneath the man's Adam's apple, the place that housed so much pain, where Mickey had deeply pushed his finger against Frankie Archembault's windpipe last month when Frankie's headlock had blurred his eyes with tears and his face scraped the cold March earth. It was not a fight; Frankie simply got too rough, then released Mickey and rolled away, red-faced and gasping and rubbing his throat. When Mickey stood facing his father he looked directly at the two lower ribs, above the solar plexus. His father stood near-motionless, his limbs still, quiet, like his voice; the strength Mickey felt from him was in his eyes.

The man had lit a cigarette and was smoking it fast, looking at the cars passing; Mickey watched the side of his face. Below it, on the reddened bicep of his right arm that brought the cigarette to his mouth and down again, was the tattoo, and Mickey stared at it as he might at a dead animal, a road kill of something wild he had never seen alive, a fox or a fisher, with more than curiosity: fascination and a nuance of baseless horror. The Marine Corps globe and anchor were blue, and permanent as the man's flesh. Beneath the globe was an unfurled rectangular banner that appeared to flap gently in a soft breeze; between its borders, written in script that filled the banner, was *Semper Fidelis*. Under the banner were block letters: USMC. The man still gazed across the street, and Mickey stepped around him, between him and the bar, to walk up the street and over the bridge; he would stop and look down at the moving water and imagine salmon swimming upriver before he walked the final two miles, most of it uphill and steep, to the tree-shaded street and his home. But the man turned and held his shoulder. The man did not tightly grip him; it was the man's quick movement that parted Mickey's lips with fear. They stood facing each other, Mickey's back to the door of the bar, and the man looked at his eyes then drew on his cigarette and flicked it up the sidewalk. Mickey watched it land beyond the corner of the bar, on the exit driveway of McDonald's. The hand was rubbing his shoulder.

"You just got out. Ah. So it's not July. Three fucking something o'clock in April. I believe I have missed a very important appointment." He withdrew his left hand from Mickey's shoulder and turned the wrist between their faces. "No watch, see? Can't wear a wristwatch. Get me the most expensive fucking wristwatch in the world, I can't wear it. Agent Orange, man. I'm walking talking drinking fucking fighting Agent Orange. Know what I mean? My cock is lethal. I put on a watch, zap, it stops."

"You were a Marine?"

"Oh yes. Oh yes, Charlie. See?" He turned and flexed his right arm so the tattoo on muscles faced Mickey. "U-S-M-C. Know what that means? Uncle Sam's Misguided Children. So fuck it, Charlie. Come on in."

"Where?"

"Where? The fucking bar, man. Let's go. It's springtime in New England. Crocuses and other shit."

"I can't."

"What do you mean you can't? Charlie goes where Charlie wants to go. Ask anybody that was there." He lowered his face close to Mickey's, so Mickey could see only the mouth in the beard, the nose, the blue eyes that seemed to burn slowly, like a pilot light. His voice was low, conspiratorial: "There's another one in there. From 'Nam. First Air Cav. Pussies. Flying golf carts. Come on. We'll bust his balls."

"I can't go in a bar."

The man straightened, stood erect, his chest out and his stomach pulled in, his fists on his hips. His face moved from left to right, his eyes intent, as though he were speaking to a group, and his voice was firm but without anger or threat, a voice of authority: "Charlie. You are allowed to enter a drinking establishment. Once therein you are allowed to drink non-alcoholic beverages. In this particular establishment there is pizza heated in a microwave. There are also bags of various foods, including potato chips, beer nuts, and nachos. There are also steamed hot dogs. But no fucking rice, Charlie. After you, my man."

The left arm moved quickly as a jab past Mickey's face, and he flinched, then heard the doorknob turn, and the man's right hand touched the side of his waist and turned him to face the door and gently pushed him out of the sun, into the long dark room. First he saw its lights: the yellow and red of a jukebox at the rear wall, and soft yellow lights above and behind the bar. Then he breathed its odors: alcohol and cigarette smoke and the vague and general smell of a closed and occupied room, darkened on a spring afternoon. A man stood behind the bar. He glanced at them, then turned and faced the rear wall. Three men stood at the bar, neither together nor apart; between each of them was room for two more people, yet they looked at each other and talked. The hand was still on Mickey's back, guiding more than pushing, moving him to the near corner of the bar, close to the large window beside the door. Through the glass Mickey looked at the parked and moving cars in the light; he had been only paces from the window when the man had turned and held his shoulder. The pressure on his back stopped when Mickey's chest touched the bar, then the man stepped around its corner, rested his arms on the short leg of its L, his back to the window, so now he looked down the length of the bar at the faces and sides of the three men, and at the bartender's back. There was a long space between Mickey and the first man to his left. He placed his books and binder in a stack on the bar and held its edge and looked at his face in the mirror, and his shirt like green leaves.

"Hey Fletcher," the man said. "I thought you'd hit the deck. When old Charlie came walking in." Mickey looked to his left: the three faces turned to the man and then to him, two looking interested, amused, and the third leaning forward over the bar, looking past the one man separating him from Mickey, looking slowly at Mickey's pants and probably the web belt too and the tee shirt. The man's face was neither angry nor friendly, more like that of a professional ballplayer stepping to the plate or a boxer ducking through the ropes into the ring. He had a brown handlebar mustache and hair that hung to his shoulders and moved, like a girl's, with his head. When his eyes rose from Mickey's clothing to his face, Mickey saw a glimmer of scorn; then the face showed nothing. Fletcher raised his beer mug to the man and, in a deep grating voice, said: "Body count, Duffy."

Then he looked ahead at the bottles behind the bar, finished his half mug with two swallows, and pushed the mug toward the bartender, who turned now and took it and held it slanted under a tap. Mickey watched the rising foam.

Duffy. Somehow knowing the man's name, or at least one of them, the first or last, made him seem less strange. He was Duffy, and he was with men who knew him, and Mickey eased away from his first sight of the man who had stepped onto the sidewalk and held him, a man who had never existed until the moment Mickey drew near the door of Timmy's. Mickey looked down, saw a brass rail, and rested his right foot on it; he pushed his books between him and Duffy, and folded his arms on the bar.

"Hey, Al. You working, or what?"

The bartender was smoking a cigarette. He looked over his shoulder at Duffy.

"Who's the kid?"

"The kid? It's Charlie, man. Fletcher never saw one this close. That's why he's so fucking quiet. Waiting for the choppers to come."

Then Duffy's hand was squeezing Mickey's throat: too suddenly, too tightly. Duffy leaned over the corner between them, his breath on Mickey's face, his eyes close to Mickey's, more threatening than the fingers and thumb pressing the sides of his throat. They seemed to look into his brain, and down into the depths of his heart, and to know him, all eleven years of him, and Mickey felt his being, and whatever strength it had, leaving him as if drawn through his eyes into Duffy's, and down into Duffy's body. The hand left his throat and patted his shoulder and Duffy was grinning.

"For Christ sake, Al, a rum and tonic. And a Coke for Charlie. And something to eat. Chips. And a hot dog. Want a hot dog, Charlie?"

"Mickey."

"What the fuck's a mickey?"

"My name."

"Oh. Jesus: your name."

Mickey watched Al make a rum and tonic and hold a glass of ice under the Coca-Cola tap.

"I never knew a Charlie named Mickey. So how come you're dressed up like a fucking jungle?"

Mickey shrugged. He did not move his eyes from Al, bringing the Coke and Duffy's drink and two paper cocktail napkins and the potato chips. He dropped the napkins in front of Mickey and Duffy, placed the Coke on Mickey's napkin and the potato chips beside it, and then held the drink on Duffy's napkin and said: "Three seventy-five."

"The tab, Al."

Al stood looking at Duffy, and holding the glass. He was taller than Duffy but not as broad, and he seemed to be the oldest man in the bar; but Mickey could not tell whether he was in his forties or fifties or even sixties. Nor could he guess the ages of the other men: he thought he could place them within a decade of their lives, but even about that he was uncertain. College boys seemed old to him. His father was forty-nine, yet his face appeared younger than any of these.

"Hey, Al. If you're going to hold it all fucking day, bring me a straw so I can drink."

"Three seventy-five, Duffy."

"Ah. The gentleman wants cash, Charlie."

He took the chained wallet from his rear pocket, unfolded

it, peered in at the bills, and laid four ones on the bar. Then he looked at Al, his unblinking eyes not angry, nearly as calm as his motions and posture and voice, but that light was in them again, and Mickey looked up at the sunglasses on Duffy's hair. Then he watched Al.

"Keep the change, Al. For your courtesy. Your generosity. Your general fucking outstanding attitude."

It seemed that Al had not heard him, and that nothing Mickey saw and felt between the two men was real. Al took the money, went to the cash register against the wall behind the center of the bar, and punched it open, its ringing the only sound in the room. He put the bills in the drawer, slid a quarter up from another one, and dropped it in a beer mug beside the register. It landed softly on dollar bills. Mickey looked at Al's back as he spread mustard on a bun and with tongs took a frankfurter from the steamer, placed it on the bun, and brought it on a napkin to Mickey.

"Duffy." It was Fletcher, the man in the middle. "Don't touch the kid again."

Duffy smiled, nodded at him over his raised glass, then drank. He turned to Mickey, but his eyes were not truly focused on him; they seemed to be listening, waiting for Fletcher.

"Cavalry," he said. "Remember, Charlie Mickey? Fucking guys in blue coming over the hill and kicking shit out of Indians. Twentieth century gets here, they still got horses. No shit. Fucking officers with big boots. Riding crops. No way. Technology, man. Modern fucking war. Bye-bye horsie. Tanks." He stood straight, folded his arms across his chest, and bobbed up and down, his arms rising and falling, and Mickey smiled, seeing Duffy in the turret of a tank, his sunglasses pushed-up goggles. "Which one was your old man in? WW Two or—how did they put it?—the Korean Conflict. Conflict. I have conflict with cunts. Not a million fucking Chinese."

"He wasn't in either of them."

"What the fuck is he? A politician?"

"A landscaper. He's forty-nine. He was too young for those wars."

"Ah."

"He would have gone."

"How do you know? You were out drinking with him or something? When he found out they didn't let first-graders join up?"

Mickey's mouth opened to exclaim surprise, but he did not speak: Duffy was drunk, perhaps even crazy, yet with no sign of calculation in his eyes he had known at once that Mickey's father was six when the Japanese bombed Pearl Harbor.

"He told me."

"He told you."

"That's right."

"And he was too old for 'Nam, right? No wonder he lets you wear that shit."

"I have to go."

"You didn't finish your hot dog. I buy you a hot dog and you don't even taste it."

Mickey lifted the hot dog with both hands, took a large bite, and looked above the bar as he chewed, at a painting high on the center of the wall. A woman lay on a couch, her eyes looking down at the bar. She was from another time, maybe even the last century. She was large and pretty, and he could see her cleavage and the sides of her breasts, and she wore a nightgown that opened up the middle but was closed.

"Duffy."

It was Fletcher, his voice low, perhaps even soft for him; but it came to Mickey like the sound of a steel file on rough wood. Mickey was right about Duffy's eyes; they and his face turned to Fletcher, with the quickness of a man countering a striking fist. Mickey lowered his foot from the bar rail and stood balanced. He looked to his left at Al, his back against a shelf at the rear of the bar, his face as distant as though he were listening to music. Then Mickey glanced at Fletcher and the men Fletcher stood between. Who were these men? Fathers? On a weekday afternoon, a day of work, drinking in a dark bar, the two whose names he had not heard talking past Fletcher about fishing, save when Duffy or Fletcher spoke. He looked at Duffy: his body was relaxed, his hands resting on either side of his drink on the bar. Now his body tautened out of its slump, and he lifted his glass and drank till only the lime wedge and ice touched his teeth; he swung the glass down hard on the bar and said: "Do it again, Al."

But as he pulled out his chained wallet and felt in it for bills and laid two on the bar, he was looking at Fletcher; and when Al brought the drink and took the money to the register and returned with coins, Duffy waved him away, never looking at him, and Al dropped the money into the mug, then moved to his left until he was close to Duffy, and stood with his hands at his sides. He did not lean against the shelf behind him, and he was gazing over Mickey's head. Mickey took a second bite of the hot dog; he could finish it with one more. Chewing the bun and mustard and meat that filled his mouth, he put his right hand on his stack of books. With his tongue he shifted bun and meat to his jaws.

"Fletcher," Duffy said.

Fletcher did not look at him.

"Hey, Fletcher. How many did you kill? Huh? How many kids. From your fucking choppers."

Now Fletcher looked at him. Mickey chewed and swallowed, and drank the last of his Coke; his mouth and throat were still dry, and he chewed ice.

"You fuckers were better on horseback. Had to look at them." Duffy raised his tattooed arm and swung it in a downward arc, as though slashing with a saber. "Wooosh. Whack. Fuckers killed them anyway. Look a Cheyenne kid in the face, then waste him. I'm talking Washita River, pal. Same shit. Maybe they had balls, though. What do you think, Fletcher? Does it take more balls to kill a kid while you're looking at him?"

Fletcher finished his beer, lowered it quietly to the bar, looked away from Duffy and slowly took a cigarette pack from his shirt pocket, shook one out, and lit it. He left the pack and lighter on the bar. Then he took off his wristwatch, slowly still, pulling the silver expansion band over his left hand. He placed the watch beside his cigarettes and lighter, drew on the cigarette, blew smoke straight over the bar, where he was staring; but Mickey knew from the set of his profiled face that his eyes were like Duffy's earlier: they waited. Duffy took the sunglasses from his hair and folded them, lenses up, on the bar.

"You drinking on time, Fletcher? The old lady got your balls in her purse? Only guys worse than you fuckers were pilots. Air Force the worst of all. Cocksucking bus drivers. Couldn't even see the fucking hootch. Just colors, man. Squares on Mother Earth. Drop their big fucking load, go home, good dinner, get drunk. Piece of ass. If they could get it up. After getting off with their fucking bombs. Then nice bed, clean sheets, roof, walls. Fucking windows. The whole shit. Go to sleep like they spent the day—" He glanced at Mickey, or his face shifted to Mickey's; his eyes were seeing something else. Then his voice was soft: a distant tenderness whose source was not Mickey, and Mickey knew it was not in the bar either. "Landscaping." Mickey put the last third of the hot dog into his mouth, and wished for a Coke to help him with it; he looked at Al, who was still gazing above his head, so intently that Mickey nearly turned to look at the wall behind him. The other two men were silent. They drank, looked into their mugs, drank. When they emptied the mugs they did not ask for more, and Al did not move.

"All those fucking pilots," Duffy said, looking again down the bar at the side of Fletcher's face. "Navy. Marines. All the motherfuckers. Go out for a little drive on a sunny day. Barbecue some kids. Their mothers. Farmers about a hundred years old. Skinny old ladies even older. Fly back to the ship. Wardroom. Pat each other on the ass. Sleep. Fucking children. Fletcher used to be a little boy. Al never was. But *I* was." His arms rose above his head, poised there, his fingers straight, his palms facing Fletcher. Then he shouted, slapping his palms hard on the bar, and Mickey jerked upright: "*Chil*dren, man. You never smelled a napalmed kid. You never even *saw* one, fucking chopper-bound son of a bitch."

Fletcher turned his body so he faced Duffy.

"Take your shit out of here," he said. "God gave me one asshole. I don't need two."

"Fuck you. You never looked. You never saw shit."

"We came down. We got out. We did the job."

"The *job*. Good word, for a pussy from the Air fucking *Cav*."

"There's a sergeant from the First Air Cav's about to kick your ass from here to the river."

"You better bring in help, pal. That's what you guys were good at. All wars—" He drank, and Mickey watched his uptilted head, his moving throat, till his upper lip stopped the lime, and ice clicked on his teeth. Duffy held the glass in front of him, just above the bar, squeezing it; his fingertips were red. "All fucking wars should be fought on the ground. Man to man. Soldier to soldier. None of this flying shit. I've got dreams. Oh yes, Charlie." But he did not look at Mickey. "I've got them. Because they won't go away." Again, though he looked at Fletcher, that distance was in his eyes, as if he were staring at time itself: the past, the future; and Mickey remembered the tattoo, and looked at the edges of it he could see beyond Duffy's chest: the end of the eagle's left wing, a part of the globe, the hole for line at the anchor's end, and *lis* written on the fluttering banner. He could not see the block letters. "I tell them I'm wasted, gentlemen. The dreams: I tell them to fuck off. They can't live with Agent Orange. They just don't know it yet. But fucking pilots. In clean beds. Sleeping. Like dogs. Like little kids. Girls with the wedding cake. Put a piece under your pillow. Fuckers put dreams under their pillows. Slept on them. Without dreams too. Not nightmares. Charlie Mickey here, he thinks he's had nightmares. Shit. I ate chow with nightmares. Pilots dreamed of pussy. Railroad tracks on their collars. Gold oak leaves. Silver oak leaves. Silver eagles. Eight hours' sleep on the dreams of burning children."

"Jesus Christ. Al, will you shut off that shithead so we can drink in peace?"

Al neither looked nor moved.

"Duffy," Fletcher said. "What's this Agent Orange shit. At Khe San, for Christ sake. You never got near it."

"Fuck do you know? How far did *you* walk in 'Nam, man? You rode taxis, that's all. Did you sit on your helmet, man? Or did your old lady already have your balls stateside?"

"I hear you didn't do much walking at Khe San."

"We took some hills."

"Yeah? What did you do with them?"

"Gave them back. That's what it was about. You'd know that if you were a grunt."

"I heard you assholes never dug in up there."

"Deep enough to hold water."

"And your shit."

Duffy stepped back once from the bar. He was holding the glass and the ice slid in it, but he held it loosely now, the blood receding from his fingertips.

"You want to smell some grunt shit, Fletcher? Come over here. We'll see what a load of yours smells like."

"That's it," Al said, and moved toward Duffy as he threw the glass and Mickey heard it strike and break and felt a piece of ice miss his face and cool drops hitting it. Fletcher was pressing a hand to his forehead and a thin line of blood dripped from under his fingers to his eyebrow, where it stayed. Then Fletcher was coming, not running, not even walking fast; but coming with his chin lowered, his arms at his sides, and his hands closed to fists. Mickey swept his books toward him, was gripping them to carry, when two hands slapped his chest so hard he would have fallen if the hands had not held his collar. He was aware of Fletcher coming from his left, and Duffy's face, and the moment would not pass, would not become the next one, and the ones afterward, the ones that would get him home. Then Duffy's two fists, bunching the shirt at its collar, jerked downward, and Mickey's chest was bare. He had sleeves still, and the shirt's back and part of its collar. But the shirt was gone.

"Fucking little asshole. You want jungle? Take your fucking jungle, Charlie."

With both hands Duffy shoved his chest and he went backward, his feet off the floor, then on it, trying to stop his motion, his arms reaching out for balance, waving in the air as he struck the wall, slid down it, and was sitting on the floor. From the pain in his head he saw Duffy and Fletcher. He could see only Fletcher's back, and his arms swinging, and his head jerking when Duffy hit him. Al had gone to the far end of the bar, to Mickey's left, and through the opening there, and was striding, nearly running, past the two men who stood watching Duffy and Fletcher. Mickey tried to stand, to push himself up with the palms of his hands. Beneath the pain moving through his head from the rear of his skull, he felt the faint nausea, the weakened legs, of shock. He turned on his side on the floor, then onto his belly, and bent his legs and with them and his hands and arms he pushed himself up, and stood. He was facing the wall. He turned and saw Al holding Duffy from behind, Al's hands clasped in front of Duffy's chest, and Mickey saw the swelling of muscles in Duffy's twisting, pulling arms, and Al's reddened face and gritted teeth, and Fletcher's back and lowered head and shoulders turning with each blow to Duffy's body and bleeding, cursing face.

His weakness and nausea were gone. He was too near the door to run to it; in two steps he had his hand on its knob and remembered his books and binder. They were on the bar, or they had fallen to the floor when Duffy grabbed him. He opened the door, and in the sunlight he still did not run; yet his breath was deep and quick. Walking slowly toward the bridge, he looked down at his pale chest, and the one long piece of shirt hanging before his right leg, moving with it, blending with the colors of his pants. He would never wear the pants again, and he wished they were torn too. He wanted to walk home that way, like a tattered soldier.

LAND WHERE MY FATHERS DIED

For James Crumley

GEORGE KARAMBELAS

IT WAS A COLD NIGHT, and I was drunk. I couldn't get a ride at Timmy's when they closed, and I had a long way to walk. It was after one o'clock, and I kept thinking of my warm bed. I could see it in front of me, like it was ahead of me on the sidewalk, like those guys in a desert that see water that isn't there. A mirage, it's called. You can see it sometimes on a highway in summer. I thought about summer.

I lost my car. It was an old Pontiac, eight years old next year, that sucked gas. First the exhaust system went, rusted out, and I paid for that. Then it was a new starter, then the carburetor had to be rebuilt and I paid for all that and was broke. Then the transmission started to go and I said fuck it and sold it for junk. Fuck them at Timmy's. Fuck Steve. Fuck Laurie. Fuck George, they say, let him walk a hundred miles in fifty below just to sleep. Well, fuck them too, I said.

Maybe out loud. I was that drunk. I wished I wasn't. I wished I had gone right home soon as I got all the dishes washed and the pots scrubbed out and hung from the beam. I still would have frozen to death walking home, but I'd be in bed. And Timmy's is on the other side of the river so it was a longer ways to walk and I had to cross the bridge going and coming back, and the bridge is long on foot, and the wind was coming down the river. It's the chill factor. You never know how cold it is. The thermometer outside the window will say nineteen, but then you go outside and the cold comes blowing and it's like twenty below. That's the story: it's nineteen but it's *like* twenty below.

I tried to walk straight, looking down at the sidewalk like it was a board over a big hole, but I was zigging and zagging from one snowbank to another. Once I slipped on ice and landed on my ass. I thought about if I had hit my head I could have stayed there and froze to death. But still I couldn't get sober. I walked through the square about a mile above the river. Even the pizza shop was closed. We got a lot of pizza shops in this little town, mostly Italian, some Greek.

When Steve gave last call at Timmy's I started asking around for a ride. Nobody going my way. Who are they shitting? A night like this you can go out of your way for somebody. Up above the square I was walking past houses. Trees were in the yards in the snow and next to the sidewalk. Face it, George, I said to myself. Nobody's ever gone your way. I didn't like hearing that. I'm twenty-three. I started thinking about people that liked me. I got back to eighth grade, there was this Irish kid, but nobody liked him either. I got very sad walking under the big trees. No girl, not ever, and I don't know why. I look in the mirror and I don't know why. I've been laid, sure, but with sluts. It's a wonder I never caught herpes or something. I saw the light on in Dr. Clark's office. I was walking past it, and it was on my right, the road on my left. Then I stopped because I saw that I was seeing the light through the window but through the door too. Hey, I looked around: up and down the street, no cars, and up and down the sidewalk, of course nobody was out. Who would be but Eskimos and a dumb Greek.

I went up his walk slow and casual, like a dude coming home. There was salt on it. I was doing everything but whistling, a Greek dishwasher coming home to sleep in a doctor's office. It was a one-story brick building set back in the trees, a small office, a one-man operation. This was a neighborhood of big old wooden houses. They were dark. At the two front steps I stopped and looked again. I went up the steps and in the door, breathing hard with the booze. Everything was hard to do. This was the waiting room, and it was dark. Or the lights were off, but I could see the desk by the office door and the chairs along the walls; because the light was coming from the office and that door was open. I could see part of his desk in there, a corner and some of the top. To this day I don't know what I had in mind. I was thinking money, but I think about money all the time. Every day, every night. I think I was hoping for drugs. But I was too drunk for any of it to make any sense and if I hadn't been drunk I would have walked right on by. If I hadn't been drunk maybe somebody would have given me a ride, maybe that's it, maybe I drink too much. But that's not it because in high school I wasn't drunk or not much of the time and it didn't matter. I'd go to the smoking area outside where the faggots made us go even if it was a blizzard and I'd look at the girls shivering around their cigarettes and they'd either look at me like the smoke made them blind or like instead of a mouth I had a boil under my nose. I'd go over to the guys and they'd start busting balls on me. Sometimes it's friendly, it depends on how you say things. Bob the chef busts them on me all the time, but it's friendly; he likes me, and he's an old man. The guys at school weren't friendly. *So George, you going to ever shave, or what? He plucks them. All three, every week.* I'd laugh with them. But I wouldn't say anything back.

I was still not walking straight. I got across the waiting room on a slant toward the door and stepped in and saw a dead man. I knew he was dead when I saw him. I've only seen my grandparents, all four, laid out in the coffins. But I knew he was dead. I think I said something out loud. I remember hearing somebody. It did not get me sober but it got me sober as I could get. He was on his back, dressed up in a suit, and there was blood dried on his mouth. It was open. I've never seen a mouth look so open, looser than somebody sleeping. His eyes were closed. One hand was resting on his belt buckle. He was not a very big man, on the thin side. I had never been to see him, we always went to Papadopoulos, our family, but I knew it was Dr. Clark. I had seen him around town in his Mercedes, and sometimes when I was washing dishes I'd look through the window to the dining room and he'd be there eating lobsters with his scrawny old lady. I started to get out of there when I saw the big pistol on the floor. It was lying right beside his face. I bent over and picked it up and I kept my eyes away from his that were shut. I put it in my coat pocket, a pea coat. A prescription pad was on his desk and I put that in the other pocket. Then I got out of there.

I turned off the light switch by his door, and the office was dark. I had to feel my way across the waiting room. I think I was walking straight then. I had my arms out in front of me and moving, like a breaststroke, like I was swimming through the dark. My hands hit the front door. I opened it a little and looked at the street. A car passed. Then it was empty, and I was gone, shutting the door, and down the steps, holding the metal rail cold under my glove. Down his walk to the sidewalk.

I didn't think about the cold anymore. I didn't feel it. I didn't see my bed either. I saw his face on the floor looking up at the ceiling except his lids were down and there was nobody behind them. I saw his hand covering his belt buckle. The pistol was heavy in my pocket, and I was weaving again. I live in an old house that used to be one family's house, all three stories, and now it is a lot of apartments. I went up to mine on the second floor and pissed, shivering, for a long time. Then I swallowed some anisette from the bottle and drank a beer while I took off my clothes. I put the coat over a chair, and left the gun in it. When I got in bed I could still see him and I was tense and breathing fast, curled up on my side under the covers, and I thought I would not sleep. Next thing I knew the sun was in the room and I had a dry mouth and a headache and I had to piss but I lay there remembering everything and thinking here I was with a dead doctor's script pad and a big pistol I didn't want to see. Then I got up and took it out of the coat pocket. It was an Army .45, and the hammer was cocked. I looked some more. The safety was off.

ARCHIMEDES NIONAKIS

Because it was probably not murder—someone hit Francis Clark on the jaw and apparently his head struck the desk as he fell—and because it seemed to involve bad luck more than volition, I sometimes thought George had done it, but it was a thought I could only hold in the abstract, for a few moments, until I imagined him in the flesh. Then I could not believe it, could not see George Karambelas punching anybody, much less a man with a loaded pistol.

Then I believed the story he had just told me. I could still smell his story as I drove back to town from the prison. My car windows were up, and my clothes smelled of George's cigarette smoke trapped in the counseling room, and also the vanished smoke, and words and breath it seemed, of the others who had sat or paced in that room with its two straight wooden chairs and old wooden desk with an ashtray long overflowed, and butts scattered on the desk top with burns at its edges where live cigarettes had lain, and burns on its top where they had been put out. I did not sit at the desk. I leaned against a wall without windows, and said: "I can't believe how dumb you are."

"Don't say that," he said. "You got to make the jury believe it."

He did try to smile, as he tried to be friendly, but in his circumstance it is hard to do either. I don't mean simply incarceration; or being charged with second-degree murder. George is one of those people who have nothing specific wrong with them, except that they are disliked, and it's difficult to understand why. I don't even know why I don't like him. He is not very bright, but it isn't that. So I stood breathing in that room and told him I would represent him, and that is why: I couldn't bear disliking him for no just reason, and seeing him in that room too, and imagining him in the cell where probably already his cellmates didn't like him either. I did not mention money, any more than I would look for a fish in a tree, but he said he would raise it. He did not go so far as to ask how much he ought to raise. I told him we'd talk about that when the time came. I listened to his foolish story again, and congratulated him again on at least burning the prescription pad, forced my hand into his, and fled.

In my old Volvo, once I opened the window a bit to cold air and got past the weariness I feel when I do something good that I don't want to, I was suddenly glad he had called me. This surprised me, then disturbed me, for at thirty-three I should not be able to surprise myself. But there it was: that part of me I can't silence or even fully please, that will sometimes, while I'm in bed with a woman, leave us and stand dressed in the room, laughing or scowling: the little bastard was active again. I know he's the one who makes me an insomniac, when I'm too tired to read, and have no worries about money or family: I have money because I don't have a family, and I live alone by choice so am not lonely; still he keeps me awake, feeling that I'm worrying. Though I'm not. Except about getting to sleep. Now he hoped for some complicated work. Probably, for him, there had been too many times lately when I would stop what I was doing and look around me at my life—or the little bastard would—and feel it was not enough. Not enough for what? was the question I couldn't answer, except to say it wasn't using enough of me. I run a lot.

In the detectives' office, Dom Schiavoni sat on the secretary's desk. He sat on its edge, profiled to her; in winter clothes he looked even bigger, a V-necked blue sweater pulled tight over his belly and chest, his shoulders looking squeezed into an old dark suit coat. His complexion, in winter, changed from dark to pale olive, so he always looked like a swarthy man who had just had the flu. He introduced me to the secretary, Roberta Ford, a buxom woman in her fifties with fleshy cheeks and probably arms too under the sleeves of her sweater; her hair was red and looked like it had been done by one of my brothers, who had colored it for her too. Dom introduced me, and she said: "Your brother Kosta does my hair."

We came over on the boat when I was five, the youngest; my brothers own their shop and work very hard, from seven in the morning till six or seven at night, every day but Sunday; they tell me they could have women in the chairs at five in the morning if they wanted to start that early. There are many Greeks in beauty parlors in the Merrimack Valley; it was work they could learn quickly and could do in Greek while they were learning English, and it paid well. My brothers put me through school and every day they turn, in seriousness, to the stock-exchange section of the *Boston Globe*.

"You still running?" Dom said.

"Yes."

"You look like it. You going to run the Marathon again?"

I told him yes and that I was representing George. I watched his mouth, waiting for the smile; but there was none in his eyes either. Then he said: "Good."

"Why?"

"Somebody ought to."

"You want coffee?" Roberta said.

I told her I hadn't had breakfast and would take anything.

"This is early for him," Dom said. "Maybe there's a dough-nut left." He looked at his watch. "Nine-thirty. What's it feel like?"

"Dawn. You don't think he did it?"

Roberta gave me a Styrofoam cup of coffee and a glazed doughnut.

"I *think* he did it. Problem is, I don't *know* he did it."

Then he told me how it took less than forty-eight hours for the arrest because the receptionist found the doctor when she opened Thursday morning and later in the day did a quick inventory for Schiavoni and told him the gun and a prescrip-tion pad were gone. Schiavoni found the receipt for the pistol in a desk drawer, and talked to Mayfield, the narcotics officer. Mayfield started talking to punks, and on Saturday one told him who had bought a .45 Thursday.

"So we went to see the new owner. He never heard of the .45 till I told him the name of the previous owner, then he's giving me the gun, seven rounds of ammo, and the name and address of George Karambelas."

"Who didn't even deny it."

"No."

Roberta shook her head, repeating the no.

"The dumb bastard," Dom said. Roberta nodded.

"Why was Clark in his office at night? And on a Wednesday?"

This town has an old custom: a lot of stores close on Wednesday afternoons, and no doctors work. Neither do I.

"The receptionist doesn't know. Maybe his wife will tell you."

Then he smiled.

"They're separated, right?" I said.

"Why do you say that?" He smiled again.

"Because the receptionist found him."

"Archimedes," and he reached out and laid his big hand on my shoulder, smiling that mischievous way, and said: "They're not separated."

"Where was she? In Moscow?"

"About five miles from here."

"So you went Thursday morning and told her why her husband didn't come home last night?"

"Kind of grabs you, doesn't it?"

"What did she say?"

"She designated a funeral home."

Roberta was nodding.

I drove to the address Dom gave me. It was a clear February day, with deep snow bright on the ground in the sunlight. The downtown part of our city, on the riverbank, is ugly, and there's nothing more to say about that. They tell me this place used to thrive; that was back when my uncle brought us over and put my brothers to work in his factory. They made parts for women's shoes: bows, and an arrangement of straps called vamps; these vamps and bows, when attached to an arched and high-heeled sole, formed an absolutely functionless shoe. My uncle shipped the bows and vamps my brothers helped make to another factory in another state, and there they were attached to soles.

There are neighborhoods of big, old houses that prove someone was making money, but I don't believe this town ever thrived; I think people mean the shoe business was good and the factory-owners made a lot of money and most of the poor were employed poor. They still are; there are no union factories, and unskilled workers—many of them Greek and Hispanic and now, since the war, some Vietnamese—work for minimum wage. Our better neighborhoods have many old trees, and these places are lovely when the leaves change colors in the fall. As I drove under them on the way to Lillian Clark's, there were enough pines to scatter green against the blue sky, and sometimes the sun glinted from ice on the branches of naked trees. I skirted a frozen lake bordered on one side by a public woods that has a good running road under its trees, following the bank of the lake. I entered countryside: woods, and fields of snow with tufts of brown dead weeds. Dr. Clark had a rural mailbox at the road, at the entrance of a paved driveway that curved up through evergreens. I shifted down and went up it, thinking of the good smell he had had in spring and summer, when a breeze went from the pines into his house. It was not an old one but one he had either built or bought from its first owner: two stories of stones and brown wood and A-shaped peaks enclosing windows. The garage was built onto one side, its door was raised, and inside, in one of the two spaces, was a fucking Porsche. The little bastard got excited by that sculpted-looking piece of steel that could feed a family across town in the tenement streets for five years or more; he liked knowing that the big surprises of pain and death infiltrated so impartially. I told him to show some compassion for Christ sake, and got out and pressed the cold button for the bell.

Lillian Clark had bags under her eyes, and they were not the recent kind that let you know someone's had a bad night. They were permanent knolls on the landscape of her face. She was a thin woman who could have been dissipated in her forties or poised in her fifties for a final decline. There was gray in her brown hair; her eyes were brown and angry, so that I apologized and felt my cheeks flush as I introduced myself and asked if I could speak with her; then I realized the anger was permanent too. Or guessed it, because of the rest of her face, its lines in her cheeks and about her eyes, that appeared set in some epiphany of bitterness. You have seen them, when you spy on people in airport lounges or pedestrians walking toward you: their eyes focus on things, and you wonder what they could be looking at to cause such anger; then you know it is being fed to them from inside their skulls. Her skin was the pallid tan of Dom's, but hers was not genetic; this was a woman of the sun who had probably had a winter vacation a month ago in Florida or the Caribbean. Wherever it is they go. Her voice was soft, though a bit crisp at the edges, and probably that was permanent too, a chord telling the world that was all the control she could muster. In the living room I sat in an armchair that was too deep and soft, so only my toes touched the floor. She sat opposite me; our chairs were half-turned toward a cold fireplace with ashes between the andirons. She drank sherry from a stemmed glass, and flicked a hand, as though backhanding a gnat, toward a bottle of Dry Sack on the table beside her, and asked if I wanted some. There was no question mark in her voice, so the invitation had the tone of a statement like: Your socks don't match. I said no and repeated the condolences I had offered at the door, while she sipped and gazed at the fireplace. I offered to light a fire, and she said: "I can make fires."

I said something about chimney drafts and the trick of holding a torch of burning paper up the chimney to start it drawing, and I began telling her about a bricklayer I knew who built a chimney for a man with a bad reputation for paying bills, and halfway up the chimney he laid a plate of glass across it, but her head jerked toward me, and this time her eyes glared. I liked the story and had believed it when I heard it, though it was one of those I stopped believing the first time I told it; still, I wanted to tell her about the man calling to complain about the smoke backing up in his living room and the bricklayer telling him he would fix it when he got paid for the chimney, in cash, and driving to the man's house and, with the money in his pocket, going up his ladder with a brick in his hand and dropping it down the chimney. But I said: "Can you tell me why your husband was at his office on a Wednesday night?"

"He took Wednesdays off."

"The afternoons?"

"Yes. He went to the hospital in the morning."

She was looking at the fireplace. So did I. I kept seeing George in prison, suspended in dismay, but not one sentence, not one word, came to me.

"Why did he do it?" she said.

I looked at the side of her face, and an attractive streak of gray above her left ear.

"George didn't do it."

"You don't think so?"

"No."

"Would you defend him if he had?"

"No."

"Really? Why?"

"I couldn't enjoy it."

"You couldn't enjoy it."

"No."

Now she did look at my socks, which matched and were folded over the tops of hiking boots. Her eyes moved up my legs, or slacks, and shirt and coat to my face.

"I like you with a mustache."

I was about to ask when she had seen me without one, but caught that in time and said: "He didn't know Dr. Clark."

"He could be angry at him without knowing him."

"Is that why your husband had a gun?"

"Probably."

"Did he see patients on Wednesday nights?"

"That's what he said."

She was looking at my eyes, and I wished she would turn to the fireplace again.

"Because they needed him?" I said. "Because of the afternoons off?"

"Some. He said."

"So why not work on Wednesday afternoons and take the evenings off?"

She was watching my eyes. I had heard or read about recent widows being angry at their husbands for dying. I had not understood it, though I recognized that it must have something to do with grief; but those were widows of husbands who had died of what we call natural causes. Their husbands had not been murdered. Yet there was nothing of sorrow, of memory, in Lillian Clark's eyes.

"For the receptionist?" I said. "So she could have time off? Or did she work on Wednesday nights?"

"You could ask her."

"You don't know, then?"

"I never phoned the office on Wednesday nights."

"Was she a nurse?"

"You mean is she. Francis was killed, not Beverly. Yes, she's a nurse."

"She would have to be there, wouldn't she?"

"Would she?"

"For female patients. Doesn't there have to be a nurse in the examining room?"

"I suppose."

"All this is very strange."

Finally she looked away, back at the fireplace. So did I.

"Did he ever talk about trouble with a patient?"

"Trouble?"

"Someone who might have got angry and hit him. I think it was an accident. His death, I mean."

"Depends on what you call an accident."

"I suppose it does. Are you the executrix of the estate?"

"That's funny."

"What is?"

"My new title. Yes."

"Could I look at his files?"

Looking into the fireplace she called Te*resa*, with Spanish pronunciation, and my thighs jumped taut. I looked behind me, stretching to see over the back of the chair, at the sounds of footsteps. Teresa was young and too thin.

"Bring my purse down from the bedroom."

She left, and I listened to her climbing stairs and walking above us, and I looked around the room. A model of a yacht was on the mantelpiece. In one corner was a small bookcase with a glass door; the corner was dark, and I could not read the titles. More furniture was behind us and against the walls. The floor was carpeted, and Teresa crossed it now with the purse, then was gone. Lillian took out a key ring, and worked one of them to the top.

"Where's the other car?" I said.

"He had a Mercedes. I gave it to my daughter."

"What was his practice?"

"Internal medicine. Here."

I took the key and thanked her.

"Mrs. Clark?" I stood up, looking down at her face gazing at the fireplace. "Did you call anyone when he didn't come home Wednesday night?"

"I was asleep."

"What about next morning?"

"I slept late. I always do."

"So Detective Schiavoni woke you up?"

"No."

"I don't understand."

She looked at me.

"You don't understand what?"

"Why you didn't know."

"I always woke up alone. He got up at seven."

"You couldn't tell he hadn't slept there?"

"How?" She was still looking at me.

"The blankets. The way the pillows were. Teresa must make a tight bed."

"Why are you upset?"

"I'm not."

"Yes, you are. I suppose I didn't look."

I thanked her, told her I'd bring back the key, and left. In the car I felt I had a hangover: the weariness, the confusion. On the way to my office I bought two meatball subs and four half-pint cartons of milk. My office is small, the waiting room no larger, and the receptionist's desk was empty, its surface bare save for a covered typewriter. I did not have a regular secretary, and was using interns from the small college in town. I gave them work to do and even taught them, and the college paid them with credits. My intern was Paula Reynolds, a lovely girl with healthy skin and long blond hair. I opened the office door. She was lying on the leather couch my brothers gave me. She wore a sweater, and jeans tucked into high boots, and was smoking a French cigarette.

"Jesus," I said, and opened the window behind my desk. A pack of Gitanes was on the floor beside her. Sometimes she does this, shows up with Gauloises or Gitanes, and I accuse her of affectation; but the truth is she spent a year in France before college, and now and then she has the urge. While she finished smoking I told her about my morning, then she took her milk and sandwich to the couch, managed to eat daintily, a good trick with a meatball sub, and she was smoking again as we left the office and I drove us to Dr. Clark's.

He was either a yachtsman or simply loved boats. What had been a model of a yacht, painted white, was on his desk, the bow split and crumpled, the masts snapped in two and held together only by sails; it looked as though a storm had driven it against rocks. I thought of all the concentration he had put into it and the one on his mantelpiece at home. Then I imagined the ocean rushing through the hole with its splinters, unpainted on the inside, and I looked away. On the wall were three color photographs of the same yacht, at anchor.

Paula stood beside me, looking down at the yacht, and when I turned our arms brushed, her sweater and my jacket and shirtsleeve padding our muscles and bones. I unbuckled her belt, turned her toward me, and, kissing her, slipped her jeans down her hips. Her pants were pale blue and already moist. We undressed and, as she lay on the floor, she said: Isn't this where—and I said Yes, and was in her.

We dozed for half an hour on the carpet, then dressed and stood at the filing cabinets against one wall. Paula started with the As, on my right, and I crouched to the Zs, three of them, and sat on the floor and read about a man named Zachary who was fifty-eight years old, had seasonal allergies, got an annual physical, and since five years ago, when he had asthmatic bronchitis, had either not been sick or had treated himself at home. Paula went to the reception room to look for an ashtray and came back empty-handed except for her unlit cigarette and said: "Goddamn doctors."

"Just chew it. Then I can breathe."

"Goddamn joggers."

"I'm not a *jogger*."

"Goddamn runners then. Why don't you put pictures of running shoes on your office wall? And a bronze pair on your desk."

"My bronze pair is between my legs."

Then she was bending over me, her fingers coming like claws at my crotch, and I quickly shut my legs. She put the cigarette between her lips, untied my hiking boot, pulled it off, took it to her end of the cabinets, and set it on top of the As. I put away Zachary and opened Zecchini. Florence Zecchini was not doing well: she was sixty-three and had high blood pressure, bursitis in the left shoulder, and every year, from November to April, she contracted a mélange of viruses.

"The Zs are all old." I watched her flicking ashes into my boot. "What happened to wastebaskets?"

"It has paper in it. What are we looking for?"

"Are you going to put it out in my boot?"

"The toilet." She went there, through the examining room

beside the files. When she came back, I said: "I don't know. Anything that'll help George. The poor fuck."

She looked at me over a file. She was still standing, working at the top drawer.

"You're not a poor fuck," she said.

"Neither are you."

I was thinking about the endless money from her parents, but her eyes looking at me were brown and lovely, so I did not clarify.

I was in the Ps, still wearing one boot, when the sun shone on the windows behind Clark's desk and on its glass top, and the bow of his broken white boat. The sun was very low, and I had missed my run. When we finished, Paula's smoke lay in the air, and the sun was behind the houses and trees beyond the windows, a rose glow beneath the dark sky. In the car I said I would run before dinner, and Paula told me I was crazy, that I would twist an ankle or slip on ice or get hit by a car; I said I needed a run after an afternoon shut up in an office reading files, and she said It wasn't *all* reading files, and a drink would do as well. I have never run at night, for the reasons Paula gave, and I crossed the bridge over the Merrimack as the last glow of sunset faded to dusk, and stopped at Timmy's, where we stood at the bar and had two vodka martinis, and talked with Steve Buckland, the bartender, who has a long thick reddish-blond beard and is one of the biggest men I've ever known; he is also a merry one.

We had planned to go to my apartment and cook steaks and spend a quiet evening; she had her schoolbooks with her, and I was reading *Anna Karenina*, although I meant to watch a Burt Reynolds movie on television at eight. I had not told her this because she might have the discipline to go to the dormitory to study. I was going to glance at the paper after dinner and say, Oh: *Hustle* is on, then she would watch it with me, tensely for a while, but she would stop worrying about her work, and after the movie, because the television is at the foot of my bed, we would make love, and soon she would fall asleep studying beside me and I would read *Anna Karenina* until two or three, when I would sleep. But we had our third martini at an Italian restaurant south of town, and the young woman tending bar made them so well that we violated the sensible rule, whether we had one or not, about martinis, and drank a fourth. We shared a bottle of chianti with dinner; Paula eats well and does not exercise but is flat-bellied and firm. Of course, as she approaches thirty, six or seven years from now, her flesh will soften, then sag. We each drank Sambuca with three floating coffee beans, and she drank coffee. I didn't dare.

I do not record this drinking as some laurel for hedonism, but because the alcohol gave us a distance from the afternoon, as surely as air travel would have, and during dinner we were able to see clearly what had, in Clark's office, been blurred by names (I knew some of them), and ages, and ailments. We were talking generally about mortality and the distillation of its whisperings that we had confronted in the files, when Paula stopped talking, and stopped listening to me, though she watched me still as she twirled spaghetti in oil and garlic around her fork.

"Jesus," she said. "He was a script doctor."

And there it was, as though rising to the surface of a dream, the truth coming as it so often does in that last hour of drunkenness when all that is unessential falls away and suddenly you see clearly. Soon after that you are truly drunk and may not remember next day what it was that you saw. But we had it now, the truth—or a truth out of all the pneumonia, flu, strep throat, two cases of gout that had made me feel I was in the nineteenth century watching Anna Karenina's eight rings sparkle in candlelight, cancer and heart disease and strokes, an afternoon of illness and injury and their treatment recorded in Francis Clark's scribbled sentences that began with verbs: *Complains of chest pains. Took EKG*—a truth that seemed tangible and shimmering on the table between us, among the odors of wine and garlic and Paula's lipsticked unfiltered Gitanes in the ashtray: a number of girls and young women whose only complaint was fat, and whose treatment was diet and prescriptions. Speed, Paula said. That's what they get, so they won't eat. And downers so they can function. Which did not really mean he was a script doctor, for neither of us could recall whether the patients were fat or simply getting drugs. There was also the matter of his Wednesday nights, and I knew they involved a woman, or women, and believed Paula knew it too, though was too loyal to what her sex has told itself it has become to admit it, and she argued that both my age and my Greek heritage had combined to blind me as surely as the famous Greek motherfucker; that Lillian Clark's bitter and unhappy face and Francis Clark's Wednesday nights did not add up to adultery.

"She may be unhappy for a *to*tally different reason," she said, waving a cool and hardened chunk of garlic bread. "Something that has *noth*ing to do with a man."

"Right," I said. "One morning she woke up and looked under the hood of her Porsche and found an engine there instead of God."

"I knew you'd see the truth. You don't know how hard it is to be a rich woman."

"A rich lovely woman."

"Yes."

"A rich lovely sensual woman."

"With a balding Greek for a lover. Yes."

"It runs in my family."

"Why don't I ever meet them?"

"Saturday."

"This Saturday?"

"There's a Greek dance."

"Will you teach me how, before we go?"

"I don't know if WASPs can learn it."

We left the epiphanic phase with Sambuca, and had a second one, and I drove carefully home, turned on the eleven-o'clock news, found that I could not understand it and was drinking a bottle of Moosehead beer; so was Paula; then I remembered bringing them to the bedroom. I turned off the television and lights and we undressed and got into bed and talked for a while, about snow I believe, or rain, and forgot to make love. I woke early, at eight-fifteen, with a hangover, and got the *Boston Globe* from the front steps, and after aspirins and orange juice and a long time in the bathroom with the paper, I ran ten miles and returned sweating and clearheaded to the smells of dripping coffee and the last of Paula's Gitanes.

Beverly Strater lived on the second floor of an apartment building that had been a house, and the front door did not unlock from inside her apartment. About ten years ago, in this town, that would have been customary, but whatever was loose in the land had reached us too, a city of under fifty thousand where old people living in converted factory buildings, renting good apartments for small portions of their incomes, boasted of the buildings' security. Beverly Strater was neither old nor young, and had the look about her of a divorcee whose children had grown: that is, she looked neither barren nor discontented, had a good smile and some lines of merriment in her face, and a briskness to her walk and gestures that seemed to come from energy, not nerves. I had simply climbed the stairs and knocked on her door, and I wished she were not so accessible; I did not think she could afford thieves, and she was certainly not too old to discourage any aesthetic considerations a rapist might have. She dispelled my worries before I mentioned them, as, over tea in her kitchen, she told me about Francis Clark's gun, and that she kept a loaded .38 at her bedside, and took it with her when she went places that would keep her out after dark. Her husband had taught her about guns, and it was his revolver she had now; she had reared three children and gone back to nursing six years ago, after he died. Because of her husband's attitude—and her own—about guns, she had not thought it unusual of Dr. Clark to own one and keep it in his office. Sometimes he left the office after dark, always in the winter months of short days, and she assumed he armed himself before walking to his car.

"It's just the times," she said. "And you see, poor man, he was right."

In winter I am condemned to sit in rooms of smoke. Beverly was filling the kitchen, and her lungs too, and watching her inhale, I shuddered. Or perhaps I shuddered at the image of Clark putting a .45 in his pocket to walk out to his car, and Beverly's seeing that as something of no more significance than wearing a hat or a pair of sunglasses. Yet I liked her. She was one of those women whom, if I had children, I would trust to care for them. I liked her stockiness, which reminded me of my mother, who was at that time visiting Greece, and reminded me also of women in a Greek village, not of a stout American. I have never held a gun, and would be frightened if I did, and as I was about to tell her that, I thought of something else, of the fear and anger I would feel if anyone pointed a gun at me and what I would do if I could get that gun from him, and I said, "It may have got him killed."

"That's true too. My husband always said: Don't ever use it for a bluff. He meant—"

"I know what he meant. Did he ever use it?"

"Oh, Lord, no: he was a mailman. He had a spray for dogs. The gun was to protect our home at night."

There are days, and this was one of them, when I cannot bear the company of my countrymen. I wished Paula were not at classes. My God, you can stay more or less happy doing your work and enjoying the flesh and the company of friends until you get a glimpse of the way people perceive the world. Once in a psychology journal I read an article on suicides in New Hampshire during the decade from 1960 to 1970; there were graphs showing that suicides by women were on the rise; the two authors did not mention it, but I noticed that suicides by both women and men increased each election year. My own notion is that my neighbors to the north were incurably shocked to see the evidence of what the majority of people were not simply content with, but strove for. I often feel the same, and conclude that most of us are not worth the dead

trees it takes to wipe our asses one summer. I was feeling this
now, watching Beverly's motherly face talking about life as
though it were lived in a sod hut in Kansas in 1881 or in a city
slum where teenaged criminals routinely sacked apartments.

I asked her about Wednesday nights. She was truly surprised, and she remained so, went from surprise to puzzle-
ment and was still frowning with it when I left. Before doing
that, I asked her about the girls and young women on diets.
She answered absently, still trying to understand the Wednesday nights. A few, she said. He wasn't a *diet* doctor, but there
were a few patients—girls—who came to him with a weight
problem. I have noticed that women of the working class call
each other girls, as men say "the boys." I asked only one more
question, at the door: "Were they really fat?"

"If they weren't, they *thought* they were. It's the same
thing, isn't it?"

Paula and I met for lunch in my office, then went to Clark's.
Because she does not exercise, she still had a hangover. In
front of the filing cabinet, she touched me, but I shook my
head, starting to explain, but then said nothing, knowing I
was too despondent to give meaningful words to my despon-
dency and my dread, so muted that it was lethargic, as impossible as that sounds. But it was lethargic, my dread, and it
made me think of summer and lying on the beach in the sun,
so that I wanted to lie on the floor and sleep, for I was beginning to know that in simply trying to save George Karambelas
I was going to confront nothing as pure and recognizable as
evil but a sorrowful litany of flaws, of failures, of mediocre
hopes, and of vanity. We wrote the names and addresses of
the twelve, and Paula said That's what Jesus started with, and
I said So did Castro, and at the sound of my voice, she said,
"Are you all right?"

She stood at Clark's desk, holding the notebook, and
looking at me in a way that would have been solemn if it
weren't tender too.

"Sure," I said. "Let's start."

We did, in midafternoon, in the low winter sun of that Tuesday. The sun lasted through Wednesday, and that night we lay in the dark and watched snow blowing against the windows and listened to Alicia de Larrocha play Chopin Preludes. We spoke to one woman on Tuesday, three on Wednesday, three on Thursday, and two Friday; then we did not need the other three. Paula rescheduled some of my appointments, mostly for tax returns and wills, work that could wait, though I felt like a gambler when we changed the appointments for wills, and since the gamble did not involve me, I felt a frightening sense of power I did not want. Wednesday morning we brought the key back to Lillian; Paula wanted to see her. But Teresa answered the door and said She is busy, and I gave her the key, looking at her brown eyes and thinking of her making Lillian's bed, and cooking her meals, and cleaning her house.

The first woman was a florist, or she worked in a florist's shop, and she took us to the office at the rear of the store and gave us coffee while the owner stayed in front with his flowers. Ada Cleary was twenty-five years old, one of those women whose days for years have been an agony about the weight of her body, or how much of it she could pinch. She looked at Paula, with polite glances to include me, as she spoke of her eight years of diets. I could not see the results, since I did not know what she had looked like before she had started seeing Clark a month ago. What I saw was a woman in a sweater and skirt, neither fat nor thin, but with wide hips and a protrusion of rump that looked soft enough to sink a fist into; I did not dare look at her legs, though I tried to spy on them but was blocked by the desk she stood behind. Her cheeks, though, were concave, and the flesh beneath her jaw was firm, and her torso looked disproportionate, as though it were accustomed to resting on smaller hips; or, the truth, it had recently been larger. Dr. Clark was very nice, she said, very understanding. And for the first time she was able to say no to food. It was the drugs.

"Speed," Paula said.

"Yes. And I take the others. You know, to get me down."

"Don't you worry about your head?" Paula said.

"I can't. Once I get down to one hundred and six pounds, that's when I'll stop the drugs. And see if I can make it on my own. You know: throw away my clothes, buy some new ones."

"Why one-oh-six?" I said.

"That's what I weighed in high school. Junior year. Before I turned into an elephant."

"What will you do without Clark?" I said.

"Oh, Gawd, find another doctor. I still have some pills left."

"Will he be hard to find?"

"Oh, no. It's like sleeping pills. I've never had trouble sleeping, but a friend of mine does. You just have to shop around. Some are strict, some are—helpful."

"Understanding," I said. "I don't sleep well either."

"Oh? What do you take?"

"Moosehead," Paula said.

"Really? You don't look it."

"Sometimes," I said. "Sometimes I just read."

"He runs a lot," Paula said.

"It's all legal," Ada said. "I mean, wasn't it?"

"Sure," I said. "Good luck with the one-oh-six."

In the car, Paula said: "You shouldn't have looked at her like that."

"Like what?"

"Angry."

"Was I?"

"Weren't you?"

"Yes."

"Why?"

She opened her purse and went through the smoker's elaborate motions, whose rhythm was disrupted by her hurriedly lifting and pushing aside whatever things had found or lost their way into her deep purse, until her hands emerged with the pack and lighter, and with thumb and forefinger she tore open the cellophane, opened the box, removed the top foil, put it and the crumpled cellophane into her purse, and so on. I have never wanted to smoke, but I would enjoy opening those pretty little boxes, as I would enjoy filling a pipe. My brother Kosta carries worry beads, but at work he is too busy to play with them. If he smoked, he would have to pause to give his attention to the cellophane, the cardboard, the foil. I thought of telling him he should stop every half hour to play for five minutes with his beads, and opened my window a few inches. Her cigarette was American.

"Well?" she said.

"Because it's bullshit."

"What is?"

"All that dieting."

"You should feel sorry for her."

"I do."

We passed the college where she lived and, on some nights, slept.

"Describe her," she said.

"Okay."

"Well. Go ahead."

"I mean okay, I get your point."

"Do you really?"

"I don't want to, but I do."

"*You* look at women that way."

"You couldn't let it go, could you?"

We passed the Common, a small park with a white fence and scattered old trees. On Thursday nights in summer an orchestra of old men plays old popular songs and marching tunes, and old people bring their lawn chairs and listen. At other times, young people gather under the trees. In the summer afternoons they are still-lifes, except for an occasional Frisbee game. I have never understood why they cup their hands and lower their heads when smoking dope, since those are the only signs giving them away to anyone passing by. They should pretend to be smoking cigarettes, but then no one cares anyway, until night when the police cruiser disperses them.

"You just had to say it."

"Yes."

"Okay."

At the Square that is not a square but a street and one parking lot in front of commercial places, I parked and we crossed the street and looked in the window of the young Greek's fish market. He waved from behind the counter where he was wrapping and weighing white fillets of fish for a woman taking bills from her wallet and wiping her nose with Kleenex. We waved and went to Timmy's.

"Does it bother you?" I said at the bar.

"Why should it? I'm not fat."

"It bothers me," I said, and big Steve Buckland came and greeted us and took our orders. Steve has a grand belly, but his chest is even larger, by eight or ten inches, and if he didn't have the belly he would look like those body builders who seem involved with their bodies to the point of foolishness, so I don't like looking at them. It gets confusing. We drank beer, then went to my apartment for the steaks we had not cooked the night before.

When I look back on that week, I see a series of female faces and gesturing hands, and I hear their voices, and I remember the constriction I felt, as though I had left the world and its parts I recognized, and was immersed in only one of those parts, and it blinded and deafened me to the others. All I could see was female flesh, all I could hear was female voices: they were intense, as from long anger; they were embittered yet resolute; they were self-effacing, with a forced note of humor; they were lyric in their plaintiveness, abrupt with considered despair; they were hopeful. Their hands held pencils, pens, cigarettes, black coffee, diet drinks, and moved in front of and beneath their faces, hovered and swooped over laps and desks, and darted to the mouth that sucked or chewed, smoked or drank. Their faces, I realized, were the faces of the obsessed. Always, behind their eyes, I could see another life being lived. They spoke to us of Dexedrine balanced by Seconal, Nembutal, or Quāāludes and, before the drugs, water diets, grapefruit diets, carbohydrates, calories, diuretics, laxatives, vomiting— every one of them but Ada had forced herself, until Clark's treatment, to vomit at least three times a week, usually more, so we assumed Ada had too, and I liked her for not disclosing that, for keeping private at least that humiliating detail, and also the other one these women did not spare us: images of frequent and liquid emptying of the bowels, whose imagined sounds and smells destroyed, for me, whatever beauty the women did have (none of them was truly fat), as well as that ideal of weight and proportion they strove for. Yet, while they turned their bodies, before my eyes, into bowels, intestines, adipose, digestive juices, piss, shit, and vomit, there was that other life visible in the light of their eyes. Perhaps they strode across the room of their consciousness, graceful, svelte; or sat naked, their stomachs flat, unwrinkled, the skin as taut as the soles of their feet; or, with slender arms, whose only curves were those of athletic muscles, whose flesh did not shake or hang, they reached for steaming bowls of food and piled it on their plates.

That week, except for the martini and Sambuca night, I kept my usual discipline and drank only a few Mooseheads in the evening. So I was sober all those nights after our talks with the women, and I lay awake long after Paula slept, and the little bastard spoke to me of flesh, of food, of dresses, of Lillian's Porsche and my brothers bent over bows and vamps, and I tried to shut him up with the word *vanity*, but he was persistent. *It always connects*, he said. *Everything connects. You have only to look.* I got up to drink milk in the dark living room; I rolled from side to side on the bed and lay still, listening to Paula breathing, and I thought of my brothers fleeing the shoe factory and the future my uncle had planned for them: to learn English while they learned the work of every room and bench in the factory, from the designer in the basement, whose ideas were stolen from Italian shoes bought or photographed in Italy by my uncle, or clipped from magazines, to the cutting room, the stitching room, and so forth, to the room where women inspected and boxed and shipped the pieces of leather that would be the tops of shoes, and then perhaps my brothers would become foremen, certainly not partners, for my uncle had his own sons (has: they now own the factory), though maybe he would have left them a share. Fled to beautician school, then borrowed money and opened a shop and married Greek women, lovely Greek women who bore children who are respectful, beautiful, and well behaved, not at all like American children, though they speak English without the accents of their parents. Anyone visiting my brothers' houses will be given a drink and food, and always there is feta cheese and olives, and my brothers' wives keep stuffed grapeleaves and spinach pies in the freezer. They proudly sent me through school, and now, with love and less pride, they look at my life, and sometimes they ask me, as the little bastard did those nights of the week of the dieting women, why I am, at thirty-three, still living in a three-room apartment (including the kitchen, with the table where I eat) and going to work at ten in the morning and taking Wednesday afternoons off and spending so much time running and fucking young girls. They are not opposed to running but that I do it during my long lunch break and so return late for the afternoon's work; nor are they opposed to the young girls, but insist that I could have them and marriage and a family. I have no answers. But when they tell me I'm thirty-three, I am for moments, even minutes, frightened. It is strange: no one is Christian anymore, but every man I've known reach the age of thirty-three has been afraid that he will not see thirty-four, as if none of us can forget that the most famous death of our culture occurred at thirty-three. I do tell them I don't need more money, but they say I do, I should be investing in stock, in bonds, and buying a house, and I shiver at this and grow silent until they laugh and clap my shoulder and hug me, and I am the baby brother again, whom they care for and indulge.

The little bastard is not so gentle, and those nights he demanded answers and got none, and he kept saying, *It all connects; it all connects*, as I tried to sleep and tried to read, but *Anna Karenina* took me back to, rather than away from,

the women; for if she had lived now and had believed she was
fat because her stomach creased, because she could pinch
flesh over her ribs, because she could not wear her size eight
or ten, she would have been among them, taking pills and getting through the day on black coffee and cigarettes, nibbling
food while her face tautened and her heart beat faster, creeping down to the kitchen at night to eat a half-gallon of ice
cream, then rushing in remorse to the bathroom to jam fingers down her throat and vomit the colors of that food children and dieting women so love, if I can take as a microcosm
the women we interviewed, for each of them confessed ice
cream as her secret wickedness. These images of shitting and
vomiting induced by laxatives and fingers interrupted me
whenever, that week, I touched Paula: to teach her a Greek
dance in my living room, standing side by side, hands on each
other's shoulders, as I counted one-two one-two; to make
love with her before she slept and I lay staring opposite the
bed, at the dark window, its glass fogged and moist.

We simply happened, on Friday, to be free at two-thirty,
so we drove to the public high school, whose crowded halls
and rooms I had endured for four years. I parked at the front
of the building. They would all come out there, to the waiting
buses in line ahead of us, to the cars in the lot. A large statue
of *The Thinker* was on the schoolground, between us and the
building. A bell rang loudly, and as they came out, some singly,
most in hurried groups, lighting cigarettes, Paula got out of
the car, stopped several of them until one boy turned back to
the grounds and pointed at a girl alone, lighting a cigarette in
the lee of *The Thinker*. Paula went to her, and I watched them
talking. Then they came to the car. I watched Paula talking,
smiling; when they got closer I could see that the girl was
doing neither, and as she slid into the back seat and looked at
me, I thought she wouldn't, not in this car, not with us.

"Who's your father?" I said.

"Jake."

"Jake? I know Jake."

KAREN ARAKELIAN

They said they would take me home, but could we go by his office first and talk where it was comfortable so him and the girl didn't have to stay twisted around to look at me. I knew who he was, I had seen him a lot in town, but he didn't recognize me, because I kept growing up while he stayed the same. Except he had lost more hair. He drove, and I just watched his bald head and the hair at the back and sides and smoked two cigarettes. I didn't say anything, and I didn't know if I would or not in his office; I wouldn't know till it was over. But I felt like it was all over and nobody would understand what it's like when they're all so thin. Everybody, even Heidi, even though she's always talking about how fat she is, but I know it's so we'll look at how thin she is and be jealous. And we are. Anyways I am.

I think it was money. I even thought of shoplifting and trying to sell things, but after I figured out how I could do it and where, and that took hours and hours, for days and nights, a lot of time thinking about the different stores and what they had in them and where the clerks were. I even went to some of them and looked around. Then after I planned how to do it and what to take, I realized there was no one to sell it to. Because if they could afford to buy the stuff, then they didn't have to buy it cheaper from me, and if they were my friends, or people like them, they couldn't buy anything anyways.

I was relieved, but I was at the bottom again, like the times when I wanted to be dead, because the pills were working but I couldn't afford a second prescription. I had saved for the first one, and for the first visit to Francis too, and there were no jobs, not unless I quit school and worked full time, which I would do, but my parents would never let me. All of us were supposed to go to college, my Dad was very proud about that, and I could see why: he had worked so hard at that shitty place, and his father had come over from Armenia to get away from the Turks. I have heard those stories, about them killing my great-grandparents, and other stories, and I hate fucking Turks. Everyone else went to college, and I'm the youngest. So I couldn't get a job.

I went to Francis for my second appointment in January, when school had just started and my Christmas job at the department store was over and I was down to my last two days of pills. He weighed me; then I started crying, and he told me to get dressed and he sent the nurse out. When I was dressed he sat me down in his office and said, "You lost seven pounds. Why did you cry?"

So I told him, and I see now that's when he knew my parents didn't know I was going to him, didn't know about the pills and the vomiting. You know how they are, the doctors: they handle you so fast they hardly look at you, and even if they do, even if they touch you with their stethoscope and their fingers, you feel like they haven't. But he was definitely looking at me, and I couldn't believe it: there it was in his face; he wanted me, the first time almost anybody ever looked at me like that, anybody but punks in the halls and at parties, the first time ever that the guy was a grown man. An old one too. So I looked back. And saw that he was old but not too old. He was probably fifty or more, but he was distinguished-looking; he had a nice haircut, not too short, and blow-dried hair, dark brown with some gray at the sides and temples; and he was tall and trim, athletic-looking, probably racquetball and tennis. I knew he sailed his boat. The lines in his face must have come from the boat; they looked like outdoor lines. I watched him watching me; then I took out a cigarette, which I'd always been afraid to do in a doctor's office, and I lit it and he didn't say anything. After a while he got up and gave me his Styrofoam cup for an ashtray. A few drops of coffee were in the bottom. He drank it with cream. Then he said: "I can help you."

He was standing right in front of me, his legs nearly touching my knees, and I moved my cigarette out to the side so the smoke wouldn't go up to his face.

"Please do," I said.

"Come here tomorrow night at eight."

Tomorrow was Wednesday. I said I would. He kept standing there. I finished my cigarette, blowing the smoke off to my side and watching him talk to me. We would have to be careful, he said. He could get into very bad trouble. But he could give me the pills. But I mustn't ever say a word. I nodded. Then, I don't know why, I knew he was hard. When I put out my cigarette I glanced at it. His pants stretched across its top, and it was like it was trying to push through the pants and touch my eyes.

On Wednesday night it was very big, and I knew I had never really fucked before. I had done it in the yard and in cars at parties, when I was loaded on drugs and beer. But this was slow getting undressed, and his hands weren't a doctor's anymore, they were slow and gentle and everything took a long time. He liked eating me and he stayed down there till I came; then he sat on the floor beside the couch and touched me till I was ready again. Then he put on a rubber, and for a long slow time he was in me and I came again and finally he did: when it happened to him he groaned and shuddered and cried out in a high soft voice like a girl. That night he gave me birth-control pills too.

So I had all these pills to take, and I hid them in my underwear drawer where I keep my cigarettes and grass, and I should have kept them all in my purse, but I'm so careless about my purse—I keep dropping it on the kitchen table with my books, or leaving it in the living room, on top of the television or on the couch—that I was always afraid, when it was just grass and cigarettes, that my mother or father would pick it up wrong, just to move it, and everything would fall out on the table or floor: my Newports and my dope, and then it was speed and downs and the birth-control pills, so everything was under my pants. Still I should have been safe. I do my own laundry and fold it in the basement and put it away.

But that night Heidi was over and we were up in my room, and I was putting away my clothes when Dad knocked on the door. I said come in. He opened the door and stood in the doorway a while, talking to us. He always liked to talk to us kids and our friends. That night we talked about school, and he said we had to work hard and try to get scholarships but that he'd see to it I went to any place I could get into. He could always get money, he said, and I was the last one, so it was easier. Then he was talking about when he went to the high school and the trouble he and the guys got into, getting wise with old Mrs. Fletcher (she still teaches English, even though we think she's senile the way she keeps reciting "Snow-Bound" every year on the first day it snows because Whittier was born here and lived here), and he and his buddies would get sent to the principal; and talking Armenian in French class; and sneaking fishing rods out of the house in the morning and walking down to the bus stop with the rods in two parts down their pants legs, so they walked stiff-legged, and when they were around the corner they took out the rods and went to the pond—and it was all so tame and old-fashioned I felt sorry for him.

I've told him there are guards in the halls and patrolling the lavs for pushers, and he knows, because every kid in the family has told him, about kids smoking dope and drinking on the bus at seven in the morning, but it's like to him it's some-thing that's going on, but it's out *there* somewhere, with the Puerto Ricans and Italians, but it's not here, in this nice house he's buying every month, like we have our own world here. And Goddamn me, that's when I put the panties in my drawer, while he was laughing about him and his buddies growing up. He had moved into the room, by then, and was standing on the rug under the ceiling light, and what I didn't think of is how tall he is. If I were standing there, I could not see into the back of my drawer. I can't even see into it when I'm standing beside it; I have to sort of raise up and look toward the back. But he could look straight down in it. Not that he was. He was talking to us, Heidi sitting on the bed and me standing between the bed and the chest of drawers, and I suppose his eyes just naturally followed my hands as they took clothes from the bed and put them in the drawers, and when I put a stack of pants in the top drawer, all he did was glance that way, and what he saw wasn't the cellophane of grass or the two bottles of pills or the birth control pills, but the Goddamn turquoise of the Newport pack, and he stopped talking and I saw his face change; he said "Uh-oh," and I shoved the drawer closed.

"Karen," he said, and I looked at Heidi. She said later she thought it was the grass. She didn't know about the pills, none of them, and she still doesn't.

"It's for me," Heidi said. Her face was red, and her mouth and eyes were scared-looking, and I will never forget what she did for me, or tried to. Because she knows my Dad has a temper, and telling him you smoke dope is like telling some of these other parents you're on heroin. "Karen doesn't smoke it," she said. She looked like she was about to cry.

Then he knew. He lives at home like he doesn't know anything but the leather factory—he's a foreman there—but he is not dumb. I wish for him and me both, and Mom, and Francis, that he was. Because then he said: "You better go on home now, Heidi."

She got her parka and was gone, looking at the floor as she walked past him; at the door she looked back, and her face was still red and her eyes were bright and wet. Then she went down the hall and I heard her on the stairs and my mom calling good night and Heidi said it too, and I could tell it was over her shoulder as she went out the door. I heard it, and then the storm door, and was looking at Dad's shoes.

"Open it," he said.

I shook my head. If I spoke I would blubber. He turned his head and shouted, "Marsha!"

Mom didn't answer. She came up the stairs, her footsteps heavy like running, but she was only climbing fast. She stood at the door a moment looking at me and at Dad's back; then she came in and stood beside him.

"She's smoking dope," he said. "Cigarettes too. Show your mother the drawer, Karen."

Then I was lying on the bed, face-down, like I had fainted, because I didn't remember deciding to do it or getting there:

one second I was standing looking at them, then I was crying into the bedspread, and I knew from the footsteps and the slow way the drawer opened that it was Mom who did it. Then she was crying over me, hugging me from behind, her hands squeezed between my shoulders and the bed, and Dad was talking loud but not yelling yet, and I started talking into all that, babbling I guess, but it wasn't about Francis and me. I said that too, but it was like a small detail when you're describing a wreck you were in, telling the police, and Francis and me were just the rain or the car that stopped to help: sometimes I screamed, but mostly I moaned and cried about vomiting my dinner and hiding that from them and laxatives and having to go at school and holding it and holding it till the bell, then hurrying to the lav and the sick sounds I made in the stall with the girls smoking just on the other side of it and saying *gross gross*, and my fat ugly legs and my fat ugly bottom and my fat ugly face and my fat ugly floppy boobs and how I wanted to be dead I was so fat and ugly, and some time in there my dad stopped talking, stopped making any sound at all, except once when he said, like he was going to cry too, like Mom was the whole time: "Oh, my God."

ARCHIMEDES NIONAKIS

I said it too. I didn't say much more as I stood at the window looking from Karen to the twilit traffic to Karen again while she talked and wept and Paula's eyes brimmed over and she wiped her cheeks. Then Paula took her to the bathroom behind the waiting room, and they worked on their faces and came out cleansed of tears and made-up again, walking arm in arm. Karen was plump. But, like all those others—and I know all is hyperbolic for only eight women, nine with Karen, but on that Friday afternoon their number seemed legion—she was not fat.

Looking out my window at people driving home from work in the lingering sunset, the snow having stopped Thursday morning and the sky cleared overnight, I listened to

Karen and thought of my brothers, perhaps the happiest
Americans I know. I barely remember my father—I am not
certain whether I recall him or merely have images from stories my brothers and mother have told—but my brothers
remember him and the village where we lived. My father
owned a small café and was also the mayor of the town, so
when the Communist guerrillas came they took him with
them, to the hills. They all knew him, and they said We have
to take you because you are the mayor. Some months later
one of them came through town and stopped at our house to
tell my mother her husband was well. Kosta was ten, and my
mother sent him with the man and a knapsack of food and
wine, and they walked for two days to the camp in the mountains, where Kosta spent a day and a night with my father,
who showed him to everyone in the camp and boasted of his
son who had come to visit. It was, Kosta says, a gentle captiv-
ity. They treated my father well, and he could do whatever he
pleased except escape. Kosta walked back alone, stopping at
houses along the way. Later a guerrilla came to tell my mother
that my father had died, probably of pneumonia, and they had
properly buried him, with a marker, in the hills. She managed
the café and cared for me, playing among the tables, and worried about her older sons and wrote to her brother in America
to sponsor us.

So my brothers have built a business and houses, and
when I go visit them or, more important, when, unobserved,
I see them driving in town, and I watch from the sidewalk,
I know they are happy, as I do when I go to their shop and
wait for one of them to trim what is left of my hair. They laugh
and talk; for eleven or twelve hours a day, six days a week,
they do this, and they make a lot of money from those women,
as though, immigrants that they are, they had seen right away
in the shoe factory where the heart of the nation was and left
that bleak building and women's feet and moved up to their
own building, and later their homes, paid for by women's hair.
And remained untouched, unscathed: swam and skied and
played tennis with their wives and children, indeed lived ath-

letic lives as naturally as animals and never considered the burning of fat or the prolonging of life. As I run, not for my waist or longevity, but to maintain some proportion of my *homo duplex*, to keep some balance between the self I recognize and the little bastard who recognizes nothing as familiar, a quotidian foreigner in the land. My brothers watched with amusement, if even that, as their hair fell out. They celebrate all Greek holidays, as I do with them, and on Greek Easter we cook a lamb on a spit; they take their families to the Greek church, and I do not know whether they believe in God as much as they believe a father should take his family to church. They visit Greece, where now my father's bones lie in a cemetery in our village, and I go there too, having no memories save those of a tourist who speaks the language and shares the blood, so that I have no desire for a Greek household as my brothers have made with their marriages here, nor do I have a desire for an American one. So this year in my apartment I have Paula, and I have a law practice that is only an avocation, and my only vocation is running each year in Boston the long run from my father's country.

Still Karen talked, seated at my desk, leaning over it, her hands outstretched, held and stroked by Paula's. I looked at Paula sitting in the chair she had pulled up to a corner of the desk, and I thought I could tell my brothers now; it was clear to me, and I could explain it to them, could show them why I would not, could not, work twelve or eight or even six hours a day five or six days a week for any life this nation offered. I had not fled a village where I would roam without education till I died. I had simply been a five-year-old boy placed on a ship. I looked out the window again and thought of Lillian Clark and those terrible eyes and the Puerto Rican girl she had to free her of her work, so that she had nothing at all to do, while in the garage the steel of the Porsche drew into itself the February cold. I spun from the window in a moment of near glee, so that Karen stopped and sniffed and looked at me, wiping her eyes. But I stopped myself and turned back to the window. I had been about to tell her I was glad Jake had done it.

She did not mention once, that entire time, the killing of Francis Clark. Nor did I ask her to. When she finished I told her we would take her home and saw at once in her eyes what I knew as soon as I had spoken: we could not do that, we could not enter or even drive to the front of Jake's home, and I felt affection and respect like love for her then, saw her as a sixteen-year-old daughter who not only loved Jake but understood him too. She would have done everything again so she could clothe herself in smaller and smaller pants and skirts and dresses and blouses, but she would have done it with more care. And I remembered from somewhere, someone, in my boyhood: *Don't shit where you eat*. It was the way my brothers ran their households, and perhaps one of them had said it to me. I told Karen that Paula would drive her to her street-corner and I would phone her father. They both nodded and went to the bathroom. When they came out, I held Karen's parka for her and told Paula I would see her at my apartment.

I sat at the desk in the smoky and shadowed room—we had not turned on a light—then I looked up Jake's number, closed the book, gazed at the window and the slow cars, forgot the number, and opened the book again. His street was not far away, and I wanted to give him time to leave before Karen walked into the house. Marsha answered, and I heard the quaver of guilt in my voice and heard it again when Jake took the phone, and beneath the warmth in his voice I heard what I knew I would see in his eyes. I asked him if we could have a talk.

"Sure, Archimedes, sure. I'm on the way."

I waited outside, in the waning light now, and watched every car coming from his direction. His was large, and American, and I peered at him through the window, then got in. He drove us to the ocean. I do not know why. Perhaps it was for the expanse of it, or some instinct sent him to the shore. But I do not want to impose on Jake my own musing of that day: perhaps he wanted a bar where no one knew us. He drove for half an hour, and we talked about my brothers and his and his sisters and his work at the factory. We did not mention my work or Karen or Marsha or his grown children. Now and then I looked at his face, lit by the dashboard, and his eyes watching cars and trucks, while they stared at his new life.

He stopped at a restaurant across the road from the ocean; on the beach side of the road, a seawall blocked our view of the water, but night had come, and we could only have seen the breakers' white foam. The empty tables in the restaurant were set for dinner, their glass-encased candles burning over red tablecloths; we went through a door into the darkened lounge and stood for a few moments until we could see, then moved to a booth at the wall, across the room from the bar. The other drinkers were at the bar, four men, separate, drinking quietly. The bartender, a young woman, came for the order. Jake said a shot of CC and a draft, so I did too and had money on the table when she came back, but he covered it with his hand, said, No, Archimedes, and paid her and tipped a dollar. He raised his shot glass to me, and I touched it with mine. He drank his in one motion; I swallowed some and said, "I'm defending George Karambelas."

"Yes."

"I've just talked to Karen."

"Ah."

He drank from the mug of draft and called to the bar: "Dear? Two more shots, please."

So I drank the rest of my whiskey, and we watched her cross the floor with the bottle and pour, and he gave her money again before I saw it in his hand, but I said: My round, Jake, and gave her my ten and told her to keep one. We watched her until she was behind the bar again, then touched glasses, and I sipped and looked at his wide neck as he drank. Then I said: "I've been wondering about the boat."

"The boat?"

"That model. How did it break?"

"I broke it. With my fist, on the desk."

"Why?"

"How do you think he paid for it, Archimedes? You think he was a good man? An honest man? A good *doc*tor?"

"No."

"That's why I broke it."

"Then what?"

"He was sitting behind his desk when I broke it. He was waiting for—you know what he was waiting for."

"Yes."

He turned toward the bar, lifting his glass.

"No," I said. "Finish first. Please."

"Okay. That's when he took out the gun. From his drawer. He took it out and he worked it, so he had a bullet in there, in the barrel, and it was cocked. You know something? I looked at that big hole in the barrel, pointed at me, and I looked at that son of a bitch's face, and I wasn't scared of that gun. I think because if I died I didn't care. I can't tell you how bad I felt. You don't know; I can't say it."

"I know."

I took our shot glasses to the bar and she filled them and he said loudly, to my back: "Archimedes. That's my round."

"I'll run a tab," she said. I noticed then that she wore glasses, and in the light behind the bar was pretty, and I wanted to be home with Paula, only to lie beside her, and to sleep. I spilled whiskey on both hands going back to the booth.

"She's keeping a tab," I said.

Jake nodded, and raised his glass to mine, and I smelled more whiskey than I drank.

"He told me to leave. How do you like that? He's doing that to my daughter and giving her those pills, and he says to me, leave. Go home. So I didn't move. I came to talk to that son of a bitch —"

"He was certainly that, Jake."

"Yes. And you know how they are, those rich doctors, all the rich people, they're used to saying leave, go home, and everybody goes. So what's he going to do, Archimedes? Shoot me? Of course not. He's got the gun and he's behind his desk, but *still* he has to listen. Because I'm talking to him, Archimedes; I'm telling him things. So he gets mad. *Him.* And he comes around the desk with that gun, and I tell him I'll shove that thing up his ass. Then I hit him. But, Goddammit, he hit his head. On the corner of his desk there, when he went down. Just that once. I hit him just that once, and the son of a bitch cracked his head. I can't feel bad. For him. But let me tell you, since that night nobody talks in my house. Marsha and Karen, they just go around sad. And quiet. Jesus, it's quiet. We talk, you know; we say this and that, hello, good morning, you want some more rice? But, oh Jesus, it's quiet, and me too. I've just been waiting. You see, when they blamed it on George, I knew I had to go tell them. Every night, I'd say to myself: Tomorrow, Jake. After work, tomorrow, you go down to the station. Then I'd go to work next day, and when five o'clock came I'd drive home. I couldn't leave them. My family. I don't mind being punished. You kill somebody, you go to jail, even if he's a son of a bitch. But every day I couldn't leave my family."

"Monday," I said.

"What about Monday?"

"Let's do it Monday. That'll give you two days to raise bail."

He drank the rest of his beer, then leaned over the table. "How much?"

"Probably five thousand for the bondsman."

"I can get it."

"I could ask my brothers," I said. "You might need ten, but I doubt it."

"No. I have some family. And I have friends."

He slid out of the booth, stood at the table's end, held two mugs in one hand, the glasses in the other.

"Well," he said. "Okay. Yes: Monday."

He went to the bar, tall and wide and walking steadily, and I wanted to tell him not to bring me another shot, but I could not keep that distance from him, though my legs under the table felt weak, as if they alone, of my body, were drunk. Then he paid her, so this was our last drink, and I imagined Paula in the warm bedroom, lying on the bed reading her philosophy book, glancing at her watch. When Jake sat across from me, we raised the glasses, and I said, To Monday; then we touched them and I drank mine in one long swallow, exhaled, and drank some beer.

"You said let's," he said.

"What?"

" 'Let's do it Monday.' What did you mean?"

"I don't charge much," I said. "I don't charge anything at all, for a good Armenian."

"Really? You? You want to be my lawyer?"

"Jake, you'll never see the inside of a prison."

"*No.*"

"I'm sure of it."

"Really?"

"Really."

"What about George?"

"He won't be my client anymore."

"But this weekend. He stays in jail?"

"Only till Monday. What the hell: he shouldn't drink so much."

His smile came slowly and then was laughter that rose and fell and rose again as we walked out of the dark lounge, to the parking lot and the smack of breakers beyond the seawall and into his car, where pulling down his seat belt, he turned to me and said, "Come to the house and have dinner."

"Another time," I said. "I've got a woman waiting at home."

He squeezed my shoulder, reached across me and pulled my seat belt over my chest and snapped it locked, then started the car and turned on its headlights and slowly drove us home.

MOLLY

for George Gibson

ONE

WHEN CLAIRE'S HUSBAND left her and their daughter, she was twenty-five years old and Molly was three. By the time she was thirty Claire knew other men like Norman, knew them because their sad wives were her friends. These men were absolutely competent in their work, even excellent, better than others because more committed or obsessed. Or possessed. But they and Norman could not be husbands and fathers, unless their wives and children wanted little more than nothing, or little more than what money gave them. So Norman had left to be free, to work as an anthropologist all the way across the country in California, as if he needed that distance between him and Massachusetts to make final his leaving. Every month he sent Claire a check drawn on the Wells Fargo Bank in Pacifica. After receiving the third check, she divorced him.

Norman was a tall, angular man who appeared clumsy: a coffee cup in his large and bony hands seemed to be in its last moments before fragmentation; a car in his control looked alive, like a horse that senses his rider is a novice and is deciding whether to be gentle and patient, or a rascal. But he was not clumsy. He moved that way, looked that way even at rest in a chair, because he seemed to live always in a world that was not physical. Or nearly always. At his long table in his large cluttered den he studied artifacts and catalogued them, and his hands and face then, his sloping shoulders and long arms, reminded her of a pianist's. To him, his den was not cluttered: it was perfectly in order; but that order was for Claire an accumulation of objects that she knew were part of her own history in America and with Norman but now, unearthed and collected, had no connection with the world she lived in.

She prepared meals that he ate as a pet dog eats its dry food, out of hunger while knowing there is better food he would gobble if only he could get it. But for Norman there was no better food. He did not smoke, and before dinner he drank whatever she did, and he took his alcohol as he did his food: quickly, and without visible pleasure or lack of it, and always moderately. Some evenings, with what she believed at the time was mischievous curiosity, she mixed herself a bloody mary or salty dog and gave him only the seasoned tomato juice or salted grapefruit juice, and he drank these, fooled and never knowing it. Then she realized he would not care if he did know it, and with scorn but fear too she saw him not as a fool but as a creature who needed almost nothing that she did. After that she nightly gave him juice and doubled the vodka in her own drinks, wanting to drink his portion as she sat across the living room from him, and Molly played on the floor between them and Claire drank until she was drunk: a drunkenness she masked so well that he could neither see nor hear it. She sat talking as though sober and smelling the food on the stove and in the oven and wishing he would suddenly die, drinking grapefruit juice in his large chair where he could not look comfortable, where his long arms and legs shifted and jutted out and would not rest in the chair's sturdy depth.

He touched and held Molly, and spoke to her, as absently as he ate and drank and drove and touched everything that was part of their lives. Before she began wishing for his death, she had at times felt compassion for him as she watched him with Molly, saw him as though deprived of his sense of touch and so removed from the world and condemned to move in it on a chair with motor and wheels. Also, during that time, she often read in his den while he worked at night, after his work-day was over, and he had drunk his two drinks and eaten his dinner. She sat in a chair across the room from him, facing his profile at the table, and sometimes she lowered the book to her lap and with yearning sorrow that dampened her eyes she watched him fondle the old bottles and potsherds and crusted iron, the only things she ever saw him fondle, and she wanted his hands like that on her flesh. This was early enough in the marriage for her sorrow to include him, for her to feel that his steadfast lack of proportion was a curse on him too, and gave him pain he could neither voice nor heal. And then her sorrow included hope too: that as he grew older, toward thirty, and attained some of the achievement he wanted, he would change, would become a whole man whose pleasures as husband and father were two-thirds of his fulfillment instead of the third or fourth or even less they were now.

On one of those evenings she admitted they were less. She did not admit this so much as she was finally no longer able to deny it: the truth of it rose in her and she fought it, tensed her muscles against it; then she tired and with a sigh he did not hear at his table, she surrendered to it. She and Molly could vanish tonight, and his life would move on, move in the direction he believed was forward. This man, whose only physical appetite was sexual, who left his desk for bed and her body and excited her with the extremity of his only passion away from his work, who plunged and panted and gasped and groaned, was nothing more than an anthropologist who was beyond hardworking, who was even a bit mad, and after his work he was a good fuck. Soon she started serving him juice before dinner and watched him from her secret and vengeful drunkenness, and spoke to him, made the sounds of marital exchange that she had once loved, those words whose function was not so much to inform but to assure, to celebrate even, the communion between a woman and a man;

and she looked at him dangling in his chair and wished he were dead.

So he had left her and Molly long before he took his body and artifacts and other possessions with him, took them from Massachusetts to California. Always he sent the monthly check, inside a folded and blank page of white stationery. She assumed the checks would stop arriving on the first of each month when he realized that Molly was eighteen or twenty-one, whatever age he had in mind. Or perhaps the money was for her, and it would keep coming until he died or she did, and if she died first whoever did such things would find him through his bank (there was no return address on his envelopes) and tell him it was over now, he could stop. He might have married out there, but she could not imagine it. Because he had left to be free, and for him freedom was selfishness, while for her it was being able to live each day without violating her conscience. She came to believe this after he left, when for the first time in her life without parents or a husband, and so without another adult between her and the world, she had needed a conscience, a place in her spirit where she could stand with strength, and say yes or no. When Molly was nine, Claire told her: "I grew up when he left."

This was during their time before dinner, when each evening they sat in the living room of the house Norman had left, and during Claire's cocktail hour they talked.

"I had to learn to sell real estate, then I had to sell it. And I learned something else. This was during Vietnam. That it wasn't just the Pentagon and the President and Congress that lied. And were cowards. And were evil. Doing terrible things and calling them something else. It was people everywhere, little people. They made money and maybe thought they had power but whether they lived or died wouldn't make any difference. Not to the world. They were people with jobs. It's how they got the jobs and made money. They're cowardly with their bosses and they call it being shrewd. Smart. They call lying 'business.' They always call something by another name. I think it's because people know. They know what's right and what's wrong. And they want to be good. So when they do something evil they say it was something good. It was justified. I've never heard anyone say, 'I did this terrible thing to somebody and I loved it.' Except a boy I knew who'd been to Vietnam. But that's different, and we can't understand it. So it wasn't just Johnson and Nixon and Kissinger and all the rest of them. The country was at war over there, and it was a war here too, of beliefs, and every day it was with me. A confrontation—a fight—between good and evil, truth and lies. People marching in the streets. And there I was with my little life. Working with real-estate agents, and lawyers, and banks—Jesus: *banks*—and architects and building contractors. And I think everything would have been blurred. For me, anyway, if it weren't for the war. I think I would have figured, this is the way the world is. And maybe that's how these people got that way when they were young. Maybe they just figured this was it: lying and fucking over people. And they either had to do it or go live in the desert on locusts and honey. But the war gave me a—moral energy, maybe. Or maybe it just woke me up. Because everything connected in the war. You could hardly buy anything without supporting some corporation that made money on killing people. And your taxes. And the money you earned: you never knew where it came from. What stocks. What profits. So there was always blood on it. None of this got to Norman. He almost cried at the My Lai pictures. The ones I showed you. I never saw him cry but that night he looked like he would. Then he went upstairs to work. And I sat downstairs with the *Life* magazine. The same one we threw away last year. I was pregnant with you. And I sat there and knew we did not live alone anymore, me and you inside of me. I was part of the war. So I was part of everything. I had paid for bullets, and I started imagining money I had spent working itself through the economy. From the counter at the store to the people who made what I bought and made bullets too, and I saw my money finally buying bullets for Calley's gun. And I saw my money spent on those bullets coming back to us—you and me—in Norman's paycheck. I didn't do anything. I didn't stop buying, or paying taxes, or go to jail or march in the streets. But by the time Norman left I had at least learned something. So I'm glad I went to work late in my life. I didn't connect it right away with the war. But I do now. I've never done anything at work I'm ashamed of. I'm ashamed of a lot of things I've done as your mother. But I'll keep learning how to do that, all my life. I don't lie to my clients."

A year after Norman left, when it was clear that he would not be a father for Molly, she changed their names from Thornton back to Cousteau. It did not feel like a change. Even early in the marriage, when she wanted his name, it was strange on her tongue and in her ears; at times she felt pride and love, yes, but she also felt separated from the name, as though it were an acquired title that did not touch all the depths of Claire Cousteau. By that time she was working and Molly was with sitters during the day, so after work Claire gave her the attention she would have shared with a man, if she had been with Molly all day, and if she had had a man. Now her companion for cocktail hour and dinner was Molly. And Claire did not go out in the evenings before she and Molly had eaten dinner together and Molly was asleep. At work Claire missed her, and called home and spoke to the sitter and then to Molly: the pleased and confused child holding the phone to her face, repeating Claire's greetings and the promptings from the sitter: *We played in the snow; I ate pea soup.* After work she drove home to a daughter whose company she dearly wanted.

By the time Molly was nine she was a sensitive and eager listener who understood everything, it seemed, that Claire told her of work, of what she had learned and was learning about people, how much of themselves they would give away for money or simply to avoid standing their ground, even when the issue was trifling and the consequence they feared was only embarrassment. You could see in their eyes the cages they had built between their lives and their beliefs.

"It's what makes people age," she said to Molly. "I'm sure of it. Not wrinkles, or gray hair, or getting flabby or dull. It's that compromise, over and over for years. That's what you see in those tired old faces. You and I—only our skin and hair will age."

Molly was able to connect her own moral landscape with Claire's: the disloyalty of children at school, and their fear of teachers and other children, and their willingness to do anything, say anything, so they would not seem foolish, or separate from the others. Molly could listen to Claire talking about a man she was seeing: what Claire liked about him, what she was uncertain about, what she found amusing, and Molly could talk about him, and on these evenings the two of them were like roommates as they recounted and mimed the comic flaws of Claire's lovers.

She never had more than one at a time. In her affairs she obeyed a pattern she had lived with before marriage and was comfortable with as a divorced woman: a series of dates, a ritual of drinking and eating and talking and touching and kissing that allowed her to believe that she and the man were learning to know each other rather than simply increasing their excitement by conducting foreplay while clothed in restaurants and movie theaters and bars. Norman had been her first lover, and from her marriage she had learned that the desire to know another, and to be known by him, was futile. But she could live with the illusion of it. She believed there was nothing harmful in living a lie if you knew you were. It was, in fact, good. For how else could you live, except to will yourself into an alteration of the truth you were dealt at birth?

When Molly was twelve, her curiosity about sex became concrete and personal. Until then, beginning years earlier, Claire had given her long answers to her questions about procreation, pregnancy, menstruation, childbirth, nursing, and these lessons had seemed to Claire abstract and general, like their talks about death. Now Molly knew girls only a year or two older who kissed and let boys touch them and even touched the boys. Some old instinct urged Claire to lie: to tell Molly it was wrong. But she knew the emotions of that instinct were fear and a desire to protect Molly, and she resisted them because the truth was that girls no longer had to worry about either pregnancy or bad reputations, they were as free as boys now, and so there was little to fear, little need to protect Molly. The world she was growing into held in waiting far more complex and dangerous threats to her young spirit. And women, even girls, had always been more sane about sex than men, than boys: women's instincts were sound, and saved most of them from the damages of promiscuity or guilt.

She forced herself to look across the dinner table at Molly's eyes: at their curiosity, their fascination. And gratitude too, for being able to talk to her mother, with the confidence that her mother would tell her the truth. So Claire felt blessed, sitting in candlelight, pleasantly well-fed, drinking wine; and oblivious of their soiled plates on the table and the pots waiting in the kitchen to be emptied and cleaned, she sank warmly into the deep pleasure of motherhood. She said that she discovered after Norman left—always she called him Norman when she spoke to Molly—that you had to find some answers for yourself. And after a long and painful and frightening time—about six months, while men invited her on dates and she said no—she decided she did not have to either marry again or be doomed to loneliness only because as a young woman she had loved, then married, a man who believed he wanted marriage and children and learned too late that he did not. But as soon as she said the word loneliness, it jarred her. She said to Molly: "No. I didn't mean loneliness."

She believed she said this so Molly would not feel that Claire could live with her and still be lonely. Then she knew that wasn't the reason either, and for the first time since divorce she went beyond that word she had used for years as a name for her desires. Now she felt as though she were actually removing the word from her tongue, or from the air between her and Molly, and holding it before the candles' flames, turning it in her hands, squeezing and probing it, finding that it was not the truth, was not even close to it.

"No," she said to Molly. "I was never lonely. Not after Norman left. I was lonely when he was here, around the end of him being here. Because there were three of us, and we had a home. But the truth is there were only two of us, and we had a house and a two-legged pet I fed. Not a domestic animal, though. Norman was never domestic, except like an ashtray is, or a vegetable bin. Something that's in a house, and only receives. Maybe he was a Goddamn Christmas tree. When he left us I wasn't lonely. I wanted a man. It's—" She looked over the candle flames at their moving light on Molly's eyes. Molly had dark skin, like Claire's, and her black hair too, as though pallid Norman had truly left his daughter without a trace. "It's wanting to be wanted. Listened to. Really listened to. The way a man listens when he's attracted to you. Soon you'll know what I mean. You say something—anything, the stuff people are always saying to each other, and none of it's important. Except that it's you saying it to someone you care about, and who cares about you. *I never remember my dreams. I need a new raincoat.* It's the way a man listens. The way he looks at you when you talk. You're not talking about a raincoat anymore. It's as though you're showing him everything you remember about yourself: the girls you used to jump rope with, the tree you lay under as a child and daydreamed, your first crush on a boy in second grade. And the way a man will notice you. The gestures you make all day, every day. The way you push your hair back from your face. Or knit your brows or tighten your lips when you're trying to remember something. Your different smiles. When you do one of these, you can see it in their faces—it's a sudden look of appreciation. Or satisfaction. That they anticipated what you'd do. They notice everything, so you dress for them, you bathe for them, put on perfume and make-up for them. They do their own version of that for us too. And you feel known. Then you're not just one person among everyone. You're one woman among all women. You're you. That's what it feels like to be loved. And when you're not loved you become worse than part of a crowd. It's like you don't have a body anymore. You become abstract: just your voice inside you talking to yourself, and you feel like you don't even occupy the space you're standing in, like you're weightless. You're standing on a spot on the earth, but your feet are like air. *You* give me weight," she said to Molly, the child's face intense still, curious still, fascinated and grateful still, with a shade of fear too in her eyes: but always you had to tell your children something that brought that fear to their eyes, that awakening to what waited for them. "And I hope I give it to you." Molly nodded twice, three times. "And you need it from your friends too, your teachers, right?" Again the nod: a quick motion of agreement that asked Claire for more of this knowledge, this disclosure in candlelight and her mother's cigarette smoke, and the scents of melting wax and her mother's Burgundy. "And I need it from my woman friends. And from a man. From a man it's not really love. Not true love. But it has all the feelings of it."

"Why isn't it love?"

"Because love is a vocation."

"A what?"

"Work. Work that you love. That you must do to be whole. That you devote your life to. They don't teach it in school, but they should. I learned it with Norman. We got married thinking marriage was the happy ending, like in the movies; we had to learn it was the beginning of a vocation. He never did. He didn't want to. So with men—for me, anyway—it's not love. But it's close enough. And there's the pleasure."

For this she needed a cigarette, and as she lit it she glanced at Molly and saw in her daughter's face, watching Claire inhale and blow out smoke, an expression of desire, and she knew that Molly wanted to smoke and was twelve years old but would do it anyway; remembering now her own girlhood, watching her parents and their friends smoking and waiting for the time, only a little longer but so long in childhood, when she would have the courage to steal and smoke one, the knowledge that she had to wait based not simply on fear of being caught when she was so young that her parents' anger would be even worse, but also on an instinct in her very flesh that told her you spared your body certain pleasures, and smoking was one of them, until you were older. Her recognition of Molly's yearning disrupted the excitement and reward of talking to her daughter about love, and although Claire was silent she felt she was stammering. She rose and went to the kitchen for a demitasse, and in that movement performed only to regain the rhythm of their talk she at once saw clearly, even as she poured coffee into her small cup, that the look of desire she had caught in Molly's face was not a break from that rhythm at all, but was part of it. Remembering again herself as a girl, waiting for the time, the day, the moment when there would be an open pack in an empty room and she would take a cigarette into the woods behind their home. It had nothing to do with wanting to look grown up, as adults liked to say, perhaps needed to say. It was being a child, and children perceived everything in their homes, so Claire had seen, then wanted, the sensation smoking gave her parents. When she returned to the table to sit and face Molly she was afraid again, as she had been earlier when she overcame the urge to lie about men and women, and men and herself. But she was more afraid of yielding to her fear than of what she meant to tell Molly.

"I'm going to tell you something else, and thank God you'll hear it first from me. Or at least completely from me. I can't tell you not to share this with your friends. But I'm going to ask you. I'm going to ask you please not to. Because this is for families. For you and me. And your friends should hear it and talk about it at home. We've no right to violate that. Each girl has her own timing for this, and you've got no way of knowing what a girl should know, and when. Okay?"

The nod again, the young eyes oblivious now of Claire's smoking, as though knowing what Claire was about to say and already intent on that; the same desire, though, was in her face, and the shyness, and Claire did not know whether to see this as a sign of the deep and trusting comfort between them, or a sign that already she had said too much; and, entrapped by herself, was about to say far, far too much.

"It's the pleasure too," she said. "With a man. Making love with a man. You know how his seed gets into a woman. You looked worried, afraid, when we talked about that. Because you could only imagine pain. That part of his body going into you. But now you know girls who are experimenting. Touching boys there. Letting boys touch their vaginas. Maybe put in their fingers?"

This time Molly's nod was slow, and she blushed.

"They don't talk about pain, do they? Those girls."

"No."

"Only the first time. When the hymen breaks. When a man—or a boy—breaks it with his penis. But it's worth it. It's one of the most wonderful pleasures we can have. Maybe the most intense. Surely the most intense. Making love with a man you care for. It's everything I was talking about before, the way you feel like you, yourself alone among everyone else, and you feel it with your body *and* your heart. Damnit, I'm not going to lie to you. Mostly it's the body. The man's orgasm is his deepest pleasure, and that's when he ejaculates his seed. Our orgasm is even more intense, it lasts longer, and it's better than theirs." She paused, looking at Molly's puzzled, quizzical eyes. "Climax," she said. "Coming. Orgasm is coming."

"Oh. I thought it was—" She looked at her plate, then back at Claire's eyes, blushing again.

"What?"

"Getting pregnant."

"No. It's the completion of lovemaking. And when your body matures, you need it. Not *all* the time. It's not the most important thing in our lives. It's a very small part. But I need it. And that's what I thought and thought about when Norman left. There's masturbation, but it's not the same. It's like seeing only the end of a movie. So I decided back then that I could make love with a man—not any man, not *just* for the body, but a man I felt something for. Respected. Cared about. Could be myself with. And *feel* I was myself with. I hadn't listened to some snake and talked somebody into eating an apple. I was too young to know better, so I married a snake and he crawled away, to California. And left me to get banished like Eve. It wasn't right. Your generation won't go through all that worrying. But it was different for me. Being a young mother. I had to think things through, be sure I was right." Like a narrow beam of white light through a cloud of colors and images in her mind, a discovery came to her: she had either drunk too much, or had become too excited by talking like this to Molly; but something was spurring her to a volubility beyond Molly's reach, beyond her age and experience, and so beyond her ability to comprehend with comfort, with confidence. Then with a heedless shrug or a brave leap of her heart she ignored the light and opened her mind again to the flow of images from her memory and her ideas that she wanted to form into sound, into words.

"Good Lord," she said.

"What?"

"The grape. I'm talking too much. Listen: here's what I want you to know. Since sometime in the first year Norman left, I've had lovers." Molly's body showed nothing, was still, even relaxed; her eyes looking into Claire's were patient and calm. Claire sighed, audibly, louder than she needed to: a sign to Molly that a gift had passed between them, through the fire of the candles. "They've been nice men, good men. I don't hang out in bars and—" Molly quickly shook her head. "Thank you. As long as you don't think I go around looking for them. It's a pleasure I need sometimes." Then she smiled, and then her shoulders and abdomen shook with laughter that she tried to keep behind her closed lips, but it forced open her mouth, and she sat laughing, and as her face rose and fell with it she saw, through the tears in her eyes, Molly's smile. The smile was not forced, yet could not become laughter either. "Woo," Claire said. "Sorry. I just remembered a man who had been in the Navy. On a ship. He told me one night after they'd been at sea for a good while, they anchored off some island. Okinawa. Whatever. Their first night ashore. So you know what they did, besides get drunk. They went by a small boat from the ship to the island and back. They were coming back to the ship at midnight, and an old sailor looked around at all the drunk young men and said: 'Sex is the one thing you can get behind on the most, and catch up on the quickest'—" Then she was laughing again, her legs tightening with it, her torso and head swaying to and fro with it; and across the table Molly was laughing too, doubling over her cold dinner plate; and Claire knew their talk had ended, in this crescendo of laughter, and she gave herself to it until it ended too, then stood and gathered up dishes and carried them to the sink. Then Molly was beside her with glasses and a serving bowl, and she felt Molly's body touching her thigh and hip and ribs, and she placed a hand on Molly's long soft hair; then she gently pressed Molly's head against her side, and she said: "When you're ready—in high school, college, whenever—we'll get you a diaphragm."

She did not have a lover then, but two months later she did, and after twice going to his apartment and then coming home to Molly and the sitter, she told Molly about him. This was in winter at their cocktail hour, Molly with her cup of tea and Claire with the second martini she allowed herself before dinner.

"He's a nice man. Divorced. Or just separated now, getting divorced. I sold him their house three years ago. Now she has it. Some couples do that, you know: their marriage is going under, so they make a leap: buy a new house, or have a baby. It's sad. I had a hunch, when I was showing them houses. There was a sadness about them. And a shyness between them. A fragile commitment to stake their marriage on doing something new together. Now she has the house and the kids and the poor guy—Stephen, his name is Stephen—has the mortgage payments and a little apartment above a dentist's office. He pays rent to the dentist. Are you all right?"

"Sure."

"Hearing this, I mean. Knowing it's where I was last night. I go to his apartment."

"I don't mind."

Molly was twelve still, in the seventh grade; next summer she would be thirteen, and her body was shaping itself toward those numbers, her waist lengthening, becoming distinct and

slender, and her breasts giving her sweater two small contours of fertile hope. She wore the subdued lipstick, a delicate
deepening of her lips' color, that Claire allowed her for school
and parties. On these winter days, when she came in from the
cold, with her cheeks reddened, the lipstick looked from
across a room like the true coloring of her mouth.

"Would you like to meet him? Have him come here for
dinner?"

"Yes."

"What if he stayed?"

"I don't mind."

"To sleep with me."

"I know."

"Are you sure? You wouldn't be embarrassed? Or something else? When you went up to bed and—"

"Mom. It's okay."

"Or at breakfast? Think about it. I'm very serious about
this. *It's* not serious, me and Stephen. But our home is. It's
more important than me and Stephen, and how you feel about
your home is more important. So tell me the absolute truth.
Because, Molly, if there's ever anything but the absolute truth
between us, then we've failed. And the failure is mine."

Molly had different smiles: some private, some distracted,
some childish, some courteous, and she had one that for years
had warmed Claire, as though it came to her on wings over
whatever space lay between her and her daughter, and touched
her; it was the smile of an old and intimate friend who loved
you, trusted you, and did not have to forgive you. She was
smiling that way now. For moments she did not speak. Then
she said: "I better make you a third one tonight. You're like
me in the principal's office."

"Do you know how?"

Molly crossed the room, took Claire's glass.

"It's gin and vermouth, right?"

"Not much vermouth. And four olives."

"Two ounces of gin. A few drops of vermouth. Stir."

Claire watched her walk into the kitchen, listened to her

tossing ice from the glass into the sink, then working with the ice tray and dropping new cubes into the glass. She lit a cigarette and leaned back in her chair and closed her eyes. Her body felt relieved, as though she had just completed a task. She opened her eyes to a tinkling martini. Then Molly sat across from her on the couch and sipped her tea and frowned because it had cooled.

"Why were you at the principal's office?"

"Smoking."

Claire straightened, her arms rigid in front of her, and cold martini dropped onto her fingers.

"*Dope?*"

"Yuk. I'll never smoke that stuff."

Claire eased back into the chair, and lowered her arms.

"Molly, don't smoke."

"We just passed one around. I didn't even in*hale*."

"Whose was it?"

"Belinda's."

"Do you smoke?"

"*Mom.*" Molly lifted her purse from the cushion beside her, the purse filled, bulging. "Want to look?"

"No. No, of course I don't."

"I took a drag and Conway came in. The French teacher. They've got their own lavs. She just likes to catch people. What kind of grown-ups like to do that anyway?"

"Lord knows, sweetie. Not me, anyway. But please don't start, and get hooked."

Molly's smile now was sly, teasing, and they both looked at Claire's cigarette poised over the ashtray, her finger raised to tap ashes.

"Okay," Claire said. "Hell with spaghetti. Want to go out for dinner?"

The dinners, the evenings, and the breakfasts with Stephen were more comfortable than she had expected them to be; were even as comfortable as she had hoped they would be. On the first night, two nights after Claire had talked to Molly, Stephen came to dinner, and Claire was shy. She heard it in her voice too, and felt it in her cheeks, and glimpsed it in Molly's watching eyes. Molly watched them both as the three of them sat in the living room before dinner, and at dinner, and afterward as they lingered at the dining-room table, then as all of them cleared it and filled the dishwasher. But mostly she watched Claire, and Claire remembered Molly years ago watching her put on make-up. For in Molly's eyes now there was that same look of an astute apprentice. And there was a nuance too of collusion, the look of a female roommate who shares dinner with you and your lover before going to a movie, or to her room for the evening. When the kitchen surfaces were clean and the dishes were in the dishwasher, they went to the living room, and as Claire finished her coffee and offered Stephen more cognac, she realized that she did not control the evening; Molly did. For Claire did not have the courage to send her to bed. So, sitting with Stephen on the couch, she kept talking, including Molly, and hearing her own discomfort in her voice, feeling it warming her face. At ten o'clock Molly stood and said goodnight and came to the couch and kissed her. She shook Stephen's hand as he rose and told her goodnight. Then she left them.

Claire did not want to make love, did not want to climb the stairs with Stephen and take him into her bed where she had slept alone since Norman left. On the couch they kissed and touched until the second floor of the house was quiet. Still she kept Stephen on the couch until her passion overcame her; or nearly did; and she led him creeping up the carpeted stairs and down the carpeted hall and into her bedroom, and behind them she eased the door shut, and slowly turned the knob. She had not made love for so long in this bed that she could not remember whether it was audible or silent. It was silent, as silent as the one down the hall, behind the closed door: her daughter's bed she listened for as Molly slept on it or lay awake listening too, imagining, in the darkened knowledge of her bedroom. Then Claire's body surprised her, left her alone with her caution; yet as she came she clamped her teeth on her voice, panted through her nostrils, then held

Stephen to her breasts, and kissed him. At early breakfast, feeding Stephen and Molly before the school bus came to the driveway, she was no longer shy.

That summer Molly celebrated her thirteenth birthday. She and Claire planned a party: after dinner, friends to come for snacks and music, maybe dancing if the boys could be coaxed. Claire and Molly ate dinner in the evening sunlight, the two candles between them: always at dinner Claire burned candles. When they finished dinner Claire went to the kitchen for her coffee and returned to sit with Molly. She lit a cigarette. Then Molly reached across the table for the pack, took a cigarette, tapped it, smiling at Claire; and as Claire watched, with the old cooling fear rising from her calves to her heart, Molly placed the cigarette between her lips, pulled a candle closer, leaned toward it, and drew from its flame—and oh not like an experimenting child with lips curled clumsily inward but with her lips delicately pursed, then she leaned back from the candle, and two fingers gracefully took the cigarette from her mouth and held it beside her cheek as she inhaled.

"Very sexy," Claire said, and heard the bitterness, the angry sense of betrayal in her voice, before she knew it was in her heart too. Molly smiled. Then Claire's bitterness was gone, and the fear too: it was sadness now, and resignation to it.

"Oh shit," she said. "You told me you wouldn't."

"No I didn't. You asked me not to."

"That's true. Well. I guess I can't tell you not to, while I'm sitting here smoking."

"You could. I could keep hiding it."

"How long have you hidden it?"

"Just this summer."

"Why didn't you tell me? When you started."

"I don't know. I guess because I wasn't a teenager yet."

"Jesus."

"What?"

"I don't know." She watched Molly smoke. "I started at thirteen. But it was before the Surgeon General's report."

"Thirteen?"

"It was different. We did it in attics. In basements. We chewed gum so our parents wouldn't know. Cleaned our fingers with lemon juice."

"Would you rather that?"

"No. Aren't you even a little afraid of cancer?"

"No. Are you?"

"I don't think about it. Are you just smoking to look sexy?"

Molly shrugged. "I like it."

Claire did not want to see the cigarette moving again to Molly's lips, but she forced herself to watch. Then she said: "Oh shit. You don't look thirteen anymore."

She pretended not to see Molly's hand coming across the table to touch hers, and she quickly rose with her plate and glass, and her cigarette like steel between her fingers, and hurried to the kitchen before her eyes brimmed and tears trickled on her cheeks. With a dishcloth she dried her face, and when Molly came in with her cigarette and plate and glass, Claire took the plate and glass from her, put them in the sink, and hugged Molly tightly, and rubbed her back, and stroked her hair.

And that was it, the reason for her sorrow; she realized this more deeply at the party that night: Molly did not look thirteen anymore. And it seemed to Claire that all she had shared with Molly until now had been mere words spoken to a child who was still little Molly, lovely Molly, her little girl she loved so much, and wanted to teach as well. Now a simple burning white cylinder between Molly's fingers and lips gave Claire a sense of dread she did not understand. But there it was, each time she looked in on the party of girls and boys in the living room, most of the girls smoking, only two of the boys, and she knew that Molly was the only child who could smoke at home, with her mother, and so now the others could smoke here too. Why so many of the girls, and so few boys? It was becoming a female vice.

She told herself that the dread and sorrow she felt were irrational. Hadn't Molly said she would never smoke dope? She was an intelligent girl, wise enough to see and scornfully

avoid the stoned and perhaps forever ruined lives of the classmates she had talked about with Claire. But when the party
ended and she and Molly picked up the soft-drink bottles,
and emptied ashtrays, and vacuumed pieces and crumbs of
cake and cookies and potato chips, and filled the dishwasher
with glasses and plates, and bowls for dips, and the cake plate,
and wistfully dropped the thirteen candles into the garbage,
she felt that Molly working beside her was more like a grown
daughter visiting home than the girl she had come home to
from work, and had, with love and pride, watched grow: her
young body assuming grace, her mind becoming perceptive
and singular, moving toward a character all her own in its
intellectual and moral solidity. But she knew that, with time,
this sad distance would pass. A night and a day. Two or three
days. And she was able, without willing it, to smile at Molly
when their cleaning was done and they stood in the kitchen,
in the sound of the dishwasher, and to hand Molly a clay ashtray for her room. And at the top of the stairs, when they
kissed goodnight, and Molly went down the hall, with the
ashtray and her Marlboros and red disposable lighter, and
opened her bedroom door, Claire said: "Don't smoke in bed,
sweetie. We could do without a fire."

Molly turned and blew her a kiss. Then Claire went to
bed and lay awake and tried to clear her mind, to empty it so
it could receive, and finally when nothing came she turned on
the bedside lamp and got out of bed and crouched before a
bookshelf at one wall. It held her books from college, and
among the Fs she found the novel she had read twice more
since graduation, and brought it to her bed. It was *The Good
Soldier* by Ford Madox Ford. She knew the passage was near
the end of the book, and that she had long ago underlined it in
ink, and she found it and read it: *Is there then any terrestrial
paradise where, amidst the whispering of the olive-leaves, people can be with whom they like and have what they like and
take their ease in shadows and in coolness?*

TWO

Belinda was blond and her cheeks were pink, her blue eyes glistening, and she was laughing and calling to Molly that she was smoking two cigarettes. Belinda was three feet away, across the long coffee table, sitting on the couch, laughing and pointing at her, and Molly looked at the cigarette between her fingers and then down at the one resting in the ashtray on the table, both of them just lit, and she shrugged and smiled but did not miss a note. She was in love with her voice. Like a precious discovery she had not been looking for, it rose from her diaphragm to her cheekbones, and they tingled; her mouth opened widely and the sound from it was beautiful. She was fifteen and she had sung in the chorale at school. She had sung alone at home, or with her mother, but softly. She had sung loudly with her friends. She had never sung loudly, alone, in front of anyone; and now, though she could hear rock music from the record player across the large basement room, her voice was louder and there were twenty people in the room, and on the couch with Belinda were Dotty and Wanda and Belinda's brother Bruce, a senior, and others were gathering around her: senior girls and boys, and her sopho-more friends. And she knew the songs. She had not known she knew them. She spread her hands outward from her uplifted face, her eyes leaving their faces to focus on the top of the wall, where it joined the ceiling, to focus there on the images of the song: the sad lady alone in her apartment high above a city, holding a drink in a stemmed glass, staring across the darkened room at the window, and beyond it at the lights blinking like a heartbeat:

> "Maybe I won't find someone
> As lovely as youuu
> I should care
> And I dooooo—"

They shouted and clapped and without a pause, her eyes closed now, she swayed and sang:

> "I used to visit all the very gay places
> Those come what may places
> Where one relaxes on the axis of the wheel of life
> To get the feel of life
> from jazz and cocktails—"

She was in their center, yet somewhere above them; beyond her closed eyes she felt their bodies, but as a snake senses body heat; and she felt their spirits drawn into hers, and hers leaving her body, moving in song out of her mouth:

> "I know that if
> I took even one sniff—"

She opened her eyes to their laughter, flipped a hand downward and gestured with upturned palm at the mirror on the table, the razor blade, the straws—

> "It would bore me
> Terrif-ically too—"

She did not want to stop and she could not stop; she danced backward away from the table and couch, spun into the center of the room, spreading her arms. Someone put a can of Budweiser in her hand.

> "—just one of those fabulous flights
> a trip to the moon on gossamer wings—"

She looked at the can, frowned with disdain, held it out and someone took it and gave her a bottle of Dos Equis. She nodded, drank from it, and sang. Bruce was holding her; tall Bruce. He was at her side, his arm around her waist, moving with her, his body with hers, swaying with her melody, his feet moving with hers and her rhythm. She sang "Something Cool" and "Laura" and "Autumn Leaves" and "Moonlight in Vermont." And she kept singing: these songs she had heard on the evenings and nights and weekend mornings and afternoons of her childhood, and she saw her mother's pretty face with the faces in the songs, for all the songs had faces, and Molly's was in them too. Her body was weightless as music and had boundless energy; and everything—the summer night, the party, the people there and herself there, Molly in the basement room and on the earth and in her breath of eternity—was as clear and lovely as a long high note on a trumpet.

She stopped when the songs did. They simply stopped rising inside her. She was not tired. And she did not care whether people had heard too much of her; she did not even consider it. She ended with "It Could Happen to You" and took a cold Dos Equis from an extended hand, a girl's hand, a senior's, and moved with Bruce, his arm at her waist, her body weightless still, her heart racing, through applause and shouts of surprise and delight, to the coffee table, to Belinda beaming at her from the couch, pretty Belinda holding out her arms, standing now, and coming around the coffee table, losing her balance and snatching it back with a quick shift of feet, Belinda hugging her tightly, prying Bruce away, saying at her ear: "God *damn*, Molly."

Belinda moved back, looked at her eyes, kissed her lips.

"You're beautiful. Where did you get those *songs*?"

"My mother's songbook."

"Songbook?" Bruce said. His hand was on her hip, his arm resting across the back of her waist.

"You know. Her records."

"She's a great mom," Belinda said to Bruce.

Wanda and Dotty appeared from behind her. They stood on either side of Belinda. They wanted to know where Molly learned all those songs, and how come they never knew she could sing like that. Wanda was drunk, and the color was leaving her face; she weaved and stared and drank from her bottle of beer, and Molly knew she would be in the bathroom soon, on her knees, hugging the bowl, riding the porcelain bus. Dotty said she had heard that Janis Joplin got started at a party, just like this; Janis hadn't known till then she was such a good singer.

"Me and Southern Comfort," Molly said.

"Smack and death," Bruce said.

"Somebody change the subject," Belinda said.

"Dos Equis," Molly said, and turned away from Bruce to get one, but he said he would, and he left for the ice chest across the room. Time stopped, or sped. She was leaning against a wall with Dotty, and Bruce stood facing them, talking, and Molly saw that he only remembered now and then to look at Dotty; and Wanda had been in the bathroom since she first hurried there a cigarette ago, or two, or an hour. A girl kneeled at the coffee table, bent over the mirror, holding a straw in her nostril and bending farther, following the straw as the white line vanished into it.

"Vanished," Molly said.

"What?" Bruce said.

Molly shrugged. Somehow she knew people were upstairs, in bedrooms. She remembered a girl and boy going up the stairs. Then another girl and boy. And others. In her mind she saw them as clearly as if she were watching them now, across the room, holding each other and climbing the stairs, their faces flushed, their eyes bright and glazed. But she could not place them among her images of the party, could not establish a sequence. The entire night seemed to be in the present, moving in concentric circles. But she felt them up there in the many bedrooms of this house and on the sunporch couch and living-room couch, her spirit cringing yet fascinated as she watched them, her spirit up there in the enchanted forest where demons made vicious love, their faces neither soothed nor ecstatic: they hissed through clamped teeth, and their eyes shone with the vengeful and raging hate of lust. Belinda came from dancing, sweat dripping on her face, as Molly heard her mother's moans through the wall and down the hall to her bedroom door and through it to her ears, her face on her satin-covered pillow; saw her mother's face next morning, lovelier in a different way, private but not secret, as though her cheeks and eyes were nourished by lovemaking, as a flower by the sun. Her lovers' faces looked only comfortable, contented. Belinda said, "My parents should stay in Maine all week. Think of it. Think of the party we'd have."

"Is Wanda still throwing up?" Molly said.

"Wanda? Is she sick?"

Bruce pointed at the end of the room where it became L-shaped; in that leg with the ping-pong table was the bathroom. Belinda said she would go check on her and Molly said Maybe she's upstairs and Bruce smiled and shook his head and said he didn't think so.

"A lot of people upstairs," Molly said to Belinda.

"Wicked," Belinda said, and left them, walked between clustered people, walked slowly, swaying when she had to change direction to skirt a dancing couple or a group standing and drinking. It was strange for Molly to be so drunk yet to see clearly how drunk Belinda was, how much effort she expended on controlling the balance of each step.

"Let's go upstairs," she said to Bruce, and felt in her purse for cigarettes. He leaned to kiss her but she lowered her face, looked into the open box: two cigarettes. "I can't believe this. I came with one open pack and another whole one and I still ran out and Belinda gave me these. Look. I must have smoked fifty cigarettes."

"It's the cocaine."

"What is?"

"You smoke a lot. And you can drink all night."

"No more of that shit."

"You sang too."

"Yes. I sang." He took the cigarette from her and lit it and put it between her lips. "Come on," she said.

She took his hand and, bumped by dancers, led him through the room; she climbed the stairs, pulling him behind her. They would always follow you. She knew that. Their cocks got hard and their faces looked helpless, no matter how they tried to disguise it, and they would follow you anywhere. She had never let any of them follow her to nakedness. No. And she was not a tease. She simply had not let any of them follow her to where they thought they were leading. She emerged from the stairs into the dark kitchen and turned into the living room, dark too; Bruce was beside her now, holding her hand between them. She went down a hall to the stairs, and stopped. Her fingers flicked ashes before she could tell it not to, and with the sole of her shoe she rubbed the carpet and hoped her foot had found the ashes.

"You guys are so rich," she said.

"It doesn't matter."

"I know. Let's go to the woods."

"What woods?"

"Upstairs."

He moved to her front to kiss her, but she stepped around him and pulled him up the stairs. At their top she looked down the dark hall past closed doors. She looked at him and raised a forefinger to her lips and whispered: "They're so quiet." She looked down the hall. "My mother's not. Probably she thinks she is."

"What are we doing?"

"Ssshhh. Whisper."

Holding his hand, she moved down the carpeted hall. The music in the basement room was faint, and she did not know whether she heard its repetitive bass or felt it through the soles of her sneakers. She stopped at the first door and heard nothing but the music and her clandestine breathing, and Bruce's, faster and louder beside her. She went to the next door and flicked ashes again and when she realized it, her foot moved over the carpet. She followed the hall, turning into another wing, past doors closed to silent rooms, and stopped at the master bedroom at the end of the hall. Behind it the mattress was moving, and Bruce whispered: "It's Goldilocks." She wanted to hear a girl's voice from the bed.

"Your parents' room. They shouldn't do it in there."

"Why not? No: I guess you're right."

She caught his wrist as he lifted his arm to knock on the door. She pulled him away, and all down the hall to its corner she listened behind her for a girl's voice. She imagined hissing, in there on the huge bed. She turned into the first wing, hurrying, pulling him; the heat of her cigarette was near her fingers. One of the doors was open now, and she glanced through it at the dark and the bed's silhouette and smelled marijuana smoke. At the top of the stairs she drew him beside her for the descent. She said aloud: "Get me to an ashtray."

Now he led: into the empty living room with its large windows, and he leaned away from her, then an ashtray was in her hand. Her fingers burned as she put out the cigarette. He took the ashtray and put it on a lamp table beside them. Then he was holding her, kissing her with his open mouth, his tongue, and he was hard against her pelvis. Slowly she was moving backward with the pressure of his weight, and when her calves touched the couch she lay on it and held and kissed him as he moved on top of her and mimed lovemaking between her legs that she spread and then lifted around his waist, her sneakers crossed above him. She had done this before and she would do it now with him, let him come against her in his jeans, listen to the soft cries and groans from his throat and receive his weight as he collapsed on her. But he stopped and shifted and was beside her; with closed eyes she saw herself singing, saw the mirror and the line and the straw from her nostril, and Belinda hugging her, and the smoke of fifty cigarettes pluming from her lips, and Wanda's face so pale just before she pushed herself from the wall and into the crowd between her and the bathroom; Bruce unbuttoned her jeans and carefully, slowly, eased down the zipper; she raised her hips and he slid the jeans down to her ankles, then he was off the couch, squatting, working at the laces of her sneakers and taking them off, one at a time, a hand holding her heel; then he pulled off her jeans and laid them on the floor. She waited for his hands to move up her legs for her pants, waited to twist away from them, and to close her thighs. But he rose and, standing on one leg at a time, pulled off his sneakers;

then he unbuckled and unzipped and pushed his jeans down his hips and stepped out of them. His erection was white cotton. He pulled his tee shirt over his head. When his hands touched the waistband of his jockey shorts she turned toward the floor and found her purse on it and lit her last cigarette. She reached to the coffee table for an ashtray and lay on her back again and placed the ashtray on her skin and the front of her bikini pants. She remembered they were pale blue. He lay on his side, at the edge of the couch, the cock pressing her left thigh. She held her cigarette to his lips, then said:

"Can we just lie here?"

"Sure."

But when they finished smoking he moved the ashtray to the floor and kissed her. For a long time he kissed her in the dark and the distant music and low beat from the basement and once the steps and voices of a couple descending the stairs and in the hall and through the dining room and kitchen, music rising through the basement door as they opened it, then they closed it and her sounds again were those of kissing and fast breath, and his hand was gentle on her breasts, under her loose white Mexican blouse. When he pushed it above her breasts she raised her shoulders and head and arms, and for an instant her face was inside its white, then it was gone and she was naked with him, save for her pants. When his hand went there she closed her legs and he kissed and softly sucked her breasts and she opened her legs to his hand, and lifted her hips; he pulled her pants away from her, then pushed them past her knees, and she drew one leg out of them and with that foot she pushed them down and over the other foot. He was on top of her, kissing, hard against her, and she drew back and twisted away.

"I can't."

"Please."

"I can't."

"Why?"

"I don't have anything."

"I do."

"No you don't."

She held him tightly and kissed him and it was touching her again; she moved with it, felt it slip between her lips, and she jerked back from it.

"In my room," he said. "I'll go get one."

"No. I can't. I won't."

"Please. I can't stop."

"Here. Move."

Holding his waist, she tenderly pushed him toward the back of the couch, and she shifted to its edge. When she held the cock, he lay on his back. She kissed him. She had never touched one, and its surface was smooth. She moved her hand up and down and he moaned. Now that she was not afraid, she wanted to give him his pleasure or his release from it; and warmly she kissed him, gently she moved her hand. Then he said: "Molly. Your mouth. Please."

She did not want to and she wanted to and this made her feel her drunkenness again, and the cocaine, and she moved with them, between his legs, and said What if I don't like it? then knew she had not said it aloud and she did not; she lowered her face, her hair falling down her cheeks and forehead, her jaws widening, and she saw a large bird, a swan, eating from the earth; then, as if she were beside the couch, she saw her mouth moving down and up. He squirmed and gasped and moaned, then it twitched: only a tiny spurt of salty liquid, it was nothing and it was over; but then she felt the rush beneath its skin and it convulsed and warm bitter liquid softly slapped the roof of her mouth, and then again, her mouth filled with it and the bitterness of lemon rind; she swallowed and oh shit oh God she had done it, it was in her, and her soul recoiled from her throat, from her heart, and lay soiled and sticky in her stomach while she swallowed again, then did not move. In her mouth it throbbed. She did not move; she kept her face hidden in her soft hair. Then his hands were on her cheeks, her shoulders, and he pulled her up to him, her face to his, and kissed her: her dirty mouth and fouled breath and her soul lying cold beneath her heart. She felt both abused

and unworthy, so she gratefully received his kisses, and wept.
He licked her tears. He was murmuring to her. She was beautiful, she was wonderful. His tongue went from her tears to
her breasts, and he moved, and licked her belly and moved
again and was licking her, she could hear him lapping juice,
his tongue inside her, then on it, oh on it where at night in her
bed and in the morning in her bed and afternoon in her bed
her finger— She moved against and with his tongue and
pressed his hair and head with her hands. Then she heard her
voice, the girl's voice above her with its deep strange cry like a
prayer as she became her climax and her voice grew louder
with its chant: "Oh God —"

In the morning, heat woke her. She was naked and she got up
and turned on the oscillating fan on her bureau at the foot of
her bed, and knew from the angle of sunlight in her room that
it was between eight and nine; as she went to the fan and back
to bed she did not look at the clock. She opened her eyes only
to the sunlight and the fan's switch, and closed them as she
walked to the bed and lay on it and saw through her headache
and nausea the cock in her mouth. His semen was in her blood.
She was nearly asleep again; she had to piss and she tried to
will her bladder to sleep too but it was insistent and now she
was fully awake to the day she did not want to wake to. She
got up and lit a cigarette and went to her bathroom and sat
and sighed and shut her eyes and smoked. Then her bowels
held her there, the Dos Equis leaving her with more solidity
than they had in their bottles, all those bottles she had drunk,
and with a stench that repulsed even her. Pain moved laterally through her stomach, and the next release weakened her,
and her legs quivered. She sat and waited for her body to set
her free so she could sleep, and regain that freedom too, from
her knowledge that she deserved this punishment. Then she
washed her hands and face, and studied its pallor and her dark
eyes for a sign. There was none: only the fatigue in her eyes,
and the drained skin and the expression of painless damage

on her face. Only a hangover. *Gueule de bois*, the French called it. Mug of wood, Mrs. Conway said. Wooden face.

But she wanted a mark: deserved one, had earned one as Dorian Gray earned his. Late one night she had watched the old movie on television, in black and white until he pulled the cover from his portrait and it was in color; and sitting in the dark living room, she had exclaimed in horror; or her flesh had, her body tightening upright in the chair, and sending from her mouth an articulated gasp: *oh*. She rinsed her tooth-brush glass and filled it with water and imagined her photograph on her mother's dresser: that eternal smile when she was fourteen changed by a downward turn of one corner of the mouth. She almost believed it, and felt the picture draw-ing her to her mother's bedroom, to gaze at the grim set of her lips. Then she saw her mother's mouth going down and up on a cock. From a bottle in the medicine cabinet she took three aspirins and swallowed them and gagged, on the tablets or the water, but she held her breath, then slowly released it, and leaning on the sink she told her body to relax, and she did not vomit.

In bed she smoked, to blend the flavor with the taste of toothpaste, to soothe her nerves and heart in their hung-over acceleration. Melted lemon rind in her mother's mouth, in her mother's breath and blood. *You feel like yourself alone among everyone else*, her mother had said. *With your body and your heart*. Then why did she feel like ashes? And not even five feet and four inches and a hundred and twelve pounds of contained ashes, but ashes scattered and blown among others, everywhere and so nowhere, and all that was left on her bed was her soul steeping in bitter semen. She slid her hand under the sheet she had pulled above her hips because even alone in her room she needed to cover her vagina. She closed her eyes to the sound of Bruce licking, to the image of them on the couch; she watched them from above and from the side and a close-up of his tongue on her like in the movie they had gath-ered the courage to rent, the four of them together in the store, and they watched it in Belinda's dark basement, Molly and Belinda and Dotty and Wanda: *They've got to be on drugs. That is sick!* and laughing and joking, then after the movie, in the first moments of dark, the four of them suddenly quiet on the couch, disgust and sorrow spreading like gas from their bodies pressed together, and all at once they each lit a cigarette and Belinda said *I guess nobody wants to suck a cock tonight* and the gas was compressed and released in jets of laughter. Now her finger was helpless against her mind, and she focused again on Bruce's tongue and inhaled from her cigarette as she came, the two pleasures drawing from her the moans she controlled from habit, muted to sighs of smoke.

Now she could sleep. But she took the ashtray to the wastebasket beside her dressing table and emptied it so she would not wake to its smell. She watched the ashes floating down to settle on wads of Kleenex and a crumpled shopping bag; yesterday she had bought music, cassettes in that bag. Yesterday: a Wednesday in summer. She looked at the mirror attached to the table. Not a mark. Even her hymen was in place. How could it be a Thursday you did not want to wake for, and how could you want it to be Wednesday again and buying Rickie Lee Jones, and nothing of those wishes showed, not even in your eyes? Her body was faithless. It only showed eating and colds and flu and the sun. *Yourself alone among everyone else. Your body and your heart.* Bullshit, she said to her eyes in the mirror, and turned from her reflected nakedness and went to bed, drew the sheet to her waist, and in the breeze of the fan, she slept.

Noon light was in her room when she woke. It was on the sheet and her breasts, her face in shadow still. She thought she was nauseated again, then knew it was hunger. She imagined the kitchen and her mother standing in it, and she wanted her mother there to smile at her, kiss her. Kiss her? She had given away her mouth. It would never be the same mouth for her mother; never, never. *If I don't get out of this bed I'm going to cry all afternoon.* Then she let it come, lying on her back, a forearm covering her eyes. When it stopped she was very hungry. She would eat on the sundeck and lie all afternoon in the sun. She would read. Choose a book that would make her forget, for those hours in the sun, last night and today and seeing Bruce tonight; would make her forget even her body, and her name. A book by a woman. She liked Edna O'Brien. She did not always understand the stories, but she loved their music. But she would not spend this afternoon with Edna O'Brien; she wanted the people in the book to have clothes on, and to be outdoors in sunlight.

Her stomach's demand was a childish distraction, and she denied it. She made the bed and gathered last night's clothes from the floor and stuffed them into the wicker basket in her bathroom. She would have to shower tonight to see Bruce, but she showered now for her soul, and when she stepped out of the tub her clean wet skin gave her a portion of hope, like a scent on the breeze. Showers were a delightful mystery: water, soap, water, and some transition occurred, something deeper than clean flesh. Her morning was in the past now. She could dress, move about the house, eat and drink; afternoon was here; night would come. Time had started its motion again, and she could enter it, with interest, with anticipation, and soon—she was sure of it now, as she dried before the steamed mirror and thought of what she would eat—she could enjoy again what time held for her: tonight with Bruce the ocean glittering and blue in the last of the sun, then darkening under the first stars in the fading color of the sky. She put on a maroon bikini bathing suit and went barefoot to her mother's room. The door was open. The bed was made, the windows behind it open to the smell of trees. She did not look at her photograph on the dressing table. She crouched at the bookcase and scanned the spines, then went downstairs. The living room was sunlit, warm; she moved slowly past the large bookcase, looking for a woman's name. But in the Hs she stopped at the five Hemingway books. Her mother had asked her to read *The Old Man and the Sea*, and she had liked it and had cried, last winter with snow. When she was a virgin. She was still a virgin. So last winter when she felt like one. Her mother's favorite was *For Whom the Bell Tolls*, but Molly had not wanted to read it because it was long. But this afternoon was long. She took it from the shelf and went to the kitchen.

Its emptiness felt larger than the room itself. She wanted her mother there. She had not realized how often she thought of her mother as the cheerful and pretty woman in the kitchen. Suddenly the emptiness within the walls shifted, spread out laterally, and extended itself beyond the house and lawn, out into the world, and it drew her with it as powerfully as an undertow. She dropped the book and her cigarettes and lighter on the table and gripped the edge of it. She could feel California beside her, and her father out there, living his morning. With her first tears the room became itself again, walls that contained her and sunlight, and air to breathe. When she stopped crying she said: "Fuck him."

But her words and her voice in the empty kitchen pierced her, and she sat at the table and her face dropped to her folded arms and she cried on her flesh: for having no memory of Norman, for Norman not loving her and not giving her even a memory, and never a visit or a phone call or even a letter; cried on her brown forearm for herself at three kissing her daddy goodbye. Her father. She had no memory of that, but her mother told her she had kissed him, he had held her in his arms and hugged her and she had hugged him around his neck with her little arms and kissed his mouth and said *Bye-bye, Daddy*, and her mother told her she had looked puzzled and frightened but not sad. *And how did he look? Very sad. Did he cry? No; but he never did.* But later she was sad, as days passed and each morning she asked *Where's Daddy?* and her mother told her again he was gone and her mother cried, not for herself, she said, but for Molly. Then it was weeks and she was not eating well and sometimes she was quiet for too long and other times she was ill-tempered and yelled at her mother and struck her. Her father. Norman. How could he leave that little girl and break her heart so soon? And not be here now. To see her. Not to know about last night, not even to know her as her mother did, but to be here with his man's voice and

smells and touch, to look at her with love. She felt the loneliness of one who is not even hated, but worse: ignored; and
she grieved too much for Molly at three to be angry, to hate
him for giving her life, then only three years later turning
away from her and leaving so he could be alone and, having
that, still not giving her himself again, even for a Christmas or
summer visit, not even a voice on the phone to love, an image
of him to keep alive in school and with her friends and here in
this house with her mother. No wonder her mother had never
married again. He had done the same to her. The—. But she
could not curse him again, could not bear the sorrow of it, the
knowledge that he deserved her curse.

   She rubbed her eyes on her forearm, then with her palms
rubbed them again, and her cheeks, and left the table. In the
refrigerator she found slices of ham and a small wheel of Vermont cheddar and made a sandwich. She took it to the sundeck with a Coke instead of the diet cola she had reached for,
had even touched before realizing the comedy of drinking so
many Dos Equis and then a Tab. She nearly smiled, even felt
the beginning of laughter, the first breath of it in her breast.
And it was not just the paradox of debauchery at night and
vanity at noon. Something deeper that she could not define,
could only know: after last night, in today's sun, the weight of
her body, and whether her flesh was taut or flabby, had no
importance at all. She read while she ate and she finished the
sandwich and Coke and wanted a cigarette but they were in
the kitchen and she did not move to get them. Not until she
finished the first chapter, then she put her plate in the dishwasher and her bottle in the carton in the broomcloset and
went out again, into the sun; but it was in Spain, and she was
too, settled in the hammock, smoking, the sun glaring on the
page that became in moments not white paper with black
words but the smells of pine and garlic and tobacco smoke
and wine, and cool dry air high in the hills, and a cave, and a
magnificent ugly woman named Pilar, and a man with a strong
and gentle heart, and a young woman only a few years older
than Molly, a woman whose soul had been wounded too, and

near mortally, through her body too; and the sun and the sky, and wood smoke from the fire in the cave where Molly lived too as her own sun moved in her sky; and between Maria and Robert the sudden and certain feeling that was falling in love. Pausing once, closing the book on her finger, she looked at the sky and saw their embrace in Spain, and death always so near that only the heft and length of the book assured her that it would not come; not yet. She closed her eyes and saw Maria and Robert making love, with death a very part of the air and trees around them, and not even birth control, as though indeed, for the first time in Molly's life, the old saying was true, was as solid and lasting as the large stone among the stand of poplars behind her house, was in fact the absolute and only truth: There's no tomorrow.

Then her own tomorrow, this day after last night's drugged and drunken filth on the couch, moved like this morning's nausea from her loins to her throat. She opened the book. At once, in the sag and scant sway of the hammock, she was in another country with people she loved. Her mother's car climbing the gravel driveway seemed not an intrusion but a sound from within the book, as though it came from a road beneath the hill and the cave. Then it was her mother's car, and the door of it opening and closing, and her mother's steps on the gravel, then silent on grass, and the screen door of the kitchen opening and closing, and steps again on the floor, then her name called into the rooms, the two floors of the house. She left the hammock, looked once more at the book as barefooted she crossed the warm floor of the sundeck, committed to memory the number of the page, and entered the kitchen: the cool of it, the diminished light. Her mother smiled and kissed her.

"*For Whom the Bell Tolls?* Well. Do you like it?"

"I love it."

"Sweetie? Are you all right?"

"No."

"What is it?"

"It's long. Maybe you'd better get your drink."

Her mother studied her face, then reached out, placed her palm on Molly's cheek.

"Okay. I'll get one."

She watched her mother make a gimlet, and she wanted one too, or wanted to want one. She did not want to drink. Leaving Maria and Robert and the hammock had aroused her hangover: the lethargy of her body and the anxiety of her mind, and her stomach's promise that if she swallowed alcohol it would spurt it back up her throat. But she liked the green-tinged color of the gimlet, and the cool and soothing look of the moist glass and ice and wedge of lime, and she wanted its effect: wanted the words for her mother to flow from her, without the fetters of shame. And she did not want to cry. She filled a tall glass with ice, took a Coke from the refrigerator, followed her mother to the couch, and as soon as she could free her hands of glass and bottle, lowering them to the coffee table, she lit a cigarette, and held the lighter for her mother, and felt that this small flame between them was a pact. She looked across the room, out the window at the crest of the wooded hill beyond the road. She heard her mother sip the drink; then her mother leaned forward and put the glass on the table and sat back again, and laid a hand on Molly's thigh.

"Tell me."

"I did coke last night. I've never done it before. I'll never do it again."

Her mother's hand gently patted. Molly saw the trees and hill through mist now; the afternoon was gone, Spain and Maria and Robert and danger were only a book she had been reading; the living room seemed to move in on her, a trick of distance and time, its walls and ceiling and floor shutting her in, severing her from the afternoon in the sun, distorting her memory so all she had felt for and with the people in the book was as distant as an aimless afternoon with friends a year ago. So were this morning's headache, and her humiliation on the toilet, her lust, and sleep again, and the shower. And Bruce was not a grateful boy murmuring *You're beautiful, you're wonderful*, and then in his gratitude and passion giving to her until she cried out in the dark that surrounded the couch. He was only it, in her mouth.

"I—"

Her mother's hand left her thigh, moved to her right shoulder, and the arm pressed her to her mother's body: the side of a breast, and soft flesh over ribs. She smiled against the mist that became droplets on the rims of her eyes.

"I turned into Ella Fitzgerald."

"You sang?"

"Your songs. A lot of them. I didn't even know I knew them." She sighed, and swallowed. The tears did not drip down her cheeks. She blinked, flicked once at each eye with a finger, and there was only mist again. She breathed deeply once and knew that at least she would not cry. She looked into her mother's brown eyes, waiting like calm water for her to float on, or immerse herself in.

"I did fellatio."

The eyes received her; then her mother's flesh did, turning to her, holding her now with both arms, breasts pressing and yielding with hers; then gently the body drew back, the arms slid from her, and she was looking again into her mother's eyes.

"The first time?"

Molly nodded.

"Have you been with a boy before? Made love?"

"No. I would have told you."

"Do you love him?"

"It's Bruce."

Her mother nodded. They turned from each other, smoked, and together their hands descended to the ashtray, flicked ashes, and Molly watched their fingers, her mother's longer, more slender; then she looked at her mother's mouth, her eyes. Her mother's face was so near her own that Molly felt they shared the same air, their lungs synchronized so one exhaled as the other breathed in.

"Do you love him?"

"I don't know."

"It was just cocaine?"

"And beer."

"I mean why you did it."

"The cocaine. Yes. But maybe him too."

"What are you going to do? About him, I mean."

"We're going out tonight. To the beach. For the sunset."

"How is he? With you?"

"I don't know. I guess he's nice. There's just one thing I know. If doing that isn't wrong, then I don't know what is."

"It's my fault."

"Nothing's your fault."

"I'll tell you why it's my fault. If I'm wrong, stop me. Oral sex is—oh shit: I'm sorry I'm embarrassed. It's not you, do you understand? I don't feel *any* differently about you. You're my Molly. Just like yesterday. Always. I'm embarrassed because of what we're talking about, not what you did. You see the difference?"

"I think so."

"Because when I talk to you like this, I'm sharing with you. My own experiences with men. It's all I know. And it makes me blush, that's all. Am I blushing?"

"You were."

"Oral sex. Fellatio, cunnilingus—" Molly felt now the warmth rising to her own cheeks, and saw the recognition in her mother's eyes before they quickly lowered to her cigarette and she drew from it and looked again at Molly. "They're more advanced. God, what a word. They're for lovers. Who are in love with each other. Who need to explore each other. Each other's bodies. Give each other different pleasures. Receive them. There's nothing dirty about it. In the right context. And that's always the people. Just intercourse is dirty— I'm not talking about you, I've done it too, long ago, years ago—it can be dirty when you hardly know each other and you're drunk or—whatever: cocaine, other drugs—anything that makes you silent."

"Silent?"

"The deepest part of you. That wants to complete itself

with another human being. When we silence that part we just become—we *can* just become—our sex organs. Not even our bodies. Just a meaningless desire between our legs. No heart; no brain."

"That's how it was. I think."

"No wonder you feel terrible. And it's my fault, because I should have known it would happen. You *are* a woman, in a lot of ways. Certainly you look like one. So I should have faced it. Faced *you*. I should have gotten you a diaphragm. Because— stop me if I'm wrong—I think you got carried away, you weren't sober, and Bruce is a good-looking boy, and he seems nice—you said he was nice to you?"

"Yes. He was nice."

"Okay. And you went too far, and you couldn't stop, and you were afraid of getting pregnant. So instead of— Instead of *mak*ing love, in the usual way, for a girl and boy, so young, you did the other. And—Molly, it's all good, when the two people are. But it takes a while, sometimes a very long while, for *that* to be good. Because it has to be your idea. Sometime when you know it's time, when you want to do it. Until then, it can be—I guess as awful as it was for you."

"He did it to me too."

"I thought so. And?"

She felt the blush again, and lowered her eyes.

"He was nice."

"Are you going to be his lover?"

"I don't know yet."

"Think about it. If it was just beer and cocaine, make yourself forget it. Like doing something silly you wouldn't do sober. I'm saying forgive yourself."

"I just don't know."

"Are you sure you should see him tonight?"

"I want to. I want to know things."

"What things?"

"About Bruce. Without beer or drugs."

"I think you should wait."

"For what?"

"I want to call Harry and get you fitted for a diaphragm."

"I'm not going to do anything tonight."

"That's easy to say in daylight. At night we change."

"I won't."

"I'll call Harry in the morning."

Molly looked out the window at the trees on the crest of the hill.

"He'll make time for you tomorrow."

"All right."

She was watching a crow perched on a branch near the top of a pine. Something in the book this afternoon: a bird flying.

"I wish you were happy," her mother said. "Not that you should be. Today."

"I will be."

"You're not just saying that?"

"No. I will be."

The crow was restless, watching for something.

"I wouldn't want you on the pill. Or an IUD. I've read too much about them; heard too much."

Molly nodded, and the crow spread its wings and climbed, large and glistening black against the blue sky.

"There used to be a rubber generation. I mean boys carried them. Before the pill. But a diaphragm's better. With the cream. It's—"

"Mom." The crow had risen out of her vision, above the window.

"What?"

She watched the pine tree.

"What's going to happen?"

"I don't know."

"I mean what's going to happen to me?"

"It looks like—I guess you're going to have your first affair."

"My first affair."

"I guess, sweetie."

"Then what?"

"Maybe you'll learn something."

"And then I'll get married."

"Of course you will."

"So did you."

"It'll be different for you."

"Why?"

"You'll know more than I did."

"About sex?"

"About men. About yourself, most of all."

"I'm not off to a good start."

"You don't have to be. You're young. And Molly: this is a shitty time to say it, but I have to. I've let you drink at home. Wine at dinner. A beer sometimes. We even smoked a joint once."

"Twice."

"Twice. I wasn't very good at it."

"Neither am I. I don't smoke it anymore."

"Really? Not since then?"

"No."

"*That* makes me feel good. Since they were yours." Her mother's hand was on Molly's shoulder now, kneading it, and Molly knew from that touch that her mother's voice, when she spoke again, would be friendly, teasing, and it was: "Since you had these *joints* with you."

"That was last year. I smoked for a while. Then I thought it would be fun to turn you on." She looked at her mother, and blinked away the distant light and color of the pine against the sky. "To turn on with you."

"We got awfully hungry."

"It's dumb. A lot of stuff is dumb."

"I hope you mean that."

"Why else would I say it?"

"Sorry. I just want to ask you not to get drunk again. Or stoned, or whatever cocaine does."

"I told you I won't."

"I just have to say it. I know you and your friends drink a few beers."

"That's all. For me. From now on."

Her mother's arm was around her again, hugging, their temples and cheekbones touching, then pressing too.

"You'll be all right, Molly. You're strong. And you're wise. God, I was a silly, shallow little thing at fifteen."

Her mother's face moved back, then she stood and, holding Molly's hands, drew her up from the couch, and kissed her forehead, her eyes, her nose, and then her lips, and with that kiss Molly was inside her mother's mind—or was it only her own?—seeing her lips encircling Bruce's cock, and moving down and up, and sucking.

"And you'll be happy too."

"Yes," Molly said. "I will."

THREE

Molly sat at her dressing table, and when the polish on her fingernails had dried dark pink, she licked a finger and moistened an eyelid, chose the green eyeshadow, and colored her skin. When she finished her other eyelid, she lit a cigarette, then leaned forward and brushed mascara up onto her eyelashes. She squinted and with a finger pushed her lashes upward. She spread dark pink lipstick on her lips, then brushed the skin beneath her cheekbones with blush. She took the cigarette from the ashtray and drew on it, watching in the mirror, and as she returned the cigarette to its notch she looked at the lipstick on its filter. That stain of pink on the fawn tip, and the smoke rising between her face and the mirror that showed her brightened lashes and colored eyelids and, on her dark skin, the diagonal brushstrokes of pink rising to her cheekbones, and her lips like rose petals, made her sit erectly, and take a calm deep breath; and she felt that with the inhaled air, and its scents of cosmetics, and the aroma of cigarette smoke, she breathed an affirmation of her womanhood.

Her straightened back and shoulders pushed her breasts against her tight black shirt, so the button pulled against its hole at her cleavage. She did not wear a brassiere, and her

nipples shaped the soft cotton of the shirt. They were small breasts, but certainly enough; certainly not flat; their proportion to her chest and shoulders and waist was good. *You're beautiful, you're wonderful.* She held the cigarette angling from her closed lips, and placed her hands on the table, tilted her head to the right, and lowered her face, so her black hair moved to her cheek and the corner of her left eye. Slightly she raised her eyes, watching Molly Cousteau in the glass. She withdrew the cigarette a moment before its lengthening ash changed her image from alluring to slovenly. She upturned a bottle of perfume onto her finger, and dabbed it behind her ears and on the arteries on either side of her neck and on the veins of her wrists. For a while longer she looked at herself, and turned her head from left to right to see fully the turquoise-on-silver earrings at her lobes. She was putting her make-up into her leather purse when she heard Bruce's car turning from the road and climbing the gravel driveway. She stood, in long soft leather boots under the tight legs of her jeans. The boots were dark brown, with high heels and toes that were sharply rounded, but not quite western. She went down the hall and stopped at her mother's door. Her mother sat at her dressing table, her back to Molly; she wore a beige dress and high heels and was applying lipstick. She stood and looked at Molly and said: "I'm glad I'm not one of those jealous mothers."

"Are there any?"

"So I've heard."

"Pretty shitty."

"I might not think so if you were a few years older."

"How many?"

The doorbell chimed.

"Ten?" her mother said. "Six? Face it: probably two. The way some of these men are. Is that Bruce?"

"In shining armor. If it's two, why not one?"

"What."

"Years."

"Oh."

"Or none."

"Because," her mother said, crossing the room now, pointing the tube of lipstick at Molly, a smile in her mother's eyes, and her lips mimicking scorn. "Because," she said, stopping, looking down, but with less angle of her neck now; soon, in a year, or two, they would look into each other's eyes. "You are an empty-headed girl. You could not talk to a grown man. You just want to eat junk, and listen to rock music—" But when she said eat junk the smile darted from her eyes, driven out by shame and guilt, and Molly felt them in her own eyes, and quickly said: "And get *stoned*, man; get wasted just all day long. And pop pimples."

Her mother's eyes, and her own, she knew, showed nothing now; but they would, in a second, and here it was and she felt it in her eyes too: the light of jest and merriment. Her mother said, "You're going to the beach? Don't you want to take a sweater? Or your shawl?"

"Maybe the shawl."

"Molly? Speaking of shining armor. Make him stop at a drugstore."

"He already has them."

"He has them." It was not a statement; it seemed to want to be a question, but her mother had controlled it, and was thinking now. Molly could see the images in her mind, hear the questions her mother would not allow to have sound: *If you know that, then he showed you or told you, so why fellatio? Or was it afterward? Did he say next time he would have rubbers? Because you— What did you do afterward? Spit it out? Cry? Get sick?*

"But he won't need them," Molly said.

"Molly."

"I'll be all right."

"I love you."

"I love you too."

"Should I go and tell Bruce hello?"

"No need."

"Give me a kiss, then."

Molly lifted her face and puckered her lips and they kissed, and Molly felt she was kissing from behind glass, not separating their lips but glass between her own heart and breasts.

"Bye-bye," she said.

"Twelve o'clock, sweetie."

As she went down the hall and stairs, she wondered how much she had lost or given away last night, or whether she had given or lost anything at all, and most of all she wondered how long she would feel like scattered pieces that were only contained in one body and soul when she was oblivious: asleep or lying in the sun on the hammock with Maria and Robert in Spain, among the smell of pines and the cool breath of dying in the sunlit air. It was her, not her mother; in her mother's eyes and mouth, in her voice and touch, there was nothing of accusation, or shame, or sorrow. Nothing but love, friendship—and yes: alliance, encouragement—in the face that had nearly wept two years ago when, after the birthday dinner, Molly had taken one of her mother's Winstons, and slowly, calmly, had tapped it and lit it: a performance that had concealed her fear of anger or, worse, ridicule, embarrassment; and Molly did not know that night when she gave in to her impulse, allowed it to become a choice that directed her fingers and lips, and still she did not know whether she was testing their friendship, or showing her trust in it.

Bruce stood looking out at the road, not at the screen, not into the kitchen, and tenderly she knew it was a pose, tenderly because at once she knew that he was not certain she would come to the door, and go with him. She stepped out and they stood on the concrete slab, close yet not touching, though her hands, her arms, started to rise and reach out to embrace him, but they stayed tensely at her sides. Then they spoke, the hello and how are you so tentative that quickly they laughed, with reddening cheeks, and they walked to the car, with between them a space, a foot or two of late-afternoon summer air and light that asserted itself, so Molly wanted to penetrate it, thrust her hand through it. But at the front of the blue Subaru they separated.

The interior of the car began to restore her, to draw back

into her what had been dispersed. For here there was the ritual of pulling the seat belt over her shoulder and across her
hips, watching their four juxtaposed hands pulling straps,
pushing them into buckles; and lighting a cigarette and looking out her window and to the rear as he backed down the long
driveway and paused, then backed into the road and shifted
gears and drove away from the sun; past trees and the dairy
farm, to the river, and east on the road where old trees grew
on the bank, and across the road mowed hills rose to large
houses. She had last seen him in this car, and sitting here in
the passenger seat, with Dotty and Wanda in back, Wanda
drinking a can of ginger ale and saying oh God it was good she
puked, at least she wasn't sick anymore, and if she'd thrown
up like that at home her mother might have heard her, and
come to see if she had the flu or something, and one smell of
her breath and it'd be all over, grounded, probably till she went
to college. And she would never drink that much beer again.
Never. It wasn't worth it. Bruce took her home first, then Dotty,
quietly smoking a joint in the back seat, offering it again and
again to Molly and Bruce, holding it between their shoulders,
but they said no. At Dotty's house he waited at the curb, as he
had at Wanda's, and watched Dotty standing under the lit
porch light and unlocking the door and going inside. Then he
drove to Molly's. But her house should have been first, it was
between his and Dotty's and Wanda's. She was the one, though,
who had taken the front seat. He had not arranged that, had
only said he would drive the three of them home; he had
brought them to the party, so there was nothing there either.

Nothing for any of her friends to see (yet she had chosen
the front seat, and had not spoken when he drove toward
Wanda's); and she thought and hoped there had been nothing
they could see after she and Bruce dressed in the dark and, in
a half-bathroom near the foot of the stairs leading to the bedrooms, she combed her hair and lipsticked her new mouth. Or
perhaps old. For it felt older than she was, older than her time
on earth, as if it had joined the mouths of women long dead,
centuries dead, beyond electric lights and houses, all the way

back to the dark of tents on deserts, beneath skies whose only light was the stars and moon. Bruce waited outside the bathroom door. When she came out, the light from above the mirror struck his face, and she saw her beauty in his humble eyes, his solemn lips. She switched off the light and moved a hand outward from her side in the dark and it met his moving toward her, and tightly their hands joined as they went through the dark and large dining room and through the kitchen, the bass of the music downstairs pulsing in the floor and the soles of her feet. At the door to the stairs they withdrew their hands, and he opened the door and went ahead of her down the stairs, into the light and music and smoke. As she descended, Molly looked over and beyond his shoulders scanning the people below, but she saw only dancers watching each other, and Belinda, with her back to Molly, standing at the couch across the room, talking to a seated girl, probably Wanda, though Molly could see only the girl's arms spread on top of the couch's back, one bare arm on either side of Belinda. She wondered how long she and Bruce had been upstairs. The first face to turn and look at her was a girl's, straightening up from the ice chest on the floor, twisting the cap from a Miller Lite. She was a senior, and Molly did not know her.

"I like your blouse," the girl said. "Your singing too."

"Thank you. I can't really sing. It was the coke."

"I don't do that anymore. It's dangerous shit. I've got a brother-in-law who's married to it. He's married to my sister too. But it's all shit now. You shouldn't do it anymore. You think these are addictive?" She held up her cigarette. "They're nothing. They'll maybe kill you. But my brother-in-law is soup. Babbling soup. My sister does everything: a job, the house, takes care of the kid. One day she'll walk out. When she sees it's all over. No hope. The asshole will be robbing banks soon, to pay for his shit. Maybe they'll shoot him and she can start living again. Jesus. I made a promise. I'd never *think* about them when I'm drinking. I can't take it, you know?"

"Yes."

"She's so *nice*. I'm fucked up. But not her. She's *getting* fucked. You know? It's not *right*. Shit."

Molly bent over the chest and pulled a Dos Equis from the ice. She was in the world again: that was it: you did something, then it was over and you were back in the world. She looked at the girl's face, imagined her sorrow for her sister, imagined the sister coming home from work to a man she had loved, his body and mind and heart and tongue racing about, within the walls of their home with its littered floors. She wanted to embrace the girl. She said: "He'll either get himself cured, or your sister will leave him and marry somebody good."

"That's true. I believe it. It's just waiting for her to do it. That gets me. She doesn't even cry, my sister. When she talks to me. I'll tell you something about coke, though."

"What's that?"

"It doesn't give anybody a good voice. You can really sing. I'm going to the john. How does this stuff make you fat when it doesn't even stay in your body?"

Then she was gone, a pretty brown-haired girl walking with the concentrated steadiness of a drunk, around the corner to the room with the ping-pong table no one was using, and the bathroom where Molly knew there would be people waiting. She turned toward the room, the dancers; she had not felt Bruce close to her since she left the stairs. He was across the room, standing with Belinda at the couch, and yes it was Wanda sitting, smiling, holding a can of ginger ale. So Bruce had gone from the stairs to Belinda. Meaning what? That he was finished with her? Had been the first to hold her naked, and they had— No. He was being cool. She remembered his face in the light when she stepped out of the bathroom. She warily traversed the room to join him: angled from one person or group to another, stopped to talk, to smoke a cigarette, returned once to the chest for another beer, so that when finally she stood near him, with Belinda between them, she believed she had hidden any connections of time and space between her and Bruce, and their absence from the timeless swirl of the party. But Belinda said: "Where've you been?"

"Talking to a girl." She did not look past Belinda at Bruce. "A senior. About her brother-in-law. He's hooked on coke."

"That's Shelley," Bruce said.

Molly asked Wanda if she felt better; Wanda raised the ginger ale and nodded.

"Time for the Cinderellas to go home," Bruce said.

"Is it already?" Belinda said.

"Eleven-thirty. Where's Dotty?"

"I'll get her," Wanda said. "I want to see if I can walk. In case Dad's still watching a ballgame."

"This late?" Molly said.

Wanda pushed herself up from the couch.

"They're playing in California," she said. "I *al*ways check."

So as Wanda and Dotty and Molly approached the car, Molly quickened her last three strides and opened the front door, and Wanda followed Dotty into the back seat. Bruce drove out of the circular driveway and at the road turned right instead of left and Molly said nothing, waited in the sudden and brief quickening of her heart and breath, but Wanda and Dotty said nothing about the turn and the direction Bruce took, did not even give it an instant of divining silence: they kept talking and Dotty laughed at her fingers, said they were too drunk to roll a joint. Then Wanda and Dotty were gone and Bruce was driving to her house and Molly was trying to know what she ought to feel now, alone with him, or trying to feel what she ought to feel, or know what she did feel. She was not sober, and she was shy as with a stranger, and she tried to say something in the silence, and having to try tightened her stomach, and opened her to remorse and yearning. For they ought to be touching, and gentle, and they ought to fill the car with whatever sounds lovers made.

It was Bruce who finally spoke, when he stopped at the top of her driveway and turned off the engine and put his arms around her and kissed her, his lips open but his tongue withheld, a kiss so tender that it felt shy. Then he looked at her and asked if she would like to go to the beach tomorrow, in late evening, when the sun was setting and everyone had gone home and they could walk on it with the seagulls and sandpipers. She said yes and kissed him; a kiss she willed herself to give; yet when she felt and tasted his mouth her tension dissolved and she leaned into him, held him, and for those moments felt what she had wanted to, what she had believed during the quiet ride that she ought to: a yielding of herself to him, to his knowing her, and from his hard chest against her breasts she drew the comfort she was certain now that he gave. Then she went inside and heard his car start and back down over gravel as she climbed the stairs and quietly passed her mother's closed door, and went into her room. Almost at once she slept.

Now in the car with Bruce she sat again in tactile silence, and the car seemed strange too, smelling of an engine in the summer heat, and upholstery, and summer air coming through the windows, for until she actually entered it the car smelled forever in her mind of marijuana and cigarettes and the exhaled odor of beer; last night the windows had been closed; Bruce had said: *You can't open windows when girls are in the back seat.*

"I read all afternoon," she said.

"Really?"

"In the hammock."

"What did you read?"

"*For Whom the Bell Tolls*. Or a lot of it. By Hemingway."

"I know."

"Have you read it?"

"No. We read *A Farewell to Arms*. In English."

"Is it good?"

"It's sad. But it's good."

"I think this one will be sad too. It's so exciting, I can't stop reading it. But I don't understand what's going on."

"Why?"

"It's in Spain. In a civil war. I don't even know when."

"Neither do I."

"They're fighting the fascists."

"That's good."

He climbed up away from the river, through a neighborhood with old trees, toward the highway.

"And there are Communists. And Robert Jordan is an American fighting with them. He's a Spanish teacher. Can you believe it? From University of Montana. Can you see Howell going off to war?"

"I'm trying to."

He entered the three-lane highway and drove northeast; she had never ridden alone with him, on a drive in daylight, and she was relieved when he moved into the middle lane and stayed at fifty-five miles an hour while on both sides cars and trucks passed them.

"I don't know shit about history," she said. "I've never had a history course that got up to World War I."

"Neither have I. The school year ends."

"It's crazy. There was this important war going on, and everybody's ready to *die* for it. Even this American, Robert Jordan. And I don't know anything about it."

"Maybe it doesn't matter."

"Knowing about it? Or that it happened?"

"Knowing about it. It had to be important for the people in it."

She looked out her open window at the green hills and trees, then a dirt-streaked camper passed them, moving across her vision; the rear license plate was from North Carolina.

"Heading to Maine," she said. "Or Canada."

Bruce moved behind the camper, then left the highway and drove toward the sea, and quietly she watched the houses they passed: small yards, shaded by trees, most of them pines, and small houses: a juxtaposition of Americans she knew nothing about, people who were called working people because they did the real work, whatever that was, some fathers mowing lawns, others sitting with beer on their front steps, the wives probably inside cooking the dinners. Someone had told her that blue-collar people ate before six, then drank beer. Their children were on the lawns, with gloves and baseballs or toys, and she believed she could see in their faces some predetermined life, some boundary to their dreams, enclosed as tightly as their bodies were by their lawns and small houses. They were five minutes from the beach, these families, and Molly's notion was that they never went there. That they received the ocean's weather, and its smell too when the wind blew from the east, yet some routine of their lives—work, habit, or something of the spirit—held them at home as surely as it contained their hopes. She had never seen anyone like them at the beach. In the faces of a group of teenagers who stood under a tree and watched her and Bruce passing, she saw a dullness she thought was sculpted by years of television, of parents who at meals and in the evenings had nothing to say to them, nothing to teach them; and breathing now the first salt air coming through her window, she thanked her mother. Then the houses were behind her and on both sides of the car the tall grass of a salt marsh gently swayed, its green darkening in the setting sun, and she touched Bruce's shoulder, squeezed its hard width, and said: "Maybe I'll major in history."

He looked at her, and before he looked at the road again, the relieved expectancy in his eyes reminded her that this touch was their first since last night. She left her hand resting on his shoulder, moving with its motion as he steered.

"I don't know anything," she said. "It's like the whole world started fifteen years ago. My mother told me about Vietnam. And old movies."

"And old songs."

"Oh: those. They were before her time. She likes jazz."

"I've been wanting to tell you something for a long time. I'm sorry your father took off."

"I cursed him today."

"On the phone?"

"I've never talked to him on the phone. I cursed him at the kitchen table."

"What's it like? With just a mother?"

"I don't know. She's all I've ever had. Look, the tide's in."

They crossed a bridge over a tidal stream of rapid blue water moving at the tops of the banks. With her hand on his shoulder he turned north, then east, and parked facing a sand dune. In front of the car he took her hand and they climbed the dune. He was right: the beach was empty save for gulls standing in groups, their tails to the sea, and sandpipers darting across the sand. The surf was high and loud, and washed far up the slope of the beach. Beyond the white foam of the breakers and green of the shallow water the sea was deep blue to the horizon where it met the arcing cover of the sky, a clear and lighter blue. She wished she had remembered to bring her shawl, but her legs in denim and boots were warm; and her face, and her arms and body in the cotton shirt, still held that afternoon's slow burning in the sun, and the cool salt air soothed it. But soon she would be cold.

Holding hands, they descended the dune with short quick steps, then walked toward the surf. Sandpipers flew away from them, low over the beach; the seagulls in their path became restless, walked as a group farther up the beach; one flew ahead of the rest, then a second, and they both landed, but the others walked only far enough to allow Molly and Bruce to pass behind them. At the edge of the surf, where it hissed and spent itself at their feet, Molly shivered. Bruce put his arm around her and held her against his side.

"We should have brought sweatshirts," he said.

"Nobody knows what to wear to the beach."

"In New England, anyway. Let's keep moving."

She put her arm around his waist, and they walked south; his body shielded her from the breeze; in the distance she could see the ferris wheel at Salisbury, where the beach ended at the Merrimack River; in front of them the sandpipers flew and landed, and she said: "What are we doing?"

"Walking on the beach. Getting ready to freeze our asses off. Maybe we'll get hungry."

"I don't even know you."

"Only for eight years."

"Belinda's big brother. You don't know me."

"I know you're a fox."

"For eight years?"

"Three."

"So what are we doing?"

"I don't know."

"In the book. That I was reading this afternoon. They only have three days."

"Who?"

"The lovers."

"Why?"

"He has to blow up a bridge. Probably he'll get killed."

"How does he know that?"

"He doesn't. But he feels it. And a gypsy woman sees it in his hand. If we just had three days I'd know what we were doing. Did I tell you I'm a virgin? If you can call it that now."

"No. But I knew."

She stopped, releasing his waist, and faced him.

"How?" With a new shame now, seeing Shelley at the beer cooler—*I'm fucked up*—and probably she had made love for years, did it all the time with what's-his-name, and Bruce had been with girls like her—*I'm fucked up*—and then last night she had been on the couch, a naked clumsy frightened—

"Hey. Hey, Molly." He held her biceps. "I could just tell, that's all. I was surprised. I mean that you wanted to go upstairs. I thought that's why you wanted to go. And you took *me.* Out of all those guys."

"Was I that shitty?"

"Don't say that. It's—" He looked above her head at the sky, and squinted his eyes against the last of the sun. "Sweet," he said. "You're sweet."

"Really?"

"What do you think I'm here for? Not shitty, Molly. Sweet."

"Is that what you're here for?"

"Jesus. Let's walk back. When that sun goes, we'll freeze."

He turned her and held her on his lee side and they walked north. She watched the rose and gold above the distant pine trees that hid the sun.

"I didn't come out here to make love," she said.

"Maybe I didn't either. Why did you?"

"To see if I wanted to. No. To understand last night. If it was just coke and beer. Can we just—"

Then she watched the sand ahead of their feet and listened to the roaring and smacking waves to her right and looked at the shadows cast now by the dunes. Far beyond them the pines in the sunset were darker; soon the red sky at their crowns would be twilight, the trees black.

"Just what?"

"I don't know. That's what's so bad. I don't know."

"Let's go to one of those beach stores. We'll get sweatshirts. With I Heart New Hampshire or something. Then let's go to Salisbury. Eat. Ride the roller coaster."

"No roller coaster."

"The ferris wheel."

"Okay."

Their sweatshirts were red with a white breaker on the chest and, beneath it, in white block letters: Seabrook Beach, N.H.; in the store, they pulled them over their heads, and when Bruce's hair and face pushed through the collar, he said: "Seabrook Beach, home of the nuclear power plant they can't get built; and if they do there are no—I repeat no—escape routes."

He paid for them, and as they walked to the car he said: "So maybe we just have three days anyway."

"It's not built yet," she said as he drove out of the parking lot: "And if we only had three days we wouldn't need that rubber."

"*What* rubber?"

"In your wallet."

"You didn't see that."

"I didn't have to."

"Holy shit. You know something?"

"What."

"This is the weirdest first date I've ever had in my fucking life."

"Me too," she said. "In my sucking life."

"*Molly*."

She smiled and lit a cigarette, passed it to him, and lit one for herself. She did not know what it was: the darkness spreading in the sky, the headlights now of cars, her hunger for Italian sausage and egg rolls, but now they were all she knew and wanted, those and the ferris wheel circling above the lights and crowd and at its top showing you the white breakers and black sea and the paler dark sky at the horizon; and she felt too a control, a power, new and solid: she could tease him. She could do whatever she wished. When he stopped at a red light she leaned over and kissed him, mouths open, a brief kiss, and she felt she was his girl.

Felt it too with the taste of egg rolls and hot mustard and duck sauce in her mouth as the ferris wheel began its slow circle, and she was warm in her sweatshirt—was any material softer than a new sweatshirt?—and their seat went back and up, Bruce's arm around her shoulders, hers around his waist, tightly there between him and the wood of the seat as they rose above the people in the streets and the six policemen leaning against their motorcycles, and the buildings—bars and short-order restaurants and food and game stands—above the lights, but not beyond the voices of the crowd and the roller coaster's clacking roar and disco music from one of the hurtling rides, and the smells of hot grease and sausage; up to the top of the circle where for moments she saw the sea but not as she knew and loved it. For the breakers were hidden by buildings and there were too many bright lights so all she saw was an expanse of black, too wide and its length forever, without horizon, for with so many lights there was only the low sky above the amusement park. It frightened her, that large black space that was not sea and sky at all, yet she stared at it, as though looking at the night of her death. Then the blackness was gone behind roofs and lighted walls and her legs hung over the street as backward she circled down past the man controlling the wheel, then up again, and as they rose she said to Bruce, loudly over the street voices and the roller coaster and screams from it and the cacophony of music from rides and booths and nightclubs: "Watch the ocean!"

Holding him tightly she watched it with him, her face beneath and parallel to his, and she glanced at his mouth and left eye to see if he saw it too, felt it, but she could not tell, and she looked again at that black space and tried to imagine fish in it, and ships on it, but all she saw was Molly Cousteau, not scattered ashes now, nor ashes drawn back and contained again by flesh and voice, and eyes with vision; but Molly as one tiny ash on the surface of the earth, looking into the depth of the universe, at the face of eternity.

So she told him. Not on the wheel, or when they left it and moved through the crowd on the streets to his car, and not while he slowly drove, changing gears, with the congestion of cars leaving Salisbury, then merging and increasing speed and the spaces between them, stopping once more at a traffic-lighted intersection, before dividing, taking separate roads to the north and south and west, and Bruce reached the highway and its middle lane, and she felt his body relax even as he lit a cigarette and settled in his seat. Felt like his girl again, as she told him of looking at death from the ferris wheel, felt like his girl when he listened, and said he had not felt it on the wheel, had felt only her against him, and her arm behind his waist, and her hand pressing his side, and himself holding her. But he had felt it before. Earlier in the summer, at night, in a strange mood, not sad or depressed or anything like that, but strange, and he wanted to be alone and drove without music to the sea and walked on the beach, at Seabrook, where they had walked at sunset, and he had stood looking at the ocean, at its huge deep blackness coming at him, coming straight to *him* till it stopped on the sand, and he was afraid. Really afraid. And he tried to talk himself out of it, because at first he thought what he feared was something stupid like a sudden tidal wave, the sea rising to take him and pull him away. Or that the sea could actually decide to drown him. That it was alive and could do it if it wanted to, just send in a big wave to knock him down and a current to take him under and out. Then he realized it wasn't drowning. It was that he felt so small. Tiny. And so empty. He tried to remember school, where he did well, and being class president, and having friends all around him. He did not have a girl then but he tried to remember old ones, their faces, the way they smiled at him. But he could not make the girls real so he could feel them, and he could not make school and his friends real, or even Belinda and his parents and his bedroom. So he could not feel himself. Except as that tiny empty breathing thing under stars in the biggest sky he had ever seen, frightened by the sound of the breaking waves and all that black out there. He turned his back on it and walked as quickly as he could over the sand. Only pride, as though he were being watched, kept him from running. On the ride home he played a cassette; the front windows were open, and his speakers were behind the back seat, and he turned the volume all the way up, so the music was louder than the rushing air.

She felt like his girl too when he parked on a country road not far from her house, and unbuckled his seat belt and she unbuckled hers. The car was on grass beside the road and under the branches of trees, and dark woods were on both sides of the road, a different darkness here, a quiet enclosing private dark that turned her to his lips and hands. His hands on her body were slow and as gentle as they could be, with the gearshift and hand brake between them. Then he stopped and pulled off his sweatshirt and she pulled off hers and they tossed them into the back seat. She received his tongue, and his hands unbuttoning her top button, then the next and the next until he reached her waist and she drew in her stomach muscles so he could unbutton the jeans, and with her legs she pushed herself upward so he could pull the zipper down. Then she pushed her jeans beneath her knees, until they stopped, and were crumpled at her feet, lower than the high leather calves of her boots, and she saw herself sitting on a toilet. But then he unbuttoned the lowest button of her shirt and helped her arms out of its sleeves and dropped it onto the back seat, and they embraced above the brake and gearshift, and she heard his side hitting the steering wheel. As they kissed she unbuttoned his shirt, unbuckled his belt, then he opened his door and took off his shirt and was gone, around the front of the car, his brown chest darker than the air above the road, lighter than the trees, as he moved to her door and opened it and with his toes pushed off his sneakers and stepped out of his jeans and scooped them and his shoes from the earth and shoved them behind her seat. Then he was holding the calves of her boots; and slowly still, gently, he turned her toward him, and pulled off one boot at a time and put it on the floor behind her, and lifted her jeans from her ankles and laid them in the back seat. The brake was against her back as he drew her pants down her legs and she watched them, pale in his hand above her, as he dropped them over the seat. He stepped out of his underpants and crouched to enter the car, then murmured something, not a word, only a sound like pain or anguish, a sound more intense than that of mere hurry in the quiet of the trees, and he reached into the back seat, and she listened to his wallet sliding out of denim, then the tearing of foil. Her back was still against the brake, and she said: "How do we —"

"Sit up." His voice was neither aloud nor a whisper: a moan, nearly plaintive, and her heart received it, felt the urgency that consumed him, as if the cock's tumescence drew all of him into it, diminishing his mind and soul to its length and circumference; but her body felt none of this, pinioned in static transition, seated naked, facing the windshield. She turned to watch him standing beside the car and unrolling the rubber, so white in the dark, onto his cock, and she remembered that she liked his waiting for Wanda and Dotty last night to get safely into their homes before he drove away, and she liked his walking between her and the breeze from the sea. Then he ducked and entered the car, bent over her, and he reached down between her legs and raised the lever under the seat and pushed it backward, and now he had space between her and the dashboard. She wanted to kiss him but his hand was between the door and her seat, his breath that of someone at work, and she heard plastic moving in a slot, and the back of the seat angled to the rear, but only a few degrees, and declined she sat and waited while he lifted her calves until her feet in socks pressed the dashboard.

Still he bent over her. Then he pulled her buttocks forward, and the cock touched her. He kissed her breasts. His hands pressed the back of the seat above her shoulders, and she held his swelling biceps, and wanted him now but in her bed, and was about to say: *Outside. On the ground.* So he would not be poised at the top of a push-up and they could lie together, slowly, and with grace; but then it was inside of her. Hard and pushing and she tried to jerk back from the pain but could not move; her hands left his biceps and loosely held his waist, and here it was again, the push against *her*, that small thin part that was her now; his pushes were rapid but still she had an instant to wait for each one's pain, and without seeing or even knowing numbers in her mind she counted, as if her hymen were counting and recording the assaults that would destroy it. The number was five and with that pain was a new one as the cock plunged and reamed, and she tried to move her hips and saw Belinda and Wanda and Dotty in their separate homes, or together in one, with music, and laughing—*No wonder they call it screwing.* Her jaws were tight against the pain, and the sound of it: *oh* and *oh* and *oh* held in her throat till it had the force of a scream. But she did not. Then he was saying it, his voice a boy's, high yet soft: Oh oh oh Molly oh Molly *oh*—

Then his right hand moved down, and he was out of her, holding his cock at its base, and she realized it was the rubber he held, the backflow of semen, and it just took one seed to work its way up and into her womb. Crouched above her, he stepped over her right leg, lost his balance leaving the car, but hopped and drew his other leg across her, then was standing on the grass, holding the rubber still, and in her pain she thought of blood on the seat and she swung her legs out of the car and stood facing him, standing in her socks, her feet pressing down the high and soft wild grass. Slowly he pulled off the rubber and dropped it and she looked at it lying on the grass. She wanted to step toward him and hold him, but her eyes, her face, would not move so she could not, and she looked down at that length of flat white draped over the dark blades. Then she turned to the car and leaned in to her purse on the floor in front of her seat, felt in it for Kleenex but everything she touched was hard or the leather of the purse. She looked over the seat, saw her pants lying on her clothes, and she reached around the seat and picked them up: soft cotton bikinis. They were pink. She stood and looked at Bruce's face: the same as last night when she stepped out of the bathroom and the light shone on him: not joyful or even happy, and not wicked, but humble and solemn. Then with her pants she touched the opening of her pain. Still she looked at his eyes. She dabbed the gentle warm flow; then wiped it, and her hair, and the tops of her inner thighs, but under the cotton they were dry. She looked down at the blood on her pants. Then she turned them and held Bruce's cock, hard still but angling downward, softening even as, with the clean side of her pants, she wiped it, then wiped her hand, and dropped the pants. She looked at them lying near the rubber.

When she looked up at Bruce his eyes and mouth had changed: a nuance of fear, of— Then she knew, or almost knew: something of awe, of responsibility; then she did know, felt it with a certainty as if he had spoken, had told her, or somehow his flesh naked under the dark of the trees had touched her own through the two feet of earth and air between them. He stood at the edge of remorse, and if she did not hold him, she would lightly push him over. He was all of Bruce again, his limp cock returning to him all those parts she had known for years, and perhaps now was loving as well. She stepped forward and tightly held him, her heart weeping but not with sorrow, her body quivering but without passion or fear. She kissed him, and closed her eyes, and breathed through her nose the smell of his face, and a sweetness of wild flowers, and the summer scents of grass and trees.

She would never forget holding him under those trees. The memory of the pain, renewed next morning by the doctor's cold probing and measuring while her mother sat in the waiting room, would fade until she no longer recalled it with the fear and helplessness she had felt that night. By the end of summer it seemed merely a brief and necessary suffering, and she could remember it as one remembers any rite of passage that is physically arduous and whose result is a change of the spirit, of the way one moves in the world. In fall she could laugh about it, talking with Belinda and Wanda and Dotty; mostly she talked to Belinda, though, for she was a virgin still, while Wanda and Dotty had been the first to lose their hymens and had long since lost the boys who broke them. So Molly felt closer to Belinda.

Even with Belinda she could not give words to what she had felt holding Bruce under the trees. She only knew she would never feel it again. Long after she had wept for Maria and Robert, reading in bed on a summer night, she could only think: *There is no Madrid*, but she could not say that to Belinda, or even to Bruce as they lay on her bed after school. His seed flowed from her as she sat on the toilet, and when her mother came home in the evenings Molly wondered if her own face bloomed as her mother's did the morning after a lover. But she never saw it in her face, and did not know whether this meant she was not in love, or whether her face did not change because she rarely came with Bruce, now that they made love; only when he licked her as he had on the couch last summer. But most of the time he did not pause for that, and after a while she pretended to come when he did, and though always she was impassioned on those afternoons and wanted to be naked with him and wanted him in her, she never again felt what she did that summer night when she looked up and saw in his face what he had done to her body forever, the first and last to do it, and then she held him and it was they who had done it, not just him.

On New Year's Eve her mother was at a party and Molly and Bruce were in Molly's bed and at midnight she kissed him and said Happy New Year. Then she knew. She rose from the bed and stood naked at the window and looked down at the snow on the earth, and the bare trees on the lawn. In the fall he would go to college and she would be a junior and she would lose him to a college girl. Then she knew she had always known it, and she closed her eyes and tried to see her and Bruce standing in the grass. From the bed he spoke her name. She still could not see them holding each other, with the rubber and her bloody pants near their feet, her body quivering with his. Bruce's voice gave her another image: a boy she did not even know; but faceless he waited for her, in the halls at school, and some afternoon or night he would lie on her bed and speak her name. Then she saw the others waiting, in high school and college and afterward, and she shivered and opened her eyes to the snow and the dark sky.

She tried to think of something new waiting for her, something that by her sixteenth year she had not done, but all she could imagine was pregnancy and childbirth and being a mother. She shivered again and he told her to get back under the covers. But now she was quietly crying. She would go to the bathroom and finish it there, because he was tender, he was always good to her, he would want to know why she wept, and he would kiss the tears on her cheeks, and kiss her eyes, as he did that night on Belinda's couch. And he would ask why she was sad, and as much as she wanted him to hold her, and to kiss her tears, she would hide them, because she would not be able to tell him. She wished she could. But blinking her eyes and looking once more at the snow, all she saw was her and Bruce in the car under the trees, on what she knew now was the last night of her girlhood, and she had no words to explain it to Bruce, or to herself, so she turned and hurried to the bathroom, switched on its lights, and shut the door and stood in the middle of the room and its brightness that dazzled her eyes, her heart.

ROSE

In memory of Barbara Loden

SOMETIMES, WHEN I SEE people like Rose, I imagine them as babies, as young children. I suppose many of us do. We search the aging skin of the face, the unhappy eyes and mouth. Of course I can never imagine their fat little faces at the breast, or their cheeks flushed and eyes brightened from play. I do not think of them after the age of five or six, when they are sent to kindergartens, to school. There, beyond the shadows of their families and neighborhood friends, they enter the world a second time, their eyes blinking in the light of it. They will be loved or liked or disliked, even hated; some will be ignored, others singled out for daily abuse that, with a few adult exceptions, only children have the energy and heart to inflict. Some will be corrupted, many without knowing it, save for that cooling quiver of conscience when they cheat, when they lie to save themselves, when out of fear they side with bullies or teachers, and so forsake loyalty to a friend. Soon they are small men and women, with our sins and virtues, and by the age of thirteen some have our vices too.

There are also those unforgivable children who never suffer at all: from the first grade on, they are good at school-work, at play and sports, and always they are befriended, and are the leaders of the class. Their teachers love them, and because they are humble and warm, their classmates love them too, or at least respect them, and are not envious because they assume these children will excel at whatever they touch, and have long accepted this truth. They come from all manner of families, from poor and illiterate to wealthy and what passes for literate in America, and no one knows why they are not only athletic and attractive but intelligent too. This is an injustice, and some of us pause for a few moments in our middle-aged lives to remember the pain of childhood, and then we intensely dislike these people we applauded and courted, and we hope some crack of mediocrity we could not see with our young eyes has widened and split open their lives, the home-coming queen's radiance sallowed by tranquilized bitterness, the quarterback fat at forty wheezing up a flight of stairs, and all of them living in the same small town or city neighbor-hood, laboring at vacuous work that turns their memories to those halcyon days when the classrooms and halls, the play-grounds and gymnasiums and dance floors were theirs: the last places that so obediently, even lovingly, welcomed the weight of their flesh, and its displacement of air. Then, with a smile, we rid ourselves of that evil wish, let it pass from our bodies to dissipate like smoke in the air around us, and, freed from the distraction of blaming some classmate's excellence for our childhood pain, we focus on the boy or girl we were, the small body we occupied, watch it growing through the sum-mers and school years, and we see that, save for some strengths gained here, some weaknesses there, we are the same people we first knew as ourselves; or the ones memory allows us to see, to think we know.

People like Rose make me imagine them in those few years their memories will never disclose, except through hearsay: *I was born in Austin. We lived in a garage apartment. When I was two we moved to Tuscaloosa....* Sometimes, when she is drinking at the bar, and I am standing some distance from her and can watch without her noticing, I see her as a baby, on the second or third floor of a tenement, in one of the

Massachusetts towns along the Merrimack River. She would not notice, even if she turned and looked at my face; she would know me, she would speak to me, but she would not know I had been watching. Her face, sober or drunk or on the way to it, looks constantly watched, even spoken to, by her own soul. Or by something it has spawned, something that lives always with her, hovering near her face. I see her in a tenement because I cannot imagine her coming from any but a poor family, though I sense this notion comes from my boyhood, from something I learned about America, and that belief has hardened inside me, a stone I cannot dissolve. Snobbishness is too simple a word for it. I have never had much money. Nor do I want it. No: it's an old belief, once a philosophy, which I've now outgrown: no one born to a white family with adequate money could end as Rose has.

I know it's not true. I am fifty-one years old, yet I cannot feel I am growing older because I keep repeating the awakening experiences of a child: I watch and I listen, I write in my journal, and each year I discover, with the awe of my boyhood, a part of the human spirit I had perhaps imagined, but had never seen or heard. When I was a boy, many of these discoveries thrilled me. Once in school the teacher told us of the men who volunteered to help find the cause of yellow fever. This was in the Panama Canal Zone. Some of these men lived in the room where victims of yellow fever had died; they lay on the beds, on sheets with dried black vomit, breathed and slept there. Others sat in a room with mosquitoes and gave their skin to those bites we simply curse and slap, and they waited through the itching and more bites, and then waited to die, in their agony leaving sheets like the ones that spared their comrades living in the room of the dead. This story, with its heroism, its infinite possibilities for human action, delighted me with the pure music of hope. I am afraid now to research it, for I may find that the men were convicts awaiting execution, or some other persons whose lives were so limited by stronger outside forces that the risk of death to save others could not have, for them, the clarity of a choice made with courage, and in sacrifice, but could be only a weary nod of assent to yet another fated occurrence in their lives. But their story cheered me then, and I shall cling to that. Don't you remember? When first you saw or heard or read about men and women who, in the face of some defiant circumstance, fought against themselves and won, and so achieved love, honor, courage?

I was in the Marine Corps for three years, a lieutenant during a time in our country when there was no war but all the healthy young men had to serve in the armed forces anyway. Many of us who went to college sought commissions so our service would be easier, we would have more money, and we could marry our girlfriends; in those days, a young man had to provide a roof and all that goes under it before he could make love with his girl. Of course there was lovemaking in cars, but the ring and the roof waited somewhere beyond the windshield.

Those of us who chose the Marines went to Quantico, Virginia, for two six-week training sessions in separate summers during college; we were commissioned at graduation from college, and went back to Quantico for eight months of Officers' Basic School; only then would they set us free among the troops, and into the wise care of our platoon sergeants. During the summer training, which was called Platoon Leaders' Class, sergeants led us, harrassed us, and taught us. They also tried to make some of us quit. I'm certain that when they first lined us up and looked at us, their professional eyes saw the ones who would not complete the course: saw in a young boy's stiffened shoulders and staring and blinking eyes the flaw—too much fear, lack of confidence, who knows—that would, in a few weeks, possess him. Just as, on the first day of school, the bully sees his victim and eyes him like a cat whose prey has wandered too far from safety; it is not the boy's puny body that draws the bully, but the way the boy's spirit occupies his small chest, his thin arms.

Soon the sergeants left alone the stronger among us, and focused their energy on breaking the ones they believed would break, and ought to break now, rather than later, in that future war they probably did not want but never forgot. In another platoon, that first summer, a boy from Dartmouth completed the course, though in six weeks his crew-cut black hair turned gray. The boy in our platoon was from the University of Chicago, and he should not have come to Quantico. He was physically weak. The sergeants liked the smaller ones among us, those with short lean bodies. They called them feather merchants, told them You little guys are always tough, and issued them the Browning Automatic Rifle for marches and field exercises, because it weighed twenty pounds and had a cumbersome bulk to it as well: there was no way you could comfortably carry it. But the boy from Chicago was short and thin and weak, and they despised him.

Our platoon sergeant was a staff sergeant, his assistant a buck sergeant, and from the first day they worked on making the boy quit. We all knew he would fail the course; we waited only to see whether he would quit and go home before they sent him. He did not quit. He endured five weeks before the company commander summoned him to his office. He was not there long; he came into the squad bay where he lived and changed to civilian clothes, packed the suitcase and seabag, and was gone. In those five weeks he had dropped out of conditioning marches, forcing himself up hills in the Virginia heat, carrying seventy pounds of gear—probably half his weight—until he collapsed on the trail to the sound of shouted derision from our sergeants, whom I doubt he heard.

When he came to Quantico he could not chin himself, nor do ten push-ups. By the time he left he could chin himself five quivering times, his back and shoulders jerking, and he could do twenty push-ups before his shoulders and chest rose while his small flat belly stayed on the ground. I do not remember his name, but I remember those numbers: five and twenty. The sergeants humiliated him daily, gave him long and colorful ass-chewings, but their true weapon was his own body, and they put it to use. They ran him till he fell, then ran him again, a sergeant running alongside the boy, around and around the hot blacktop parade ground. They sent him up and down the rope on the obstacle course. He never climbed it, but they sent him as far up as he could go, perhaps halfway, perhaps less, and when he froze, then worked his way down, they sent him up again. That's the phrase: *as far up as he could go.*

He should not have come to Virginia. What was he thinking? Why didn't he get himself in shape during the school year, while he waited in Chicago for what he must have known would be the physical trial of his life? I understand now why the sergeants despised him, this weak college boy who wanted to be one of their officers. Most nights they went out drinking, and once or twice a week came into our squad bay, drunk at three in the morning, to turn on the lights and shout us out of our bunks, and we stood at attention and listened to their cheerful abuse. Three hours later, when we fell out for morning chow, they waited for us: lean and tanned and immaculate in their tailored and starched dungarees and spit-shined boots. And the boy could only go so far up the rope, up the series of hills we climbed, up toward the chinning bar, up the walls and angled poles of the obstacle course, up from the grass by the strength of his arms as the rest of us reached fifty, seventy, finally a hundred push-ups.

But in truth he could do all of it, and that is the reason for this anecdote while I contemplate Rose. One night in our fifth week the boy walked in his sleep. Every night we had fire watch: one of us walked for four hours through the barracks, the three squad bays that each housed a platoon, to alert the rest in case of fire. We heard the story next day, whispered, muttered, or spoken out of the boy's hearing, in the chow hall, during the ten-minute break on a march. The fire watch was a boy from the University of Alabama, a football player whose southern accent enriched his story, heightened his surprise, his awe. He came into our squad bay at three-thirty in the morning, looked up and down the rows of bunks, and was about to leave when he heard someone speak. The voice frightened him. He had never heard, except in movies, a voice so pitched by desperation, and so eerie in its insistence. He moved toward it. Behind our bunks, against both walls, were our wall lockers. The voice came from that space between the bunks and lockers, where there was room to stand and dress, and to prepare your locker for inspection. The Alabama boy stepped between the bunks and lockers and moved toward the figure he saw now: someone squatted before a locker, white shorts and white tee shirt in the darkness. Then he heard what the voice was saying. *I can't find it. I can't find it.* He closed the distance between them, squatted, touched the boy's shoulder, and whispered: *Hey, what you looking for?* Then he saw it was the boy from Chicago. He spoke his name, but the boy bent lower and looked under his wall locker. That was when the Alabama boy saw that he was not truly looking: his eyes were shut, the lids in the repose of sleep, while the boy's head shook from side to side, in a short slow arc of exasperation. *I can't find it,* he said. He was kneeling before the wall locker, bending forward to look under it for—what? any of the several small things the sergeant demanded we care for and have with our gear: extra shoelaces, a web strap from a haversack, a metal button for dungarees, any of these things that became for us as precious as talismans. Still on his knees, the boy straightened his back, gripped the bottom of the wall locker, and lifted it from the floor, six inches or more above it, and held it there as he tried to lower his head to look under it. The locker was steel, perhaps six feet tall, and filled with his clothes, boots, and shoes, and on its top rested his packed haversack and helmet. No one in the platoon could have lifted it while kneeling, using only his arms. Most of us could have bear-hugged it up from the floor, even held it there. *Gawd damn,* the fire watch said, rising from his squat; *Gawd damn, lemmee help you with it,* and he held its sides; it was tottering, but still raised. Gently he lowered it against the boy's resistance, then crouched again and, whispering to him, *like to a baby,* he told us, he said: *All rot, now. It'll be all rot now. We'll fin' that damn thing in the mawnin';* as he tried to ease the boy's fingers from the bottom edge of the locker. Finally he pried them, one or two at a time. He pulled the boy to his feet, and with an arm around his waist, led him to his bunk. It was a lower bunk. He eased the boy downward to sit on it, then lifted his legs, covered him with the sheet, and sat down beside him. He rested a hand on the boy's chest, and spoke soothingly to him as he struggled, trying to rise. Finally the boy lay still, his hands holding the top of the sheet near his chest.

We never told him. He went home believing his body had failed; he was the only failure in our platoon, and the only one in the company who failed because he lacked physical strength and endurance. I've often wondered about him: did he ever learn what he could truly do? Has he ever absolved himself of his failure? His was another of the inspiring stories of my youth. Not *his* story so much as the story of his body. I had heard or read much about the human spirit, indomitable against suffering and death. But this was a story of a pair of thin arms, and narrow shoulders, and weak legs: freed from whatever consciousness did to them, they had lifted an unwieldy weight they could not have moved while the boy's mind was awake. It is a mystery I still do not understand.

Now, more often than not, my discoveries are bad ones, and if they inspire me at all, it is only to try to understand the unhappiness and often evil in the way we live. A friend of mine, a doctor, told me never again to believe that only the poor and uneducated and usually drunk beat their children; or parents who are insane, who hear voices commanding them to their cruelty. He has seen children, sons and daughters of doctors, bruised, their small bones broken, and he knows that the children are repeating their parents' lies: they fell down the stairs, they slipped and struck a table. He can do nothing for them but heal their injuries. The poor are frightened by authority, he said, and they will open their doors to a social worker. A doctor will not. And I have heard stories from young people, college students who come to the bar during the school year. They are rich, or their parents are, and they have about them those characteristics I associate with the rich: they look healthy, as though the power of money had a genetic influence on their very flesh; beneath their laughter and constant talk there lies always a certain poise, not sophistication, but confidence in life and their places in it. Perhaps it comes from the knowledge that they will never be stranded in a bus station with two dollars. But probably its source is more intangible: the ambience they grew up in: that strange paradox of being from birth removed, insulated, from most of the world, and its agony of survival that is, for most of us, a day-to-day life; while, at the same time, these young rich children are exposed, through travel and—some of them—culture, to more of the world than most of us will ever see.

Years ago, when the students first found Timmy's and made it their regular drinking place, I did not like them, because their lives were so distant from those of the working men who patronize the bar. Then some of them started talking to me, in pairs, or a lone boy or girl, drinking near my spot at the bar's corner. I began enjoying their warmth, their general cheer, and often I bought them drinks, and always they bought mine in return. They called me by my first name, and each new class knows me, as they know Timmy's, before they see either of us. When they were alone, or with a close friend, they talked to me about themselves, revealed beneath that underlying poise deep confusion, and abiding pain their faces belied. So I learned of the cruelties of some of the rich: of children beaten, girls fondled by fathers who were never drunk and certainly did not smoke, healthy men who were either crazy or evil beneath their suits and briefcases, and their punctuality and calm confidence that crossed the line into arrogance. I learned of neglect: children reared by live-in nurses, by housekeepers who cooked; children in summer camps and boarding schools; and I saw the selfishness that wealth allows, a selfishness beyond greed, a desire to have children yet give them nothing, or very little, of oneself. I know one boy, an only child, whose mother left home when he was ten. She no longer wanted to be a mother; she entered the world of business in a city across the country from him, and he saw her for a weekend once a year. His father worked hard at making more money, and the boy left notes on the door of his father's den, asking for a time to see him. An appointment. The father answered with notes on the boy's door, and they met. Then the boy came to college here. He is very serious, very polite, and I have never seen him with a girl, or another boy, and I have never seen him smile.

So I have no reason to imagine Rose on that old stained carpet with places of it worn thin, nearly to the floor; Rose crawling among the legs of older sisters and brothers, looking up at the great and burdened height of her parents, their capacity, their will to love long beaten or drained from them by what they had to do to keep a dwelling with food in it, and heat in it, and warm and cool clothes for their children. I have only guessed at this part of her history. There is one reason, though: Rose's face is bereft of education, of thought. It is the face of a survivor walking away from a terrible car accident: without memory or conjecture, only shock, and the surprise of knowing that she is indeed alive. I think of her body as shapeless: beneath the large and sagging curve of her breasts, she has such sparse curvature of hips and waist that she appears to be an elongated lump beneath her loose dresses in summer, her old wool overcoat in winter. At the bar she does not remove her coat; but she unbuttons it and pushes it back from her breasts, and takes the blue scarf from her head, shakes her graying brown hair, and lets the scarf hang from her neck.

She appeared in our town last summer. We saw her on the streets, or slowly walking across the bridge over the Merrimack River. Then she found Timmy's and, with money from whatever source, became a regular, along with the rest of us. Sometimes, if someone drank beside her, she spoke. If no one drank next to her, she drank alone. Always screwdrivers. Then we started talking about her and, with that ear for news that impresses me still about small communities, either towns or city neighborhoods, some of us told stories about her. Rumors: she had been in prison, or her husband, or someone else in the family had. She had children but lost them. Someone had heard of a murder: perhaps she killed her husband, or one of the children did, or he or Rose or both killed a child. There was talk of a fire. And so we talked for months, into the fall, then early winter, when our leaves are gone, the reds and golds and yellows, and the trees are bare and gray, the evergreens dark green, and beyond their conical green we have lovely early sunsets. When the sky is gray, the earth is washed with it, and the evergreens look black. Then the ponds freeze and snow comes silently one night, and we wake to a white earth. It was during an early snowstorm when one of us said that Rose worked in a leather factory in town, had been there since she had appeared last summer. He knew someone who worked there and saw her. He knew nothing else.

On a night in January, while a light and pleasant snow dusted the tops of cars, and the shoulders and hats and scarves of people coming into Timmy's, Rose told me her story. I do not know whether, afterward, she was glad or relieved; neither of us has mentioned it since. Nor have our eyes, as we greet each other, sometimes chat. And one night I was without money, or enough of it, and she said *I owe you*, and bought the drinks. But that night in January she was in the state when people finally must talk. She was drunk too, or close enough to it, but I know her need to talk was there before vodka released her. I won't try to record our conversation. It was interrupted by one or both of us going to the bathroom, or ordering drinks (I insisted on paying for them all, and after the third round she simply thanked me, and patted my hand); interrupted by people leaning between us for drinks to bring back to booths, by people who came to speak to me, happy people oblivious of Rose, men or women or students who stepped to my side and began talking with that alcoholic lack of manners or awareness of intruding that, in a neighborhood bar, is not impolite but a part of the fabric of conversation. Interrupted too by the radio behind the bar, the speakers at both ends of the room, the loud rock music from an FM station in Boston.

It was a Friday, so the bar closed at two instead of one; we started talking at eleven. Gradually, before that, Rose had pushed her way down the bar toward my corner. I had watched her move to the right to make room for a couple, again to allow a man to squeeze in beside her, and again for some college girls; then the two men to my left went home, and when someone else wedged his arms and shoulders between the standing drinkers at the bar, she stepped to her right again and we faced each other across the corner. We talked about the bartender (we liked him), the crowd (we liked them: loud, but generally peaceful) and she said she always felt safe at Timmy's because everybody knew everybody else, and they didn't allow trouble in here.

"I can't stand fighting bars," she said. "Those young punks that have to hit somebody."

We talked about the weather, the seasons. She liked fall. The factory was too hot in summer. So was her apartment. She had bought a large fan, and it was so loud you could hear it from outside, and it blew dust from the floor, ashes from ashtrays. She liked winter, the snow, and the way the cold made her feel more alive; but she was afraid of it too: she was getting old, and did not want to be one of those people who slipped on ice and broke a hip.

"The old bones," she said. "They don't mend like young ones."

"You're no older than I am."

"Oh yes I am. And you'd better watch your step too. On that ice," and she nodded at the large front window behind me.

"That's snow," I said. "A light, dry snow."

She smiled at me, her face affectionate, and coquettish with some shared secret, as though we were talking in symbols. Then she finished her drink and I tried to get Steve's attention. He is a large man, and was mixing drinks at the other end of the bar. He did not look our way, so finally I called his name, my voice loud enough to be heard, but softened with courtesy to a tenor. Off and on, through the years, I have tended bar, and I am sensitive about the matter of ordering from a bartender who is making several drinks and, from the people directly in front of him, hearing requests for more. He

heard me and glanced at us and I raised two fingers; he nodded. When I looked at Rose again she was gazing down into
her glass, as though studying the yellow-filmed ice.

"I worry about fires in winter," she said, still looking down.
"Sometimes every night."

"When you're going to sleep? You worry about a fire?"

She looked at me.

"Nearly every night."

"What kind of heat does your building have?"

"Oil furnace."

"Is something wrong with it?"

"No."

"Then—" Steve is very fast; he put my beer and her screwdriver before us, and I paid him; he spun, strode to the cash register, jabbed it, slapped in my ten, and was back with the change.
I pushed a dollar toward him, and he thanked me and was gone,
repeating an order from the other end of the bar, and a rock
group sang above the crowd, a ceiling of sound over the shouts,
the laughter, and the crescendo of juxtaposed conversations.

"Then why are you worried?" I said. "Were you in a fire?
As a child?"

"I was. Not in winter. And I sure wasn't no child. But you
hear them. The sirens. All the time in winter."

"Wood stoves," I said. "Faulty chimneys."

"They remind me. The sirens. Sometimes it isn't even the
sirens. I try not to think about them. But sometimes it's like
they think about me. They do. You know what I mean?"

"The sirens?"

"*No.*" She grabbed my wrist and squeezed it, hard as a
man might; I had not known the strength of her hands. "The
flames," she said.

"The flames?"

"I'm not doing anything. Or I'm at work, packing boxes.
With leather. Or I'm going to sleep. Or right now, just then, we
were talking about winter. I try not to think about them. But
here they come, and I can see them. I feel them. Little flames.
Big ones. Then—"

She released my wrist, swallowed from her glass, and her face changed: a quick recognition of something forgotten. She patted my hand.

"Thanks for the drink."

"I have money tonight."

"Good. Some night you won't, and I will. You'll drink on me."

"Fine."

"Unless you slip on that ice," nodding her head toward the window, the gentle snow, her eyes brightening again with that shared mystery, their luster near anger, not at me but at what we shared.

"Then what?" I said.

"What?"

"When you see them. When you feel the fire."

"My kids."

"No."

"Three kids."

"No, Rose."

"Two were upstairs. We lived on the third floor."

"Please: no stories like that tonight."

She patted my hand, as though in thanks for a drink, and said: "Did you lose a child?"

"Yes."

"In a fire?"

"A car."

"You poor man. Don't cry."

And with her tough thumbs she wiped the beginning of my tears from beneath my eyes, then standing on tiptoe she kissed my cheek, her lips dry, her cheek as it brushed mine feeling no softer than my own, save for her absence of whiskers.

"Mine got out," she said. "I got them out."

I breathed deeply and swallowed beer and wiped my eyes, but she had dried them.

"And it's the only thing I ever did. In my whole fucking life. The only thing I ever did that was worth a shit."

"Come on. Nobody's like that."

"No?"

"I hope nobody is."

I looked at the clock on the opposite wall; it was near the speaker that tilted downward, like those mirrors in stores, so cashiers can watch people between shelves. From the speaker came a loud electric guitar, repeating a series of chords, then two or more frenetic saxophones blowing their hoarse tones at the heads of the drinkers, like an indoor storm without rain. On that clock the time was two minutes till midnight, so I knew it was eleven thirty-eight; at Timmy's they keep the clock twenty minutes fast. This allows them time to give last call and still get the patrons out by closing. Rose was talking. Sometimes I watched her; sometimes I looked away, when I could do that and still hear. For when I listened while watching faces I knew, hearing some of their voices, I did not see everything she told me: I saw, but my vision was dulled, given distance, by watching bearded Steve work, or the blond student Ande laughing over the mouth of her beer bottle, or old gray-haired Lou, retired from his job as a factory foreman, drinking his shots and drafts, and smoking Camels; or the young owner Timmy, in his mid-thirties, wearing a leather jacket and leaning on the far corner of the bar, drinking club soda and watching the hockey game that was silent under the sounds of rock.

But most of the time, because of the noise, I had to look at her eyes or mouth to hear; and when I did that, I saw everything, without the distractions of sounds and faces and bodies, nor even the softening of distance, of time: I saw the two little girls, and the little boy, their pallid terrified faces; I saw their father's big arm and hand arcing down in a slap; in a blow with his fist closed; I saw the five-year-old boy, the oldest, flung through the air, across the room, to strike the wall and drop screaming to the couch against it. Toward the end, nearly his only sounds were screams; he virtually stopped talking, and lived as a frightened yet recalcitrant prisoner. And in Rose's eyes I saw the embers of death, as if the dying of her spirit had come not with a final yielding sigh, but in a blaze of recognition.

It was long ago, in a Massachusetts town on the Merri-

mack River. Her husband was a big man, with strongly mus-
cled arms, and the solid rounded belly of a man who drinks
much beer at night and works hard, with his body, five days a
week. He was handsome, too. His face was always red-
dish-brown from his outdoor work, his hair was thick and
black, and curls of it topped his forehead, and when he wore
his cap on the back of his head, the visor rested on his curls.
He had a thick but narrow mustache, and on Friday and Saturday nights, when they went out to drink and dance, he
dressed in brightly colored pants and shirts that his legs and
torso and arms filled. His name was Jim Cormier, his grandfather Jacques had come from Quebec as a young man, and his
father was Jacques Cormier too, and by Jim's generation the
last name was pronounced *Cormeer*, and he was James. Jim
was a construction worker, but his physical strength and
endurance were unequally complemented by his mind, his
spirit, whatever that element is that draws the attention of
other men. He was best at the simplest work, and would never
be a foreman, or tradesman. Other men, when he worked with
them, baffled him. He did not have the touch: could not be
entrusted to delegate work, to plan, to oversee, and to handle
men. Bricks and mortar and trowels and chalk lines baffled
him too, as did planes and levels; yet, when he drank at home
every night—they seldom went out after the children were
born—he talked about learning to operate heavy equipment.

Rose did not tell me all this at first. She told me the end,
the final night, and only in the last forty minutes or so, when
I questioned her, did she go further back, to the beginning.
Where I start her story, so I can try to understand how two
young people married, with the hope of love—even, in those
days before pandemic divorce, the certainty of love—and
within six years, when they were still young, still in their
twenties, their home had become a horror for their children,
for Rose, and yes: for Jim. A place where a boy of five, and
girls of four and three, woke, lived, and slept in isolation from
the light of a child's life: the curiosity, the questions about
birds, appliances, squirrels and trees and snow and rain, and

the first heart-quickening of love for another child, not a sister or brother, but the boy or girl in a sandbox or on a tricycle at the house down the street. They lived always in darkness, deprived even of childhood fears of ghosts in the shadowed corners of the rooms where they slept, deprived of dreams of vicious and carnivorous monsters. Their young memories and their present consciousness were the tall broad man and his reddening face that shouted and hissed, and his large hands. Rose must have had no place at all, or very little, in their dreams and in their wary and apprehensive minds when they were awake. Unless as a wish: I imagine them in their beds, in the moments before sleep, hoping for Rose to take them in her arms, carry them one by one to the car while the giant slept drunkenly in the bed she shared with him, Rose putting their toys and clothes in the car's trunk, and driving with them far away to a place—what place could they imagine? What place not circumscribed by their apartment's walls, whose very colors and hanging pictures and calendar were for them the dark gray of fear and pain? Certainly, too, in those moments before sleep, they must have wished their father gone. Simply gone. The boy may have thought of, wished for, Jim's death. The younger girls, four and three, only that he vanish, leaving no trace of himself in their home, in their hearts, not even guilt. Simply vanish.

Rose was a silent partner. If there is damnation, and a place for the damned, it must be a quiet place, where spirits turn away from each other and stand in solitude and gaze haplessly at eternity. For it must be crowded with the passive: those people whose presence in life was a paradox; for, while occupying space and moving through it and making sounds in it they were obviously present, while in truth they were not: they witnessed evil and lifted neither an arm nor a voice to stop it, as they witnessed joy and neither sang nor clapped their hands. But so often we understand them too easily, tolerate them too much: they have universality, so we forgive the man who watches injustice, a drowning, a murder, because he reminds us of ourselves, and we share with him the loyal bond of cowardice, whether once or a hundred times we have turned away from another's suffering to save ourselves: our jobs, our public selves, our bones and flesh. And these people are so easy to pity. We know fear as early as we know love, and fear is always with us. I have friends my own age who still cannot say what they believe, except in the most intimate company. Condemning the actively evil man is a simple matter, though we tend not only to forgive but cheer him if he robs banks or Brink's, and outwits authority: those unfortunate policemen, minions whose uniforms and badges and revolvers are, for many of us, a distorted symbol of what we fear: not a fascist state but a Power, a God, who knows all our truths, believes none of our lies, and with that absolute knowledge will both judge and exact punishment. For we see to it that no one absolutely knows us, so at times the passing blue figure of a policeman walking his beat can stir in us our fear of discovery. We like to see them made into dupes by the outlaw.

But if the outlaw rapes, tortures, gratuitously kills, or if he makes children suffer, we hate him with a purity we seldom feel: our hatred has no roots in prejudice, or self-righteousness, but in horror. He has done something we would never do, something we could not do even if we wished it; our bodies would not obey, would not tear the dress, or lift and swing the axe, pull the trigger, throw the screaming child across the room. So I hate Jim Cormier, and cannot understand him; cannot with my imagination cross the distance between myself and him, enter his soul and know how it felt to live even five minutes of his life. And I forgive Rose, but as I write I resist that compassion, or perhaps merely empathy, and force myself to think instead of the three children, and Rose living there, knowing what she knew. She was young.

She is Irish: a Callahan till marriage, and she and Jim were Catholic. Devout Catholics, she told me. By that, she did not mean they strived to live in imitation of Christ. She meant they did not practice artificial birth control, but rhythm, and after their third year of marriage they had three children. They left the Church then. That is, they stopped attending

Sunday Mass and receiving Communion. Do you see? I am not a Catholic, but even I know that they were never truly members of that faith, and so could not have left it. There is too much history, too much philosophy involved, for the matter of faith to rest finally and solely on the use of contraceptives. That was long ago, and now my Catholic friends tell me the priests no longer concern themselves with birth control. But we must live in our own time; Thomas More died for an issue that would have no meaning today. Rose and Jim, though, were not Thomas Mores. They could not see a single act as a renunciation or affirmation of a belief, a way of life. No. They had neither a religion nor a philosophy; like most people I know, their philosophies were simply their accumulated reactions to their daily circumstance, their lives as they lived them from one hour to the next. They were not driven, guided, by either passionate belief or strong resolve. And for that I pity them both, as I pity the others who move through life like scraps of paper in the wind.

With contraception they had what they believed were two years of freedom. There had been a time when all three of their children wore diapers, and only the boy could walk, and with him holding her coat or pants, moving so slowly beside her, Rose went daily to the laundromat, pushing two strollers, gripping a paper grocery bag of soiled diapers, with a clean bag folded in her purse. Clorox rested underneath one stroller, a box of soap underneath the other. While she waited for the diapers to wash, the boy walked among the machines, touched them, watched them, and watched the other women who waited. The oldest girl crawled about on the floor. The baby slept in Rose's lap, or nursed in those days when mothers did not expose their breasts, and Rose covered the infant's head, and her breast, with her unbuttoned shirt. The children became hungry, or tired, or restless, and they fussed, and cried, as Rose called to the boy to leave the woman alone, to stop playing with the ashtray, the soap, and she put the diapers in the dryer. And each day she felt that the other women, even those with babies, with crawling and barely walking children, with two or three children, and one pregnant with a third, had about them some grace, some calm, that kept their voices soft, their gestures tender; she watched them with shame, and a deep dislike of herself, but no envy, as if she had tried out for a dance company and on the first day had entered a room of slender professionals in leotards, dancing like cats, while she clumsily moved her heavy body clad in gray sweat-clothes. Most of the time she changed the diaper of at least one of the children, and dropped it in the bag, the beginning of tomorrow's load. If the baby slept in her stroller, and the older girl and the boy played on the floor, Rose folded the diapers on the table in the laundromat, talking and smoking with the other women. But that was rare: the chance that all three small children could at the same time be peaceful and without need, and so give her peace. Imagine: three of them with bladders and bowels, thirst, hunger, fatigue, and none of them synchronized. Most days she put the hot unfolded diapers in the clean bag and hurried home.

Finally she cried at dinner one night for a washing machine and a dryer, and Jim stared at her, not with anger, or impatience, and not refusal either: but with the resigned look of a man who knew he could neither refuse it nor pay for it. It was the washing machine; he would buy it with monthly payments, and when he had done that, he would get the dryer. He sank posts in the earth and nailed boards across their tops and stretched clotheslines between them. He said in rain or freezing cold she would have to hang the wet diapers over the backs of chairs. It was all he could do. Until he could get her a dryer. And when he came home on those days of rain or cold, he looked surprised, as if rain and cold in New England were as foreign to him as the diapers that seemed to occupy the house. He removed them from the rod for the shower curtain, and when he had cleaned his work from his body, he hung them again. He took them from the arms and back of his chair and laid them on top of others, on a chair, or the edges of the kitchen table. Then he sat in the chair whose purpose he had restored; he drank beer and gazed at the drying diapers, as if

they were not cotton at all, but the whitest of white shades of
the dead, come to haunt him, to assault him, an inch at a time,
a foot, until they won, surrounded him where he stood in
some corner of the bedroom, the bathroom, in the last place
in his home that was his. His *quercençia:* his cool or
blood-smelling sand, the only spot in the bull-ring where he
wanted to stand and defend, to lower his head and wait.

He struck the boy first, before contraception and the
freedom and new life it promised, as money does. Rose was in
the kitchen, chopping onions, now and then turning her face
to wipe, with the back of her wrist, the tears from her eyes.
The younger girl was asleep; the older one crawled between
and around Rose's legs. The boy was three. She had nearly
finished the onions and could put them in the skillet and stop
crying, when she heard the slap, and knew what it was in that
instant before the boy cried: a different cry: in it she heard not
only startled fear, but a new sound: a wail of betrayal, of pain
from the heart. Wiping her hands on her apron, she went
quickly to the living room, into that long and loudening cry, as
if the boy, with each moment of deeper recognition, raised his
voice until it howled. He stood in front of his seated father.
Before she reached him, he looked at her, as though without
hearing footsteps or seeing her from the corner of his blurred
wet vision, he knew she was there. She was his mother. Yet
when he turned his face to her, it was not with appeal: above
his small reddened cheeks he looked into her eyes; and in his,
as tears ran from them, was that look whose sound she had
heard in the kitchen. Betrayal. Accusing her of it, and without
anger, only with dismay. In her heart she felt something fall
between herself and her son, like a glass wall, or a space that
spanned only a few paces, yet was infinite, and she could
never cross it again. Now his voice had attained the howl, and
though his cheeks were wet, his eyes were dry now; or anyway tearless, for they looked wet and bright as pools that
could reflect her face. The baby was awake, crying in her crib.
Rose looked from her son's eyes to her husband's. They were

dark, and simpler than the boy's: in them she saw only the ebb of his fury: anger, and a resolve to preserve and defend it.

"I told him not to," he said.

"Not to what?"

"Climbing on my legs. Look." He pointed to a dark wet spot on the carpet. "He spilled the beer."

She stared at the spot. She could not take her eyes from it. The baby was crying, and the muscles of her legs tried to move toward that sound. Then she realized her son was silent. She felt him watching her, and she would not look at him.

"It's nothing to cry about," Jim said.

"You *slapped* him."

"Not *him*. You."

"Me? That's onions."

She wiped her hands on her apron, brushed her eyes with the back of her wrist.

"Jesus," she said. She looked at her son. She had to look away from those eyes. Then she saw the older girl: she had come to the doorway, and was standing on the threshold, her thumb in her mouth; above her small closed fist and nose, her frightened eyes stared, and she looked as though she were trying not to cry. But, if she was, there could be only one reason for a child so young: she was afraid for her voice to leave her, to enter the room, where now Rose could feel her children's fear as tangibly as a cold draft blown through a cracked windowpane. Her legs, her hips, strained toward the baby's cry for food, a dry diaper, for whatever acts of love they need when they wake, and even more when they wake before they are ready, when screams smash the shell of their sleep. "Jesus," she said, and hurried out of the room where the pain in her son's heart had pierced her own, and her little girl's fearful silence pierced it again; or slashed it, for she felt as she bent over the crib that she was no longer whole, that her height and breadth and depth were in pieces that somehow held together, did not separate and drop to the floor, through it, into the earth itself.

"I should have hit him with the skillet," she said to me, so many years later, after she had told me the end and I had drawn from her the beginning, in the last half-hour of talk.

She could not hit him that night. With the heavy iron skillet, with its hot oil waiting for the onions. For by then something had flowed away from Rose, something of her spirit simply wafting willy-nilly out of her body, out of the apartment, and it never came back, not even with the diaphragm. Perhaps it began to leave her at the laundromat, or in bed at night, at the long day's end not too tired for lust, for rutting, but too tired for an evening of desire that began with dinner and crested and fell and crested again through the hours as they lay close and naked in bed, from early in the night until finally they slept. On the car seat of courtship she had dreamed of this, and in the first year of marriage she lived the dream: joined him in the shower and made love with him, still damp, before they went to the dinner kept warm on the stove, then back to the bed's tossed sheets to lie in the dark, smoking, talking, touching, and they made love again; and, later, again, until they could only lie side by side waiting for their breathing to slow, before they slept. Now at the tired ends of days they took release from each other, and she anxiously slept, waiting for a baby to cry.

Or perhaps it left her between the shelves of a supermarket. His payday was Thursday, and by then the refrigerator and cupboard were nearly empty. She shopped on Friday. Unless a neighbor could watch the children, Rose shopped at night, when Jim was home; they ate early and she hurried to the store to shop before it closed. Later, months after he slapped the boy, she believed his rage had started then, alone in the house with them, changing the baby and putting her in the crib while the other girl and the boy spat and flung food from their highchairs where she had left them, in her race with time to fill a cart with food Jim could afford: she looked at the price of everything she took from a shelf. She did not believe, later, that he struck them on those nights. But there must have been rage, the frightening voice of it; for he was tired, and confused, and overwhelmed by three small people with wills of their own, and no control over the needs of their bodies and their spirits. Certainly he must have yelled; maybe he squeezed an arm, or slapped a rump. When she returned with the groceries, the apartment was quiet: the children slept, and he sat in the kitchen, with the light out, drinking beer. A light from the living room behind him and around a corner showed her his silhouette: large and silent, a cigarette glowing at his mouth, a beer bottle rising to it. Then he would turn on the light and put down his beer and walk past her, to the old car, to carry in the rest of the groceries.

When finally two of the children could walk, Rose went to the supermarket during the day, the boy and girl walking beside her, behind her, away from her voice whose desperate pitch embarrassed her, as though its sound were a sign to the other women with children that she was incompetent, unworthy to be numbered among them. The boy and girl took from shelves cookies, crackers, cereal boxes, cans of vegetables and fruit, sometimes to play with them, but at other times to bring to her, where holding the cart they pulled themselves up on the balls of their feet and dropped in the box, or the can. Still she scolded them, jerked the can or box from the cart, brought it back to its proper place; and when she did this, her heart sank as though pulled by a sigh deeper into her body. For she saw. She saw that when the children played with these things whose colors or shapes drew them so they wanted to sit on the floor and hold or turn in their hands the box or can, they were simply being children whom she could patiently teach, if patience were still an element in her spirit. And that when they brought things to her, to put into the cart, repeating the motions of their mother, they were joining, without fully knowing it, the struggle of the family, and without knowing the struggle that was their parents' lives. Their hearts, though, must have expected praise; or at least an affectionate voice, a gentle hand, to show that their mother did not need what they had brought her. If only there were time: one extra hour of grocery shopping to spend in this gentle instruction.

Or if she had strength to steal the hour anyway, despite the wet and tired and staring baby in the cart. But she could not: she scolded, she jerked from the cart or their hands the things they had brought, and the boy became quiet, the girl sucked her thumb and held Rose's pants as the four of them moved with the cart between the long shelves. The baby fussed, with that unceasing low cry that was not truly crying, only word-less sounds of fatigue. Rose recognized it, understood it, for by now she had learned the awful lesson of fatigue, which as a young girl she had never felt. She knew that it was worse than the flu, whose enforced rest at least left you the capacity to care for someone else, to mutter words of love; but that, healthy, you could be so tired that all you wanted was to lie down, alone, shut off from everyone. And you would snap at your husband, or your children, if they entered the room, probed the solace of your complete surrender to silence and the mattress that seductively held your body. So she under-stood the baby's helpless sounds for *I want to lie in my crib and put my thumb in my mouth and hold Raggedy Ann's dirty old apron and sleep*. The apron was long removed from the doll, and the baby would not sleep without its presence in her hand. Rose understood this, but could not soothe the baby. She could not have soothed her anyway; only sleep could. But Rose could not try, with hugs, with petting, with her softened voice. She was young.

Perhaps her knowledge of her own failures dulled her ears and eyes to Jim after he first struck the boy, and on that night lost for the rest of his life any paternal control he might have exerted in the past over his hands, finally his fists. Because more and more now he spanked them; with a chill Rose tried to deny, a resonant quiver up through her body, she remem-bered that her parents had spanked her too. That all, or prob-ably all, parents spanked their children. And usually it was the father, the man of the house, the authority and judge, and enforcer of rules and discipline the children would need when they reached their teens. But now, too, he held them by the shoulders, and shook their small bodies, the children sometimes wailing, sometimes frighteningly silent, until it seemed their heads would fly across the room then roll to rest on the floor, while he shook a body whose neck had snapped in two like a dried branch. He slapped their faces, and sometimes he punched the boy, who was four, then five, with his fist. They were not bad children; not disobedient; certainly they were not loud. When Jim yelled and shook them, or slapped or punched, they had done no more than they had in the supermarket, where her voice, her snatching from their hands, betrayed her to the other women. So maybe that kept her silent.

But there was more: she could no longer feel love, or what she had believed love to be. On the few nights when she and Jim could afford both a sitter and a nightclub, they did not dance. They sat drinking, their talk desultory: about household chores, about Jim's work, pushing wheelbarrows, swinging a sledgehammer, thrusting a spade into the earth or a pile of gravel or sand. They listened to the music, watched the band, even drummed their fingers on the table dampened by the bottoms of the glasses they emptied like thirsty people drinking water; but they thirsted for a time they had lost. Or not even that: for respite from their time now, and their knowledge that, from one day to the next, year after year, their lives would not change. Each day would be like the one they had lived before last night's sleep; and tomorrow was a certain and already draining repetition of today. They did not decide to sit rather than dance. They simply did not dance. They sat and drank and watched the band and the dancing couples, as if their reason for dancing had been stolen from them while their eyes had been jointly focused on something else.

She could no longer feel love. She ate too much and smoked too much and drank too much coffee, so all day she felt either lethargic from eating or stimulated by coffee and cigarettes, and she could not recall her body as it had once been, only a few years ago, when she was dating Jim, and had played softball and volleyball, had danced, and had run into the ocean to swim beyond the breakers. The ocean was a half-hour away from her home, yet she had not seen it in six years.

Rather than love, she felt that she and Jim only worked together, exhausted, toward a nebulous end, as if they were digging a large hole, wide as a house, deeper than a well. Side by side they dug, and threw the dirt up and out of the hole, pausing now and then to look at each other, to wait while their breathing slowed, and to feel in those kindred moments something of why they labored, of why they had begun it so long ago—not in years, not long at all—with their dancing and lovemaking and finally marriage: to pause and look at each other's flushed and sweating faces with as much love as they could feel before they commenced again to dig deeper, away from the light above them.

On a summer night in that last year, Jim threw the boy across the living room. Rose was washing the dishes after dinner. Jim was watching television, and the boy, five now, was playing on the floor between Jim and the set. He was on the floor with his sisters and wooden blocks and toy cars and trucks. He seldom spoke directly to his father anymore; seldom spoke at all to anyone but his sisters. The girls were too young, or hopeful, or were still in love. They spoke to Jim, sat on his lap, hugged his legs, and when he hugged them, lifted them in the air, talked with affection and laughter, their faces showed a happiness without memory. And when he yelled at them, or shook or spanked them, or slapped their faces, their memory failed them again, and they were startled, frightened, and Rose could sense their spirits weeping beneath the sounds of their crying. But they kept turning to him, with open arms, and believing faces.

"Little flowers," she said to me. "They were like little flowers in the sun. They never could remember the frost."

Not the boy, though. But that night his game with his sisters absorbed him, and for a short while—nearly an hour—he was a child in a home. He forgot. Several times his father told him and the girls to be quiet or play in another room. Then for a while, a long while for playing children, they were quiet: perhaps five minutes, perhaps ten. Each time their voices rose, Jim's command for quiet was abrupt, and each time it was louder. At the kitchen sink Rose's muscles tensed, told her it was coming, and she must go to the living room now, take the children and their blocks and cars and trucks to the boy's bedroom. But she breathed deeply and rubbed a dish with a sponge. When she finished, she would go down to the basement of the apartment building, descend past the two floors of families and single people whose only sounds were music from radios, voices from television, and sometimes children loudly playing and once in a while a quarrel between a husband and wife. She would go into the damp basement and take the clothes from the washing machine, put them in the dryer that Jim was now paying for with monthly installments. Then she heard his voice again, and was certain it was coming, but could not follow the urging of her muscles. She sponged another dish. Then her hands came out of the dishwater with a glass: it had been a jelly jar, and humanly smiling animals were on it, and flowers, and her children liked to drink from it, looked for it first when they were thirsty, and only if it was dirty in the sink would they settle for an ordinary glass for their water, their juice, or Kool-Aid or milk. She washed it slowly, and was for those moments removed; she was oblivious of the living room, the children's voices rising again to the peak that would bring either Jim's voice or his body from his chair. Her hands moved gently on the glass. She could have been washing one of her babies. Her heart had long ago ceased its signals to her; it lay dormant in despair beyond sorrow; standing at the sink, in a silence of her own making, lightly rubbing the glass with the sponge, and her fingers and palms, she did not know she was crying until the tears reached her lips, salted her tongue.

With their wooden blocks, the children were building a village, and a bridge leading out of it to the country: the open spaces of the living-room carpet, and the chairs and couch that were distant mountains. More adept with his hands, and more absorbed too in the work, the boy often stood to adjust a block on a roof, or the bridge. Each time he stood between his father and the television screen, he heard the quick command,

and moved out of the way. They had no slanted blocks, so the
bridge had to end with two sheer walls; the boy wanted to
build ramps at either end, for the cars and trucks to use, and
he had only rectangles and squares to work with. He stood to
look down at the bridge. His father spoke. He heard the voice,
but a few seconds passed before it penetrated his concentration and spread through him. It was too late. What he heard
next was not words, or a roar, but a sustained guttural cry, a
sound that could be either anguish or rage. Then his father's
hands were on him: on him and squeezing his left thigh and
left bicep so tightly that he opened his mouth to cry out in
pain. But he did not. For then he was above his father's head,
above the floor and his sisters, high above the room itself and
near the ceiling he glimpsed; and he felt his father's grip and
weight shifting and saw the wall across the room, the wall
above the couch, so that when finally he made a sound it was
of terror, and it came from him in a high scream he heard as
he hurtled across the room, seeing always the wall, and hearing his own scream, as though his flight were prolonged by
the horror of what he saw and heard. Then he struck it. He
heard that, and the bone in his right forearm snap, and he fell
to the couch. Now he cried with pain, staring at the swollen
flesh where the bone tried to protrude, staring with astonish-
ment and grief at this part of his body. Nothing in his body
had ever broken before. He touched the flesh, the bone
beneath it. He was crying as, in his memory, he had never
cried before, and he not only did not try to stop, as he always
had, with pride, with anger; but he wanted to cry this deeply,
his body shuddering with it, doubling at his waist with it,
until he attained oblivion, invisibility, death. Somehow he
knew his childhood had ended. In his pain, he felt relief too:
now on this couch his life would end.

He saw through tears but more strongly felt his sisters
standing before him, touching him, crying. Then he heard his
mother. She was screaming. And in rage. At his father. He had
never heard her do that, but still her scream did not come to
him as a saving trumpet. He did not want to live to see revenge.

Not even victory. Then he heard his father slap her. Through his crying he listened then for her silence. But her voice grew, its volume filled the world. Still he felt nothing of hope, of vengeance; he had left that world, and lived now for what he hoped and believed would be only a very short time. He was beginning to feel the pain in his head and back and shoulders, his elbows and neck. He knew he would only have to linger a while in this pain, until his heart left him, as though disgorged by tears, and went wherever hearts went. A sister's hand held his, and he squeezed it.

When he was above his father's head, the boy had not seen Rose. But she was there, behind Jim, behind the lifted boy, and she had cried out too, and moved: as Jim regained his balance from throwing the boy, she turned him, her hand jerking his shoulder, and when she could see his face she pounded it with her fists. She was yelling, and the yell was words, but she did not know what they were. She hit him until he pushed her back, hard, so she nearly fell. She looked at his face, the cheeks reddened by her blows, saw a trickle of blood from his lower lip, and charged it: swinging at the blood, the lip. He slapped her so hard that she was sitting on the floor, with no memory of falling, and holding and shaking her stunned and buzzing head. She stood, yelling words again that she could not hear, as if their utterance had been so long coming, from whatever depth in her, that her mind could not even record them as they rushed through her lips. She went past Jim, pushing his belly, and he fell backward into his chair. She paused to look at that. Her breath was deep and fast, and he sat glaring, his breathing hard too, and she neither knew nor cared whether he had desisted or was preparing himself for more. At the bottom of her vision, she saw his beer bottle on the floor beside the chair. She snatched it up, by its neck, beer hissing onto her arm and breast, and in one motion she turned away from Jim and flung the bottle smashing through the television screen. He was up and yelling behind her, but she was crouched over the boy.

She felt again what she had felt in the kitchen, in the

silence she had made for herself while she bathed the glass. Behind and above her was the sound of Jim's fury; yet she stroked the boy's face: his forehead, the tears beneath his eyes; she touched the girls too, their hair, their wet faces; and she heard her own voice: soft and soothing, so soft and soothing that she even believed the peace it promised. Then she saw, beneath the boy's hand, the swollen flesh; gently she lifted his hand, then was on her feet. She stood into Jim's presence again: his voice behind her, the feel of his large body inches from her back. Then he gripped her hair, at the back of her head, and she shook her head but still he held on.

"His *arm's* broken."

She ran from him, felt hair pulling from her scalp, heard it, and ran to her bedroom for her purse but not a blanket, not from the bed where she slept with Jim; for that she went to the boy's, and pulled his thin summer blanket from his bed, and ran back to the living room. Where she stopped. Jim stood at the couch, not looking at the boy, or the girls, but at the doorway where now she stood holding the blanket. He was waiting for her.

"You crazy fucking bitch."

"*What?*"

"The fucking TV. Who's going to buy one? You? You fucking cunt. You've never had a fucking job in your life."

It was madness. She was looking at madness, and it calmed her. She had nothing to say to it. She went to the couch, opening the blanket to wrap around the boy.

"It's the only fucking peace I've *got.*"

She heard him, but it was like overhearing someone else, in another apartment, another life. She crouched and was working the blanket under the boy's body when a fist knocked loudly on the door. She did not pause, or look up. More knocking, then a voice in the hall: "Hey! Everybody all right in there?"

"Get the fuck away from my door."

"You tell me everybody's all right."

"Get the fuck *away.*"

"I want to hear the woman. And the kid."

"You want me to throw you down the fucking stairs?"

"I'm calling the cops."

"Fuck you."

She had the boy in her arms now. He was crying still, and as she carried him past Jim, she kissed his cheeks, his eyes. Then Jim was beside her. He opened the door, swung it back for them. She did not realize until weeks later that he was frightened. His voice was low: "Tell them he fell."

She did not answer. She went out and down the stairs, past apartments; in one of them someone was phoning the police. At the bottom of the stairs she stopped short of the door, to shift the boy's weight in her arms, to free a hand for the knob. Then an old woman stepped out of her apartment, into the hall, and said: "I'll get it."

An old woman with white hair and a face that knew everything, not only tonight, but the years before this too, yet the face was neither stern nor kind; it looked at Rose with some tolerant recognition of evil, of madness, of despair, like a warrior who has seen and done too much to condemn, or even try to judge; can only nod in assent at what he sees. The woman opened the door and held it, and Rose went out, across the small lawn to the car parked on the road. There were only two other cars at the curb; then she remembered that it was Saturday, and had been hot, and before noon she had heard most of the tenants separately leaving for beaches or picnic grounds. They would be driving home now, or stopping to eat. The sun had just set, but most windows of the tenements on the street were dark. She stopped at the passenger door, started to shift the weeping boy's weight, then the old woman was beside her, trying the door, asking for the key. Rose's purse hung from her wrist. The woman's hands went into it, moved in there, came out with the ring of keys, held them up toward the streetlight, and found the one for the car. She opened the door, and Rose leaned in and laid the boy on the front seat. She turned to thank the woman but she was already at the front door of the building, a square back and short body topped by hair like cotton.

Rose gently closed the car door, holding it, making certain it was not touching the boy before she pushed it into place. She ran to the driver's side, and got in, and put the key in the ignition slot. But she could not turn it. She sat in the boy's crying, poised in the moment of action the car had become. But she could not start it.

"Jimmy," she said. "Jimmy, listen. Just hang on. I'll be right back. I can't leave the girls. Do you hear me?"

His face, profiled on the seat, nodded.

"I've got to get them."

She pushed open the door, left the car, closed the door, the keys in her hands, not out of habit this time; no, she clung to them as she might to a tiny weapon, her last chance to be saved. She was running to the building when she saw the flames at her windows, a flare of them where an instant before there had been only lamplight. Her legs now, her body, were weightless as the wind. She heard the girls screaming. Then the front door opened and Jim ran out of it, collided with her, and she fell on her back as he stumbled and sidestepped and tried to regain balance and speed and go around her. Her left hand grabbed his left ankle. Then she turned with his pulling, his weight, and, on her stomach now, she held his ankle with her right hand too, and pulled it back and up. He fell. She dived onto his back, saw and smelled the gasoline can in his hand, and in her mind she saw him going down to the basement for it, and back up the stairs. She twisted it away from his fingers on the handle, and kneeled with his back between her legs, and as he lifted his head and shoulders and tried to stand, she raised the can high with both hands and brought it down, leaning with it, into it, as it struck his skull. For a moment he was still, his face in the grass. Then he began to struggle again, and said into the earth: "Over now. All over."

She hit him three more times, the sounds hollow, metallic. Then he was still, save for the rise and fall of his back. Beneath his other hand she saw his set of car keys. She scooped them from the grass and stood and threw them across the

lawn, whirling now into the screams of the girls, and windows of fire. She ran up the stairs. The white-haired woman
was on the second-floor landing. Rose passed her, felt her following, and the others: she did not know how many, nor who
they were. She only heard them behind her. No one passed
her. She was at the door, trying to turn the knob, while her left
arm and hand pressed hot wood.

"I called the fire department," a man said, behind her in
the hall.

"So did we," a woman said.

Rose was calling to the girls to open the door.

"They can't," another man said. "That's where the fire is."
Then he said: "Fuck this," and pulled her away from the door
where she was turning the knob back and forth and calling
through the wood to the screams from the rear of the apartment, their bedroom. She was about to spring back to the
door, but stopped: the man faced it, then stepped away. She
knew his name, or had known it; she could not say it. He lived
on the second floor; it was his wife who had said *So did we.*
He stepped twice toward the door, then kicked, his leg horizontal, the bottom of his shoe striking the door, and it swung
open, through the flames that filled the threshold and climbed
the doorjambs. The man leaped backward, his forearms covering his face, while Rose yelled to the girls: *We're coming,
we're coming.* The man lowered his head and sprinted forward.
Or it would have been a sprint. Certainly he believed that,
believed he would run through fire to the girls and get them
out. But in his third stride his legs stopped, so suddenly and
autonomously that he nearly fell forward into the fire. Then
he backed up.

"They'll have a net," he said. He was panting. "We'll get
them to jump. We'll get them to a window, and get them
to jump."

A man behind Rose was holding her. She had not known
it till now. Nor had she known she was straining forward. The
man tightly held her biceps. He was talking to her and now

she heard that too, and was also aware that people were moving away, slowly but away, down the hall toward the stairs. He was saying, "You can't. All you'll do is get yourself killed."

Then she was out of his hands, as though his fingers were those of a child, and, with her breath held and her arms shielding her face, and her head down, she was in motion, through the flames and into the burning living room. She did not feel the fire, but even as she ran through the living room, dodging flames, running through them, she knew that very soon she would. It meant no more to her than knowing that she was getting wet in a sudden rain. The girls were standing on the older one's bed, at the far side of the room, holding each other, screaming, and watching their door and the hall beyond it where the fire would come. She filled the door, their vision, then was at the bed and they were crying: *Mommy! Mommy!* She did not speak. She did not touch them either. She pulled the blanket from under them, and they fell onto the bed. Running again, she grabbed the blanket from the younger girl's bed, and went into the hall where there was smoke but not fire yet, and across it to the bathroom where she turned on the shower and held the blankets under the spray. They soaked heavily in her hands. She held her breath leaving the bathroom and exhaled in the girls' room. They were standing again, holding each other. Now she spoke to them. Again, as when she had crouched with them in front of Jimmy, her voice somehow came softly from her. It was unhurried, calm, soothing: she could have been helping them put on snowsuits. They stopped screaming, even crying; they only sniffled and gasped as she wound a blanket around each of them, covering their feet and heads too, then lifted them, pressing one to each breast. Then she stopped talking, stopped telling them that very soon, before they even knew it, they would be safe outside. She turned and ran through smoke in the hall, and into the living room. She did not try to dodge flames: if they were in front of her, she spun and ran backward through them, hugging the girls against each other, so nothing of their bodies would protrude past her back, her

sides; then spun and ran forward again, fearful of an image
that entered her mind, though in an instant she expelled it:
that she would fall with them, into fire. She ran backward
through the door, and her back hit the wall. She bounced off
it; there was fire in the hall now, moving at her ankles, and she
ran, leaping, and when she reached the stairs she smelled the
scorched blankets that steamed around the girls in her arms.
She smelled her burned hair, sensed that it was burning still,
crackling flames on her head. It could wait. She could wait.
She was running down the stairs, and the fire was behind her,
above her, and she felt she could run with her girls all night.
Then she was on the lawn, and her arms took the girls, and a
man wrestled her to the ground and rolled with her, rolled
over and over on the grass. When she stood, someone was
telling her an ambulance would— But she picked up her girls,
unwrapped now, and looked at their faces: pale with terror,
with shock, yes; but no burns. She carried them to the car.

"*No*," she heard. It was a man's voice, but one she did not
know. Not for a few moments, as she laid the girls side by side
on the back seat. Then she knew it was Jim. She was startled,
as though she had not seen him for ten years. She ran around
the car, got behind the wheel, reached over Jimmy, who was
silent now and she thought unconscious until she saw his
eyes staring at the dashboard, his teeth gritting against his
pain. Leaning over his face, she pushed down the latch on his
side. Then she locked her door. It was a two-door car, and
they were safe now and they were going to the hospital. She
started the engine.

Jim was at her window, a raging face, but a desperate one
too, as though standing outside he was locked in a room without air. Then he was motion, on her left, to her front, and he
stood at the middle of the car, slapped his hands onto the
hood, and pushed. He bulged: his arms and chest and reddened face. With all his strength he pushed, and she felt the
car rock backward. She turned on the headlights. The car
rocked forward as he eased his pushing and drew breath.
Then he pushed again, leaning, so all she could see of him was

his face, his shoulders, his arms. The car rocked back and stopped. She pushed the accelerator pedal to the floor, waited two or three seconds in which she either did not breathe or held what breath she had, and watched his face above the sound of the racing engine. Then, in one quick motion, she lifted her foot from the clutch pedal. He was gone as she felt the bumper and grille leap through his resistance. She stopped and looked in the rear-view mirror; she saw the backs of the girls' heads, their long hair; they were kneeling on the seat, looking quietly out the back window. He lay on his back. Rose turned her wheels to the right, as though to back into a parking space, shifted to reverse, and this time without racing the engine, she slowly drove. She did not look through the rear window; she looked straight ahead, at the street, the tenements, the darkening sky. Only the rear tires rolled over him, then struck the curb. She straightened the front wheels and drove forward again. The car bumped over him. She stopped, shifted gears, and backed up: the bump, then the tires hitting the curb. She was still driving back and forth over his body, while beyond her closed windows people shouted or stared, when the sirens broke the summer sky: the higher wail of the police called by the neighbor, and the lower and louder one of the fire engine.

She was in the hospital, and by the time she got out, her three brothers and two sisters had found money for bail. Her parents were dead. Waiting for the trial, she lived with a married sister; there were children in the house, and Rose shied away from them. Her court-appointed lawyer called it justifiable homicide, and the jury agreed. Long before the trial, before she even left the hospital, she had lost the children. The last time she saw them was that night in the car, when finally she took them away: the boy lying on the front seat, his left cheek resting on it as he stared. He did not move while she drove back and forth over his father. She still does not know whether he knew then, or learned it from his sisters. And the two girls kneeling, their chests leaning on the back of the seat, watching their father appear, then vanish as a bump beneath them. They all went to the same foster home. She did not know where it was.

"Thanks for the drinks," she said, and patted my hand. "Next time you're broke, let me know."

"I will."

She adjusted the blue scarf over her hair, knotted it under her face, buttoned her coat, and put on her gloves. She stepped away from the bar, and walked around and between people. I ordered a beer, and watched her go out the door. I paid and tipped Steve, then left the bottle and glass with my coat and hat on the bar, and moved through the crowd. I stepped outside and watched her, a half-block away now. She was walking carefully in the lightly falling snow, her head down, watching the sidewalk, and I remembered her eyes when she talked about slipping on ice. But what had she been sharing with me? Age? Death? I don't think so. I believe it was the unexpected: chance, and its indiscriminate testing of our bodies, our wills, our spirits. She was walking toward the bridge over the Merrimack. It is a long bridge, and crossing it in that open air she would be cold. I was shivering. She was at the bridge now, her silhouette diminishing as she walked on it. I watched until she disappeared.

I had asked her if she had tried to find her children, had tried an appeal to get them back. She did not deserve them, she said. And after the testimony of her neighbors, she knew she had little hope anyway. She should have hit him with the skillet, she said; the first time he slapped the boy. I said nothing. As I have written, we have talked often since then, but we do not mention her history, and she does not ask for mine, though I know she guesses some of it. All of this is blurred; nothing stands out with purity. By talking to social workers, her neighbors condemned her to lose her children; talking in the courtroom, they helped save her from conviction.

I imagine again those men long ago, sitting among mosquitoes in a room, or sleeping on the fouled sheets. Certainly each of them hoped that it was not the mosquito biting his arm, or the bed he slept on, that would end his life. So he hoped for the men in the other room to die. Unless he hoped that it was neither sheets nor mosquitoes, but then he would be hoping for the experiment to fail, for yellow fever to flourish. And he had volunteered to stop it. Perhaps though, among those men, there was one, or even more, who hoped that he alone would die, and his death would be a discovery for all.

The boy from Chicago and Rose were volunteers too. I hope that by now the man from Chicago has succeeded at something—love, work—that has allowed him to outgrow the shame of failure. I have often imagined him returning home a week early that summer, to a mother, to a father; and having to watch his father's face as the boy told him he had failed because he was weak. A trifling incident in a whole lifetime, you may say. Not true. It could have changed him forever, his life with other men, with women, with daughters, and especially sons. We like to believe that in this last quarter of the century, we know and are untouched by everything; yet it takes only a very small jolt, at the right time, to knock us off balance for the rest of our lives. Maybe—and I hope so—the boy learned what his body and will could do: some occurrence he did not have time to consider, something that made him act before he knew he was in action.

Like Rose. Who volunteered to marry; even, to a degree, to practice rhythm, for her Catholic beliefs were not strong and deep, else she could not have so easily turned away from them after the third child, or even early in that pregnancy. So the life she chose slowly turned on her, pressed against her from all sides, invisible, motionless, but with the force of wind she could not breast. She stood at the sink, holding the children's glass. But *then*—and now finally I know why I write this, and what does stand out with purity—she reentered motherhood, and the unity we all must gain against human suffering. This is why I did not answer, at the bar, when she told me she did not deserve the children. For I believe she did, and does. She redeemed herself, with action, and with less than thirty minutes of it. But she could not see that, and still cannot. She sees herself in the laundromat, the supermarket, listlessly drunk in a nightclub where only her fingers on the table moved to the music. I see her young and strong and swift, wrapping the soaked blankets around her little girls, and hugging them to her, and running and spinning and running through the living room, on that summer night when she was touched and blessed by flames.

PREVIOUSLY UNCOLLECTED
STORIES BY ANDRE DUBUS

THE CROSS COUNTRY RUNNER

Of ALL THE FORCES in his life, Paul Ritchey thought that passion and fertility had done him the most harm. He and Jeannie had planned to postpone marriage until they had both earned Master's Degrees. But midway through their senior year at Louisiana State University, after making love for only the second time in three years of dating, Jeannie became pregnant. She found a job, left college, and they were married. Her job would last only until the child was born. Their parents offered to support them while Paul went to graduate school, but knowing that neither her parents or his could afford it, he refused.

So after graduation, with Jeannie still pregnant, he joined the Marine Corps; they would save money, he told Jeannie, and after his service he would go to graduate school. He served three years as a lieutenant and, when released at Camp Pendleton, California, they had four hundred dollars in the bank and three children. Paul got a job teaching English in a high school in San Diego, so they would be near the La Jolla Playhouse, the bullfights in Tijuana, and the sea. He was now in his fourth year of teaching. They were in debt, they could rarely afford plays or bullfights, and they had five children. For two weeks of every month they did not touch each other in bed.

Then on a Monday afternoon in April, Paul quit his job. He had not planned to. He quit because he had just finished his Introduction to Literature class and he was walking across the lawn to the gym, where he would change clothes for his noon run, when Alfred Keith caught up with him. Keith was the principal.

"I'd like you to come to my office," Keith said. "Mrs. Andrews is coming to see me."

Paul did not answer. He looked at Keith: a thin man, approaching fifty; Paul had once remarked to Jeannie that if Keith ever screamed—a really good scream—his jaws and lips might relax and maybe even the veins at his temples would lose their prominence.

"She's worried about Camilla's grades," Keith said.

"Is she? Well, maybe she just ought to worry about Camilla."

"I assume that's her reason for coming."

Paul was looking at the track behind the school and thinking of Camilla Andrews. She had given him a ride home one rainy winter afternoon. Before leaving the school parking lot she had asked him for a light; almost shamefully, he had told her he didn't smoke anymore and didn't carry matches. She had smiled at him: too womanly, too aware of his discomfort. Then she had found matches in her purse. Driving to his house, she had talked to him as if he were another of her boy friends, as if the Mister Ritchey of the classroom was not the real Mister Ritchey at all. He had answered shyly, wishing he could change the conversation to literature. But, afraid she would give him that smile again and go on with her chatting, he hadn't tried. When she let him out at his house, he had been depressed.

"Grades," he said to Keith. "Tell her Camilla should stop bleaching her hair and she shouldn't have an MG and she ought to stay home at night and keep her legs together."

"I hardly think we'll tell her that."

"No, I suppose we won't," Paul said. "All right: I'll be there in a few minutes."

Keith walked back to the school building. When he had gone inside, Paul turned and went to the gym and put on his sweat suit and track shoes. As he stepped onto the cindered track, he thought of Keith and Mrs. Andrews waiting for him in the office. Then he started running.

He had always been a runner: in high school and college he had run the cross-country, in the Marine Corps he was an infantry officer and proudly and mercilessly he ran his platoon over the dusty fire trails at Camp Pendleton. For four years now he had been splitting his teaching day by running two miles at noon. It rarely failed to have a cathartic effect: somewhere after the first half mile, the jarring of his feet would shatter all his thoughts and they would be sloughed off, as if each bead of sweat contained a fragment of thought, of memory.

Finishing the first lap, Paul looked at the back of the school building, half-expecting to see Keith standing at the door and motioning for him. A boy and girl were sitting on the steps, their heads close. Keith would be in his office, his face tightening, his voice nervously high as he tried to explain Paul's absence. In an instant of sorrow he thought of Jeannie, feeding the children their lunch now and not knowing how vulnerable she was, not knowing that he was probably losing his job.

That morning Paul had been waked by a loud irregular pounding, then he heard Jeannie cursing the washing machine. She called it a son of a bitch and a bastard and finally a God-damned son of a bitch. Then she started kicking it again. Paul got out of bed and went to the bathroom, where he had to clean and remove a diaper from the toilet before he could uri-nate. In the kitchen, Jeannie was leaning over the washing machine and manipulating the hoses with both hands. She wore blue jeans and a large sweat shirt which made her appear fat; her short black hair was tousled, and a cigarette hung from her lips.

"What's wrong with it?" he said.

"It won't fill. It just keeps draining."

She released the hoses and faced him and he wished he had enough money so that she would never have to look like this, her face without make-up and swollen from sinus; he wanted her to wake in a large bed and spend half an hour before a mirror while servants prepared breakfast and dressed the children. She was tall and dark-skinned, a Cajun girl, and she had gained only a pound or so with each of her five pregnancies; she had needed the weight, for she was very lean when they had married, and her face was still lovely. But he was afraid her beauty could not stand many more years of low income and pregnancy and, fleetingly, he wondered if the Church would ever change its view on artificial birth control.

"Can we afford to get it fixed?" she said.

"Of course not. But we have to."

"I'm so tired of this."

"So am I," Paul said.

He was standing at the sink, looking through the window at the fog: in another hour or so, it would lift and Jeannie's sinuses would clear.

"And I'm tired of California," he said.

"Then why don't we go home?"

"Because I'd make even less money teaching in Louisiana and we can't afford to move anyway."

"We could sell all this junk and bring the books in a U-Haul. You could get a job as a nightwatchman or something and go to graduate school."

He thought of crossing Arizona and New Mexico and Texas with five children and little cash and an oil-burning Chevrolet that was six years old.

"It wouldn't work," he said.

He sat at the table and she poured him some coffee: a strong, dark-roasted brand which they ordered twice monthly from Louisiana. She lit a cigarette and, watching her, he stood and hurriedly drank his coffee. He had stopped smoking three months before, in January, and now every cup of coffee was a test of his will. He went to the bathroom to shave. The children were stirring in their bedrooms, the two younger ones crying because they were wet.

With the taste of coffee in his mouth and wanting a cigarette, he remembered the day the Surgeon General's report was broadcast and he had sat listening to it, thinking of death before fifty; Jeannie was not interested in the report. That afternoon Paul had given up cigarettes and advised Jeannie to also; she replied that she had committed herself to smoking long before the report and she did not particularly care what finally caused her death, as long as it wasn't violent, and anyway she didn't believe you could bargain with God, trading smoking for ten more years of life. Paul had felt there was something more: that she had grasped some truth which gave her a perspective he did not have. In the weeks following the report, when friends came to their house, Paul watched the men constantly re-lighting and puffing on their new quick-drying pipes, while he (who was proud of shunning pipes and cigars) sat drinking beer and longing for one of the cigarettes which the women enjoyed with bold immoderation. He thought all of them must have the secret, not only Jeannie, and everywhere in the world women were gaily lighting cigarettes while men switched to unsatisfying substitutes.

There was an exception: one young woman, Charlotte Hunt, childless after five years of marriage (she was a legal secretary; her husband worked at a stock exchange), whose ambition was to live in a ranch house at a desert resort. At a party a week after the report Terry, her husband, complained of an irritated tongue; he had been breaking in four pipes during the week. Charlotte ate crackers and dip with every drink.

"I'm afraid to weigh myself," she said to Paul. "I've been stuffing ever since I quit smoking. But it's worth a few pounds—my God, I was smoking two packs a day. The odds were terrible."

Paul looked at her red hair, her shaded eyelids above green eyes, and her mouth closing on another cracker with dip; he glanced at her fine large breasts which babies had never suckled and probably never would, and he thought of her lungs, denied cigarette smoke so they could finally and for a long time breathe desert air. Then he knew the answer. The women were smoking because they were satisfied: they enjoyed reciprocal love, they had borne children. The men—and Charlotte Hunt—wanted longevity; there were things they had not accomplished and they needed time. Smiling at Charlotte, he said:

"Yes. A misfit has to live long enough to stop being a misfit."

She returned his smile.

"Are you talking about me?"

"No," he said, "about myself."

When he was ready to leave the house that morning Jeannie was calling a repair man for the washing machine. She lowered the phone long enough to give him a quick kiss, then he kissed the children at the breakfast table and, wiping milk and egg yolk and toast crumbs from his mouth, he went outside.

The fog was beginning to lift. Paul drove out of the residential section and joined the traffic, his hands and feet and eyes functioning as if they were part of the car, while in his mind he saw Jeannie, her face still without make-up, talking into the phone and sending him off with a tepid kiss.

He passed the drugstore where he had a charge account and thought of the hours he had spent there, looking at paperbacks—reading titles and skimming through pages—while his mind was filled with images of himself standing at the drug counter and, for the first time in his life, buying contraceptives. Once, after their fourth child, he had bought them: for nearly an hour he had pretended to read while he watched the pharmacist, waiting for a time when no one was near the drug counter. Finally he had approached the counter and, in a low voice, asked for them; and even after hurrying from the store, he was afraid some Catholic had seen it all and had recognized him as the man who, every Sunday at eleven o'clock Mass, received Holy Communion.

They had used them for a week, their passion intensified by freedom and joint evil; but each night, after the lovemaking, they lapsed into silent remorse. Then at Sunday Mass Paul had kneeled beside Jeannie, painfully watching others going to the altar rail for Holy Communion, and after Mass he was grateful when Jeannie had said:

"I can't stand it, not going to Communion."

"Neither can I."

They had practiced rhythm ever since: two years of thermometer and chart, anxiety when her period was due, a fifth child, the strain of abstinence, and, perhaps worse, the despairing knowledge that it had never been accurate and probably never would be. So he still couldn't enter a drugstore without thinking longingly of all the accessible contraceptives; often he walked slowly past the counter of foams and jellies, staring, reading brand names.

He stopped at a traffic light. Next to him a sun-tanned blonde in a white Thunderbird was lighting a cigarette. She was not wearing a ring; a girl going to work, he thought, and tonight there would be martinis and steaks and then back to her apartment where she would take her young man to bed. That's what she would be thinking about now, on a foggy Monday morning, drawing on her cigarette and looking at the traffic light. She wouldn't be thinking about her job, for it meant nothing to her: it was something she did so she could buy clothes and make the payments on the Thunderbird.

When the light changed she darted ahead of him and he stomped the accelerator, shifting quickly and reaching an engine-pinging forty miles an hour in second gear before shifting to third. But she was gone. He stopped at the next light and saw her Thunderbird disappearing in the traffic ahead...

Now he was well into his third lap around the track, his leg muscles were warm and eager, his breathing steady; for the first time that day, he approached a degree of peace. He was beginning to forget his morning: in composition class he was forced to teach grammar and spelling, in grammar class he not only had to teach spelling but also try to convince them that grammar was a worthy subject, and in the Introduction to Literature class he tried to teach high school seniors to read. In that class though, he had a good half hour telling them why Hollywood movies were not art. A discussion nearly began; it was like trying to start a fire with green logs: there were small flames, the bark smoldered, but no crackling fire. When the class ended he felt that he had convinced them. Then walking to the gym at noon, he knew they would continue seeing movies, holding hands and eating popcorn, and at home they would watch television. Only the wounded would go into a corner with a book.

He wished he could teach them four or five years later, when they would be ready for him. More than that, he wished he could drive wedge-like into their minds now; but he knew he could not. They were all like Camilla Andrews: they wanted to dance and dress well and be attractive and loved.

By the end of his fourth lap, it was all behind him: the classes and Keith in the office with Mrs. Andrews and being twenty-eight years old and trapped because he had slept with the woman he loved—just running now, no more thinking, as if he were a horse and all he had to do was run and sweat. He got his second wind and increased his pace. When he finished the second mile, he decided to run a third.

He was conscious only of the hot sun on his head and the aching burning muscles in his thighs and calves and now his shoulders and biceps too. His lungs worked desperately. He looked at the cinders in front of his feet, watching in nearly hopeless fascination as one leg strode ahead of the other—and for an instant he thought he couldn't make three miles, not at this pace. But he didn't slow down. His legs kept going and he knew they could take him farther and faster than his lungs wanted to go, farther and faster than he wanted to go. He let them take him.

Halfway through the third mile, his breathing steadied; he moved a hand over his firm waist and chest and felt that he would have a long life. On the final lap he lengthened his stride, breathing hard but well, running happily through the cool air.

Alfred Keith was waiting in the corridor when Paul came in from running; very quietly, he told Paul to come to his office. They went in, Paul following, and Keith sat in the swivel chair behind his desk; he turned the chair sideways so he was profiled to Paul, rarely looking at him.

At first, Paul instinctively stood before the desk, as if he were being reprimanded by a battalion commander. But after a minute or two he sat down. Keith was no battalion commander: his eyes never met Paul's, he kept pausing to light his pipe (he had been a cigarette smoker), and he talked on and on about teacher-parent relationships and teacher-student relationships until Paul didn't know whether he was being admonished or fired. Soon he didn't care. He watched the side of Keith's face and thought of teaching in a college in Louisiana: seminars with students who came to him because they wanted to. Finally Keith turned the chair and looked at him, his voice still controlled but the color of his face changing, reddening, as he said:

"But you wanted to run. Mister Ritchey, I skipped lunch today so I could see Mrs. Andrews. I'm afraid I fail to understand your lack of responsibility."

Then Paul stood up.

"Oh, come on, Keith. Responsibility for what? What the hell did you tell her?"

"Mister Ritchey—"

"—Lies, that's what. And I *refuse* to play that game with a woman who apparently doesn't have an idea in her head, not one moral value—if Camilla's any indication, and I believe she is—"

"Mister Ritchey, I suggest you calm down and—"

"No! Do you really *believe* all these lies? Do you really think all Camilla needs is her mother proofreading for grammar? And spelling too. Good Lord, I forgot spelling. You can't be *that* stupid—"

Keith's face reddened again, then paled, and he stood up and opened his mouth to speak but Paul didn't stop:

"You *must* see Camilla doesn't want to know anything, she just wants to be pretty and have money and a nice uncomplicated life and orgasms that don't make babies—and that's what her mother wants too and all they want from this school is *grades*—"

Then he stopped, shutting his mouth on rushing obscenities; from the other side of the wall he heard the secretary typing.

"I dislike reminding you," Keith said quietly, "that I am the principal of this school. And, as such, I am entitled to a little more—"

"As such you can *shove* it. I resign."

Paul wheeled and strode to the door; he reached it as Keith said:

"Mister Ritchey."

"What?"

"At the moment I couldn't care less if you ever teach here again. But that will pass. I'm aware of your frustrations, we've all been through them at one time or another. I'm also aware of your responsibility to your family. Think it over tonight and give me your decision in the morning."

Paul walked out.

Stopping first to buy a six-pack of beer, he drove to the ocean. He opened a beer and walked on the beach. Near the horizon a ship was headed north. He tried to see what kind it was, but could not. Whatever its type, though, it had a crew: there would be young men who had gone to sea and now wished they had not, older men who longed for a different ship or retirement. But he was free: he could walk on the beach and sip beer, sell his furniture and drive east (he was momentarily uneasy, thinking of his car), work as a night-watchman—perhaps a policeman on a four to midnight shift; police departments were replete with ex-Marines—go to graduate school and for the rest of his life teach college students. He finished the beer and cocked his arm to throw the can into the sea—but paused, thinking of litterbug slogans; then joyfully he threw it into the approaching waves.

He drove home. Jeannie met him at the door, wearing slacks, her face made-up; when he kissed her he smelled perfume. The children came from the back yard and hugged his

legs and shouted to him that one had fallen from a tree, they
wanted a dog, they had seen a fire truck. They all went inside.

Several toys and an open newspaper were on the living
room floor, a broom and dust pan were in the dining room, and
in the kitchen the breakfast and lunch dishes were stacked
unwashed beside the sink. Paul said nothing and tried to keep
the disapproval from his face; since their fifth child he had
learned to accept two choices: coming home to a pretty wife
and happy children or to a clean house. When the house was
clean and orderly Jeannie and the children were usually tense,
for she would have to scold them, keeping them out of her
way, making them pick up toys. Today she had probably spent
time with them—reading to them, watching them perform—
and then finished the book she had started the night before.

While he was opening two cans of beer and putting the
others in the refrigerator Jeannie told him the repair man
had come and the washing machine was fixed and it would
cost twenty-two dollars and eighty cents.

"For crying out loud," he said.

He looked out the window at the blue sky and flowered
lawns and felt utterly alone and far from home, like a fugitive
standing in a final afternoon of freedom with the knowledge
that telephones and office intercoms were at that moment
transmitting instructions for his capture.

"It comes at a bad time," he said.

Then he sent the children outside to play and took Jeannie to the living room and told her. She listened quietly, fre-
quently drinking her beer. Paul had expected her to be excited,
but her face showed nothing; when he finished she said:

"Well, I'm glad."

"Are you really? You sound worried."

"Naturally I'm worried but I'm glad too, if you're going to
be happy."

"Don't you think I did the right thing?"

"Yes. When do we leave?"

"I haven't thought about it."

She finished her beer and went to the kitchen for another

one. Then she sat on the couch and, looking at the carpet, she said:

"Was he going to fire you anyway?"

"I don't think so. But I just couldn't take anymore of that crap. I *had* to resign."

Now she looked at him.

"I know. Oh, I hope you can get your degree in Louisiana so you can teach college where you belong."

"I'll get it."

"Do you think the car will make the trip?"

"It'll have to."

"Shouldn't we borrow a little so we'll have something to hold us over until you get a job?"

"I don't know. We could."

"You work that out," she said. "I'll start figuring what we can take in a U-Haul. And I should put an ad in the paper and see if we can sell the rest. Maybe we can scrape up enough cash to buy some old furniture when we get home."

"We probably can. Where are your cigarettes?"

"Are you starting again?"

"No. I just need one now."

"Here."

"Course it's not too late," he said. "Keith *did* say I could think it over."

"You couldn't crawl back to that idiot."

"I wouldn't want to. But if you're worried—"

"I'm happy here and I'll be happy in Louisiana too. Do what *you* want to do, whatever will make *you* happy."

That night in bed she repeated it. They lay smoking and she asked if he were smoking because he was satisfied with his life now and he said no, it was because he could not relax, he could only think of debts and insurance premiums and the old car and going home without a job. She moved close to him and told him not to worry, then he became passionate but it was the wrong time of the month, so she said let's go to sleep, and briefly kissed his cheek with her lips closed like a mother, then said:

"Do what you want to do. Whatever will make you happy."

He lay awake wondering whether anyone but children were happy.

Later he prayed. He began with *dear God*, then smoking again, he talked: sometimes to God and sometimes to himself.

It had been a terrible curse when He drove them from the garden and said: *with labor and toil shalt thou eat*...People didn't love their work: they wanted afternoons off, vacations. Maybe Hollywood was right. What about the Errol Flynns of the world? A philosophy professor in college had said it once: *Virtue is* NOT *its own reward: the virtuous man plods along through his days burdened with responsibility while Errol Flynn swings aboard the pirate ship, rapier in hand, then leaves the set for wine, women, and song.* And wasn't it true? All around them at college young couples had remorseless sex lives that were probably as regular as his own now; yet he and Jeannie had tried to be chaste. Again and again they had pulled away from each other on the car seat, breathed deeply, lit cigarettes, and driven home. Twice, they had been unable to stop and the second time—a tormented month after the first—she conceived, while the other couples went on with their beer, their raucous laughter, their planned sex.

And now again having to pull away from each other in bed, abstaining two weeks out of every month, while Charlotte Hunt remained purposely barren and she and Terry made over a thousand a month, still in their twenties, and probably someday they would live suntanned and healthy in a desert resort. They would all pass him, these Californians: filled wallets and tanned skin and dyed hair, their big automobiles headed south for Mexico, east for the desert—tequila, gin, adultery. Were they happy? Would his students be happy?— those girls with platinum hair who drove sports cars to school, their Winstons in their purses (and what else? how many already had diaphragms?) And Alfred Keith wanted to talk to Mrs. Andrews about grammar and spelling.

He had until tomorrow to change his mind.

He didn't want the Errol Flynn life; he wanted to go

home to Louisiana and rear his children where teen-agers at least looked young, he wanted to teach in college and read and have some peace.

The trip was impossible. The car was burning oil now; in the desert heat something would go wrong and he would have to submit to a mechanic who could tell him anything—it needed a valve job, a ring job, the engine had to be rebuilt—and Paul would have to accept it.

The grass is always greener.

He could get his degree from San Diego State and work at night. He reached for a cigarette on the bedside table; the bedsprings squeaked, the old mattress sagged with his shifting weight. A night job in San Diego. That would mean looking tomorrow. One probably started with the want-ads; if there was nothing, then—Then what? Go to the police department. Whom should he ask for a job? The chief of police? The mayor? He had no idea. And would the police actually have a four to midnight to eight job, when could he study? For that matter, when could he study if he were working from four to midnight?

A policeman in San Diego could be killed.

It wasn't dying he feared: it was the terrible senseless injustice of being killed while performing an alien role. He saw himself stopping a car speeding back from a night in Tijuana; he parked behind the car (never stop in front of them; he knew that: they may run over you), approached it wearily and stooped toward the driver's window to see a hopped-up teen-ager's face and the suddenly potent bore of a boy's plaything: a .22 automatic. Then those absurdly tiny slugs pierced his face, ricocheted inside his skull.

God show me what to do.

Jeannie finally sobbing after she put the children to bed (she would tell them tomorrow: Daddy has gone to heaven), calling home now: Daddy can you come get us and bring us home? We need a U-Haul, everything else is junk but I want to keep his books, he loved them so much, he has notes in the margins Oh Daddy he was so brave, they said he didn't have time to get his gun out...

Lord why do You put Alfred Keiths in the world? Errol Flynns?

Was there no sweet middle ground between the two? Couldn't one have the responsibility of Keith and, in one's own way, the freedom of Flynn?

The responsibility of being loved.

Thinking of debts, costly illness, and pregnancy he finally slept.

Before the alarm clock rang he woke, with no lingering drowsiness but an immediate opening of his eyes and quickened beating of his heart. It was six o'clock. He went to the kitchen, smoking a cigarette even before the coffee was dripped. He told himself that he would quit again, after this one, or perhaps one more with his coffee.

Jeannie had washed the dishes the night before but the living and dining rooms were still disorderly. He sat in the living room drinking coffee and looking at the wooden arm of his chair, scratches showing its original finish through several coats of paint. The sofa seat had the contours of two gentle hills with a saddle between. A cover that Jeannie had made hid the exposed springs and stuffing of the couch. The legs of two dining room chairs were held on by Elmer's glue. He looked at all of it and the toys and newspaper on the floor and thought it was a hell of a thing to sell out for.

But he was not certain that he was selling out. There had to be some nobility of purpose in keeping a job, paying one's bills, buying insurance to provide for one's widow and children. Perhaps it was God's will—hadn't he prayed last night and waked this morning knowing he would see Keith? It did not have to be defeat. Maybe at school he would accomplish something; next year or the year after there might come to his class a student who needed him. One of those blondes with a maroon MG would approach him and say: Since you talked about *Heart of Darkness* I've been wanting to read it. He would lend her one of his own books with marginal comments and underlined passages and she would read it and return for more: Conrad, Tolstoy, Dostoievski. Years later, she would still be reading.

And he would have seven children.

He rose and shaved. At seven-thirty, wearing a suit and tie, he brought coffee to Jeannie.

"Where are you going?" she said.

"To school."

"*Why?*"

"To see Keith."

"Paul, don't."

"I've thought it over."

"Paul—"

"We have to keep living: we have commitments. We can't just cut them off."

"Is it because of me?" she said.

"Of course not."

"It is."

"No!"

"Are you sure this is what you want to do?"

"No, it's not what I *want* to do. It's what I have to do."

"You don't have to do anything."

He picked up the cigarettes from the bedside table.

"I'll get the degree someday," he said.

He dropped the cigarettes onto the table; he had not taken one.

"I shouldn't have smoked. Now I'll have to quit again."

He looked at her face: the sleep was gone from it and it was beautiful, her eyes sorrowful. She knew: the responsibility of being loved. At least there was that: she was aware, and it was like having a companion in purgatory.

"Someday," he said.

"Yes."

"Someday someday *someday*! I prayed and thought and prayed again and woke up, I —Ah, Jeannie."

She came to him, her bare arms encircling him, her soft-clad breasts an assuaging pressure against his chest. He kissed her, then left the house.

The sky was clear, the sun cast shadows on his front lawn, and the air was cool. He decided to walk. He felt like running: on a day like this he could run five miles. He would have to be firm with himself about cigarettes, though; he still needed them, so he must be careful never to lapse again.

Keith knew.

For twenty minutes he walked, looking at the bright cars passing him, and thinking that Alfred Keith knew he would come back.

He arrived at Keith's office at eight-fifteen and stood waiting while the secretary announced him. She returned and said Mister Keith would see him in a moment. She offered him a seat then continued her typing. Paul stood at the window and looked out at the students' cars in the parking lot. He stood there for half an hour before Keith's voice on the intercom said to send in Mister Ritchey.

LOVE IS THE SKY

but love is the sky and i am for you
just so long and long enough
E. E. CUMMINGS

THE NOVEMBER SUN was distant and the sky hazy pale blue and, although it was not two o'clock yet and the Scottish Highlanders were still doing their pre-game show on the field, the afternoon seemed to be fading into evening. Curtis Boudreaux was not watching the Highlanders. He was fifty-four years old, short and bulky, and his brown topcoat tightened across his back and shoulders whenever he leaned forward to pour from his flask. His neck was large and seemed to be straining against his starched white collar, as if trying to burst free, and he did not look like a man who wore a necktie six days a week, though he was. His face was red and brown and had been for years, and a shock of his thick dry greying hair jutted out over his forehead. The sounds of drums and bagpipe music were somehow in his mind and he was breathing the cold late fall air, but he was sensuously conscious of little save the taste of bourbon (he was sipping it) and its pleasing heartburning descent from his throat to stomach.

Sitting as he was, his paunch pressed against his belt and protruded over it; that squeezing at his waist usually made him think of heart attacks, but now he was not aware of his constricted belly, nor even of his own mortality. He was watching the director of the all-girl Scottish Highlanders. The director stood on the sidelines, wearing a light grey suit and a dark unbuttoned topcoat and a bow tie; he had white hair and a thin white mustache and his pale face, Curtis thought, was the face of a man in pain. He was smiling at his girls on the field. Curtis was sitting beside Doctor Dwight Landry on the fifty yard line, bottom row, and Dwight had just told him the band director was dying of cancer.

The Highlanders marched to the north end zone, where the university band was already waiting, then the crowd roared and Curtis looked across the field at the green-and-gold visiting team running out, single file; and he looked to his right and saw the home team coming from that end of the grandstand: white pants and red helmets and red jerseys with large white numerals, and they reminded him of power and strength, of hard men moving Westward. He looked away from them: leaned over and slipped the flask from his inside coat pocket and, holding the paper cup down between his ankles, he poured. When he straightened again he looked for the band director and found him standing at one end of the players' bench, looking across the field at his Highlanders in the end zone, then moving backward until his legs touched the bench and, with his arms stretched down behind him, he eased himself downward and sat.

He didn't sit long. The announcer asked the crowd to stand for the National Anthem and Curtis watched the director as he pushed up slowly from the bench, stood erectly, and removed his hat and placed it over his heart. From where Curtis stood, he looked over the director's white head and past the red jerseys of the players, at the university band in solid red uniforms, their gold instruments shining and flashing, and at the Highlanders in plaid and red. Beyond them were the pale blue sky and cold sun. With his hand over his heart— quickened by more hours of drinking than he had done in years—Curtis felt that a bond far greater than blood joined him and the director and Dwight Landry. For just as Dwight knew of the fatal growth in the director's stomach, he also knew of Curtis's pain and had in fact prescribed the pint of bourbon which filled his flask.

Nearly two hours earlier, when Curtis called him to ask if he still had an extra ticket, Dwight had been kind enough to merely answer the question and not to ask why, on Dad's Day, Curtis was not going to the game with his son. When Dwight picked him up at the motel Curtis had told him anyway, not wanting to but unable to stop himself, cursing angrily to keep from crying, and never once looking at Dwight behind the wheel of the Lincoln. *Oh my God*, Dwight had said, *are you sure?* Curtis had rolled down the window and thrown out his cigar and said: *Sure as my own name*—and Dwight had pulled in at a liquor store and looked down at the nearly empty fifth in Curtis's hand and said: *You better get refueled. It'll be a long afternoon.*

2

In Curtis Boudreaux's home in Baton Rouge, on the wall of what Martha called the library, there were four portraits of equal size. The first was his paternal grandfather who had been a doctor in a small town in Louisiana and had sired four daughters and two sons and was—as Curtis's father told it—a caustic but loving patriarch whose children never properly returned that love until they were old enough to understand his manner. Perhaps because of that, Curtis's father—whose portrait was next—had been a companion as well as a molder of character. He had been a building contractor and, when a heart attack killed him one summer afternoon on the clipped lawn of his house in Baton Rouge, he was wealthy. In memories made suddenly vivid by a couple of drinks or by leaving his house on black early mornings for a day of hunting or fishing, Curtis recalled his father as the man standing beside him in duck blinds or sitting at the opposite end of a skiff.

His own portrait was next, painted in 1940 when he was twenty-nine years old and had three daughters. That year he had placed an empty frame on the wall beside his portrait. It hung there for six years. He joined the Navy in January 1942, leaving Martha pregnant, and she had their fourth daughter while he was on a destroyer in the Pacific.

Then in 1946 she delivered a son. Curtis drove home from the hospital that night, removed the frame from the wall, told his daughters that Jack (named for Curtis's father) was ugly as hell but boys weren't supposed to be pretty anyway, and called some friends to come over for a stag celebration.

When Jack's portrait was painted eighteen years later and hung where the empty frame had been, Curtis knew little more about his son than he had known when the boy was three hours old: he knew his height and weight. He knew some history too but he did not understand it.

Now Jack was in a college about a hundred miles from Baton Rouge and for the first six week-ends he had not come home. Then he surprised Curtis by asking him to the football game on Dad's Day. The letter was addressed to Curtis only, not Mr. and Mrs., and it was mailed to Curtis's office: a short letter, but in Jack's voice—so much his voice that Curtis got up and crossed his carpeted office and closed the door and returned to his desk where he sat for a while, reading the letter again, holding it flat on the glass-topped desk. Then he answered it.

He wrote on a small sheet of paper. In its upper left hand corner was the name of the insurance company whose Louisiana branch he managed. *A note from Curtis Boudreaux* was written in script at the top of the paper, and Curtis's picture was in the upper right hand corner. There was not much space for a letter.

Still, after the first easy and even spontaneous sentence— *I'll be very happy to come for Dad's Day*—Curtis paused. Then he wrote. *I'll come Friday night and*—He looked at Jack's picture on the desk, then at the large picture of Jefferson Davis on the knotty pine wall, and remembered bringing Jack to the office two years ago, when he was sixteen.

The one-story Jefferson Davis Building had been a month old then, and Curtis owned half of it. He and his employees occupied that half. He had shown Jack all of it and introduced him to young energetic agents who said afterward he was a nice kid and they reckoned he was a chip off the old block and would be selling any time now, and to the young secretaries who said he was cute and would break many a heart before he settled down. And Jack had smiled and said *Glad to meet you* and had walked quietly through the air-conditioned carpeted rooms and looked at the picture of Jefferson Davis and the slogans about success and ambition which hung in the corridor. He said it certainly was a nice building.

Then Curtis had taken him outside and down the sidewalk in the June heat, trying to recall his own childhood, wondering if he and his father had really been so close or if he just remembered it that way. But still he remembered not only doing things with his father but talking as well. Often he had gone to look at buildings under construction and he had drunk ice water from dippers hanging on sweating water cans and asked his father questions, not to be polite but because he wanted to know: why were steel rods laid in the ditches before cement foundations were poured, and why did men belong to unions and why couldn't one man do all kinds of work and how much was a foreman paid. That was what he remembered and he knew it was true. He glanced at Jack walking beside him, his thin soft arms pink from the first sunburn of summer, his profiled face oblivious of Curtis, who suddenly felt as if for sixteen years he and Jack had been walking side by side, without a word. He said *Let's get some coffee* and they went into a cafe and ordered it with doughnuts. The waitress was young and had on too much make-up so that she wasn't really pretty, but she was friendly and Curtis called her *Sunshine* and winked at Jack, who smiled—either at the flirtation or the wink, and for a shameful moment Curtis was certain it was the wink. While they blew on their coffee and sipped it and ate doughnuts, Curtis explained to Jack that life insurance

was more than just selling: it was service, and a good insurance agent was an extra member of a policy holder's family.

Now at his desk he read the beginning of his sentence: *I'll
come on Friday night and—* He thought for a while longer then
wrote: *we can eat crawfish bisque and have a few drinks.* Then
he was about to ask if maybe Jack had plans for Friday night
and, if so, to let him know and he would come Saturday in
time for the game. But he did not. He wrote: *Love, Daddy*, and
mailed it.

3

The college Jack was attending had integrated its dormitories
for the first time that year and they allowed freshmen to live
off campus if they wished. Three weeks after school started,
Jack had explained this in a letter and asked for an increase in
his allowance so he could move into an apartment with a
friend. It wasn't that he minded living with Negroes, he wrote,
but he thought a nice apartment would be more conducive to
studying. Curtis had mailed him a check immediately and
said he was glad Jack was getting out.

It was a small low-roofed brick apartment on the corner
of a street of large old houses and trees stripped by autumn.
On the Friday evening before the game Curtis was sitting in
the living room, drinking bourbon and water while Jack
dressed in the bedroom. He reached over and turned down
the stereo, which had been playing something classical and
somber when he arrived, and now there was a piano without
melody and a frenzied saxophone.

"Is your roommate going out with us?" he called.

"No."

"Where did you say he was?"

"Supper, I guess."

There was something about the way he said that, and
Curtis squinted in a mock frown and looked around the room.

Its order had surprised him when he first entered. He had expected dirty clothes on the floor and school books on the furniture and beer cans emptied a week ago. But everything was in place and, except for the one he was using, even the ash trays were clean.

He finished the drink and went to the kitchen for another. When he opened the refrigerator he was certain. There was a ham under waxed paper, and through the glass top of the vegetable bin he could see carrots and lettuce and tomatoes and— yes: even a head of cabbage—and behind the ham was a portion of apple pie, homemade if he had ever seen one, with strips of pastry laid on the brown sugared apples. He was grinning when he slid the ice tray from the freezer compartment.

The little bastard, he thought warmly, *it only took him three weeks.*

He mixed the drink and went to the bathroom and stood in the doorway and watched Jack knotting his tie at the mirror.

"Beats hell out of the seminary, don't it?" he said.

"Beats hell out of the seminary," Jack said, finishing his knot, then going past Curtis, into the bedroom.

Curtis followed him. Except for the paperbacks on both bedside tables and a barbell on the floor, it could have been a motel room. Curtis looked slyly at the double bed and the books, thinking she must be a student—and of course she was, because Jack had always gone for the intellectual type—and he hoped this one was better looking and a bit more down to earth than the others.

"You and your buddy share the bed?" Curtis said.

Jack was getting a coat from the closet and he answered with his back turned:

"He sleeps on the couch."

"Yeah, how'd you manage that?"

"Tough guy," Jack said, facing him now and smiling as he flexed his right arm.

"I noticed. When did you start the weights?"

"A while back. Sharpens the mind, I think."

Curtis finished the drink and they left. As Jack circled

the front of the Cadillac to get in the other side, Curtis looked at his shoulders: they seemed broader and his chest thicker and his face was tanned.

Curtis drove to a seafood restaurant and they ordered drinks and oysters on the half shell and crawfish bisque. Half-way through his second drink, Curtis said:

"I saw the stuff in your refrigerator. Who does all the cooking?"

"My roommate's a bit of a gourmet."

"Gourmet, huh? He bake that pie?"

"Oh, yes."

"Must be nice."

After the oysters, while they were waiting for the bisque, Curtis went to the phone booth and called Dwight Landry.

"How you doing, pro?" he said.

"Pro, hell: I hadn't broke eighty in a month. Who's that? Boudreaux?"

"That's me."

"Making money all the time too. Look, you just the man—I got two tickets for the fifty tomorrow, front row. You want to make it?"

"I'm going with Jack. For Dad's Day. That is, if he don't spend all afternoon engaging in *in*door sport."

"That right?"

"I don't know, Dwight. I tell you, these kids catch on fast."

Then he chuckled and asked Dwight to bring his wife to Baton Rouge for the week-end of the Tulane-L.S.U. game. Dwight said that was a fine plan and he would come a day early so they could play golf and they talked about it until Curtis said he had to go eat his bisque.

"You tell Jack to be careful," Dwight said. "I got more maternity cases than I can handle now."

"I'll tell him, pro. I'm beginning to see why he didn't become a priest."

When he walked back to the table he was grinning at Jack, who two years earlier had announced that he was going to be a priest. And though Curtis had been greatly disappointed at having produced a celibate son, he had not objected. He had remembered his own father's refusal to interfere in his children's affairs; he had reminded himself that it was a blessing to have a son become a priest; and, most of all, he had tried to make a final gesture. Perhaps Jack would remember him as an understanding father. Then after nine months in the seminary Jack had a nervous breakdown and came home. For a while Curtis had been concerned about his health, but soon he was only relieved and hopeful.

Curtis finished his bisque and said:

"You still going to be a psychiatrist?"

"Yes."

"Long time in school. Course you'll make good money once you get out—" He paused, thinking maybe he wouldn't say it after all, but he had drunk too much and he said it, with a bitterness he had not intended: "But your man Johnson got elected. Maybe by the time you start practice he'll have *psychiatry* socialized too."

Jack blushed and, holding a crawfish with two fingers, he dug the stuffing out with his spoon.

"Oh, I don't think so," he said.

"Well, those letters you wrote—and they were *good mature* letters—but I think you're misinformed on some of the issues."

"Not the big one. There's this ROTC colonel—"

"You in the ROTC?"

"No, but Ed and I were chatting with him and some of his Bircher minions—"

"Who's Ed?"

"My roommate."

"Oh?" Curtis said, and unwrapped a cigar and offered one to Jack, who shook his head and lit a cigarette. "Okay, but look—there's no use talking politics. You're young and away from home and thinking for yourself, and that's healthy. I never fought politics with *my* daddy, but that was 'cause I didn't know anything. I was too busy trying to drink all the bars dry and get in the gals' britches."

He leaned back, grinning around his cigar, and watched Jack draining his coffee cup. Then he drank his own and they left.

On the sidewalk a group of students, perhaps five couples, walked past Curtis and Jack and turned into a bar. Past their heads and shoulders and through the open door, Curtis saw that the bar was dark and crowded with young people and he heard jukebox music. He slapped Jack's shoulder lightly, not as spontaneously as he had wanted to.

"Want to go in?" he said.

"It's not the most peaceful place in the world."

"Hell, I might *wear* out but I won't rust. I don't need peace—and I'm not talking about Goldwater, either."

He laughed and took Jack's elbow and guided him to the door. They found a small booth and sat opposite each other and ordered bourbon and water. Beside them, about three feet away, the couples they had followed in were sitting at a round table. Jack nodded to them and a girl smiled and two boys lifted their hands, briefly and quietly.

"Friends of yours?" Curtis said.

"Not really."

Curtis watched a girl with long blonde hair sitting between two boys at the table, moving her body to the music as she talked. She noticed Curtis and he grinned and winked and she looked surprised; then she turned away. Curtis glanced at Jack, but apparently he had not seen. He looked at the girl again: she was still turned, profiled to him, accepting a light from a tall boy with a crewcut. Curtis sipped his drink and watched her with paternal fondness. She was only a child and she had thought he was an old lecher making a pass. She could have been one of his own daughters.

All his married life Curtis had thought being a father necessarily meant having a son. He had felt that his four daughters were sweet little people whom he should praise and watch lovingly as they grew. His only real concern had been with their virginity, and when the last girl married he had assumed that each daughter, as she held his arm and strode up the aisle to the waiting priest and groom, had been innocent.

You didn't worry about that with boys, as long as they were careful: you worried about what sort of men they would be. And now—well, now he looked proudly at Jack, thinking they had never done anything together, but that didn't count anyway: what really mattered was a successful psychiatrist in Baton Rouge or New Orleans maybe and some knot-headed grandsons (*her* children? no: boys outgrew those girls) and he said loudly, over the music:

"Did you join a fraternity?"

"No."

Curtis looked at the couples beside them. He had done it again. Before leaving Baton Rouge that day he had resolved to avoid two subjects: politics and fraternities. The first had been mentioned too often in Jack's letters, especially in the last week before election, and the second had not been mentioned at all.

"Oh, I was rushed," Jack said, "but I refused to even attend rush parties. It's all so phony."

The two boys flanking the blonde were staring coldly at Curtis. He swallowed from his drink and relit his cigar. By God, had she told them he was making a pass? He had a horrifying image of the boys picking a fight with him, and Jack shamed but having to defend him anyway.

"Hey," he said, "how did you get so tan in November?"

Jack lit a cigarette before answering quietly:

"A heat lamp."

"A heat lamp? How come?"

"I'm afraid I'll have to admit it's nothing but vanity."

Curtis chuckled and said warmly:

"Hell, I know what you mean. I used to spend more time in front of the mirror than my sisters."

"I have to get rid of some booze," Jack said, and slid out of the booth and went to the men's room, walking gracefully around the dancers on the floor: couples facing each other, their bodies twitching and somehow jerking smoothly. Curtis

grinned and shook his head. Then he looked at the blonde
again and the boys beside her. They were across the table and
he did not want to raise his voice, so he reached out and
touched the shoulder of a boy sitting with his back turned.
The boy looked around and Curtis signalled to the waitress
and said:

"Let me buy you kids a round."

The boy said nothing. He was looking angrily at Curtis's
hand on his shoulder, and Curtis withdrew it and looked
across the table at the blonde. She stared back scornfully, and
the boy Curtis had touched said:

"No thanks, buddy. We're integrated."

"Integrated?"

All the young faces were quietly watching him. Only the
blonde's face changed: as his eyes met hers she grinned and
bit her lip.

"That's right," the boy said. "Girls and boys at this table."

He was already turning his back on Curtis when he said:

"Stick to your friend there."

And Curtis pulled back, recoiled, then sat with his shoulders hunched forward and clutched his glass, trembling furiously, and after a while he saw Jack coming around the
dancing couples again, gliding like a halfback past the jerking
buttocks of a girl.

"Funny way to dance," Curtis said when Jack sat down.

"Sublimation," Jack said.

They finished their drinks and left and Curtis felt the
couples watching him as he walked to the door.

4

He did not tell Jack. He drove silently, thinking he had been
afraid of shaming Jack if someone accused him of making a
pass at a girl—but that was nothing: those kids had thought he
was a *queer*. Never, never in his life—why, Goddammit, never.
He had been approached a few times in bars when he was

Jack's age and even now the memory of those persistent voices disgusted him. When he was twenty years old he had hit one: had just slipped off the bar stool and swung in outrage and revulsion, and the man had backed away, a handkerchief pressed against his bleeding nose, petulantly cursing as he left the bar and Curtis's life.

The little sonsobitches—

Then he stopped at Jack's apartment. There was a light inside, and Curtis's heart quickened and his throat went dry just as if he were a boy again, about to meet his blind date. But Jack was saying:

"I've got the tickets. Why don't you just pick me up for early lunch and—"

"Hold on. Can't a man get a nightcap?"

"Well—"

Curtis turned off the ignition and slid out of the car, saying:

"Hell, it's early yet."

While he waited for Jack to get out of the car and come to the sidewalk he had time to unwrap a cigar and light it. As they walked up the sidewalk to the front steps Curtis straightened his tie. On the steps he paused and took Jack's arm.

"Listen, Son. Don't worry about me telling your mother. I could see a girl's touch in that apartment from a mile off."

Jack was looking at the door. Then he opened it and walked in and Curtis followed, having only in that instant decided exactly what was the best thing to do: he would just be his old natural self, just shake her hand and sit down for a short drink and make some talk then get up and tell them *well, I'll see you kids tomorrow* and go back to the motel.

Then he was inside, blinking at a short middle-aged man wearing a tieless white dress shirt and slacks, rising from the chair where he had been reading. The man was looking at Jack, his eyes puzzled—and afraid; Curtis saw that—then he smiled and extended his hand as Jack said:

"Daddy, this is Ed Gabbert."

The cuff of Ed Gabbert's sleeve was rolled up twice, his wrist was veined and hairless, and his hand was small. Curtis saw that. Jack was saying: "And this is my father." Ed Gabbert's shoulders were narrow and sloping and his face was large and the skin red where he shaved and his eyes were scared again. Curtis saw that too. But he did not take Ed Gabbert's hand.

"He teaches psych," Jack said, and started for the kitchen. "I'll fix some—"

"Jack!" Curtis cried, and Jack turned, his mouth still open, his tan face paling, and Curtis crossed the room and started to grab Jack's lapels but didn't: he let his hands fall to his sides.

"Those kids at that table," he said. "They took me for a queer."

Behind him, Curtis heard the front door shut.

"He left?"

Jack nodded. Then Curtis turned fast and went to the easy chair and dropped in it and, looking at his hands, he said:

"Fix me that Goddamn drink."

He did not think of anything at all. Then he heard the ice tray sliding from the freezing compartment and water running and cubes dropping into the sink, and in a voice he hadn't heard coming from his own throat in a long time—two years ago when he had told his last daughter and her groom goodbye, just before they left under tossed rice and laughter and, before that, when he had phoned Martha from his father's house and said: *Honey, Daddy just died*—he said:

"They got a cure for it."

Ice cubes dropped into the glass—one, then another—and after a pause the faucet ran again.

"I can afford it, no matter how long it takes."

Then he heard Jack coming and he looked down at the rug and as Jack's shoes and trousers came into his vision he reached up for the drink. When his fingers touched Jack's he quickly took the glass. Finally he lifted his face to drink. Jack was standing in the kitchen doorway, his back turned.

"You could even go to a different state."

Jack turned and leaned his forehead against the doorjamb. Then he began to cry and Curtis had put down the glass and got up from the chair and was going to him when Jack said:

"I *told* you to come Saturday."

Curtis stopped.

"What?"

"Why didn't you come *Saturday!* I told you to come *Saturday!* I *wanted* you to come but why couldn't you have—"

"You *want* to be a queer!"

Jack was crying hard and rubbing his forehead against the doorjamb.

"*Jack?* Is that what you *want?*"

He waited, swaying, his right arm moving back and forth at his side.

"Do you want to be a queer?"

Then he was moving forward and he grabbed Jack's shoulder, the wool bunched in his hand and his fingers squeezing bone, and he jerked and spun Jack around, cocking his right arm. But he did not swing. He released the bone and wool and slowly backed to the door.

"How long you been that way?" he said, still backing.

Jack's head was lowered, his chin covering his tie knot; he had stopped crying and he was sniffling and wiping his eyes. Curtis reached the door.

"I'll keep sending money," he said. "Even if he's got enough for—" He waved his hand at the furniture and books and stereo. "He's old. He's old enough to—"

He opened the door.

"Don't you come home," he said. "Don't you ever come home again."

He left Jack standing at the kitchen door, his head lowered, one hand wiping his eyes, the other tugging at the bottom of his coat.

5

So on that fading afternoon of sun and color Curtis sat drunk beside Dwight Landry and at half-time, when the Scottish Highlanders marched on the field again, he watched the director smiling at his girls on the field and pacing gingerly up and down the sidelines, as if cancer were something you must not jar. And maybe it was. Curtis didn't know.

"The poor bastard," he said.

He sipped from his paper cup and watched the Highlanders moving about like people hurrying across a downtown intersection, then they emerged into a square formation, facing him. They began to play.

"Maybe I was too hard on him," Curtis said.

In seconds, as Dwight's hand came to his shoulder and squeezed it, he groped back through time. But he could not remember being severe. He had tried to do everything properly: had disciplined as his own father had, fairly and calmly.

"You'll go crazy, you keep trying to figure it out," Dwight said.

"They say it's the father."

"It don't have to be anybody."

Then Dwight was clapping and the crowd behind them was and Curtis did too. The Highlanders were marching off the field, coming straight toward Curtis and stepping onto the cinder track at the fifty-yard line, and turning right. The director smiled and spoke to them as they passed. Then he followed them to the end of the grandstand.

"Look, pro. Look, I'll tell you: I always knew he was a sissy. But I swear to God I never pushed him. I never even said a word."

"Take it easy, Boudreaux. It wasn't you."

The second half started and, standing for the kick-off and buttoning his topcoat which he had opened to get his flask,

Curtis resolved to be quiet for the rest of the game. He pretended to watch it and he cheered or groaned or stood when Dwight did. Then in the fourth quarter Dwight said:

"That's me."

"Huh?"

"The P.A. I got a call."

And he was gone, up the concrete steps. Curtis blinked at the speeding and bumping colors on the field, red-and-white and green-and-gold, and realized that he did not even know the score. It seemed that only enough time passed for him to realize that before he was looking up at Dwight's panting worried face framed by the cold sky.

"He's gone, Dwight. It's all over, old pro. He's—"

"Look. I got to run. You okay?"

"You know me, pro."

"If I'm not back you get a cab to the house. Okay?"

He was gone again. On the field the colors moved and exploded and fell and Curtis was thinking he could get a cab and go to Jack's apartment and sit in the easy chair and say: *Well, Son, I guess I must have done something, I guess no matter how hard I tried I got off on the wrong track.* No. He would not go inside. He would merely stand at the door and say: *Son, I was kind of hasty last night. I hope you'll forget about it. It's your home and at Thanksgiving I want you to*—That wasn't it either. He would go in, whether Gabbert was there or not, and when they offered him a drink he would say: *Now, I can't stay but a minute. I got to drop by Dwight Landry's for a while. I went to the game, it was*—Then he stopped trying.

The horn was loud in his ears and the crowd was roaring behind him and, near midfield, the colors slowed and became men again and they clustered and moved off the field. The roaring changed: voices moving forward and past him as people climbed the rail and dropped to the ground and joined the players on the field. Curtis climbed the rail too: straddled it for a steadying moment and saw himself at home—tonight if he could get sober enough to drive—and he would take Martha to the living room, knowing he shouldn't but having to anyway, and set her down and get a fire going and say: *He's gone, Martha; I told him not to come home again.* Then he saw himself dead: lying fully clothed on their bedroom floor, the old heart having finally stopped (and sitting on the rail he thought it was heating faster and skipping too) and Martha would find him there, lying on his back with his arms outstretched and his head tilted back and, if by that time she still knew where Jack was, she would call him home. Then he swung a leg over and dropped to the ground, falling to his knees on the cold earth.

He was on the cinder track. Girls were all around him, their shoulders and breasts and backs gently bumping him: pink cheeks and parted red lips under black caps, long blonde and black and brown hair falling to shoulders of red jackets, and he moved with them and their laughing voices onto the field.

Then there was a man: white hair and his face even paler when it was only two feet away and a trim white mustache following the downward line of his upper lip, and Curtis grabbed his arm. It was shrunken and dying. The director began to smile and his mustache spread straight over his lips and Curtis looked at his brown questioning eyes and said:

"Wasted."

He waved his arm at the girls in kilts moving around them and the director's smile ceased, his mustache drooping again, and his eyes shifted to Curtis's hand on his arm as Curtis spoke louder, over the girls' soprano voices:

"You poor bastard. You poor—"

"Leave me *alone.*"

He tried to jerk his arm free, but Curtis held it, and the director's hand closed on Curtis's wrist and pulled. Then Curtis released him.

"Get *away* from me," the director said, and turned and walked quickly through his girls and started across the field. He did not look back. When he was past the girls and the crowd, into the open, he slowed and walked with his hands in the pockets of his topcoat, his head lowered. Curtis stood watching him, the Highlanders skirting and jostling past him, until a policeman took his elbow and roughly led him off the field.

THE BLACKBERRY PATCH

AFTER HIS LUNCH in the student lounge David Wallace read the front page of the morning newspaper, then turned to the second page and saw the story. He read it, at first appalled, then thinking that he had to go home and be with Marian. He had told the paper boy not to deliver the paper for a month and, as he had hoped, Marian apparently did not miss it; if she did, she said nothing. But still she could know: she could have seen it on the local news or heard it on the radio or even from some tactless neighbor.

So he taught his Survey of World Literature class at one o'clock, then went to his office and got his briefcase. He was turning to leave when he saw the girl standing at his open door. She was one of his World Literature students, a pretty girl who sat three times a week in his class, her eyes intently following his lips and eyes and gesticulations. But when he asked her a question she would invariably disappoint him with a blush and a stammered irrelevancy, as if his question had dispelled all her accumulated fragments of knowledge.

"What can I do for you?" he said.

"Nothing—I mean it's not about school. I wanted to tell you I had a Mass said for your daughter."

"Oh. Oh yes: that's very thoughtful of you."

"I just wanted you to know."

He nodded, started to walk past her, then paused.

"I appreciate it," he said.

Then he went down the corridor and across the campus, trying to forgive her, telling himself that to her a Mass was important or even essential and she had probably thought she was giving him some consolation, like assuring the father of a Greek soldier that his son's body has been properly burned. Surely the Mass was as essential as the burning and just as much in vain.

When he reached his car he was sweating. He took off his coat and got into the car—its body hot and shining in the sun—and drove away from the campus.

This time he went to the blackberry patch. He had avoided it for three weeks, driving past the corner where he had always turned and going home by another route. But now he turned at that corner, drove three blocks, and parked at the field—in the entire block the only area where no house was built—and stood leaning against his car, looking at the black-berry bushes. There were perhaps twenty of them, some taller than he was. Then he looked at the entrance of a dozen labyrinthine paths worn through the weeds by blackberry pickers and he thought of Linda dragged over one of those paths, a hand over her mouth— He had a fleeting urge to fol-low the paths and try to find the spot: the flattened grass, per-haps blood. No: there had been rain—three times—since then. There would be no blood. He began to cry, silent and with his abdomen almost still, calm: no longer capable of the cathartic heavy crying that he had done at first.

He did not move from the car. Leaning against its fender he stared at the tall pale green weeds in the sunlight and the bushes where even now in September blackberries glistened, unpicked. And who could pick them now, pluck them from bushes which had hidden such horror? But he knew he was crediting people with too much: even these blackberries would end in someone's kitchen. He remembered a hurricane and tidal wave six years ago surprising a town on the Gulf Coast; over a hundred bodies were never found and for months no one would eat crabs—not compassion but squeamishness.

He got into his car, twice smoothed back the thin hair that combed over the bald spot on the top of his head, and started the engine. He turned on the radio and filled a pipe, wondering if ever again he could remember Linda as a thin quiet eleven-year-old girl without seeing also the final violent images and the awful juxtaposition of that other face: the newspaper photograph with the caption SEX KILLER CONFESSES (they caught him the same night)—the slight chest clad in what appeared to be a blue denim shirt, the lean trapped but musing face, as if he had no fear, no remorse. He had studied the picture, thinking the man was frail, that with rage—rare for him—he could kill him without a weapon.

He drove home. When he opened the front door the house was quiet; he waited a moment, then called, and Marian answered from the bedroom.

She wore only a slip and she lay on her back with one arm over her eyes. An oscillating fan on the dressing table blew at the edge of the slip above her knees. She moved her arm from her face and looked at him: she was not wearing make-up and her face looked oily and tired. The blinds were drawn so he could not see in her dark hair the gray strands at her temples and forehead; but looking at her face he was deeply aware of them, and of his own aging hair.

"You're early," she said.

"A little. Were you sleeping?"

"Just resting."

She watched him remove his coat and tie and shirt, putting on a short-sleeved shirt which he did not tuck into his trousers, so that hanging loosely it partially concealed his nascent paunch. While he sat on the bed and put on a pair of slippers, she rose and dressed. Standing at the mirror and combing her hair she said:

"The women in the neighborhood are going to cut down the blackberry patch."

He looked at her; she was still looking in the mirror, combing.

"They've petitioned the city," she said. "They'll do the work; they just want permission."

"Who told you?"

"I read it in the paper."

She opened the blinds, then returned to the mirror and began powdering her face.

"I bought it at the corner."

Now she turned and looked at him.

"Did you think I wouldn't miss the paper?"

"I hoped you wouldn't."

She looked at the mirror again, starting with the lipstick now.

"Why don't you have it delivered again?" she said.

"I suppose I will. I was only trying to spare you the details."

"I know. But I want them. I've walked to the corner every day to buy a paper, then put them in the garbage so you wouldn't know."

"It was stupid of me, I guess."

"No: not at all. But I want to know everything. I know all about him: paroled child molester—paroled by *whom*, I'd like to know but I don't know that—and the trial's in January. I don't know if I can go to it but if—"

"*Go* to it?"

"Yes. But I don't know if I could stand it. I'll follow it in the paper, though: every bit of it."

"Marian—"

"I want him electrocuted."

"Marian, he's sick."

She turned to him.

"Don't *you* want him killed?" she said.

"I can't."

"Why can't you?"

"Because it's senseless."

"But in *here*—" she jabbed a finger twice at her breast "—you want him killed, don't you?"

"All right. In *there* I suppose I do. But I can't submit to it."

"David, he *raped Linda and stabbed her twenty-seven times!* I'd pull the switch myself."

He went to her. She turned to the mirror and he stood behind her, his hands on her hips.

"I'm all right," she said. "Don't worry about me. I just want him killed; I want the trial to end quickly and him to be dead."

"He probably will be."

"And I want to help them cut down that blackberry patch."

He stepped back from her and went to the chest of drawers for a pipe.

"Do you mean that?" he said.

"Yes."

"Marian, it's senseless. Clearing that field won't accomplish a thing."

"Maybe it will. They're doing it so children can walk home safely at night. Who can say? Maybe it *will* save someone; it's better than doing nothing, just sitting by while things happen."

"I'm sure they don't expect you to help."

"Well, I'm going to."

"All right."

She faced him, prettier now but still looking tired, older.

"You understand, don't you?" she said.

"Yes."

"You go off and teach and go to meetings and you come home and read and grade papers. I don't do anything."

"I know."

"I was hoping you'd come with me."

"Where?"

"When we clear the field."

"Marian—"

"You don't have to."

"It's just so—so useless. Matrons arming themselves with brush hooks, trying to destroy evil."

"I said you don't have to."

"I'll think about it. Would you like a beer?"

"Yes. Don't be shocked at the kitchen: I haven't touched it."

"I don't blame you. It's too hot."

That night she watched television while David read. At eleven o'clock he was sleepy but he did not go to bed; he wanted to be with her as long as she was awake, for that was the only comfort he could offer: his presence. For three weeks his mind and tongue had failed him. Like an obsequious subordinate he had watched silently while she cleaned Linda's bedroom, lifting the comb and brush and mirror from the dressing table and dusting and setting them down again; pushing the vacuum cleaner over the floor of the closet while inches from her face Linda's pastel dresses hung like grieving children.

He had wanted to stop her: to tell her they must give the clothes to the poor, move his desk in and transform her bedroom to a den. But he could not. And now more: the blackberry patch. Yet he felt powerless to stop her, as if all his talent for showing truth to others had been exhausted by his hundreds of students in the past twenty years. He looked at her sitting with her hands in her lap, oblivious of him and probably of the television too, and he thought: *like Patroklos— stripped of armor and left helpless on the battlefield; we are all stripped and helpless.*

At midnight she turned off the television and they went to bed. Lying quietly on his back and listening to her breathing, David knew that something more was coming; that even this late, after hours of mesmeric television, she was not ready to sleep. Then she said:

"I want to have a baby."

He found her hand and held it.

"I want to try," she said.

"Don't do this to yourself. You know you can't."

"That's not true. It's not impossible—it's just hard."

"It took nine years."

"No: it only took a second—just at the right time. Maybe this is the time again: tonight."

"Don't, Marian. Spare yourself; give yourself some peace."

"I want to try."

"Darling—"

"Won't you even let me?"

"Of course I will, but don't hope. Please don't hope."

Taking him, she whispered furiously:

"I *will* hope. I *will*."

The next day—Tuesday—he telephoned the paper boy and told him to start delivery again. Friday morning at breakfast he read that the petition had been approved and the blackberry patch would be cut down Saturday. He assumed that Marian had read it, but he did not mention it nor did she.

He came home in the hot evening sun and they sat on the screened front porch and drank beer and still she said nothing about it, so finally he said:

"I thought we could take a drive tomorrow, if you'd like. To the Gulf maybe."

"I'm working on the blackberry patch tomorrow."

He paused, drank twice from his beer can before speaking:

"You've decided then?"

"There was nothing to decide."

"Marian—"

But he stopped. He reached across the space between their chairs and laid his hand on her shoulder, ran it lightly over her sweat-moistened cheek; then he squeezed her shoulder once before returning his hand to his lap. He never finished what he was going to say—never even started it. He quietly drank his beer, thinking of himself standing before Marian here on the porch, looking down at her and speaking with masculine firmness, gesturing with his hand gripping the can of beer: *Linda is dead. You will never see her again and you will never have another baby, not of your own flesh—our flesh; you must accept that. Throw away her things and give the dresses to the poor and change her room. Forget the trial. Forget the blackberry patch. Forget all these rituals of grief. They're as useless as that girl's innocuous Mass, as the burning of the warriors. You must start a new life.* Then he reached over again and held her hand and quietly finished his beer.

After breakfast Saturday he sat in the living room with a cup of coffee and Marian went to their bedroom and came out wearing old slacks and sneakers and one of his khaki shirts, the tail hanging, the sleeves rolled to her elbows.

"You're going?" he said.

"Yes. I'll walk, in case you want the car."

"I don't."

"I feel like walking anyway."

She opened the door.

"Wait," he said. "I'll go with you."

He put on old clothes and they went outside, blinking in the sun, and walked to the field. David counted eleven women and four men. He knew only two of the men; they came and shook his hand and spoke to him. He did not know the women but several waved at Marian.

One man was distributing tools; at the periphery of the blackberry patch, men and women were already chopping. David took two brush hooks, giving one to Marian, and walked toward the bushes, sorrowfully watching the jerking backs and swinging tools. Beside him Marian began to cut. He looked at the blackberry patch, listening to the sounds of chopping and breathing, thinking: *we are all stripped, left helpless* ... Then he lifted the brush hook and swung. His strokes were awkward at first, but soon they were rhythmic and he stopped thinking and expended himself in the sweat and heat and the futile arc of the blade.

MADELINE SHEPPARD

Last week I went to my sister's for lunch and she told me that Madeline had written to her, saying she was pregnant again.

"I never can remember her husband's name," I said.

"Jack Dauterive. With Sun Oil."

"Right. And how many children will that be?"

"Four."

When I left my sister's I sat in the car for a few moments— it was a cold day, and raining—and I thought how Madeline is a Protestant and I am a Catholic, yet I have been married nearly five years and have only one child, a frail boy. I am a disc jockey and sometimes he listens to me on the radio. Then I thought of Alice, my wife, who is frail too and nervous and in winter she usually has a head cold and is forced to breathe through her mouth and continually wipe her nose. Pregnancy had made her very nervous, delivery had been difficult, and, once finished with it, she resolved never to have another child. She is a Protestant and I have not been able to change her mind.

Then driving back to the station, watching the rain hitting the windshield, I thought of Madeline Sheppard, now Madeline Dauterive.

Madeline and my sister were college roommates for four years, but I did not meet her until their senior year when Tish brought her home for a week-end in September. I was a sophomore then, attending a small college in our town in southern Louisiana while Tish (her name at Baptism was Letitia, but she retained it for only the first three years of her life) enjoyed herself at a larger school eighty miles from home.

They came on a Friday night by bus and I met them. They stepped down from the bus, carrying purses and overnight bags and fashion magazines. Looking at Madeline for the first time I saw two things at once: she had large interested grey eyes and an attractive mole on her chin. For a moment her eyes held mine, then the flesh at their corners crinkled as she smiled; but the eyes did something else, something more than a smile, as if in that moment she knew that two days later on a cloudy Sunday afternoon she would stretch upward, standing on the balls of her feet, and kiss me.

I liked her immediately. The next afternoon when they decided to go to town I offered to drive them. We spent the afternoon in a book store, a music store, and a women's clothing store. Madeline bought *The Sun Also Rises* when I told her it was splendid (that was the word used), she listened to jazz then bought a Brubeck album, and in the clothing store she said aloud that everything was too expensive and bought nothing. By evening I loved her.

That night we went to a movie then drank beer in a college bar. Afterward I lay in bed listening to their low voices in Tish's bedroom, adjacent to mine, as they prepared their faces and hair for sleep. Often, rising gently above their voices, was Madeline's laughter.

Sunday afternoon we sat in the living room and drank coffee, waiting for a friend who was to take them back to school. When the friend arrived I saw gratefully that he had a girl sitting beside him. Tish went to the car; Madeline went to the bedroom and I followed her. Her suitcase lay open on the bed. She snapped it shut and with an incongruously masculine motion grasped the handle with one hand and jerked the suitcase off the bed and lowered it to the floor.

"I'll take it," I said.

I stood holding the suitcase and looking at her; but I did

nothing, said nothing, and if she had let the moment pass we might have been spared. But slowly her face rose to mine and she kissed me; I lowered the suitcase and held her.

"Can I take you out?" I said.

"I wish you would."

"Next week-end. I'll come on the bus."

"There's a football game," she said.

"Do you want to go?"

"I'd love it."

I squeezed her hand and we hurried from the room, for my mother was somewhere in the house.

2

It was a night game. I had sat close to her—our bodies touching, in fact—for two quarters and the half-time performance and now the band was leaving the field and soon the players would jog single file from the far end of the grandstand, but still I had not overcome the nervousness that had begun almost an hour before I called for Madeline at the dormitory. Sitting beside her I watched the players lined up for the kick-off and tried to assume the spirit of the crowd: the young men and women, standing now, smiling and laughing, their breath vaporific; I inhaled their aromas of whiskey, perfume, coffee, tobacco smoke and peanuts—then yelled encouragement to a halfback who didn't seem to need it. But I was thinking of Billy Travis, who had been a friend of mine in high school and was now attending the same college as Madeline. I was to spend the night in his room in the dormitory. In the afternoon I had seen him only briefly, while he was dressing for a pre-game party.

"Madeline Sheppard," he had said, standing at the mirror and combing his long hair.

Then he snickered. When he finished combing his hair he turned and smiled and shook water from the comb.

"Old Shep's been around some," he said.

"I've just met her."

That was all he said about her. Now I remembered it as the quarterback faded and was tackled before he could throw and they carried him from the field. Shep. The boys called her that when they stopped to speak to her or called to her from several seats away. Old Shep.

When the game ended we went to a night club; we were double-dating with a friend of Madeline and her fiance. We danced and after some drinks I talked about Hemingway. Madeline recited the first paragraph of "The Fall of the House of Usher," saying it was her favorite piece of prose. She asked whether I read poetry and I said that I didn't, but when I was five my father had hung Kipling's "If" on my wall and I had memorized it some time ago. Edna St. Vincent Millay was her favorite, she said, and she recited "Thursday," her face becoming vindictive as she said:

"'And why you come complaining
 Is more than I can see.
 I loved you Wednesday,—yes—but what
 Is that to me?'"

Then she said:

"Hard."

"Right. Like nails."

"You're not," she said.

"No. Neither are you."

"I should be."

"Why?"

She waved a hand toward the students on the dance floor.

"My lovely friends," she said. "You're young—"

"—Nineteen."

"Don't say it like that, like an apology. You're young and fresh and —*clean*."

"No, I'm not."

But I was, or I thought so; I was unaware of the asexual and more usual methods by which we make ourselves dirty and I thought of *clean* as a quality directly related to one's sex life. We virgins were clean.

"Yes, you are," she said. "But I'm not."

I thought of Billy Travis shaking water from his comb.

"I don't believe it," I said.

"You don't know me."

"I don't care: I don't believe it."

"Let's go outside."

We went out, shivering as we reached the car; we hugged each other for warmth and soon I was kissing her. Then she stopped.

"I want to talk to you."

We lit cigarettes.

"I've never known a man like you."

"I'm not a man."

"Stop talking like that: I'm only nineteen, I'm not a man—"

"All right."

"You're so innocent."

"So I can't marry you."

She sat erectly, drawing away from me.

"Why not?"

"Because you know more than I do. So I'll have to be like Hemingway first: I'll travel all over and have three wives and when I divorce the third one, I'll wire you from Madrid or someplace and tell you I'm ready for you."

"It's a deal."

"Fine. And I'll be good to you."

"I know you would. Have you ever hurt a girl?"

"I've never *had* a girl."

"You're kidding."

"No. Matter of fact, I'm even a virgin."

"Are you?"

"Afraid so."

"How did that happen?"

"I didn't want the first time to be with a whore, and no one else has given me a chance."

"That's wonderful."

"You think so?"

"Of course I do."

"Sometimes I like the idea myself."

She kissed my forehead, then my eyes.

"Tish's little brother," she said.

"Why do people hurt you?"

"Because I'm bad."

"Don't say that."

"I am. I'm a whore."

"If you say that again—"

I paused.

"You'll what?" she said.

"Slap you."

"I'm a whore."

She looked at me, waiting.

"Go ahead. I'm a whore, I'm a whore, I'm—"

I slapped her with my left hand, not hard, and she began to cry, her face on my chest. I held her, kissing her wet cheeks and eyes. We stayed in the car until her friends came out and drove us to the campus.

I woke early Sunday morning and walked to Mass at the chapel. When I returned to the dormitory Billy Travis was awake, lying in bed.

"How was Shep?" he said.

"Fine."

He smiled. I began to pack.

"I like her," I said.

I zipped the overnight bag and put it near the door.

"A hell of a lot," I said.

"What time's your bus?"

He dressed and drove me to the bus station, then went to his girl's house for dinner. In the bus station I sat in a chair against the wall and watched a stout red-faced woman of about fifty, carrying a large brown paper bag in place of luggage and wearing a wrinkled black dress. She bought her ticket and, counting her change and putting it in a worn coin purse which she dropped into a large straw purse dangling from her wrist, she walked to the wall and sat to my right. She adjusted her skirt over her spread knees—she was too obese to cross her legs—then pressed a finger across her nostrils; she waited a moment, then lowered the hand to her lap. On my other side was a thin unshaven man, his elbows on his knees, a sweet-smelling hand-rolled cigarette cupped in his hand. He stared at the floor and mumbled to himself. A boy of about ten sat beside him: one of those country boys whose faces look twice the age of their lean bodies. Looking from the man to the woman I imagined the foul acts they must have performed in their lives, these two old devils—they were so unkempt, soiled … Behind a separating glass door I saw Negroes in the colored waiting room, their ribald laughter exposing teeth and pink gums; soon they would board a bus and go quietly to the seats in its rear. Then I heard the bus and rose, turning my eyes from the Negroes as I moved toward the door but still thinking of them: illegitimacy and common law bigamy and cheap wine and a sudden terrible razor on Saturday night.

On the bus I closed my eyes and thought of Madeline, how after I slapped her she clung to me with much need, such dependence. I saw us as Brett and Jake, but without the wound; that afternoon I was sure we would marry and cross the ocean and live in France and Spain where I would write great novels. Perhaps she would even become a Catholic.

Across the aisle, the man I had watched in the waiting room was sleeping. Then he moaned. His boy sat beside him, looking out the window. The moan grew louder, grieving, as though his dream were of terrible loss. Disgusted, I closed my eyes and thought of Madeline, whom I would hold in my arms and shelter forever.

3

During the week we exchanged warm letters and the follow-ing week-end she came home with Tish. Several times as I talked to Madeline in the living room I caught my mother looking at me with scarcely concealed worry. Saturday night Tish had a date; Madeline and I bought a six-pack of beer and went to a drive-in movie. After drinking the beer we started kissing, leaving Richard Widmark in a fairly untenable position; when we next looked at the screen it was prompting us to eat pizza during the intermission. We left and drove to a country road and parked and there, for the second time in two dates, I made her cry. Recalling it now I am disturbed by my naivete in asking the question at all, for she had already called herself a whore. But remembering my attitudes at nineteen I realize that, for me, a whore could have been a girl who allowed certain hands into her blouse. So perhaps I asked her because I wasn't really certain. It was at some moment during the kissing; I drew back and said:

"Are you a virgin?"

She turned from me, looking out the windshield, and in a low intense whisper she gave me much more of an answer than I wanted, so that even now I can hear her sibilant words cutting through the passion of that front seat, dispelling it, leaving me then (and now) frail and exposed:

"*No.* No, I'm *not*—" Now she was crying "—*Oh* I'm going someplace— to *China* or someplace where they don't ask if you're a virgin on the second date—" Still she was not looking at me, her face lowered, her hands clenched in her lap "—oh they're so nice, they want to marry you, they give you presents and take you out and tell you they love you and one night you think this is it, this is the real thing, and you make love to them and then they go home and say that *whore*. I hate all of you."

I told her I did not care. I told her I loved her. She kissed and held me and soon we were cheerful again and passion returned, with its illusions, to the front seat.

4

On this same front seat two weeks later I could have lost my virginity. For two weeks we did not see each other. We wrote love letters. At the bottom of each was a postscript, something like this (the first one I wrote to her): *Have divorced third wife.*

Meet me Madrid. I love you, Papa. Madeline answered: *Arriving Madrid Sunday morning. Get bullfight tickets. Love, Number Four.* And another time: *When you're ninety-eight I'll be ninety-six,* to which she replied: *With me you are quite old. I need you very much.* She sent me a wallet-sized photograph; on the back she had written: *To Papa, with all my love, Number Four* (when I married Alice I burned it and have regretted it ever since). Then my father surprised me by letting me take the family car for the week-end.

Madeline and I went driving and ate a hamburger Saturday afternoon, then I left her at the dormitory and went to Billy Travis's room to change clothes. Billy and I did not talk about her.

She came down the dormitory stairs wearing a white sheath. I looked at her so lovingly that finally, smiling and her face coloring, she handed me her fur cape and turned from me and I carefully placed it around her shoulders. In the car she sat close to me, her aphrodisiac scents filling my head. I started to kiss her but she said:

"Not now. You'll mess me up."

We went to a night club crowded with students. Just inside the door she said: Wait a second, and stood looking at the dance floor and tables. As her eyes swept the room, people began to notice us. I took her hand.

"When I walk into a place," she said, "I want everyone there to love me or hate me. Either one—as long as I'm not ignored."

I thought of the cartoon she had told me was pinned to her wall in the dormitory: a meek violated man standing in a barrel and looking out, and under it was written: *People are no damned good.* Then I said:

"Be hard."

"Like nails."

This was a time when jitterbugging was in vogue, and that night Madeline put on a show. After a couple of drinks I was able to enjoy it, and I lead her into spaces on the dance floor where she could be watched. And, from the tables, they watched her. She danced seductively, telling them clearly enough that she was not a good girl, she did not intend to be, she was going to be bad tonight, and she did not care what they thought or even said about her. So they also watched us as we left the club, and certainly they believed that old Shep was at it again, this time with her roommate's little brother. They were right about that much, and looking back through seven years I wish I had given her my innocence—Alice swapped hers for mine, with somewhat of a fuss, six weeks before our wedding—but I did not.

Lying on the car seat, her hands moving in my hair, she said:

"I think I'll seduce you."

"I don't think you could."

For a moment she looked at me, then she smiled.

"I probably couldn't," she said.

That wasn't entirely true, but it was true enough, and I thought my motive was pure. She believed in me: I loved her and had never even attempted to touch her breasts; I spoke of marriage; I was also her friend. So we did not make love. We kissed with long breaks for cigarettes and talk, and since we had turned away from intimacy our talking turned back to it. She told me about the first man: Tommy Bertrand, a weight-lifter who owned a local gymnasium where he conducted classes for men and had recently begun calisthenics for women. He had the gymnasium when he met Madeline five years earlier, when he was twenty-four and she was sixteen. He launched a smooth steady offensive: bought her sweaters and dresses and golf clubs and finally made love to her. All this in a small town: a high school senior who was in the steady company of an older man, who sat close to him under sunlight and God and the eyes of everyone as his Oldsmobile convertible hummed through their streets. She was seventeen now, on the crest of a long affair that she thought would conclude with—or continue into—marriage. She did not know when this would happen. Then she became pregnant and knew.

He was gone. That was the first thing people saw. Next

she was gone; two weeks later she returned to a town that had guessed or even invented but somehow knew the truth: that her folks had arranged an abortion and now she was back among them as if nothing had ever happened. But it had. In their eyes she could do nothing but what she had done before, could be nothing but what she was. So she did just that. Except she did not become pregnant again.

She said that she and Tommy still exchanged birthday and Christmas cards. She did not hate him, she said; he was a man, and she should have known better. When I took her home that night I said:

"Madeline, we *will* go to Madrid."

"I believe you," she said.

Next morning she went to Mass with me. Some students were there. I received Communion, thinking if they saw Madeline with me, and I was receiving, they must know she hadn't sinned .....

5

The next week I began dating Alice, who was my age, an English major. We usually had serious conversations and kissed goodnight at her door. I had only meant to date her on weekends when I could not go see Madeline. We became close, and one night I told her about Madeline. I believed that my feelings and the tone of my voice allowed me to tell everything, and I did.

"Silly boy," Alice said, "Don't you understand what's happening?"

"What?"

"Never mind. I'll let you find out for yourself."

On a week-end in early December I went on the bus to date Madeline. We walked to a movie then several bars and planned to go to a New Year's Eve party with her friends. When I returned from Mass Sunday morning Steve Landry, another of my high school friends, was in Billy's room.

"How's Shep?" Steve said.

"Good."

"You get into that yet?" Billy said.

"Nope."

"Come on, man: no lie now. You making out?"

"No!"

"You're not screwing that?" Steve said.

"Y'all knock it off. I like Shep."

"Sure you like her," Billy said. "I do too. But you're not serious about that broad, are you?"

"I don't know."

"Steve, tell the man how many guys laid Shep."

"Who can count 'em? Nathan Shexneyder, Pat Mouton, Howie Thomas—them's steady ones. That weight-lifter knocked her up, what's his name—"

"Tommy Bertrand," Billy said.

"Yeah: him. Hell, I can't count 'em."

"All right," I said. "That's enough."

"You ought to get some of that," Billy said.

"I said that's enough."

"They say she's hot as hell," Steve said.

"Shut up! I don't care! I don't *care* about those lying son of a bitches."

"Lies?" Billy said. "Come on, man: you know better."

"I still don't care. I like her, and that's it."

"All right," Billy said. "Man wants to marry a broad that's laid everybody on the campus, let him go ahead and do it."

And suddenly I knew my other motive on the night I had not made love to her: I was afraid of failure, afraid that compared to her others I would be a mere fumbling boy. Looking at Billy and Steve my anger diminished as I thought of the grinning faces of former lovers watching Madeline walk up the aisle to marry me, and these same faces would haunt my passion with her forever.

I picked up my bag and started to leave.

"Forget it," Billy said. "I'll take you to the bus."

I paused.

"All right," I said.

That night I called Alice and took her out for a Coke.

6

I did not write to Madeline until Wednesday. For the first time since we started writing to each other, I wrote with effort, because now I did not see only Madeline when I looked at the stationery. Juxtaposed with her were shades: unknown hard faces (and bodies) who were named Nathan Shexneyder, Pat Mouton, Howie Thomas, Tommy Bertrand—and others whom even Steve could not remember. I saw her face transformed by passion in their parked cars, saw her body with theirs ...

Friday night she called me.

"I don't like your letter," she said.

"Why?"

"Something's wrong."

"No, everything's fine. I was a little distracted, studying and all."

"That's not it. Is it Alice?"

"I don't know."

"I want to know."

"I'll write you a good letter tonight and tell you about it."

"That's what I want," she said. "I love you, you know."

"And I love you."

"You think you do. If you don't love Alice."

"It's not that."

"Tell me all about it. Goodnight, Papa."

"Goodnight, Shep."

I wrote to her, saying I loved her but I was also attracted to Alice and, therefore confused. I left it at that. Her answer was she wished I'd make up my mind. We exchanged Christmas presents by mail. I had a Christmas Eve date with Alice. At her door, before kissing her goodnight, I said:

"What were you going to say about Shep that night?"

"What night?"

"When you told me you'd let me find out for myself."

"Have you found out?"

"I don't understand."

"Well, you know about the rotten apple and the good apple, don't you?"

"Yes. Yes: I suppose I do."

"Are you still a good apple? Or have you picked up some brown spots?"

"No spots," I said.

My father let me use the car for the New Year's Eve party; he said if I was going to a drunken brawl he'd rather know I was driving than riding with some drunk irresponsible fool.

Madeline was staying at a friend's house. When she greeted me at the door, she knew we were finished. Since the Sunday with Billy and Steve, my letters had been imitations of the letters I had written before. At the door my face was probably as transparently spurious as those letters.

The party started at someone's house then moved to a nightclub where a Negro band was playing. Madeline and I were often separated, dancing with other people; once I went to the telephone booth and spent two dollars calling Alice to wish her a happy New Year. I told her I felt out of place at the party.

"You are," she said.

When I got through the dance floor and reached our table Madeline was kissing a tall lean boy with a ducktail haircut.

"This is Larry Fleming," she said.

"I haven't heard about you."

Madeline glanced at me, then looked for a cigarette. For an instant her glance made me recall the way it had been with us, how she had trusted me and told me things about herself that I doubt she had ever told to another boy. Then I was shaking Larry Fleming's hand and the instant had passed. He slapped my shoulder.

"Have a cool Yule and jive in '55," he said.

"Crazy."

He turned to light Madeline's cigarette.

"Hey, man—mind if I kiss her again?"

"You buying the beer?" I said.

He laughed and slapped my shoulder.

"You're all right, man. Yeah, I'm buyin'."

Madeline was glaring at me. He ordered three beers and kissed her, a long kiss that I watched her return. Then we sat and drank. Larry was a drummer, having a combo that played for high school and college dances; while he talked one hand tapped the table in time with the music. He told her about hearing Stan Getz in New Orleans. Then he stood and took her hand.

"Hey, you mind if we dance?" he said to me.

"Go ahead."

I watched them jitterbugging. Larry danced better than I; Madeline was dancing seductively, as she always did. I looked away. They danced several times before returning to the table, where they stood with arms around each other and kissed. I rose and put a hand on his shoulder.

"I'm dry," I said.

For a moment he was puzzled; then he understood.

"Oh yeah. Yeah: crazy."

He yelled at a Negro waiter to bring three beers. Madeline was looking at me.

"There's a name for people like you," she said.

"There's a name for people like you too."

"You didn't have to say that."

She kissed Larry.

Long after midnight, which came while Madeline was dancing with another old friend and I was dancing with a drunk sleepy-eyed girl whom I kissed while the band played "Auld Lang Syne," I took Madeline home. At the door she turned to face me and said:

"Well, Papa."

I held her fur collar and lightly kissed her.

"We won't be going to Madrid," she said.

"That's a different book."

"We didn't get to that one."

"No," I said.

"The sleeping bag would have been nice."

"I know."

"Damn those sweet little girls."

"It's not just Alice."

"What else?"

"I don't know—I'm too young and stupid and confused, I don't know anything. I—"

"Don't say too much. You might say something I don't want to hear."

"All right."

"Hell. Just when I was really falling in love with you."

"Shep—"

"Never mind. Don't worry about old Shep."

She smiled.

"Be hard," she said. "Like nails."

She kissed me quickly and went inside.

My mother was relieved, my father and Tish were non-committal, and Alice was smug: she kept me waiting four months before telling me she loved me. We finished school before marrying: during our courtship we studied hard; our social life was moderate, and we did not make love until the wedding was planned. Six weeks later we got married, and her father gave us the down payment on a house. It is a nice house, just outside of this town where I have lived for twenty-six years and where I now live with my son and Alice. She is what I deserve.

THEY NOW LIVE IN TEXAS

for Peggy

WHEN THEY LEFT the party near midnight she felt sober enough to drive, but in the heated car on the way home she knew she was not. Her husband was driving with both hands, leaning forward, and she could see space between his shoulders and upper back and the car seat. She looked through the windshield at the moving reach of their headlights; on both sides of the road were snowbanks, then woods. She said: "Stephen told me about his religious experience."

"He had one of those?"

"Before AA."

"Whatever it was, it worked."

When they approached their house, free of neighbors for three acres, she told her husband she was not drunk but she was not sober, and asked him to drive the sitter home. He smiled and said he wasn't sober either but the car didn't seem to know it, and as he turned he shifted down then accelerated and climbed the long and sanded driveway.

The girl rose from the couch, turned off the television, and putting on her parka said the children had gone to bed on time, and had given her no trouble. The woman thanked and paid her and walked her to the door, then lay her coat beside her purse on the dining room table and went down the hall, into the room where her four-year-old daughter slept among stuffed bears. For moments she stood looking at her daughter's face in the light from the hall, then she crept out and went into the next room where the six-year-old girl slept with three animals she had loved since she was two: an elephant, a bear, and a rabbit. The woman pulled the blankets to the girl's shoulder and left.

She made a cup of tea with honey and lemon and drank it at the dining room table. She reached across her coat for the cigarettes in her purse as her husband turned into the driveway. In the kitchen he set the alarm, two high beeps behind her, then at the dining room door he stopped and said: "How are you?"

She looked over her left shoulder at him.

"Not sober yet. I'll wait till I am before I go to bed."

"Good plan." He came to her, taking off his coat, and leaned over and kissed her goodnight. Walking down the hall he said: "I should do what you're doing. But I'm wasted."

She watched him go into the girls' rooms, then the bedroom at the hall's end, and close the door. She finished her tea, then left the table and descended two steps into the living room. Last night her husband had brought home two movies because he liked her to have a choice. They had watched the Australian one, *Man of Flowers*, and she could not recall ever seeing a movie so beautiful. All of its music was from *Lucia di Lammermoor* and the movie itself achieved the splendid sadness of opera, for the man of the title was unique, bizarre: she could watch it in the way she listened to music, with a sorrow that uplifted her, for it did not demand empathy. The one they had not watched was a horror movie.

She pressed buttons and inserted the cassette, went to the kitchen and turned on flames under the kettle, then in the bathroom brushed her teeth; but as she poured boiling water into her cup she could taste again onions and tahini. She turned out the kitchen light, and those in the living room, and started the movie and settled on the couch with cigarettes and tea.

The woman in the movie was divorced and lived in Southern California with her children: a girl of about fourteen, and a boy and girl who appeared twelve and nine. They had an almost new car and a small good house and no one mentioned money; the mother did some sort of work, in an office with people, but only a few brief scenes showed it, and either because of the long and frightening action in the home or the Scotch the woman had drunk while she listened to Stephen in the kitchen, the work remained unclear.

The television was at one corner of the room and, to its right, the wall was a long window. The blinds were up, and now and then she glanced from the movie to the snow in front of the house: the white slope, and the scattered shapes of young trees, and, farther right, the sharp bank of the driveway. She knew she ought to lower the blinds, use them against the escaping heat and its cost, but she and her husband had built on this hill so they could look at the sky, and the woods and meadow across the road in front of their house, and she did not lower the blinds. But she stood and, watching the movie, lowered those on the left of the television, and covered the wide sliding glass door to the sundeck.

Something no one could see attacked the mother in her home. Its attacks were in the beginning those of a poltergeist: sounds that woke her, and the source of these sounds could only be another presence, or the malfunctioning of her mind; a jewelry box and evening bag exchanged places on her dressing table; doors closed or opened while the air was still; and sometimes there was nothing tangible, but a force the mother felt, usually in her bedroom, always at night.

Stephen had been sober for one month and four days when he heard a voice in his car as he drove alone one night, and in those moments he felt a strong but good presence in the front seat. Perhaps inside his body too. His face and voice as he told her the story made her believe now that it entered him. Probably he said it had. It loved him. He had never felt so loved, and he released himself to it, and then he wept. The flow of tears felt on his cheeks like the final drops of his agony.

The presence drew them from him, as first it had drawn from him not only his struggle against drunkenness, but his very struggle to survive: every effort he had made, every strength he had mustered, since his birth, or even conception. He joyfully surrendered himself to the gift he was receiving: he had never been strong and he would never again need the resolve to be.

Watching a close-up of the mother fearfully closing her eyes for another night, the woman began to cry. She flicked and wiped away tears and focused on the dark bedroom and the face finally asleep, then her tears stopped and her throat dried and her heart felt dry too, a heavy vessel of solid sighs, drawn downward by gravity. She touched her cheeks and knew her make-up was unmarred. If her husband should enter the room now, sit beside her and turn on a lamp, he could not know that she had cried. There was much that he did not need to know, and she envied him now, and many other times, or perhaps only longed for his certainty. He loved her and the girls and most of the time—no: enough of the time—his work. He not only expected nothing else but was content not to. She loved him and her daughters and—enough—her work, and she loved herself too. So her husband loved himself, if that meant being generally happy, and able to live without any of the drugs of her friends: liquor, or therapists or shrinks, or trying to prolong their lives with exercise and atrophied sensuality.

But certainly Stephen had always loved himself. How else explain his years of fighting and failing but always fighting, until the night a voice, a something, visited his car. He knew what the voice said. She understood that, in the kitchen where they leaned against the counter and she vaguely saw and heard friends moving, talking, pouring chablis. But she did not ask him for the words, and he did not offer them. For two years he had not drunk or missed it, and he went to daily Mass. He told her of Mass and communion in one soft, quick sentence; and though his face did not change color its flesh seemed held by a blush.

The attacks in the movie were vicious now: the thing

spoke the mother's name, cursed her, lifted her and flung her against walls and to the ceiling. Her children ran screaming to her room, to her. No one could help; only one person tried. The psychiatrist did not believe her; or he believed she was alone in her room. The medical doctor and the two scientists at the college did not believe her either. Only one man did, a friend not a lover. He sat with her on the final night, and when the thing attacked he cursed it and leaped at it and it threw him across the room. He was unconscious while, for the first time, it raped her. The children held each other just inside her doorway and cried and could not close or even avert their eyes. In the morning the mother and children got into the car and drove away from the house, and the camera moved back from their faces, the mother's last, then from a high distance showed the car traversing a landscape of brown and yellow hills. The scene faded, then words appeared on a blue background: The events you have just seen occurred in the lives of a real family. They now live in Texas.

She read the credits then stood and turned off the television and pressed the button to rewind the cassette. Listening to its sound she looked out at the snow. Then she removed the cassette and put it in its case. She sat on the couch and smoked, staring beyond the road at the meadow and trees and stars. She was looking out the window and reaching beside her for another cigarette, when suddenly she knew she was waiting. Quickly she stood and took the ash tray and her tea cup to the kitchen.

THE CURSE

Mɪᴛᴄʜᴇʟʟ Hᴀʏᴇs was forty-nine years old, but when the cops left him in the bar with Bob, the manager, he felt much older. He did not know what it was like to be very old, a shrunken and wrinkled man, but he assumed it was like this: fatigue beyond relieving by rest, by sleep. He also was not a small man: his weight moved up and down in the hundred and seventies and he was five feet, ten inches tall. But now his body seemed short and thin. Bob stood at one end of the bar; he was a large black-haired man, and there was nothing in front of him but an ash tray he was using. He looked at Mitchell at the cash register and said: "Forget it. You heard what Smitty said."

Mitchell looked away, at the front door. He had put the chairs upside down on the table. He looked from the door past Bob to the empty space of floor at the rear; sometimes people danced there, to the jukebox. Opposite Bob, on the wall behind the bar, was a telephone; Mitchell looked at it. He had told Smitty there were five guys and when he moved to the phone one of them stepped around the corner of the bar and shoved him: one hand against Mitchell's chest, and it pushed him backward; he nearly fell. That was when they were getting rough with her at the bar. When they took her to the floor Mitchell looked once at her sounds, then looked down at the duckboard he stood on, or at the belly or chest of a young man in front of him.

He knew they were not drunk. They had been drinking before they came to his place, a loud popping of motorcycles outside, then walking into the empty bar, young and sunburned and carrying helmets and wearing thick leather jackets in August. They stood in front of Mitchell and drank drafts. When he took their first order he thought they were on drugs and later, watching them, he was certain. They were not relaxed, in the way of most drinkers near closing time. Their eyes were quick, alert as wary animals, and they spoke loudly, with passion, but their passion was strange and disturbing, because they were only chatting, bantering. Mitchell knew nothing of the effects of drugs, so could not guess what was in their blood. He feared and hated drugs because of his work and because he was the stepfather of teenagers: a boy and a girl. He gave last call and served them and leaned against the counter behind him.

Then the door opened and the girl walked in from the night, a girl he had never seen, and she crossed the floor toward Mitchell. He stepped forward to tell her she had missed last call, but before he spoke she asked for change for the cigarette machine. She was young, he guessed nineteen to twenty-one, and deeply tanned and had dark hair. She was sober and wore jeans and a dark blue tee shirt. He gave her quarters but she was standing between two of the men and she did not get to the machine.

When it was over and she lay crying on the cleared circle of the floor, he left the bar and picked up the jeans and tee shirt beside her and crouched and handed them to her. She did not look at him. She lay the clothes across her breasts and what Mitchell thought of now as her wound. He left her and dialed 911, then Bob's number. He woke up Bob. Then he picked up her sneakers from the floor and placed them beside her and squatted near her face, her crying. He wanted to speak to her and touch her, hold a hand or press her brow, but he could not.

The cruiser was there quickly, the siren coming east from town, then slowing and deepening as the car stopped outside.

He was glad Smitty was one of them; he had gone to high school with Smitty. The other was Dave, and Mitchell knew him because it was a small town. When they saw the girl Dave went out to the cruiser to call for an ambulance, and when he came back he said two other cruisers had those scumbags and were taking them in. The girl was still crying and could not talk to Smitty and Dave. She was crying when a man and woman lifted her onto a stretcher and rolled her out the door and she vanished forever in a siren.

Bob came in while Smitty and Dave were sitting at the bar drinking coffee and Smitty was writing his report; Mitchell stood behind the bar. Bob sat next to Dave as Mitchell said: "I could have stopped them, Smitty."

"That's our job," Smitty said. "You want to be in the hospital now?"

Mitchell did not answer. When Smitty and Dave left, he got a glass of Coke from the cobra and had a cigarette with Bob. They did not talk. Then Mitchell washed his glass and Bob's cup and they left, turning off the lights. Outside Mitchell locked the front door, feeling the sudden night air after almost ten hours of air conditioning. When he had come to work the day had been very hot, and now he thought it would not have happened in winter. They had stopped for a beer on their way somewhere from the beach; he had heard them say that. But the beach was not the reason. He did not know the reason, but he knew it would not have happened in winter. The night was cool and now he could smell trees. He turned and looked at the road in front of the bar. Bob stood beside him on the small porch.

"If the regulars had been here," Bob said.

He turned and with his hand resting on the wooden rail he walked down the ramp to the ground. At his car he stopped and looked over its roof at Mitchell.

"You take it easy," he said.

Mitchell nodded. When Bob got in his car and left, he went down the ramp and drove home to his house on a street that he thought was neither good nor bad. The houses were small and there were old large houses used now as apartments for families. Most of the people had work, most of the mothers cared for their children, and most of the children were clean and looked like they lived in homes, not caves like some he saw in town. He worried about the older kids, one group of them anyway. They were idle. When he was a boy in a town farther up the Merrimack River, he and his friends committed every mischievous act he could recall on afternoons and nights when they were idle. His stepchildren were not part of that group. They had friends from the high school. The front porch light was on for him and one in the kitchen at the rear of the house. He went in the front door and switched off the porch light and walked through the living and dining rooms to the kitchen. He got a can of beer from the refrigerator, turned out the light, and sat at the table. When he could see, he took a cigarette from Susan's pack in front of him.

Down the hall he heard Susan move on the bed then get up and he hoped it wasn't for the bathroom but for him. He had met her eight years ago when he had given up on ever marrying and having kids, then one night she came into the bar with two of her girl friends from work. She made six dollars an hour going to homes of invalids, mostly what she called her little old ladies, and bathing them. She got the house from her marriage, and child support the guy paid for a few months till he left town and went south. She came barefoot down the hall and stood in the kitchen doorway and said: "Are you all right?"

"No."

She sat across from him, and he told her. Very soon she held his hand. She was good. He knew if he had fought all five of them and was lying in pieces in a hospital bed she would tell him he had done the right thing, as she was telling him now. He liked her strong hand on his. It was a professional hand and he wanted from her something he had never wanted before: to lie in bed while she bathed him. When they went to bed he did not think he would be able to sleep, but she kneeled beside him and massaged his shoulders and rubbed his temples and pressed her hands on his forehead. He woke to the voices of Marty and Joyce in the kitchen. They had summer jobs, and always when they woke him he went back to sleep till noon, but now he got up and dressed and went to the kitchen door. Susan was at the stove, her back to him, and Marty and Joyce were talking and smoking. He said good morning, and stepped into the room.

"What are you doing up?" Joyce said.

She was a pretty girl with her mother's wide cheekbones and Marty was a tall good-looking boy, and Mitchell felt as old as he had before he slept. Susan was watching him. Then she poured him a cup of coffee and put it at his place and he sat. Marty said: "You getting up for the day?"

"Something happened last night. At the bar." They tried to conceal their excitement, but he saw it in their eyes. "I should have stopped it. I think I *could* have stopped it. That's the point. There were these five guys. They were on motorcycles but they weren't bikers. Just punks. They came in late, when everybody else had gone home. It was a slow night anyway. Everybody was at the beach."

"They rob you?" Marty said.

"No. A girl came in. Young. Nice looking. You know: just a girl, minding her business."

They nodded, and their eyes were apprehensive.

"She wanted cigarette change, that's all. Those guys were on dope. Coke or something. You know: they were flying in place."

"Did they rape her?" Joyce said.

"Yes, honey."

"The *fuck*ers."

Susan opened her mouth then closed it and Joyce reached quickly for Susan's pack of cigarettes. Mitchell held his lighter for her and said: "When they started getting rough with her at the bar I went for the phone. One of them stopped me. He shoved me, that's all. I should have hit him with a bottle."

Marty reached over the table with his big hand and held Mitchell's shoulder.

"No, Mitch. Five guys that mean. And coked up or whatever. No way. You wouldn't be here this morning."

"I don't know. There was always a guy with me. But just one guy, taking turns."

"Great," Joyce said. Marty's hand was on Mitchell's left shoulder; she put hers on his right hand.

"They took her to the hospital," he said. "The guys are in jail."

"They are?" Joyce said.

"I called the cops. When they left."

"You'll be a good witness," Joyce said.

He looked at her proud face.

"At the trial," she said.

The day was hot but that night most of the regulars came to the bar. Some of the younger ones came on motorcycles. They were a good crowd: they all worked, except the retired ones, and no one ever bothered the women, not even the young ones with their summer tans. Everyone talked about it: some had read the newspaper story, some had heard the story in town, and they wanted to hear it from Mitchell. He told it as often as they asked but he did not finish it because he was working hard and could not stay with any group of customers long enough.

He watched their faces. Not one of them, even the women, looked at him as if he had not cared enough for the girl, or was a coward. Many of them even appeared sympathetic, making him feel for moments that he was a survivor of something horrible, and when that feeling left him he was ashamed. He felt tired and old, making drinks and change, moving and talking up and down the bar. At the stool at the far end Bob drank coffee and whenever Mitchell looked at him he smiled or nodded and once raised his right fist, with the thumb up.

Reggie was drinking too much. He did that two or three times a month and Mitchell had to shut him off and Reggie always took it humbly. He was a big gentle man with a long brown beard. But tonight shutting off Reggie demanded from Mitchell an act of will, and when the eleven o'clock news came on the television and Reggie ordered another shot and a draft, Mitchell pretended not to hear him. He served the customers at the other end of the bar, where Bob was. He could hear Reggie calling: Hey Mitch; shot and a draft, Mitch. Mitchell was close to Bob now. Bob said softly: "He's had enough."

Mitchell nodded and went to Reggie, leaned closer to him so he could speak quietly, and said: "Sorry, Reggie. Time for coffee. I don't want you dead out there."

Reggie blinked at him.

"Okay, Mitch." He pulled some bills from his pocket and put them on the bar. Mitchell glanced at them and saw at least a ten dollar tip. When he rang up Reggie's tab the change was sixteen dollars and fifty cents, and he dropped the coins and shoved the bills into the beer mug beside the cash register. The mug was full of bills, as it was on most nights, and he kept his hand in there, pressing Reggie's into the others, and saw the sunburned young men holding her down on the floor and one kneeling between her legs, spread and held, and he heard their cheering voices and her screaming and groaning and finally weeping and weeping and weeping, until she was the siren crying then fading into the night. From the floor behind him, far across the room, he felt her pain and terror and grief, then her curse upon him. The curse moved into his back and spread down and up his spine, into his stomach and legs and arms and shoulders until he quivered with it. He wished he were alone so he could kneel to receive it.

RIDING NORTH

for Lara J. K. Wilson

1

ON AN OLD SPOTTED HORSE he rode into Adrienne Beaumont's life, and took her father's: a big man with blond hair to his shoulders and a thick beard that covered his throat; she was twenty years old, wearing gray trousers and a blue shirt, and was crossing the living room when she saw him through the front window, sitting on his horse, talking to her father in the noon light of summer. She looked past them at the ocean two miles beyond green and yellow grass, then was climbing the stairs to her room when she heard the shot and ran outside, horses moving in the corral, one neighing, her father on the ground, the man standing with the revolver in his hand; she turned to run inside for the carbine, heard his feet quick behind her, then his arm was around her neck, lifting her, and throwing her to the ground on her stomach, beside her father lying on his back. Then the man's weight dropped on her, pushing out her breath. He pulled her up, so she was kneeling, and she swung her right fist up and back, turning with it, hitting his face once, his arm twice, then she felt the point of a knife at the side of her throat, and she was still, her weight on her knees, and on her arms beside her face, while he worked on her buttons, slowly, murmuring. Then he pulled her trousers and bloomers down. She cried for her father, still hoping the hole in his chest had not killed him, still hoping she could kill this man. Then it was happening to her, alone on a hill, alone in California, alone in the world, her mother dead and her sister in Texas as far away as the moon, and she cried out in pain as he grunted and said "virgin girl," the smell of his body like urine and cheese, his breath above her decaying fruit, the smells of what was happening, staining her forever, Adrienne knowing this while unable to envision forever or even life for one more minute. Sounds came from him, breath and grunts with his smell. He quickened his thrusts, then was still, then out of her; she did not open her eyes. She waited for him to push the knife into her artery. Then it was gone too; she opened her eyes, and rolled on her back and pulled up her clothes, watched him standing at her feet, putting a dagger in its sheath on his chest, pulling up his pants, buckling. He bent for his chaps and gun belt on the ground and buckled them on too. He looked at her and winked; she stared at his green eyes but saw in her mind his gun when it was on the ground at her feet; while he was pulling up his pants she could have shot him. She watched him take the bridle from his horse, then he walked toward the corral and barn behind her. She crawled to her father, looked at his dead brown eyes and the hole in his chest, then she lay against him and lifted his head and held it with both arms, her cheek on his with its whiskers grown since his early morning shave. She lay there crying till she heard a walking horse and looked up at the man leading Chief Joseph, the brown stallion, and she yelled: "He's my father's horse!"

"I'm trading."

"I'll kill you."

"I'll be back."

She sat up, was gathering her legs under her to run for the carbine; he drew the revolver, and pointed it at her face.

"You want another hole in you?"

She wanted to die; then she did not. She sat still, her breath fast, not crying now.

"Good. I like the one you got."

He holstered the gun and unsaddled his horse. Chief Joseph backed away from him, but he pulled down on the reins and swung the saddle up and on. She watched him cinch and mount, his back to her, Chief Joseph rearing once, then again, and in her grief, tiny but sharp and bright was hope and now she was waiting for Chief Joseph to throw him and she would be in the house in the instant it took her mind to see the carbine and her working the lever and coming out the door shooting him. He held the reins, one arm in the air; then she heard him, realized she had been hearing him: the same sounds he had made when he was in her, and Chief Joseph stopped rearing, snorted, jerked his head up and down, then settled. The man turned Chief Joseph toward her and grinned.

"Fine horse, pretty girl, fine day."

Then he rode north, slowly, and she began to cry, and lay on her father, covering the wound, her face above his, her left hand beneath his head; with her right she smoothed his dark brown hair. Her fingers kept combing it. Somewhere behind her or above her, or far beneath her heart, and her hot pain, somewhere she could not yet feel, was time: she would have to stand and dig a long, deep hole. She kept combing his hair, her tears falling to his face, drops on his brown and gray moustache, till she had no more, only their taste, and the sun and dry air took them from her father's cheeks and brow. Still she combed his hair, and there was no time; she did not know how much of it had passed when she heard a horse coming slowly behind her, from the south; on the dirt trail that some days was trod only by deer, the sound of hooves seized her: she stood whirling, then was still, looking at a Negro, a hundred feet away, stopped on the trail. His face was good. He looked at her, and at her father, and dismounted; he walked to her, past the spotted horse, his eyes lowered. He stopped ten or twelve paces from her, as though at a gate he would not enter. He was nearly as big as the other one, his curly hair hid the backs of his ears and touched his purple bandana; he took off his tan hat and said: "Can I help?"

2

Stephen Leness looked at her grieving eyes and the blood on her pants and shirt and knew she saw him as a man, and one she needed, the big white house to his right either empty or holding other dead; she did not see him as meat to dislike on sight, or to command, or to fear. You could tell at once, by their eyes. This one may change when things got better, but he thought she would not. He waited. She did not answer, or even move. He said: "Is anybody in the house?"

She shook her head once, tears starting. She wiped them with the back of her hand and said: "He's my father."

He put on his hat and moved slowly toward the man, knowing he was dead, he had known that when he first saw her combing his hair, but he squatted and looked, then said: "I could close his eyes."

"I will."

He watched her fingers touching the face, then the lids, closing them. She smelled clean. He stood and said: "Who did this thing?"

He looked at her back. She was combing his hair again.

"He just came riding up. Like you. Then he rode north."

Stephen looked north at hills with trees and green slopes and yellow and green crowns.

"How long ago?"

"I don't know."

"Did he cut your neck?"

She stood, her hand rising to the small wound, and she looked at the blood on her fingers.

"With a dagger."

"A dagger?"

"Narrow blade, double-edged, in a sheath on his chest. He

had the point there while he was doing what he wanted to do instead of killing me. It was all the same to him, all the same to me. Except for one thing: now I can kill him."

Suddenly he was full of sorrow for this girl, and he liked her very much; he did not know if she needed a doctor, he knew she needed the law, somebody riding after the man he was starting to hate, and he felt that she did not want either but he said it anyway, said he could go back to San Diego but she shook her head again and again till he stopped, then she did, and he knew something he was not ready to know yet.

"Well," he said, and waited for a thought, looking at her eyes. "Do you have people around?"

"No."

"Then we should bury him."

"Yes."

"Do you want me to take him inside? Dress him in something?"

"He's a retired colonel."

"You think he'd want his uniform?"

"Yes."

"All right then. Maybe a sword, if he had one. A flag?"

"The sword."

"I'll carry him inside. Want me to do anything else? Is that your horse?"

"It's his. He took my father's."

Stephen turned and looked at the horse; it was old. Who was this man, wearing a dagger with a shoulder rig and riding a horse a boy could catch with a pony? And he had not stolen anything; or he had but there was no place in the girl's heart and tongue now for the loss of things and money. This man did not earn or even steal money on horseback. But now he had a good one, like the others Stephen had seen in the corral when he rode up the trail, going to Los Angeles to see his sister and brother for a few days, maybe a few weeks, money in his pocket, enough to keep him till he wanted to work on a ranch again; till then play baseball and sit in the sun with a cigar, drink with his family and tell them about Mexico, where white people got that look in Mexicans' eyes and black people seldom did, and the women did not cook better than his sister and sister-in-law, but almost as well; he would have married one, but he never met her. Now, thinking about the man with the dagger and the old horse, he felt a touch of fear in his stomach; it left him when he turned to the girl, who was looking at the horse. He saw that she was trying not to blame the animal, though she wanted to kill it. He said: "I'll take him with me."

"Please do."

Then she walked quickly inside. He went to his horse he had named Sarah for his sister, and stroked her neck and looked down at the trail he had chosen because he had been in no hurry and had felt like riding up on the hills, seeing the ocean from up there, and now it seemed the trail had chosen him. He led Sarah to the corral and at the gate stopped, an instinct telling him to go to the house and ask permission, then he knew it would be like asking her if he could keep breathing. He brought Sarah in and to the trough. He counted fourteen horses; others could be in the barn. His hand was on the saddle. Then, with resignation coming so quickly and sharply that fatigue came with it, then left him in a sigh, he took off the deerskin bag and his canteen and rope and bedroll and saddlebag and the double-barreled shotgun in its scabbard. Then he took off the saddle, and Sarah stopped drinking and looked back at him. He put the saddle on the ground with everything he owned and pulled the blanket off and dropped it, and walked out of the corral to the spotted horse and put him in too; that had been in the girl's eyes when she was hating the horse for a few seconds: it ought to be able to live, drink. Then he went to the girl's father. He was a tall man with broad shoulders; Stephen squatted, slid his arms under the butt and back, then lifted, his legs working hard to straighten. He looked at the man's face and said: "How many bullets missed you, and you get shot in your own yard on a pretty day."

He looked about fifty, not much older; probably he fought the Confederates, when he was a young man, or maybe the

Union; but his daughter did not have a southern accent, or
any accent at all; he wondered what her name was. Her father
may have fought Indians too, after the war. It would be easier
to swing him over one shoulder, but she ought not to see him
carried into the house that way; holding him in his arms, Stephen crossed the yard, and climbed the porch's two steps; the
door was open. He smelled baking beans and burning wood.
He turned, so the man was perpendicular to the door, his head
toward it, and carried him into a big room with stairs at one
end and a fireplace with three carbines and three shotguns on
a rack above it, and books on shelves, and a glass-doored case
of revolvers, and good chairs, and portraits on the wall: the
girl three or four years younger, her father in uniform, probably the mother and a sister older than the girl. To his left the
girl stood in the dining room, at a table covered by a sheet; a
pan of water was on it, and a wash-cloth and a towel. How
many had she buried? He felt the paintings behind him, as if
they watched. He brought the colonel to the table and lowered him, trying to do it quietly; the only sound was the riding
boots hitting the table. The colonel had been a cavalryman.
He said: "Do you want help?"

"I'd like to be alone with him. Do you want some of his
whiskey?"

He did, but he said: "Maybe later. I should dig."

"I'll show you where."

He followed her through the kitchen and outside, the barn
to his left, and to his right, in the shade of an oak, the out-
house, and up the slope ahead of him the pump at the well.
This place filled him with love and longing, as though the
earth itself recognized him, wanted to hold him. Behind the
barn was a chicken coop, then vegetables growing, lettuce,
and beans and green tomatoes on stakes he imagined the girl
driving into the ground, working in peace, not knowing this
day was coming; corn still low, and ahead of him, up the slope,
were orange trees, and he knew she was leading him there.
He looked at her braid and the back of her shirt and the heels
of her black boots like the colonel's. She walked gingerly,

leaning forward, limping with each leg. To his left, pines grew on the ridge line. For a moment he forgot what he was doing here: he wanted to walk through the orange trees, look down the hill at the lowland to the east; it would be pines and oaks and scrub brush and anything you wanted to hunt. He looked back at the big white house, thin smoke rising from the stove chimney, then looked ahead and nearly walked into her back; she had stopped at the edge of the trees. Then she raised her foot and kicked back and down, gouging the earth. She did it three more times, then said: "Here. With his feet toward the ocean, and his head at the trees."

"That's a nice place."

She was still looking at the ground. She said: "I can help dig."

"I know you can. You take care of your father."

"He needs a coffin."

Then she turned and looked at him.

"And a cross. I can get someone, if you want to go."

"I don't want to."

"I'll pay you for this."

"No."

"I won't forget it."

"That's plenty." He suddenly knew that a lot of people had forgotten him; he was twenty-seven years old. "Where are the tools?"

"In the barn. On the east wall. There's wood too. He's a soldier. He likes simple things."

So it was the wife, buried someplace else, for there were no graves here, who chose or inherited the leather chairs, and wood and straw rockers, the china cupboard in the dining room, and God knew what in the bedrooms upstairs. A soldier could like books, collect those and read them, and the girl would; in his bag in the corral he had the Bible and he read a chapter every morning with his coffee; he was named for the first Christian martyr; fear moved lightly up his legs into his back, then out of him; he did not want to be the second martyr named Stephen. He looked at the ground near the orange trees;

he was sure the mother was dead. She would not have left these people, this place, not for any man. She was buried somewhere else. The girl said: "You'll need his measurements."

"Sure."

He turned toward the house, then she said: "I'm Adrienne Beaumont."

He turned to her. She held out her hand, palm down, and with his fingers and thumb he held it for a moment, a small strong hand with calluses. In Mexico he had held the soft hands of whores.

"Stephen Leness."

"I haven't heard that name."

"A Swede or a Finn. Nobody knows anymore. Not much of him left. As you can see."

For an instant she nearly smiled; or she was smiling, but her lips could not do it.

"We don't have much of the Frenchman either."

They walked down to the house, Stephen looking at the ocean, and for a few moments, gazing at the calm blue water, he felt blessed, peaceful; this is what he had ridden the trail to see, and now he was doing what he could for a sad girl. He touched the butt of his Colt, ran his fingers over the bullets in his belt, front and back, and the blessing was gone, as though it had taken him out of the world long enough to see it clearly, purely, and then put him back into it. He felt bullets and the earth under his boots, then the floor of the kitchen. He breathed the sweet smell of beans. In the dining room he stood at the table with the colonel and she went upstairs and came down with a measuring tape and gave him one end; he went to the colonel's feet, and she said: "Six-one. I knew that."

She measured from arm to arm.

"Twenty-five."

She gave him the tape, and he went to the barn. There were twenty-four stalls, horses in some, a cow in one. He found the tools and saw horses and stacked boards; they were pine. What had the colonel planned to build? By God, he had just learned the girl's name, he had not been here an hour, and everything he saw and touched was the history of a man who had been alive this morning. They could not just drop him into the grave; they could do it with ropes, poor girl helping him. Adrienne. He was hungry, but he took off his gunbelt and chaps and spurs and began to work.

3

She put his black boots on last, the polished ones from his closet. She had not looked at a clock since the man shot her father; Stephen was sawing; her blood on her legs was dry. She looked at her father in blue, the saber beside him; then she went upstairs to her room, looked in the full length mirror on the wardrobe at her father's blood on her shirt, hers on her pants; she touched the wound on her throat, then looked out the windows at the ocean. She placed her boot in the bootjack, and pulled it off, then the other, and leaned against her bedpost to remove her long socks. From a shelf in the wardrobe she took a folded blanket and trousers and a shirt she had made; she opened the blanket on the bed, put her clothes on it, and tied its corners. From the top shelf she took her revolver on the army belt she had cut and notched; the holster had a flap. She put on the belt and, carrying the bundle, we went downstairs and into the corral, then the barn. At the far end, behind stalls, Stephen was sawing; she took her bridle from its peg on the wall; she could not endure a saddle now. She walked into the sun to tall gray Missy standing at the fence and put on the bridle and led her out of the mares' corral, across the trail; then she mounted, pain blazing in her for so long now, and she started Missy walking.

The sound of the saw became faint when she was going down the slope, and she squeezed with her legs, kicked once, and Missy cantered, flushing a rabbit, then another, Adrienne looking at the ocean, the surf and waves, seeing the blood on her legs, in her pubic hair, stiff with it now; seeing the ocean; the heat of Missy's wide back soothed her pain. She skirted low brush, and the ground flattened and gently dipped and gently rose, then sloped toward the beach, Adrienne breathing fast and feeling the blood inside her now, unshed and rushing; soon she would hear the waves breaking; her soul was scattered in the sunlight, and on the ground in front of the house, and hanging tattered from the house, floating in the barn with Stephen and saw and wood and hammer and nails, and at the edge of the orange grove, and blowing in dry pieces through the twenty years she had lived. But her blood, her flesh, rode with fierce love, out of brush and grass and onto the dry sand where she let go of the reins and took off her gun and tossed it and the blanket. She rode into the surf, till it rushed over her feet, then she swung off Missy and into the water, under it on her back, and stood, the salt burning her; *another hole in you; I like the one you got; a hole in Daddy.* She unbuttoned her trousers and quickly pushed them down, bending her legs out of them, then the bloomers; she stuffed them into a trouser leg, not looking at her blood, maybe his dread semen, and walked toward the waves, unbuttoning her shirt, pulling it off, and pushed it into the leg, then tied a knot with the legs and put them over her head. The first wave broke and struck her breast, pushing her back; she kept walking; the next one lifted her from the sand and she swam as it broke behind her. She tasted salt that burned and cleansed her; in the swelling waves, she could not turn her face high enough, and she spit out water and swallowed it too. The trousers pulled at her throat. She stroked and kicked and breathed and spit, and the waves lifted and dropped her. Then she was beyond their rising and curling and breaking, and she tread water and pulled off the clothes and flung them ahead of her, watched them hit and bob. She kept watching, listening to waves breaking behind her. She was breathing quickly. She watched till her clothes sank.

She turned, swimming, looking once at the shore; it was too far away; she must only swim now and not look ahead again; only swim and breathe. Her arms and legs were tired, but not her soul; and, when she knew that, she also knew that if it were she would drown. She was swimming in the ocean and she would not drown and in a few days, no longer than a week, something would happen; it may not be something good, but it would be something strong, and she would be there. She swam toward it till she was in the breakers lifting and pushing her; then she stood and walked with the surf, to the beach. She walked up the warm sand to the blanket and opened the holster flap and took out the revolver, and on the blanket wiped sand from the butt and hammer. She looked up at the house. Then she untied and spread the blanket and sat on it, looking at the waves, then up and down the beach, and behind her, not with fear because she knew he would not come back today; he would come—if he ever would—at night when he could look through the windows and be certain she was alone, and he would not come today because she could not believe anything would ever be so easy and good as shooting him before the sun set. She did not look to right and left and behind her with shame or even modesty. She looked because she was naked, but she felt no need to cover herself. He had taken her privacy. She dried her hands and sat holding the gun, and closed her eyes.

She knew she should pray but she could not. She should pray for her father, she should pray for herself, but she could feel only sorrow and hatred, and the sun drying her body. Once her father had said: I never fought an enemy I felt right about. He had loved war, embraced the suffering, and held it always in his heart; he had loved soldiers and tactics and battle and winning, but he had fought southern men, knowing they were wrong, yet still they were from his own country; and he had believed the Nez Percé were more right than wrong, certainly more right than he was, and that probably it was God's will that they should escape north to Canada. Now she had an enemy she hated, one her father would hate too. Yet she must pray. Her father's spirit was with her mother's now, beyond all this; but she was in it and, as she silently recited The Lord's Prayer, her only images were the man's face and her father on the ground and herself on the ground on her knees while the man gored her. She could smell him too. When she prayed *forgive us our trespasses as we forgive those*, she stopped.

4

He did not go out to the corral for his canteen until he had finished the coffin and cross. He was standing by the fence, drinking with long swallows, when he heard a cantering horse coming up the hill. He dropped the canteen and pulled his shotgun from its scabbard on the ground, reached for his deerskin bag to get buckshot, fumbled in there once, but the horse was coming too fast; he kneeled at the fence and supported the gun on a rail and aimed at the crest of the hill, both barrels loaded for rabbit; the man would have to get close. Then the horse was walking, and Stephen ran into the barn and got his revolver, ran back and stood beside the door; he looked around it, and Adrienne crested the hill, riding bareback in tan shirt and pants with a gunbelt. He stepped into the corral, holding his shotgun with his left arm, his revolver down at his side; when she saw him, he went to the gate and opened it. She nodded and walked the horse in, then stopped, looking down at him. She said: "You thought I was him."

"Yes."

"I had to get rid of the clothes. They're in the ocean now. Till they rot. Why do you carry a shotgun?"

"I like rabbits." Her hair was dry; maybe she had not gone into the water, or maybe she had been gone for a long time. "I finished the coffin and the cross. I'll start digging now."

He went to his things and put the shotgun in its scabbard, then walked into the barn. The pick and spade were leaning against the wall with a scythe and a hoe. He picked up his gunbelt and the measuring tape, holstered the gun, and shouldered the pick and spade and went out the side door and up the hill. At the orange trees he did not look back at the house, only paused, listening for a horse, or her screaming—but she would not scream; if that man came riding back, Stephen would hear gunshots; six of them, he thought, all squeezed off by Adrienne. He dropped the tools, laid his gun on the grass, then lifted the pick and drove it into the earth she had gouged. Soon, raising and swinging the pick, he was sweating; he tossed his hat toward his gun, tied his bandana around his head, and worked with legs and back, arms and shoulders, liking the rhythm of this and the weight of the pick; and the shoveling, lifting dirt and piling it on the right side of the grave, so it would not be in their way when they carried the colonel from the barn. Then a chicken was squawking, and Stephen turned and looked down at the coop; Adrienne was swinging a chicken's head off; it dropped to the ground and ran dead in a circle and she threw the head over the fence and picked up the chicken, and started plucking feathers. Damn. Now she was going to cook. He remembered the smell of beans. He wanted chicken and beans, but that was only hunger, and he would like to be free of that for a while so he could just admire her working on a meal when her life had changed so quickly and irrevocably that he knew it was gone, that part of it till now, and whatever was coming may even be good; but it would certainly be different, and that limp she was doing now would stop when her body healed; but it would not end; it would go inside of her, and stay. He watched till she walked inside with the plucked chicken. He brought his gun belt with him to the corral and got his canteen and, at the edge of the grave, laid them on the ground. He picked and shoveled till the sides reached his waist; the earth was cool. He drank and looked at the house, feeling her inside it. He did not stop to drink again.

His back and arms were sore, a good pain that drew his mind to it, kept him from thinking. He was six feet tall. When the grave was level with his chest he stopped digging and climbed out. He took the bandana off his head and tied it at his throat; it was damp and cool; he put on his hat and buckled on his gun belt and brought the pick to the barn, then went to the open kitchen door and looked in at the pot of beans on the stove, chicken legs and wings and a split breast on the table, and sliced potatoes and, as hungry as he had been in a long time, he knocked on the wall. He was looking at the woodpile beside the door, seeing for the first time how many weapons there were in a household, how easily a man could kill a woman who was alone; just with a piece of firewood. In his life he had heard of more violence than he had seen; now he felt that everything was madly violent, and he had simply been spared. Adrienne came wearing a long black dress and the gunbelt. He looked at her eyes and could not speak: she was a rabbit under a diving eagle's talons; a doe in the sights of a carbine; she was a cougar; she was a soldier; and he was humbled, knowing that his body had never attracted a predator. Only the color of his skin, from a tribe and place and language in Africa forgotten by his family long before he was born, had drawn some mean-spirited people and repelled others; he was humbled too by the size and strength of his body; no man had ever hurt it. All his injuries had been to his spirit, and he could run from that; he was even good at it: there was sleep, the best of them all, and work and whiskey and whores; and, if none of these soothed him there was the ephemeral and joyful release of hitting a white man. Adrienne could defend her body, and she could give it; she could not escape from it. She said: "Is it time?"

5

Through the dining room windows she looked at the rim of the red sun on the ocean's horizon, the water and sky darkening to the east, whitecaps at the shore. Then she looked at Stephen eating in candlelight at the opposite end of the table; she had placed him in her chair, and taken her father's. He had finished his chicken and twice she had taken his plate to the kitchen and given him more beans and fried potatoes. At the grave, before he shoveled dirt on her father, she had stood beside him and asked him to say something. For a while they had stood silently, looking down at the coffin, the ropes tied at either end and lying on top of it. Then he said He only taught us one prayer, and he began The Lord's Prayer and she joined him, said all of it, knowing she could not forgive, but needing to pray aloud, for she could think of nothing to say; she wanted only to keen. But there should be words, and music too, and after the prayer she asked Stephen if he could sing. He sang "Amazing Grace" and she tried to, but the music made her cry, so she gazed at the coffin and wiped her eyes and listened to his sweet singing. Then she dropped a clod of earth onto the coffin and asked him where he had learned to sing so well and he said he had grown up in a church, his father had been a minister in Los Angeles. Then she watched the shovels of dirt fall and cover the coffin and fill the grave. Now she said to him: "I won't be able to ride for a few days. And I have to be with the horses."

He was chewing beans. He looked at her; his eyes were not curious but knowing, with fear; then it was gone.

"I could hire someone for the horses. But I need a few days. Maybe I don't. I rode to the ocean."

"You want me to find him, and bring him back."

"I have a sister in Corpus Christi. I may go there. I don't know. My father was born in this house. I want to give it to you, to do this, but I can't. But you could be its steward, all of it, the horses too. Or you can watch them now and I'll go. He wasn't going far. He only had a canteen. I could do it."

"Wait."

"There's a Mexican family, not far southeast, one of the boys could tend the horses. We could go together. Maybe in the wagon. But I can ride. It's only pain. I don't know if I can leave this house, and live in Texas."

"Wait."

"For what?"

"For a minute. Why isn't hanging good enough?"

"It is, if I do it."

"I understand that. I almost feel that way myself, and I've only been here half a day."

"What do you mean?"

But she knew. For hours she had taken his help, gratefully; now she saw that he liked her, wanted to be with her in some way, and he was cautious about it. He stuck his fork in a slice of potato. He chewed and glanced out the window and swallowed, then looked at her and said: "I mean I understand how you feel. I've needed to avenge things and I've done it. Sometimes it felt good. Most of the time it didn't."

"What things?"

"Mostly words."

"Have you killed a man?"

"No."

"But you've fought them."

"With my hands."

"Can you kill a man?"

"If I have to. Can you?"

"This one."

The living room was darkening, lit by one lamp, and here two candles lit the table and Stephen's face. He said: "I think if I killed a man, it wouldn't go away. I think it wouldn't go away from you either."

"Maybe God would give me that hell on earth and spare me the eternal one."

"You don't mean that."

"I do. I'm already in hell. I don't hope for anything else."

"You can choose something. I can ride to Fernando and tell the sheriff. It's the closest town north. Your man is probably there now."

"He's not my man."

"That's what you're making him."

"I'll ride there now."

"Two hours. You'll get there tired from hurting. You won't think clearly. If you find him, he may kill you."

"The house and the horses. Forever. They're yours. Just bring him back. On my father's horse."

She knew he would do it or try to, and she knew that everything he had said was right; but the fast motion of rage was more powerful than she was; she could neither stop it nor change its direction. She was looking at Stephen's face, but he could have been a shadow she glimpsed as she ran through a room. He said "I'll go." He looked above her head, then past her shoulder, then at her hand on the table. "I won't take your house and your horses. As much as I like them."

Her motion stopped, released her; suddenly she was only sad.

"Then why?"

Still his eyes roamed. He shook his head.

"I don't know what else to do."

She pitied him; since she had seen her father on the ground she had pitied no one but her sister Mary with her husband in Texas, not knowing her father was dead. She said: "Why are you here?"

Now he looked at her.

"Here?"

"Why were you on the trail today?"

"I just wanted to ride in the hills and look at the ocean."

"Are you sorry you did?"

"No. You would have been alone. Maybe it was meant to be."

"By God?"

"Maybe."

"Do you think He sent that man too?"

"I don't know why things happen, when people don't cause them."

"Can you do this?"

"If I find him."

"What about when you bring him back?"

"I don't know."

"I want to give you something. Horses, guns. Money."

"Just one thing. Let me tell the sheriff. If I have to."

"To protect yourself?"

He nodded.

"Yes," she said. "He's a little bigger than you. With blond hair and a beard."

He stood and said: "I'll just bring my things inside." She

sat looking at the ocean till he came back with a deerskin bag and put it on the table. He said: "Maybe you should get the Mexicans to wait with you."

"I don't need them. They can't shoot anyway."

"He could come back."

"I won't sleep."

"You will when you have to."

"I have coffee."

"You're brave and stubborn. Those are good, but I think scared people don't get hurt as much."

"I am scared. For you too. Do you want a cigar?"

He stared at her; then he smiled. She went with him to the living room and gave him a handful of cigars from the humidor, and walked with him to the porch and watched him mount and light a cigar. He wore his chaps and had his bed-roll and saddlebag and shotgun and canteen.

"Thank you," she said.

"Say a prayer."

"I will."

She watched him ride north on the ridge in the last of twilight, he and his horse becoming a silhouette, diminishing then gone in dark trees, as though into death, and she saw him lying in the dust of Fernando with a hole in his chest. She even took a step toward the corral, and another, to get Missy and ride and bring him back. She looked up at stars, then quickly went inside. She bolted the door and cleared the table and blew out the candles and took a basin to the pump. At the back door she poured out the grease from the skillet and washed the dishes and got firewood. She bolted the door, then went to the dining room and opened Stephen's bag she had first seen hanging from his saddlehorn; it was soft and new and its drawstring was deerskin. On top of folded clothes were a baseball glove and a ball, a bible and shotgun shells. She prayed: Don't let him get killed, don't let him get hurt. Then she did not know whether she was praying for him, or to relieve herself of responsibility; she could not know, anymore than she could know if she had used his attraction to her—if that was what she saw in his eyes—to send him after a man who liked to kill. He said he didn't know why things happened when people didn't cause them. She was causing this. She could have sent him for the sheriff in early afternoon. She touched his shirt at the top of the pile; it was blue cotton and soft and clean. She lit all the downstairs lamps, put the coffee pot on the stove, and lit the upstairs rooms. From the rack over the fireplace she got the three carbines, leaned her father's against the kitchen wall, then upstairs laid her mother's on the desk in the study, and hers on her bed.

She had never been alone for a night. Now in the light of a flame, in her shadowed room, all the day's sorrow tore at her, weakened her, and she sat on her four poster bed, the carbine on her lap, and waited. Rage was gone. It had left when Stephen said he would not take her house and horses. Only grief now, and fear. She had to stand. But she sat gripping the stock and handguard.

Then she left the gun on the bed and went downstairs in the foolish light drawing him to her; he could stand in the dark and look into every room. She got her cup and, with a cloth, the coffee pot, and blew out the kitchen lamp, then the one in the dining room, walking out of darkness into shadowed light in the living room and blew out two there and, upstairs, a lamp in the study and one in the bedroom no one used; in her father's she stood looking at his bed he had made that morning. She leaned to blow out the flame, but did not. Her room was at the top of the stairs, the only way he could come; the foot of her bed faced the door. She put the coffee pot and cup on the floor there, the cloth under the pot, then took the carbine from the bed and blew out her bedside lamp.

In the sudden dark she stood still for moments. Then quietly she moved to the foot of the bed and stood till she could see the pot on the floor. She pulled up her skirt and sat beside it with the gun on her lap; she took out the revolver and laid it beside her. Soon she could see the stairs. She poured coffee and sipped its hot strength, and felt her father under the dirt, in the wooden box. He had fled the rain in Oregon.

The rain had not killed her mother, but all the time she was sick rain fell, and it fell when they buried her. Mary was there, with Henry, married to him when he left the Army three weeks before cholera came one night and awakened her mother and killed her in three days of rain and mud. They stood in mud at her grave, and rain soaked them and the flowers, and fell for days, and Adrienne stared at it through windows, and it seemed to fall inside of her dry flesh. Its indifference was cruel, and Mary and Henry left, went to his family's ranch in Corpus Christi, and the rain stopped but the sky each morning was gray and one morning her father said I want to go home, to the sun.

6

In Fernando were opium and whores, and Stephen thought a man who raped a woman would want both; though riding in the dark among trees on the ridge and smoking his cigar, he thought of the times he had gone to Fernando, not for opium but whores, several of them till Judy came, then she was the only one. He had known her since they were children, seven or eight years old, in Los Angeles. When she was sixteen she ran away with a medicine man; she did not run from her family; they were good to her; she ran toward the man and the trains and cities and hotels. His name was Cal; he taught her to smoke opium and married her; in Seattle he sold a purgative to a man with pain in his joints and two mornings later the man came to their hotel room and, with a hunting knife, stabbed Cal in the stomach. The man ran and was never caught; Cal bled to death on the floor, in pajamas and a silk robe. Judy had learned some tricks from him, but not enough to earn the money she was accustomed to; she spent that in Seattle, moving to another hotel and waiting for an answer to what Stephen thought was a simple question: What could she do now? She could have gone home to her family. That was Stephen's answer, though he did not tell her. In Seattle she wanted a man with money and life in hotels and on trains, and opium. She was a pretty woman with light brown hair and freckles and she could have such a man if she truly wanted one, but she missed Cal and did not want to live with this man she imagined; or Stephen imagined, riding down from the hills now, seeing her in a hotel room, gazing out a window at Seattle's gray sky, looking not at the sky but at her parents' little house and at train compartments and hotel rooms and good dresses and opium in bed. Finally she chose parts of both: she became a whore and moved near her family, yet not so near that they might by chance see her at work. That was three years ago, and when Stephen first bought or rented her and heard her story, he believed she had known within days of her husband's death, while she smoked in her room, went out to buy clothes and eat, must have known what she would do, long before she started in a Seattle house, then worked her way south by train, stopping in Portland for a week and San Francisco for another, working one night on the train too, arriving in Los Angeles with money and opium and the face of a sweet sad widow. For a few days she stayed with her parents and young sister, smoked while they slept, talked with the two brothers and sister and their families who walked or rode in wagons to see her. Then she packed her trunk and rode the stagecoach to Fernando to run, she told her family, the café her husband had left her.

Outside Fernando he looked at the stars and three quarter moon and smelled the ocean he could not see beyond the low hills. In town he rode on the main street to the darkened sheriff's office, smelling Sarah's hide and sweat, and felt that he was breathing fear, down into his stomach, and not breathing it out, and the dirt street pulled him to it, and he wanted to yield to its gravity, dismount and sit on the sidewalk. No one was on the walks, the stores darkened; past the sheriff's office the hotel lobby was lit and some of the rooms on the first and second floors; across the street from it was the light of the saloon, and one room upstairs on the floor where Judy and the other girls did their work. He rode to the trough and

let Sarah drink, thinking of her knowing only thirst and hunger and lust and strong muscles and his affection and her
crankiness when she bled; she was only afraid of lightning
and all storms and fire. He rode across the street to the saloon,
went through its swinging doors, tasting menace in the smells
of tobacco smoke and liquor, looking at men sitting at tables
and standing at the bar and saw no one blond and bearded
and big. At a table near the end of the bar Judy in a blue dress
sat with two girls, a man standing and talking to one, taking
her hand; they went upstairs. Stephen was walking toward
her when Judy saw him and smiled and stood and left the
table and hugged him, then looked at his face and said: "How
was Mexico?"

"Good."

"You don't look it. Do you want to drink first?"

"No."

"Are you all right? Weren't there any girls down there?"

"Let's go up."

"I missed you. I'll put a different look on your face."

She took his hand; he climbed the stairs, squeezing her
palm and fingers, wanting nothing else now; not her body, but
to take off his hat and gun and chaps and boots and lie on her
bed and hold her and talk. In the room she lit candles on the
chest of drawers and said: "Undress me."

"I have to talk. I'll pay you for your time."

"No you won't. What is it?"

"I have to sit. I'm very tired."

She smiled.

"You? The black stallion?"

"Tired inside."

He sat on the bed, and took off his hat.

"Have a drink," she said.

"Not yet. I have to do something."

At the chest of drawers she poured whiskey, then sat
beside him, drinking, her hand on his left thigh.

"I have to find a man."

"Why?"

"He stole a horse."

"Yours?"

"A girl's."

"She your girlfriend?"

"No."

"You love her anyway?"

He looked at her brown eyes then down at her hand, her polished nails, resting on his leg. "I've never loved a woman." He looked at her red lips and rose cheeks. He kissed her; she was ready, and he almost was, her hands stroking his face, his chest, then one of them moving down, but he knew he was opening himself not to passion but to escape and lassitude. He drew away, and quickly but gently removed her hand. She said: "Let's take care of that."

"I have to do what I said I would."

"Go to Zack's house. He was drinking here an hour ago. He's home now."

"She doesn't want the law. This man, he killed her father and raped her."

"That's not stealing a horse."

"He did that too. Her father's. She wants me to bring him back. So she can shoot him."

"I like this girl. But you like her too much. What's she paying?"

"I wouldn't take anything. He's big and blond with a beard, and he wears a dagger on his chest. That's what he held at her throat—" But he stopped, looking at her eyes suddenly bright and mischievous, as though she were laughing.

"The Spanish dagger," she said, then she did laugh, softly, not for long, her hand squeezing his shoulder. "He calls it his Spanish dagger. Probably stole it in Mexico. Go out to his place and shoot him while he sleeps. He'll be drunk by now. People will celebrate. Nobody will go to the funeral. Zack won't care who shot him."

"Who is he?"

"Nobody. A lazy drunk. Pete Yerby. His father owned the

bank. And a ranch. Then he died. Without a wife; she left early, probably as soon as she knew Yerby was Satan. Maybe when he was two. So there was just Yerby. He sold the bank so he wouldn't have to work there, and sold the cattle so he wouldn't have to do anything. He lives at the ranch. Three miles or so west. He's got two men with him. And a thirteen year old girl."

"Why?"

"What do you think?"

"Damn."

"He's a coward, but he's mean. He'd shoot you and leave you on the porch in his puke. Get Zack or go home or shoot him in his sleep. But they'll be up drinking most of the night. You can't shoot all three. Somebody will kill you. Stay here. Talk to Zack in the morning."

He wanted to, but looking at Judy's eyes he saw Adrienne standing by the orange trees and saying she wouldn't forget him, saw her riding bareback with the gun, and now alone in the house. He saw a faceless girl out there in the night.

"Tell me where it is. I'll just go look."

"And you wouldn't take her money."

"She wanted to give me her house and twenty-three horses."

"You've wanted that since you were fourteen years old. What do you want now?"

"Peace." He did not know he would say that till he heard it.

"So you're riding to Yerby's."

"Maybe justice too."

"I think you want her."

"I'd do the same for you."

"I wouldn't ask you. And you love me. If I weren't a whore you'd want to build me a house. Or put me in the one you won't take from her."

"Maybe. Why are you?"

"Because I am. He has trees. You walk to them and look. Then come back here."

7

Now the house was not hers: it was too silent, the walls and floors and ceilings grieving for her father and for her and Mary, and upstairs in the dark she felt trapped. The living room should be lighted, so he would climb the stairs with light behind him, up into the faint and shadowed light cast in the hall by her father's lamp. She had drunk all the coffee; she had not needed it. With the carbine and revolver she stood and looked out the open window near the head of her bed, at the dark orange trees, at her father's grave she could not see; but she knew she was looking at it. She put the carbine on the bed and the revolver in its holster and took off the belt and undressed and lay her clothes on the bed. She slowly, quietly, opened a drawer of her chest and got folded pants and a shirt and put them on, and boots from the wardrobe, and buckled on the belt. She carried the carbine downstairs and in the kitchen lit a lantern, and walked in its light to the front door where she stood, listening. She held the carbine in the crook of her arm and unbolted the door, stepped outside, and gently pushed the door closed. On the porch she cocked the hammer, held the grip, her finger on the trigger, the muzzle pointed at the ground. She looked for a rattlesnake. She went down the steps and, holding the lantern high walked and looked at the ground, waiting for the rattling that sometimes came when the snake's head was already in motion, or even after it had struck. At the corral she put the lantern on a fence post and opened the gate and went in and closed it and took the lantern into the barn, and went to the stall where Missy stood sleeping. She lowered the carbine's hammer and blew out the lantern and looked out the big door at the moonlit corral, the smell of burning kerosene fading till she could smell only horses and hay and wood, and she could see the shapes of the three English saddles on the wall; her father's, her mother's, and hers. She opened the flap of her holster and held the carbine in her crossed arms, watching the corral and listening, till her arms tired, and she rested the carbine's butt on the ground, held its muzzle with her left hand. Her fear of rattle-snakes had given her respite; now the greater fear struck her again, but not as hard as the sorrow in the night air and moon-light and the dark of the barn with its breathing life.

To her left and behind her, up the slope, was her father. She saw Mary sleeping now beside Henry, happy Mary, in her mind, and at times silently forming the words with her lips, she spoke to her: Oh Mary, sweet Mary, if I am carrying that man's child I'll shoot myself unless Stephen knows a woman who can help me but even then I would shoot myself, leave this body that carried his child for even one second and when this is over—it will never be over—but when Stephen comes back or doesn't, when I know as much as God will let me know about the man who killed Daddy I will write to you, everything, what has happened and what will happen; if you were here you would hold me and say: Only cry, Adrienne, there is nothing to do but cry, let the men take care of this. If you had been here today you would have sent Stephen to the sheriff in San Diego and you'd have ridden to Ramon and asked him to send his sons to dig the grave and we would have cleaned and dressed Daddy and the man would be in jail now and we would be sleeping or sitting on the sofa crying. If you had been here he would not have done it to me, it was when you like to nap, and the shot would have wakened you and you'd have come downstairs and shot him from the door. Why did I run outside without a gun? I've had one with me ever since Stephen came and I went inside, and now I'm here with two, but why didn't I get one when I heard the shot? I can't even feel rage now, here in the barn; nor can I cry, my heart too broken, nor hope, and I am afraid I've sent Stephen to die, and I'm afraid of what I'll do if he doesn't, if he brings him back to me on Daddy's horse, I don't know what I'll do, can do, and I know what you'd tell me and Daddy would too, and Mama. I know what God would too, but I can't hear any of you now. We buried Daddy at the orange grove. He's in the shade till midday, then he lies in the sun. His feet point to the ocean. I'll have a stone made in San Diego. You could come out then, for the stone, and if Henry can get away he could come too. There will be voices in the house. Everything is silent, I can hear the horses breathe. There is a soft breeze from the southwest and I can hear it. I can hear the moonlight and the stars and smell the gun oil and my boots and the saddles and the walls—

She did not know that her carbine was holding her up, her left hand clutching its barrel, her muscles relaxing, her breath slowing, her head lowering; she did not know when her eyes closed. She saw her father, standing bareheaded in his blue uniform, his saber at his left side, but no revolver, it was an occasion, there was music, violins and brass, a ball or a wedding, and she looked for Mary but he was alone, standing in front of her, looking at her with sorrowful eyes. He wore white gloves. The carbine fell and she lurched and opened her eyes, and grabbed the gate of the stall, knowing again that her father was dead, her muscles tight and trembling, and she looked out of the dark at the pale dirt of the corral.

8

Standing in the trees, he listened to their voices and laughter, not two hundred feet away, the upstairs dark, the ground floor lighted, and in a room at the back of the house were the three men he could not see through the open door and windows. He had an unlit cigar in his mouth, and held his shotgun, loaded with buckshot. He had been here for more than an hour, Sarah tied farther down the hill at the edge of the trees, and still he waited to see someone, and waited to know what to do when they finally slept, how he would know which room was Yerby's. He knew this: he was supposed to be here, he had known it when he had dismounted on the hill and led Sarah to the trees and tied her there and began walking into the trees with one short step lowered slowly, then standing still, watching, listening, then moving his other foot. The stand of trees was small, a hundred feet or so, but he took a long time, most of it motionless, his fear now a small part of his concentration, consumed by it, his images of dying on the floor in there gone, as Adrienne was, and her dead father, and Judy. He saw only the house, imagined the men inside, listened to the voices, their tone good-humored and teasing and drunk. He could hear only a few words till one called "Lily!" and he watched a girl step into the doorway. She must have been lying on a sofa between windows and the door. He put his cigar in his shirt pocket. She was in a pale dress; she stepped onto the porch and walked to its edge and looked up at the sky.

"Lily!"

Still she looked up.

"Lily! We want *eggs*."

She looked down. Then she turned and went slowly inside, and she drew Stephen to her, out of the trees: before he knew he would move he was running across the open ground, the shotgun in his left hand, cocking both hammers, his finger on a trigger, as he drew his Colt and cocked it. At the porch he stopped, looked at the kitchen door across the living room, and put his right foot on the first step, and gave it some weight; the wood was solid, quiet. On the balls of his feet he went up the steps and crossed the porch and stood in the living room, the shotgun and Colt pointed waist-high at the kitchen door. On a hat rack beside it hung three hats and three gunbelts with revolvers. He ran into the kitchen: three men at the round table and the girl standing behind them at a counter, the men looking at him, glasses and a bottle on the table, Yerby facing him, the dagger at his chest, the other two in profile, their faces turned to him, mouths open, the girl looking at him, frightened, holding an egg in each hand. Stephen aimed the Colt at Yerby's heart, and moved the shotgun left and right at the dark-haired men. He said: "Lily. Get out from behind them."

She did not move.

"Put the eggs down and come this way. It's so you won't get hurt."

She put the eggs on the counter and circled the men and stood beside him. The man on the left said: "You don't need guns to have Cousin Lily."

"Your cousin?"

"Lost her family in a fire."

"So she got you."

The man was looking at the bores of the shotgun. Stephen said: "Yerby."

"I don't talk to niggers."

Stephen moved the Colt up and shot the wall behind Yerby's head, the three men jumping in their chairs, then raising their hands, Lily breathing loudly. He said: "Do you talk to guns?"

"Take her," Yerby said.

"I'm taking you."

"Me? What did I ever do to you?"

His face was red, and his drunken eyes looked distant, inward, and the two men looked at him. "I've never seen you before."

"Mister?" the man on the right said, "can I just leave?"

"I don't know what I did," Yerby said.

"You killed a man. His daughter wants to shoot you."

"That girl—" Then he stopped, the men watching him.

"That girl," Stephen said. "Lily? Do you like it here?"

"I hate it."

"Is there any rope in this place?"

"I need a drink," Yerby said.

"I think you've had your last one. Lily?"

"In the barn. Lots of it."

'Will you bring lots of it? Please."

She went quickly, through the living room; the man on the right said: "I don't know about a killing."

Yerby did not look at him; he stared at Stephen's eyes. Stephen was smelling burned gunpowder; the kick of the Colt had felt good; he could shoot him now, he even wanted to, seeing Adrienne with blood on her pants, seeing Yerby in her.

He believed now, fully for the first time, that Adrienne would kill him. Yerby said: "How much is she paying?"

"Nothing."

"I will."

"Probably the house too."

"That too. Let me have a drink."

"No."

"Why are you doing this?"

"Because I am," and he remembered Judy sitting on her bed.

"I didn't mean what I said."

"What?"

"You know. About you being colored."

If he were not holding cocked guns pointed at three men, he might have laughed. He said: "Funny how sorry so often means scared."

Lily came in, ropes coiled over both shoulders. He said: "Can you tie a good knot?"

"Sure."

"There's a knife in my left pocket."

She reached in, and his thigh muscles recoiled, tightening, as he imagined her hands' familiarity with the bodies of men; if Judy was right.

"Your cousin first," he said. "Tie his wrists behind the chair."

"He's not my cousin." At the back of the chair she pulled his arms down. "He just says that. He took me after the fire, when I was real young. He was my father's *friend*."

"Took care of you too," the man said. "Kept you fed."

She pulled his hair, jerking his head down, and dropped the rope, and with her fist struck his cheek three times before Stephen said: "Lily. Tie him. Then you can hit him some more."

She squatted and cut a length of rope and tied his wrists.

"Now tie him to the chair."

She cut the rope and looped it around his chest. The man was looking down, breathing hard with fury and fear too.

"Now the other one. Walk behind me."

She circled to the man and he looked at Stephen and said: "You're just going to tie us?"

Lily pulled his arms down, worked quickly with the rope, her brown hair falling over her cheek, but not before Stephen saw her eyes and mouth; she liked this.

"I'm only taking Yerby."

"We could be tied a long time. Nobody much comes up here."

She tied his wrists and lowered rope around him and tightened it over his arms. When she finished, Stephen said: "Tie Yerby's hands in front of him. So he can hold the reins."

She stood beside Yerby and said: "Who cares if he falls off?"

"A very sad lady. Do not get between him and the gun. Yerby, put your hands on the table."

She cut the rope and wound it around his wrists; she was tying it, watching it, when she said: "Are you leaving me here?"

"No."

"Where you taking me?"

"To my family."

She finished the knot and stood and looked at him, and said:

"I'd like to set this house on fire."

Such hatred in eyes so young, and he hated these men for putting it there, a young girl who would kill them, give them such fear and pain, and maybe even feel good about it.

"So would I," he said.

The man who called her cousin was staring at the table, sweat dripping on his face; the man on the right said: "I never touched her. It was them."

"It's true," Lily said. "He just drinks."

Stephen looked at Lily's dark eyes and shook his head.

"We're not burning the house. We'll just leave it. Get your things."

"I don't want them."

Yerby said: "I need a drink."

"You need a stone around your neck and be thrown in the sea. You need never to be born. Lily, saddle a horse for you, and the stallion."

He waited for her to hit the man again as she walked past him, but she did not look at him; she moved quickly, lightly, and in the living room she ran.

9

She woke, grief striking and spreading beneath her heart, seeing her father on the ground, on the dining room table as she washed the blood, his face as she held his legs and followed Stephen holding his armpits and walking backward, and they lowered him into the coffin on the sawhorses and she kissed his brow and eyelids and mouth; now she felt the cool earth she lay upon, on her side, her cheek on her arm; she heard horses coming from the north and stood, gasped at the hard burning pain, and leaving the carbine in the dust, she drew her revolver and limped past the stalls toward the light, not from the moon now but the unrisen sun; she heard the rooster and hens and birds and the horses trotting, then walking before she reached the door, where she stopped and looked at them: him in front on Chief Joseph, his hands tied, and a rope looped around his chest and arms, hanging loosely behind him to Stephen's saddle, and beside Stephen was a girl in bloomers; and a yellow dress pulled up to her thighs. They passed the corral and stopped at the house and she stepped out of the barn and called: "Stephen."

They stopped and he and the girl watched her cross the corral and open the gate; the man looked down at his hands. She walked to Stephen, looked up at his tired face. She touched his boot and said: "Are you all right?"

"I'm fine."

"Who's the girl?"

"Lily. I'm taking her to my sister." He shook his head, and leaned toward her, and said softly: "She was with him and another man."

In Stephen's eyes, in their glazed anger and fatigue, she saw what had been done to the girl. She looked at the man's back and lowered head; his body was shaking, he was making sounds, and she remembered his sounds when he was in her; now he was moaning. She circled him, glancing once at the girl, and faced him and aimed the revolver at his mouth.

"Get off my father's horse."

He looked at Chief Joseph's neck and shook and moaned. She said:

"Pull him off."

"You going to shoot him in front of Lily?"

"I want her to," Lily said.

"You do now. But you've got years ahead." He looked at her. "Good ones."

"What's his name?"

"Pete Yerby. He's got nobody, he's nobody, and nobody will care. I'll take Lily inside."

"Pull him off."

"It's been a long night. I'm tired of doing things to people. I'll help you bury him. Or is he going into the ocean?"

"Stephen—" Then her body slumped, her hand with the gun fell to her side, and she stepped forward and held Chief Joseph's bridle, and rested her cheek on his head, smelling him. What she wanted was impossible: to rest, at peace yet alive, and she saw her father's sad face in her dream, or standing with her in the barn if it were not a dream, and now she believed it was not, he had come to her, and she looked up at Yerby and said, not to him, nor to Stephen nor Lily: "I don't know what to do."

Then Stephen was standing beside her, patting her shoulder, and she would not cry, she shuddered and held it in; Yerby would not see, not ever, any more of her than he had seen yesterday in the sunlight. The sun was rising now. She moved back from Chief Joseph and looked at the blue ocean, its color seeming new, as it did every morning; she said: "I can't do it."

"No. You take care of Lily. I'll tie him in the barn, and go to San Diego."

She shook her head, and said: "You need to sleep."

"Later."

"Go to Ramon. He'll go."

"The farmer?"

"He's close. I'll cook something first."

"Yerby needs food too."

"No."

"He ought to hang. I wish somebody had shot him last week. But right now he needs food. It rains on the just and the unjust. He could use some whiskey too."

"I will not cook for him." She looked up at Yerby's red face, his damp eyes.

"I will," Stephen said. "If you'll let me use your things."

"I'll cook," Lily said. "I'm free."

Adrienne looked at her; she was thin and tired.

"I'll do it," Adrienne said. "You need a bed too." She looked at Stephen.

"You can take him to the barn."

Yerby said: "Just give me whiskey."

She raised the gun and cocked it and steadily held it aimed at his face, and for a while kept it there, not even seeing his face, only the sight on the barrel and his moustache; held it till she had felt all she needed of knowing she could squeeze the trigger and see his mouth a bleeding hole and see him jerk backward and fall. She moved the gun up and to the side, aimed above his right ear, and shot the brim of his hat; it lifted and fell behind him and hung by its strap from his neck, Chief Joseph stepping twice to the side, then calm. She holstered the gun, walked behind Yerby, held the rope and pulled; he fell backward, hit the ground with his back and head and said: "Oh," lying there, looking up at the sky. "Oh," he said. "Oh."

She dropped the rope and went to him and crouched and drew his dagger, and went to Stephen and handed it to him, hearing Yerby's sounds behind her as something behind her in time too, insignificant groans and curses of a departing spirit like the legion of demons the Lord sent into the pigs, running to their death. She whispered:

"Leave him till I get back from the barn. I don't want him to see me walk." Then she looked at his eyes; they were merry. "What," she said.

"I knew you could shoot."

She turned and took Chief Joseph's bridle and walked slowly, stiffly, then heard a moving horse and turned: Stephen, with the dagger, was riding to the ocean. She said: "Lily. Go inside. We'll eat. Stephen will take care of the horse."

She led Chief Joseph to the trough and took off the bridle and dropped it on the ground, then the saddle and blanket. She walked to Missy's stall and picked up her carbine, and stroked Missy's neck, and said: "Everyone's hungry. You'll have to wait this morning," and she saw hundreds, thousands of mornings, waking alone and coming here to feed the horses; she did not see the eighth morning when she would wake at dawn and stand and feel on her thigh the warm red flow, and she would stand looking at the east window, breathing with relief then gratitude then hope.

10

Now she lay in black on her bed in mid-afternoon, the sheriff gone with Yerby, the spotted horse with Ramon. Lily slept in one room, and Stephen was waking in her father's; she listened to his boots on the floor; she stood and stepped into the hall as he did. She said: "You're going?"

"I should."

"She's still sleeping."

"Then I'll wait."

"I'd like her to stay."

"She could help you."

"In a way, she's my sister."

He nodded. They walked downstairs and he got his bag from the dining room. She said: "Are you hungry?"

"No. I'll eat in Fernando. I have to see a friend there, tell her to send the sheriff out to Yerby's, and untie those men."

"Will you be in trouble?"

"No. He'll probably know it was me, but he won't mind."
She followed him outside and to the corral and watched him
saddle and mount. He took his baseball and glove from the
bag, then tied it to the saddlehorn. He said; "Let me show you
something."

He turned his horse, threw the ball high ahead of him,
and rode into its arc, watching it fall, catching it in front of his
chest, and, smiling, rode back to her. She said: "I want to do
that."

"I'll bring you a glove."

"Will you?"

"Sure. I want to see my family. On my way back here, I'm
going to burn that house. Tell Lily. It's evil."

"There's work here."

"I'll need it. In about two weeks."

"And food and a bed."

"Maybe ten days."

She reached up with her hand and he took it. She said:
"You were good to help me. And Lily."

"I'm sorry it happened to you. I hope the Lord comforts
you. I'll bring that glove, and a ball."

He released her hand and rode through the gate and she
went to the trail and watched him, his horse walking, Stephen
tossing the ball just above his head now, catching and tossing;
three times he turned to her and waved, the last time before
he rode down the slope of the ridge, waving with the glove
holding the sunlit ball, Adrienne's arm reaching up, moving.

CORPORAL LEWIS

At four-thirty on a summer day in California, the Marine captain left the barracks and drove past hills to the Officers' Club and, at the bar, found his friend, also a captain, among men and women in uniform, sitting and standing. The bar was brightly lit. He ordered a martini and said: "Today I lost a man, to the hospital in Philadelphia. A good corporal. He said God was talking to him."

"Out loud?"

"Yes. Something kicked it off. He was at a bar last night with some Marines. He didn't like the way his buddies were talking to the waitress. He told them they should stop. I talked to a corporal who was there. He said Lewis seemed sad."

"When did God start talking?"

"This morning. Then he walked around the barracks saying God told him to tell people they should be kind to one another. The platoon sergeant talked to him, then brought him to the platoon commander. He talked to him; the XO's on leave, so the lieutenant came to me and said Lewis was having some kind of breakdown, so I said to send him in. The S-3 called. It was eleven forty-five. Lewis came in and went to the radiator at the window. He kneeled there and looked outside. The S-3 finally stopped talking and Lewis was still kneeling and staring. So I went over there. I said: 'Lewis. Are you all right?' He said: 'Yes, sir.' He was staring at the sun. He wasn't blinking. I looked at the sun. Blink blink blink. Then he said: 'God told me to tell people to be kind.'"

The bartender brought the captain his martini, and a second for his friend, who sipped and said: "Schizophrenic."

"Or something. I'm a Catholic, I grew up with these stories, Joan of Arc, Moses, St. Paul, on and on. I believe them. But this was in my office, and it was spooky. I felt like there was something else in the room with us. I called the S-1 and took Lewis to battalion. We walked on the road. He got in step with me. I said: 'Can you hear God?' He said: 'Sometimes, sir.' I said: 'Since when?' He said: 'Since chow line this morning.' I said: 'Are you hearing Him now?' He said: 'No, sir; only you and me.' We went to the colonel and I told him and he called the doctor, and told us to sit down. He asked Lewis if he'd ever heard voices before. Lewis said: 'No, sir.' The colonel passed his cigarettes around. He paced behind his desk. He said: 'We'll take care of you, son.' I watched the side of Lewis's face. He looked the same as he did eight months ago, when he joined the company. The doctor and two corpsmen came and I shook Lewis's hand, told him he'd be fine. He said: 'Yes, sir, I will be.' He looked peaceful. The colonel patted his shoulder. They're flying him out tonight. But I wonder something. What if I hadn't done anything? Just brought him to the field tomorrow, for platoon tactics. And what if he'd done his job? What would that mean? You asked when God started talking to him. I'm wondering when He stopped talking to people. You think a Cheyenne warrior would have had a problem with Lewis?"

"Not if he was on their side."

"Nothing he said was crazy."

"It's how he said it. And hearing God."

"There's something else. He was squared away, spit and polish, he could have passed inspection by a martinet. He cared about the waitress. He looked at the sun and it didn't hurt his eyes."

SISTERS

For Pat, still steering

1

On the day before he rode back into her life, a summer day in 1890 in southern California, dark-haired, twenty year old Adrienne Beaumont was waiting for him, had been waiting for twenty-nine days since he rode north to Los Angeles to visit his family. That had been the day after a man neither she nor her father had ever seen before shot her father under the noon sun, in front of their house, and raped Adrienne beside his body, and rode away on her father's stallion; and while she lay on the ground, holding her father, alone now with the house and twenty-three horses and a cow and chickens, her mother killed by cholera in Oregon and her sister living with her husband in Corpus Christi, the Negro cowboy rode up the trail, coming from Mexico, and carried her father inside and made a coffin and a cross and dug the grave. His name was Stephen Leness, and after he and Adrienne used ropes to lower her father into the grave, they said The Lord's Prayer, Adrienne forcing herself to say *forgive us our trespasses as we forgive those who trespass against us* and, when she asked Stephen if he could sing, he sang "Amazing Grace." Her sorrow was brimming; she could not sing with him. Then she fed him supper and asked him to find the man and bring him back to her, so she could shoot him. She offered him her house and horses. He refused both, but rode north to Fernando and found the man, Pete Yerby, and two other men, and thirteen year old Lily O'Brien, an orphan Yerby and one of the men had been violating for four years. Adrienne did not shoot Yerby; she could not, maybe because in that long night, her father's first in the earth, his spirit came to her, or she dreamed it, and he looked sadly at her; maybe she simply could not shoot a man, not even Yerby, sitting on her father's horse, his hands tied in front of him, a noose around his torso, the rope going to Stephen's saddle horn, Stephen and Lily sitting in early morning on their horses, watching her aim the revolver at Yerby's mouth, Yerby shaking with fear and need of a drink, a big and bearded and mean drunk she hated, her hand and gun steady, not even twenty-four hours after he had killed her unarmed and lovely father and held a dagger at her neck and raped her; no, only one afternoon and that one long night when Adrienne was alone in the house with her carbine and revolver—I'll be back, Yerby had said, on her father's horse— and finally leaving her upstairs room and the house itself where she felt she was waiting in a cage to be raped, and going to the barn where, despite coffee and fear and will, she fell asleep first standing, then lying on the ground in front of her mare's stall, waking early to the sounds of three horses and going out into the light to shoot Yerby; but she could not. Maybe because Stephen did not want her to; Lily wanted her to, and wanted to watch. Adrienne shot the hat off his head, then pulled the rope looped around him and yanked him off her father's horse. Then she sent for the sheriff in San Diego. While Adrienne had slept in the barn, Stephen and Lily had been riding to her with Yerby; after the sheriff took him, shaking and moaning for whiskey, they slept: Stephen in her father's bed, Lily in her sister's. In late afternoon, while Lily still slept, Adrienne walked with Stephen to the corral where he mounted, and she told him she had work for him, and he said he would be back. He wore a baseball glove and tossed the ball in the air and caught it; that is how she last saw him, riding north, playing with the ball, turning to wave at her.

Now, on the twenty-ninth morning, Adrienne and Lily had fed the horses and chickens and cow, and milked her, and Lily was making pancake batter, and Adrienne told her she was taking her coffee to the porch. She wore khaki pants tucked in riding boots, and a burgundy shirt, and her hair hung close to her waist. Her house was on a hill, and when she opened the front door, she heard a crow's wings on the forward slope, in the grass she could not see, then it quickly rose and she watched it climb and turn, shining in the sun, and it flew east over her house toward her father's grave at the edge of the orange trees, near the crown of the hill. Over the ocean, two miles from where she stood, light fog was low and dissipating; she looked at the surf; *I don't ask to be spared grief, but I ask You to return me to the world, let me look at this water and sky and see them, not my pain.* She could only think that she must try; that each day she must spend some time, alone and still, smelling the air and looking at the water and sky and hill and the stretch of green and brown and yellow grass that rolled then flattened to the sand at the beach. Just make her body do this, and hope a time would come when she could see beauty, peace. Something moved on the ground, and she saw beyond the house's shade a rattlesnake, sinuous and slow, then still, lying in the sun, a diamondback as long as Lily, over five feet, and fear lanced her sorrow, broke it, and she put her cup on the porch railing and went inside and upstairs to her room for her Navy Colt. Going downstairs, smelling coffee and bacon and Lily's cigarette, she called: "I'm going to shoot a diamondback," and heard Lily's booted footsteps coming from the kitchen, through the dining room, into the living room, following her as she stepped onto the porch, quietly crossed it, and stopped at its edge. She feared all snakes; they were eerie: sudden and silent, and usually they saw you first. But this one could kill; it was motionless, thick and wide, its body curved four times, its colors too much like those of the brown grass and dust.

Her father had been a retired cavalry colonel, had fought the Confederates and the Nez Percé and had seemed to fear nothing; about rattlesnakes he had said you only needed to wear boots. She had not believed him; still did not; he had said it to soothe her. She cocked the revolver and aimed at the snake's head, took a breath, exhaled half of it and held the rest and squeezed the trigger, sweet adrenaline rushing with the explosion and the head gone in a flash of blood, the body jerking upward, coiling, then striking, spraying blood, and Adrienne breathed the smell of burned gun powder, and lowered the gun and briefly hugged her chilled and roiling stomach. Brown-haired Lily in a pink dress stepped beside her, and said: "*Damn*, you can shoot."

"I hate them. They scare me to death. Look." She held out her left hand, watched it tremble.

"You didn't shake when you shot him."

"Are you afraid of snakes?"

"I don't want one to bite me; but, no, I don't think about them."

It was uncoiled now, and moving with a crawling motion, from side to side but not forward: it was taking possession of this piece of earth where it was dead and looked alive. Her father, with the bullet in his head, had lain still. She said: "Do you mind getting rid of it? I don't want to touch it."

"Sure."

Lily went down the steps, dropped her cigarette and stepped on it, walked through the shade to the snake in the sun, and picked it up by the tail, raised her arm above her head, and the snake's neck hung a few inches above the hem of her dress, and jerked toward her.

"Eleven rattles," she said. "I could skin it, and make a pretty belt."

"Please don't."

"You can't even see their skins?"

"I'm better off if I don't. But if you want to, you can make a belt."

"I don't care about it. Where do you want him?"

"Down the hill."

Lily ran, swinging the snake in a circle above her head, and threw it; Adrienne watched it in the air, falling down the slope, and heard it hit the ground. She looked at Lily's dress for blood; there was none. Lily came up the steps and touched Adrienne's cup on the railing.

"It's still hot," she said. "Sit down with it. I'll bring you something."

"I don't want to eat out here."

"It's not food."

She went inside and Adrienne sat in a rocking chair and put the gun on the floor and sipped her coffee and shook her head once and smiled at the mystery of the soul, because fear of a snake sunning itself sixty feet from her body had burned away her sorrow as the sun was burning away fog over the surf and, for these moments, the ocean and sky were lovely. Lily came to the porch, holding a cup of coffee in one hand and, in the other, two cigarettes she had rolled. She sat in the rocking chair beside Adrienne. She struck a match and lit one of the cigarettes and held it toward Adrienne.

"Lily. It's not something a lady does."

"They don't wear pants either."

She took the cigarette, watched Lily light her own.

"You breathe it in," Lily said.

"I know."

She drew on the cigarette, sweet in her mouth, hot in her throat and lungs, and waited to cough but did not. She blew it out and watched it rise over Lily's head. She did it again; she was giddy and thrilled and soothed; she tried to compare it to other sensations, but could remember nothing like it.

"I've seen a grizzly and a cougar, up close while I was hunting deer. I shot them. I wasn't afraid."

"Drink some coffee with that. They're good together."

"My mother is turning in her grave. Not Daddy. Sometimes I smoked a cigar with him. We'd come out here after dinner. I wasn't afraid of Yerby either. I just wanted to shoot him."

"You could buy them already rolled. They're better."

Adrienne looked at her hazel eyes.

"I could. Probably you'd like some too."

"If you would."

"I haven't made you any pants yet. But you can wear a boy's. And you need dresses. You need a lot of things. After breakfast, I'll put on a dress and we'll go to San Diego."

"Smoking is all that got me through that time. And Will."

"That's all?"

"I don't know what else."

"I think you had hope."

"Maybe."

"Didn't you hope sometimes that it would end?"

"I guess I did."

"You probably had a little faith too. Maybe only for a second, once in a while."

"If I did, it sure happened. You should have seen Stephen come running into that kitchen with his Colt and double-barrel. He was like an angel."

"Daddy should be here with us. But if he were alive, Stephen would have ridden past here that day, maybe just tipped his hat, maybe stopped to water his horse and talk for a while. But he wouldn't have run like an angel into your life. I'm not saying that good comes from evil. I can never say I'm glad Yerby killed Daddy, and that got you away from those men. I wish he were sitting here now. He'd smile at me smoking and he'd love you and let you know it too. Yerby made us sisters."

Adrienne looked away from her at the ocean and sky, and she knew Lily did too, she could feel Lily's eyes move from her face. She drank sweet coffee and inhaled smoke, a frisson that blessed her: for the first time since that day when everything changed, she felt that she was embracing something, and being embraced; felt free of even mortality. Condors and vultures and coyotes would eat the snake.

"It's time for a holiday," she said. "After breakfast, I'll hitch Captain."

"I will. While you dress."

"Don't smoke in town. And try not to swear. Anyplace."

Lily smiled, and said: "I picked up some bad habits."

"You did very well. I'm proud of you." She reached down for the revolver and stood. "Now let's eat your pancakes. Tonight we can read Mark Twain."

When they came home, Lily still in her pink dress and Adrienne in black, the diamondback was scattered bones. The sun was setting and cirrus clouds were golden and rose, and light sparkled on the sea. They stopped in front of the house and, climbing the stairs three times, carried to Lily's room beside Adrienne's five dresses, a maroon one with hoops and, all with slits for riding, a yellow one, a pale blue, a forest green, and a silver; three pairs of khaki pants and two navy blue; a pair of brown shoes and one of black; brown English riding boots ("I'll teach you to ride the real way," Adrienne had said in the shop in San Diego), a wide-brimmed beige hat with brown plaited braid and chin strap; two silk bandannas, a gold one with red borders for Lily and a scarlet for Stephen; western boots, pink slippers and a blue robe, three night gowns, white, pink, and lilac, six shirts, purple, blue, brown, gray and blue checked, rose, and blue and white vertically striped; bloomers and a corset; twenty packages of Sweet Caporals they stacked on the coffee table in the living room; a Remington .22 pump-action rifle, a hunting knife, a Winchester double-barreled twelve gauge, a Colt .38 with holster and belt, rouge and lipstick, a hair brush and comb and hand mirror and bath powder and a bottle of perfume and one of cologne, Lily's eyes as delighted as they were in San Diego, where she had looked at and touched, fondled and smelled her gifts. Adrienne lit the wood in the kitchen stove while Lily went out to feed the horses. While the potatoes were baking, Lily bathed in the tub by the pump up the slope behind the house, and Adrienne watched her in the sunlight; Lily was softly singing; if it were not for Lily and the animals, many of these twenty-nine mornings, perhaps all of them, she would

not have waked and risen from her bed, and now she thanked
God for the slow healing of responsibility and love.

She floured the steaks she had bought in San Diego and
sliced tomatoes and snapped beans from her garden, and Lily
emptied the tub and came inside naked, drying herself with a
white towel, and jerking her head down and up to dry her
washed hair. Adrienne went upstairs with her. Lily powdered
her armpits and breasts, and chose the silver dress, and sat at
the dressing table mirror, looked happily at her face and dress
and, carefully, with Adrienne standing beside her, watching
her in the mirror, put rouge delicately pink on her cheeks and,
lightly, her eyebrows arching, red lipstick on her lips. Adrienne's heart filled: this was a different girl; a boy in a suit and
tie still looked like a boy; Lily was a young woman, opening a
bottle of perfume, and Adrienne told her to put it on her wrists
and throat, where her pulse beat, and watching her do this,
Adrienne saw, for the first time in these twenty-nine days,
Lily's heart, alive, pumping blood—*My God, Yerby and Frank
could have killed her but didn't and she is here alive with me;
alive; alive;* and she closed her eyes and bent down and
pressed her cheek into Lily's long clean hair, pressed it against
Lily's cheek, and reached with both arms around the chair
and hugged her small waist, then opened her eyes and looked
in the mirror at their pretty faces, at Lily's happy eyes, and
said: "We'll waltz tonight."

They did: After dinner they sat on the sofa and Lily read
aloud chapter twenty-three of *The Adventures of Huckleberry
Finn*, her voice breaking, then tears dropping from her cheeks
as she read: "'Oh, de po little thing! De Lord God Almighty
fogive po' ole Jim, kaze he never gwyne to fogive hisself as
long's he live! Oh, she was plumb deef en dumb, Huck, plumb
deef en dumb—en I'd ben a-treat'n her so!'" and sweet warm
tears came to Adrienne, for the beauty and purity of Lily's
compassion: this wonderful girl they had not broken; she
could be bitter now, long since fled from her own heart and so
from the hearts of all. Adrienne said: "I love you so much."

Lily turned to her, holding the closed book, and said: "You do?"

"Yes."

Lily hugged her, tears on their cheeks blending, and said: "I'm so glad I'm with you. I'm so sorry about your father. And you."

Adrienne stood, still holding Lily, then released her and cranked the gramophone and held Lily's hand and waist and led the waltz, saying, "*One* two three *One* two—" They danced to Chopin, and to J. T. Palmer and C. B. Ward, and to Charles Harris; and Lily, who had never danced, and danced now in a silver dress and new black shoes, moved at first stiffly, shyly; Adrienne told her to close her eyes, and they waltzed in candlelight, and with "After the Ball" the beat entered. Lily, she moved with it, smiling, whispering "*One* two three—"

Now on the porch they sat in cane rocking chairs, looking at the three-quarter moon and the ocean, drinking coffee, Adrienne's black with brandy in it; they lit cigarettes and blew smoke into the air smelling of the sea and coffee and grass and leaves and dew and Lily's perfume. Lily said: "I feel so clean. With my new clothes, and my perfume. I don't remember feeling clean. Probably I won't when I go to bed."

"What do you mean?"

Lily looked away from her, up at the moon.

"I feel dirty every night, till I go to sleep. And when I wake up in the morning."

Adrienne put her cup on the floor, and took Lily's cup and put it down and held Lily's hand, and Lily squeezed, still looking up at the moon.

"Lily. We were raped. We did nothing."

Lily turned to her.

"You don't feel dirty?"

"No. I feel mad."

"Then why won't you watch him hang?"

"Because I want to. He already violated my body and thank God I didn't get pregnant, and thank God that you didn't.

Just my body. I am not going to allow Pete Yerby into my soul.
Or yours."

"But he *is*."

"No. Anybody can hurt your body. Kill it too. But nobody
can hurt your soul unless you let him into it."

"Then why do I feel so *dirty*."

In the moonlight tears came to Lily's eyes, flowed over
her rouged cheeks.

"Good," Adrienne said. "Good. You cry now." She took
Lily's cigarette and went down the steps and stamped both of
them on the ground, went to Lily, and kneeled in front of her,
and Lily rocked into her arms and Adrienne lifted her and
lowered her to the floor, and Lily kneeled, her sweet smelling
cheek tight against Adrienne's, and Adrienne said : "We hate
him and we must not. We want to watch him hang, and we
must not want to." More deeply, shuddering, Lily wept.
"Because, listen, we must get him out of our souls. We're
unscathed, Lily, we're unscathed. I pray for him, Lily. I pray
for him, but it's for me. Only God can take him away; my work
is to try. But I can't do it alone. And it's for me, Lily. And for
you. Tonight when you pray, ask Him to take Yerby and Frank
from your soul. Think of the Lord in the desert with Satan.
Ask for His power. Not for you. His power to cast them out of
you. Ask Him to help you forgive. We can do it, Lily. We are
pure young women who have done *nothing*. And God will
send us men we will love, and we will bear children. We are
sisters, and we are soldiers. My father suffered war, and
endured it, and was kind and merry, and danced with his wife
and daughters. There was sorrow in his eyes too. We could
see it, because we loved him, we *knew* him. It was for what he
had seen, and maybe what he had done because he had to.
Will you try to do all of this, and will you talk to me when you
feel dirty, will you come wake me and tell me?"

Through tears in her mouth, Lily said: "Yes."

They kneeled till Lily's crying ceased, then they lit cigarettes and sat on the top step, the moonlight on Lily's dress.

Their legs and arms touched. Adrienne said: "How do I look when I smoke?"

"It suits you."

"You too."

"Do you like Stephen?"

"He's a very good man."

"But do you like him?"

"Yes."

"Do you think you'll love him?"

"Maybe he won't come back."

"He will. He said he would. He does what he says he'll do."

"Maybe he won't love me."

"He will."

"I might love him."

She gazed at the water and sky and stars and moon, and felt Lily watching her.

"Do you love him now?"

"My heart does. I wait for him. I see him in my mind. I talk to him, in my mind. I tell him about us. I hope he comes."

"He will. If your heart loves him, what else is there?"

"I don't know. Maybe time. I've never been in love. Are you ready to sleep?"

"No. I'm too happy."

"So am I. Have you ever seen anything as beautiful as the ocean? In the sun or rain or at night."

"Sometimes, when I'm happy, I think maybe I'm a lucky girl."

Adrienne looked at her and said: "You are. You're alive. And strong and good and smart, and I won't ever let anything happen to you."

2

Stephen Leness, too, was looking at the moon and stars, smelling the sea, riding toward the lights of Fernando; he was twenty-seven years old, tall and broad; he walked his mare on the empty street, the only lights now from the hotel lobby and the saloon and Judy's room above it. In the saloon, in the peaceful smells of liquor and tobacco smoke, the sounds of relaxed voices and laughter, Adele and Rosemary sat at a table, talking. Men were at other tables and some at the bar, and behind it was J.T., slender with curly brown hair. When he saw Stephen crossing the room he smiled and poured whiskey and smiled again when Stephen took the glass. J.T. said: "I hear you've been busy."

"Having fun with my family. Playing baseball. Drinking this. Eating."

"I hear you were busy before that."

"In Mexico. On a good ranch."

"You did a fine thing, Stephen. Judy's upstairs sick."

"I'll go up."

He paid and finished his whiskey and went upstairs. He had known Judy since they were children; when she was sixteen, she ran away with a medicine man who smoked opium, and soon she did too; in Seattle a man murdered her husband, and Judy had begun to whore; after a while she came home to Los Angeles to visit her family, and told them her husband owned a store in Fernando, and she was going there, to sell clothes, and they believed her. Stephen had paid for her body on the few nights, over the years, when he was in Fernando; it was exciting and strange, being in Judy while images of her as a girl and him as a boy were in his mind; sometimes he was sad, when he was done for the night, falling asleep in her bed. Twenty-eight nights ago he had gone to her, looking for a big blond and bearded man who wore a dagger on his chest; she had told him it was Pete Yerby, and told him where he lived outside Fernando; and the next afternoon, riding from Adrienne's to Los Angeles, he had stopped and asked Judy to send the sheriff to Yerby's house to untie the two men. Now he tapped on her door and softly she said: "I can't."

"It's Stephen."

"Stephen?"

He opened the door, looked at her lying on the bed in a pink gown and blue robe, and stepped in, closed the door, and took off his hat and dropped it on a chair. She said: "I'm sick."

"What is it?"

"I'm trying to quit opium. But going without it makes my stomach sick."

Her face seemed pale, with its freckles; but he had not seen her without rouge and lipstick since before she went to the medicine show and did not go home. He sat on the bed and held her hand and said: "I know of a man in San Diego. He can help you. You stay at his place."

"No. I'm quitting that too."

"It's just for the treatment. He gives you something else, till you're weaned."

"What's he cost?"

"I don't know. A Mexican woman told me about him."

"Was she a whore?"

"Yes."

"And she quit opium?"

"Yes."

She squeezed his hand, and moaned, then breathed deeply. He said: "What happened?"

"We lost Ginger."

"Which one is she?"

"Was. The redhead. She got pregnant and went to the Chinaman to get fixed. She bled to death in her room."

"Damn."

"That Chinaman gets us all, one way or the other."

"Yes, he does."

"I've never been pregnant. Maybe I can't. I've got to get out of this alive. I want to go home."

"I'll take you to San Diego. Can you ride?"

"No. I'll take the train in the morning."

"I'll help you pack, and I'll ride with you."

"The girls will do that. Why are you here?"

"To see you."

"Did you want me?"

"I just came to talk."

"You're going to see that girl, aren't you?"

"She offered me a job."

"The only one in all of California. You love her, Stephen."

"I don't even know her."

"Who knows anybody? You risked your life for her, when she could have sent the sheriff. Then she couldn't shoot Yerby anyway."

"Can I get something for your stomach?"

"That's not why I'm cranky. This is whore talk. I'm not smoking opium and I'm sick and I was thinking about you, and here you come knocking on the door. I was thinking I could go home. I was thinking you could court me. Don't look so sad."

He wished he had not come here; he wished he loved her; he wished he were sitting with Adrienne at her dining room table. Judy said: "It's what whores do. We think. Did you see my family?"

"Yes. I told them you were doing well. Your store too."

"Long as they don't know it's between my legs."

"They don't. Even if they did, you could go home."

"I know." She smiled, and pink tinged her cheeks. "You should have left Frank and Will some bowls of water to lap. They had a lot of water trouble. By the time Zack got there, they'd pissed in their pants. Now they've got no thirteen year old girl to wash their clothes and cook for them."

"They're still there?"

"Course they are. What are you doing?"

"I'm going to burn that house."

"What for?"

"It's evil."

"The house? What about the one you're standing in right now?"

"It's not." He thought of the whore washing the Lord's feet with her tears; or was she a whore? "That one is. It's in the wood."

"You're not a dull man. If I end up here again, will you come see me? If you don't marry that girl? Even if you do."

"You won't. I'm going to see you in San Diego. Let me give you some money for the cure."

"I've got money. And if it runs out, I can always make more. Just give me his name, and where he lives. There's paper on the chest."

"I should go with you."

"Should. You've got enough shoulds in your life."

"I want to go with you."

"You want to set Yerby's house afire, and go see that girl."

"They can wait."

"I know they can. It's you that can't. Besides, you'd be in the way."

"Where?"

"Here. If he's going to start weaning me tomorrow, I'm going to smoke tonight. And in the morning, till time for the train."

He nodded, and with his thumb and fingers stroked her hand. "Then your stomach will be all right."

"Everything will be all right. On your way out, will you send Adele up?"

"Sure."

"It'll be a good night. I feel good about this. I haven't felt good about anything since I stopped smoking. Three days ago. It feels like weeks. See? You gave me that. I don't think I would have made it. Do you really think I can go home?"

"Yes. You'll like it."

"Have you ever known a whore who quit, and got married?"

"I don't know. I may have."

"You wouldn't know if you had. You boys are easy to fool."

"Are you fooling me now about anything?"

"No. I'll smoke with Adele and Rosemary, and in the morning they'll ride with me to San Diego. How long will I be there?"

"I don't know."

"How long was she there?"

"I don't remember."

"Do you remember her name?"

He looked at Judy's eyes, then her forehead, then her light brown hair, waiting for a name to come to him. He said: "No."

"But you remember her body. Her face."

"Yes."

"That's not enough. We don't know where Ginger's family is. Just somewhere in Arizona. And how many men can't remember her name?"

"I'm glad you're going home."

"It looks uphill. But I believe someday I'll be very glad. I might like being with a man again."

"What do you mean?"

"Opium dulls you."

"It does?"

"Yes."

"You didn't like it?"

She smiled. "I like you."

"But you didn't—" He looked at her hand in his.

"I like you, Stephen. Opium eats up other pleasures. What are you going to do? Knock on the door and tell them you've come to burn the house?"

"I'll get them out,"

"Will is harmless. Frank wants to kill you. He has a lot of hate in him. Starting with colored people."

"Good. I'll give him another reason."

"Everybody knows it was you. You could probably be sheriff when Zack retires." She squeezed his hand and touched his cheek. "You be careful, Stephen. Kiss me, then send up my dope."

The house was dark. He walked Sarah uphill to the stand of trees and dismounted and tied the reins around the trunk of a sapling. He took off his spurs and put them in the saddlebag. Everything he owned was with him; in the deerskin bag hanging from the pommel were his clothes and Bible and baseball glove and ball and new gloves and a ball for Adrienne and Lily. He took the shotgun from its scabbard and walked slowly uphill through the trees, toward the house where the one named Frank had taken Lily after the fire killed her parents and brother and sister in their beds, while she crawled then ran. Frank had been her father's friend, and had taken her from the cemetery to Fernando, where in the first week they met Pete Yerby, and moved into his house. Where now there would be another fire, a good one, a cleansing one. Twenty-eight nights ago he had approached with soft and very slow steps through the trees, the house lighted, the three men's voices coming from the kitchen, and in his mind he had seen himself dead on the floor in there. Now, walking quietly in the trees, he was not afraid. They were sleeping; he had only to be silent; they were not even men; they did nothing but drink and live on Yerby's money, inherited when Yerby's father died and Yerby sold his bank and cattle; what could they do against a cowboy blessed with size and muscle, who had fought and beaten white boys when he was a boy, then men, because of looks in their eyes, the tones of their voices, or because they called him the word he wanted to burn too from the earth. Frank and Yerby were the ones who had hurt Lily; she had told him that Will was good to her and, if he had not been drunk from morning till night, he probably would have taken her away. Stephen stepped out of the trees and looked up at the dark windows of the second floor. He watched them as he slowly crossed the open space, his blood quick, as though he were hunting; but there was more, and it filled his soul and body: he was doing something absolutely simple and right and pure, something his dead father, a minister, would have done; something God would do; was doing, with him, through him. He reached the three steps and lightly climbed them and crossed the porch and slowly opened the door; then he stepped inside and stood looking at the walls and chairs and sofa till they were distinct and he could see by the kitchen door the hat rack, with two hats on it. He smelled tobacco smoke, but not fresh, and bacon grease and coffee and the trees behind him in the moonlight.

The stairs were to his left. He moved softly and started to climb, stopping at each step, waiting, looking up at the hall, listening, then lifting a foot. He heard snoring, from his right. He moved up the stairs and, with the shotgun pointed waist high, stood in the hall, and looked at the two open doors he faced, then at the two at his sides; then he crept toward the snoring, through the door, and stood at the bed, looking in the light from the window at Will, smelling whiskey on his breath, and sweat in the clothes on the floor; what a pitiful man this was. On the chest of drawers was the gunbelt; Stephen sidled to it and picked it up and backed out of the room, looking for rifles or shotguns on the walls and in corners, and turned and moved to the next room, his blood quicker now, angry now, and he turned into the room and was standing at the foot of the bed where Frank lay on his side, breathing through his nose, on this bed where he had lain with Lily, the smells of whiskey and sweat here too, and Stephen thought of the other smell, when Lily was here, a smell no man should ever breathe. The gunbelt hung on the bedpost near Frank's head, and Stephen loved walking this close to him, standing nearly within touch of his breath, and lifting the gunbelt and looking around for more guns, seeing only a chest and a chair and clothes and boots on the floor. He backed across the hall into another bedroom, probably Yerby's, the bed unmade, a pillow on the floor. He laid the guns on the bed, his shotgun too, and with both hands picked up the lamp on the bedside table, held it in front of his face, then unscrewed and emptied it on the floor. He picked up his shotgun, struck a match, crouched and lit the spreading oil, and stood, watching fire; he jerked at the bed sheet and dropped its corner in the flames. Then he left, and closed the door and walked quickly to Will's room, not loudly, not quietly either, feeling he was dancing on the balls of his feet. He leaned into Will's snoring and held his shoulder and squeezed, watched his eyes open, and said softly: "Your house is on fire. Get dressed and get the animals out of the barn."

Will was rising naked, his legs swinging to the floor, and Stephen ran to Frank's room hearing the flames now, smelling smoke, and he pressed the muzzles of his shotgun against Frank's cheek and shouted: "Your house is burning!" Frank opened his eyes and said: "You."

"Me. With fire. Get up."

Stephen stepped backward; Frank looked at the door, at the sound and smell of fire, sat up, looked at the shotgun, and stood naked. Firelight came into the room, and shadows moved, and Stephen backed into the hall; the closed door and walls were burning. He trotted to the stairs and down and across the living room and the porch to the grass; Will stood, looking at the house, his mouth open as it was when he slept; Stephen stopped beside him and watched flames on the window and walls, and said: "Get the animals out."

"It's two horses."

"Saddle them." He looked at Will. "Go."

Will trotted toward the barn, looking back at the fire, and Frank came running in pants and shirt and hat, holding his boots, then sat on the grass ten paces from Stephen and took his socks from his boots and pulled them and the boots on, watching Stephen; then he stood and turned to look at the burning house. Stephen laid his shotgun on the ground, took off his gunbelt and lowered it too. Frank was as tall as he was, but not as broad and deep; it would not take long; Sarah needed him; she was afraid down there. He said: "Turn around and protect yourself."

Frank turned, his eyes moving from Stephen's empty hands to the guns. Stephen said: "All you have to do is knock me down long enough."

"You're crazy."

"You should have gone to Fernando for your pleasures." But then he saw Judy lying sick in her gown and robe; and, before that, in a purple dress and rouge and lipstick, laughing and flirting and drinking, and pretending to enjoy him in her bed, moving with him, and gasping, and moaning praise. "You shouldn't have had any pleasures at all. You're not worthy of a woman. You're not a man. You're white and healthy, and look at you. Lily's Daddy would have killed you. I'm only going to hurt you."

In the light of the flames and the moonlit sky Stephen could see remorse, a fleeting wet light in Frank's eyes, a slackening of his lips; then anger darkened his eyes and tightened his jaw. Stephen looked up at fire curling over the eave, and moved toward Frank, smelling the whiskey and sweat, and the lovely smell of burning wood; he said: "So sometimes you know."

"Know what?"

It was in Frank's voice; soon he would fight; or try to.

"Sometimes you know you did evil things with Lily. So there's something in you. Maybe you'll be saved."

"I didn't know God was a — where's Will?"

"Getting the horses. Say it."

"Say what?"

"What you didn't know God was."

"You're lucky you came while I was sleeping."

"Say it."

"*Will.*"

"Say it." With his left hand, Stephen slapped his cheek. "Fight the nigger. Get the shotgun and kill him."

He did not see the fist coming from below Frank's waist; it struck his chin; he saw the left fist coming, and ducked, and it hit above his right eye, and twice quickly he jabbed Frank's mouth, cut the lips, Frank backing with his fists raised, and Stephen swung his right between the hands to the nose, and blood flowed from it; with his left he hit the jaw. Frank stepped backward twice, then fell, sat up, wiped blood and looked at it on his palm, started to rise, then dived at Stephen's legs, squeezing and trying to turn them, and Stephen gripped his collar and pulled him up, Frank punching Stephen's legs and missing his testicles, hitting his stomach and chest, and when he was standing, Stephen hit him in the diaphragm, released his collar and watched him bend and try to breathe.

Then holding Frank's right shoulder and pulling him straight, he swung his right arm behind him, his eyes on Frank's chin where blood dripped from his still breathless mouth and nose; when his arm was extended he started its arc, his body turning with it, and in the hot light of the fire he saw his fist hit the chin, the head jerking backward, and he let go of Frank's shoulder, let him fall. His eyes were open; Stephen knew they saw nothing but pain and wanting to breathe; they could not see beyond those to revenge or hatred, or regret. He walked to his guns, put on the belt, and picked up the shotgun. Frank lay on his back, breathing now.

Stephen ran to the barn, passing Will running between two screaming unsaddled horses, their eyes wide and white, Will holding the reins, pulling down on them. Stephen knew that Sarah's fear had begun when she first smelled smoke; now she could see the fire; she would be trembling, pulling back at the reins; if he had not tied her, she would have run down the hill, whatever distance she needed, then waited for him. In the barn he saw the blankets and saddles on the ground, thought of Will trying to saddle two terrified horses and, leaving his shotgun, lifted the blankets and saddles to his shoulders and trotted to the front of the house where Frank and Will held the rearing horses. He dropped the saddles and blankets and ran into the barn, picked up his shotgun, and ran out; Frank and Will each carried a saddle and held the reins of a horse, going away from the house, down the hill. He ran past them, hearing Sarah now, ran beside the trees, then he was with her; she was pulling at the reins, and screaming. He shoved the shotgun into its scabbard, untied her and mounted, and she stopped screaming. She was quivering, and trying to turn downhill, but he held her there, stroking her neck, leaning to her ear, whispering her name, and watched Frank and Will and the horses run by. Then he rode out, stroking Sarah, and watched them till they reached the bottom of the hill and slowed the horses and stopped them and began saddling. He took his spurs from the saddle bag and, leaning down, put them on.

He turned Sarah toward the house. There was fire in

front of it now, on the ground; the grass was dry; the barn would burn too; the trees; everything. He turned Sarah downhill, holding her to a walk so she would not hurt herself.

This time he slept, among trees on a ridge. When the first sunlight woke him, he was covered with the blanket he had pulled over himself in his sleep. He was under an oak tree, Sarah standing, sleeping, beside him. In the shade of pines, a hundred feet away, he saw a cottontail rabbit; quietly he stood in his socks and drew the shotgun from the scabbard, softly opened the breech and removed the two buckshot shells, put them in the saddlebag and, watching the motionless rabbit, found the birdshot, glancing at them, then slid them into the chambers and eased the breech shut. He touched Sarah's muzzle and she opened her eyes; as he lifted the gun, the rabbit bolted, to the left then right, and as it turned left again Stephen fired and it tumbled forward and was still. He walked under the pines, into the sun, and held the warm rabbit, looked at its open eyes; he was both excited and sad, as he always was when he killed game. He pulled off its skin and, with his pocket knife, gutted it, then cut a small pine branch and whittled a point. He put on his boots and started a fire, then facing the sun rising over ridges and trees, he lowered his trousers and squatted and evacuated; he wiped himself with leaves and rubbed his hands in dirt and washed them with water from his canteen. He made coffee and roasted the rabbit and, while he ate, he read a chapter from *The Gospel of Mark*, beginning with the sermon on the mount. He had given his tunic often enough, and the second mile, but had never turned his other cheek. Maybe someday.

Then he rolled his blanket and saddled Sarah and mounted; he would work with Adrienne and Lily today and tomorrow and Saturday and on Sunday he would go to San Diego and see Judy. He rode south, his heart there now, his mind too, with Adrienne on her porch, at her table, and with Lily. He rode down the west slope of the ridge, onto flat and grassy land with low brush, rabbits running and a slow hawk low in the sky, and kicked Sarah to a trot, breathed the smells of grass and sea and Sarah in the air cooling his face. When she began to sweat, he slowed her, and his body moved with hers as she walked toward the remaining weeks of summer, the good work in the sun and, in the evenings, Stephen and Adrienne and Lily dancing; toward the first kiss in the fall; then all the kisses and embraces while Lily slept; the autumn nights of unslaked and joyful passion and peaceful sleep in their separate, adjacent rooms, Stephen in her father's bed; then early sunlit winter, and the December day of the wedding, his family, and Judy with hers, and Adrienne's Mexican friends filling the house, singing and cooking and laughing; in early evening they left, in buggies with children and mothers and Judy, the men on horseback; they would sleep in Fernando on their way to Los Angeles; the Mexican family mounted horses, two boys and three girls on ponies, and rode to their farm two miles south.

Then he and Adrienne and Lily went to the porch and Lily pulled the three rocking chairs close to one another, and sat in the middle. Stephen looked at their land going down to the sea. He felt that he had lived a long time, a cowboy for eleven years, and he remembered the names and faces of men and women he would probably never see again, cowboys and cooks and ranchers in Mexico and Arizona and California, cattle buyers, blacksmiths, men in saloons and whores there too, and as these faces accumulated they seemed to be not only people but time: many years of it, over now; yet here he was, still young, seasoned, ready. He watched Adrienne and Lily smoking, and lit a cigar. He was calm. Passion could wait. Everything could. The night air was cool, moving out to sea.

They spoke little; Lily took his hand and Adrienne's, and gently they rocked. He told them he was happy about his family loving them, and about Judy, and the Mexicans bringing guitars and singing. They sat for a long time, mostly silent, till Lily yawned twice and rose and hugged and kissed them goodnight. He listened to her go upstairs and close her door, and Adrienne moved to Lily's chair and held his hand. He was mute, looking at the moon and stars and sea, warm blood of passion flowing downward now, in the way he had remarked it in autumn when he first kissed her; till then he had only made love with whores, or women he thought of as whores; now in his heat, and quickness of breath and heart, he felt certainty; he could not say it with words; he felt that he and Adrienne and the stars and sky and moon and earth and sea and somehow all people were one; and that one day he or Adrienne would not be: one of them would die. But his sorrow at that was strange, was lovely, and his soul filled him, pushed against his breast and skull, as though reaching for the sea and sky. He could not look at her. Then she released his hand and rose, and he did, and walked behind her into the house, watching her blowing out candles and lamps, then ascending the dark stairs. He climbed, gazing at her long black hair moving on her white dress and, for the first time, followed her into her room and closed the door and in the dark she lit one candle on her dressing table and turned to face him.

EDITOR'S NOTE

Joshua Bodwell

THERE IS PERHAPS no greater double-edged compliment in literature than the phrase "writer's writer." It is at once both high praise and an intimation of authorial obscurity. The phrase inevitably brings to mind writers of undeniable skill and power whose work has not easily or effortlessly found a large readership.

Andre Dubus was a writer's writer. His short stories and novellas have for decades been discussed regularly and reverently among other writers as exemplars of the forms. He was a master of narrative compression, a writer of unyielding compassion, and like his literary mentor Anton Chekhov, an author of far-reaching empathy. And like Chekhov, Dubus deserves to be discovered by generation after generation of new readers.

It was with all this and more in mind that I proposed this project to gather together the vast majority of Andre Dubus's short stories and novellas into three volumes with new introductions by some of those writers who most admire his work.

This volume brings together Andre Dubus's *Voices from the Moon*—his longest, most masterful novella—and *The Last Worthless Evening*—his fifth collection of short stories and novellas—with previously uncollected stories and a heart-rending new introduction by Tobias Wolff.

THE TITLE OF VOLUME THREE

We faced a unique challenge when it came time to title the books in this three-volume project: it was awkward and inelegant to simply merge the titles of two different books (such as *Voices from the Moon & The Last Worthless Evening: Collected Short Stories & Novellas, Volume 3*), yet Dubus was not alive to offer new titles.

My challenge then was to find more elegant titles while staying true to Dubus's voice. The solution arrived when I realized Dubus had, over the years, toyed with naming collections after different stories within a collection before settling on an eventual title. Scanning the table of contents for volume three, I knew we had myriad title options for the book, and they were all Dubus's very own words.

The title of the previously uncollected Dubus story "The Cross Country Runner" proved perfect for this volume. Dubus had been a lifelong runner until the tragic auto accident at age 50 that left him wheelchair-bound for the rest of his life, and this early story (first published in 1966) is run through with topics and themes Dubus would return to repeatedly during his writing life—the Marines, domestic miscommunication and strife, and navigating the complexities of Catholicism and contraception in the 1960s. Finally, I loved, too, the echo of the title with that of Alan Sillitoe's *The Loneliness of the Long-Distance Runner*, a book, coincidentally, Dubus's character Hank Allison is reading in his masterful "We Don't Live Here Anymore," the first novella in his debut collection, *Separate Flights*.

THE SHORT STORIES & NOVELLAS OF VOLUME THREE

Dubus spent a considerable amount of time contemplating the sequence of the stories in his collections. "The arrangement is important to the reading, and I do take the trouble," he told interviewer Thomas Kennedy. "I learned that from Richard Yates and assume that all short story writers take the trouble. Therefore, when I buy a book of stories, I read them in order." With this in mind, we have honored and retained Dubus's story sequencing here.

Voices from the Moon was first published in 1984. It is his longest novella and arguably his masterpiece. Articles about Dubus, biographical notes, and essays have been muddled over the years as to whether *Voices from the Moon* is "A Novel" or "A Novella." To be clear, calling *Voices from the Moon* "A Novel" rather than "A Novella" was a marketing not artistic decision.

"...Dubus can't be blamed for that curiosity," wrote former Godine editor William B. Goodman in his essay "An Editor's Salute" from the anthology *Andre Dubus: Tributes* (Xavier Review Press, 2001) "I had the book cast off in a format that got it to 126 numbered pages, enough to allow a small book that could be practically list priced and—may Chekhov forgive me!—got Dubus to let the front of the jacket say "A Novel by Andre Dubus." That small travesty did not tarnish the tale itself."

In a 1988 interview with Jennifer Levasseur and Kevin Rabalais for *Glimmer Train*, Dubus confirmed he had been given final approval on the decision to call it a novel, but didn't want to engage in the argument, as it appeared evident that "A Novel" was preferable for marketing purposes. Years later, it was Goodman who helped edit *The Selected Stories of Andre Dubus*, and said (according to Dubus) he wanted to put *Voices from the Moon* right in the middle of the anthology.

Dubus's initial inspiration for *Voices from the Moon*—the idea of a father marrying a woman his son had recently

divorced—came from an article he read in the *Boston Globe*.
Years later, Andre Dubus III would find the inspiration for his
breakout novel *House of Sand and Fog*—the story of a woman
whose home is taken by the city because of a clerical error—in
the pages of the same newspaper.

While many writers have written deeply about the
American family, few have written as well as Dubus from
every point of view *within* the American family. He inhabited
his stories not only in the voices of sons and fathers ("If They
Knew Yvonne" and "A Father's Story"), but in those of mothers
and daughters, too ("Leslie in California" and "In My Life").
In *Voices From the Moon*, Dubus—like William Faulkner in *As
I Lay Dying*—uses all of these voices, examining the story's
central conflict from multiple perspectives.

"One of *Voices from the Moon's* theological implications is
that, in seeking relief from solitude we sin and fall inevitably
into pain," wrote John Updike in his admiring *New Yorker*
review of the novella. The observation could, of course, be
attributed to any number of Dubus's stories. In a 1993 interview
with Lori Ambacher, Dubus said he agreed with Updike's
reading, though he certainly hadn't set out with the intent to
make such a direct, moral statement.

One of Dubus's most-quoted lines comes near the end of
Voices from the Moon: "We don't have to live great lives; we've
just to understand and survive the ones we've got." Dubus
said he was surprised by how many critics latched onto the
line as though it were a summary statement of the novella.
"I wouldn't take it as gospel," he said. "That line got quoted in
a lot of reviews of that book, and it puzzled me. It made me
wonder if the reviewers were trying to live great lives as hard
as they should be because it is spoken by a woman who has
given up."

Just two years after *Voices from the Moon*, Dubus's *The
Last Worthless Evening* appeared in 1986. It would be his last
collection of new stories published by Godine; the house
released his *Selected Stories* in 1988. The *New York Times*
summed up the collection this way: "Mr. Dubus's talent lies in

his love and sympathy for people—petty criminals, baseball players, single mothers, drunks and addicts—who get their hands dirty with life."

The collection opens with "Deaths at Sea." First published in *Quarterly West* issue No. 22 in 1986, the story about Naval officers and residual racism in the 1960s carries echoes of Dubus's only novel, *The Lieutenant.* For a southern-born writer whose work is at least associated with that region, if not as much as it is with hardscrabble New England mill towns, Dubus wrote very little on the topic of racism. When asked about this in a 1988 *Glimmer Train* interview, he said, "There should be more.... In the sixties and seventies, I shied away from writing about this topic because of the turmoil in our country." Interestingly, the last two stories Dubus published in his lifetime—the Western-themed "Riding North" and its sequel "Sisters"—were his first to feature a main character who is black.

"After the Game" first appeared in the now-defunct *Fiction Network* magazine in 1983, and later appeared in the Scott Walker-edited *Graywolf Annual: Short Stories* in 1985. The story continues the tale of "The Pitcher," from Dubus's third collection, *Finding a Girl in America.* In this story, the pitcher has become a major-leaguer.

"Dressed Like Summer Leaves" appeared in 1986 on the pages of longtime Dubus supporter, *The Sewanee Review.* The lyric title eschews the story's core of explosive violence.

"Land Where My Fathers Died" appeared in *Antaeus*—the literary journal that beget Daniel Halpern's Ecco Press—in the autumn of 1984, and was later collected in *The Best Short Fiction for 1985: The Editor's Choice: New American Stories, Volume 2,* edited by George E. Murphy, Jr.

While the story's form is an homage to the detective story genre—a sort of Raymond Chandler-meets-James Crumley—it's rife with Dubusian touches, such as the effect of the male-gaze and a passionate defense of the victimized. "So the only thing new, I think, is the detective story structure," Dubus told Patrick Samway in a 1986 interview for the *Xavier Review.*

The story does, however, also contain (in one short section) a rare moment of Dubus writing in the first-person voice of a female character; he also sustained this point-of-view in the short stories "In My Life" in *Separate Flights* and "Leslie in California" in *The Time Are Never So Bad*.

In 1984, publisher Stuart Wright released a standalone limited edition of "Land Where My Fathers Died" under his imprint Palaemon Press in Winston Salem, North Carolina. The 37-page hardcover was letterpress printed, bound in full-cloth with a printed-paper spine label, and the entire edition of 200 copies—of which 26 were lettered A-Z and 174 were unnumbered—were signed by Dubus. Two more fine press publishers approached Dubus in the 1980s to release limited editions of his stories: Kevin Rita of Raven Editions published "Blessings" in 1987, and Tom Tolnay of Birch Brook Press published "Leslie in California," in 1989.

"Molly" first appeared in *Crazyhorse* in the spring of 1986. Dubus told an interviewer in 1993 that the story came to him after seeing a group of fourteen-year-old girls on a park bench, smoking, all wearing excessive make-up in an attempt to look older. "I usually judge the success of a story by how hard I had to work on it," he told Patrick Samway in a 1986 interview for the *Xavier Review*. "Using that criteria, I would suggest "Adultery" and "Molly," because they took so much out of me that I didn't know I had."

"Rose," the collection's final story, first appeared in Emerson College's *Ploughshares* in 1985. The story was then selected for the Bill Henderson-edited *The Pushcart Prize, XI: Best of the Small Presses in 1986*; in the same volume were Richard Ford's "Communist" and Tobias Wolff's "Leviathan," work by two authors often associated with Dubus.

"I write a story to understand my concerns," Dubus told Amy Schildhouse in 1986 *Indiana Review* essay "Our Dinners with Andre." "In the novella "Rose," I wanted to understand child abuse."

THE UNCOLLECTED DUBUS

By the 1990s, Andre Dubus was contending with mounting medical bills. In need of additional income, Dubus finally considered something he'd refused for years: contracting with a major New York publisher for his next book. With Godine's blessing and support, Dubus's final collection of short stories, *Dancing After Hours*, was published by Alfred A. Knopf.

Dancing After Hours turned out to be Dubus's final collection of fiction. Somewhat surprisingly, while the book was published in 1996, it opens with "The Intruder," the first story Dubus ever published. He wrote the story in 1961 while still serving in the Marine Corps and before he'd attended the Iowa Writers' Workshop. *The Sewanee Review* published the story in 1963, marking the beginning of a long association with Dubus.

With the idea that Dubus was not, as some authors are, "ashamed" of his early stories—his *juvenilia*, if you will—I began researching how many early and uncollected Dubus stories existed. The scholarship of Robert E. Skinner—the longtime University Librarian at Xavier University of Louisiana—was a huge help along the way. I began to gather both the very first stories Dubus published, and the very last. Andre Dubus III confirmed that there were no other finished but unpublished stories at the time of his father's death.

Many of the journals that published Dubus in the 1960s, such as the *Midwestern University Quarterly*, are long defunct. In some cases, thanks to arduous searches and advice from rare book dealer friends such as Don Lindgren, I was able to acquire actual copies of the original Dubus publications. In cases when finding a hardcopy for sale proved impossible, I depended on the prowess of university librarians to supply me with scans of the stories from their reference copies of the journals, and I am grateful for their patience and help.

Two stories included here in the uncollected section— "They Now Live in Texas" and "The Curse"—did not appear in regular, original Dubus collections, but were gathered into his *Selected Stories*.

Without Dubus to consult with—a loss I have felt more keenly and more deeply the longer I've worked on these three volumes—I have simply arranged the uncollected stories chronologically by publication date; as was often the case with Dubus's work, publication date may wildly differ from the date of composition—in other words, it's difficult, if not impossible, to know in what order Dubus first wrote these stories.

"The Cross Country Runner" appeared in the *Midwestern University Quarterly* 1 No. 4 in 1966. The Wichita Falls, Texas-based publication then published "Love Is the Sky" in *Midwestern University Quarterly* 2 No. 2 in 1966.

"The Blackberry Patch" appeared in the anthology *Southern Writing in the Sixties: Fiction*, edited by John William Corrington and Miller Williams, and published by Louisiana State University Press in 1966. Interestingly, during this time period, Corrington was an early supporter of and regular correspondent with Charles Bukowski; Williams, a poet, read at President Bill Clinton's second inauguration, and is the father of singer-songwriter Lucinda Williams.

"The Blackberry Patch" was reprinted in *Stories of the Modern South*, edited by Benjamin Forkner and Patrick Samway, and published by Bantam in 1978. When this collection was revised and reprinted by Penguin in 1981, Dubus's story "The Blackberry Patch" was replaced with "Over the Hill" from his collection *Separate Flights*.

"Madeline Sheppard" appeared in the *Midwestern University Quarterly* 2 No. 4 in 1967, the last of his run of stories in the small journal in the course of just a few years. Many readers and critics have noted the tonal and stylistic links between Dubus's stories and the work of Ernest Hemingway. While Anton Chekhov unquestionably became Dubus's literary guide, there's no denying Hemingway's obvious influence, too, especially here in these early stories. In "Madeline Sheppard," Dubus pays blatant homage to Hemingway when a character makes reference to *The Sun Also Rises* right on page one. Later, there is playful banter between lovers referencing Madrid and bullfights, and the story's final movement is page after page of clipped dialogue that was likely an intentional nod to Papa. Years later, Dubus would have his recurring character Hank Allison make a casual reference to *A Farewell to Arms* to explain how he's feeling in the novella "Finding A Girl in America."

"They Now Live in Texas" was first published in the *Indiana Review* 10 No. 1/2 in 1987, along with Amy Schildhouse's long essay "Our Dinners with Andre." The story later appeared in Dubus's *Selected Stories*.

"The Curse" appeared in the January 1988 edition of *Playboy*, one of several Dubus stories selected by the magazine's acclaimed longtime fiction editor, Alice K. Turner. The story later appeared in Dubus's *Selected Stories*.

"Riding North" was published in *Oxford Magazine* 12 in 1998. Joseph Squance, who serves as the faculty adviser for the Miami University of Ohio publication, was generous enough to scan from the only copy of the issue he could find.

The vignette "Corporal Lewis" first appeared in *Epoch* 48 No. 3 in 1999. The piece opens the issue, which was published shortly after Dubus passed away.

In the March/April 1999 issue of *Book* Magazine, editor Jerome V. Kramer wrote a dual profile of Dubus and Andre Dubus III. During the interview for the profile at Dubus's home in Haverhill, Massachusetts, Dubus mentioned a story he just completed: "Sisters." While *Book* was known for its author profiles, book reviews, and reporting on the publishing industry, not publishing fiction, two days before Dubus's sudden death on February 24, 1999, he mailed the story to Kramer.

"Sisters" appeared in the May/June 1999 issue of *Book* Magazine, with the dedication to Dubus's first wife: "For Pat, still steering." It would be the last story Dubus completed in his life. A note from Kramer gives the story context. He writes: "The story is unedited; while there are questions an editor could have raised to its author, there was, in this case, no one to answer them. That was very much the editor's loss."

"Riding North" and "Sisters" led to a friendly, teasing debate between Dubus and his sons Andre and Jeb, both of whom were skilled carpenters. The Dubus boys told their father he'd have to do a re-write of a particular scene because one man could not build a coffin by hand and dig a grave in the length of a single afternoon. Dubus chuckled and challenged his boys to prove him wrong.

On the winter evening of Dubus's death, Andre and Jeb met in their woodshop and began to build a simple pine coffin lined with satin sheets for their father. Even with electric tools, the pair worked through the night and into the morning. Digging a grave wasn't even an option as the February freeze made the New England graveyard ground impenetrable. Dubus was eventually laid to rest—in a hole dug by his boys—on April 13, 1999, opening day at the author's beloved Fenway Park in Boston.

EDITOR'S ACKNOWLEDGMENTS

In 2007, Kevin Larimer at *Poets & Writers Magazine* accepted my pitch to write a long piece entitled "The Art of Reading Andre Dubus: We Don't Have to Live Great Lives." Kevin was, as he always is, a patient, shrewd, and thoughtful editor of that piece. The joys of writing that article became the seed of this three-volume project, and for that I will be eternally grateful to the encouragement of Kevin and *Poets & Writers Magazine.*

At David R. Godine, Publisher, the talented team of Michael Babcock, Kim Courchesne, Ally Findley, and Sue Ramin were tirelessly dedicated to this series; as was the calm, insightful George Gibson, for which I am grateful.

Greta Rybus not only made the photographs for the covers of all three new volumes of this project, but went above and beyond, reading and re-reading Dubus's story, and offering thoughtful, caring, and deeply felt creative ideas about how the photographs might speak in conversation with

Dubus's complex stories. We should all be so lucky to have the opportunity to work with collaborators as gifted and generous as Greta.

Tobias Wolff is a master of the American short story in his own right. I have read and re-read his gripping stories just as I have read Dubus's over the years: for instruction. A military veteran himself and a Catholic, Wolff's stories confront morality without judgment...*who* could be better to introduce this third volume? It's an honor to have Wolff's memories of Dubus here and I'm grateful for Toby's contribution.

Personally, my dear friends Steve Abbott, Steve Kelly, and Michael Tarabilda patiently listened to me verbally process this project for months and months. They buoyed my spirits and celebrated this project's every small success, and I'm eternally grateful. At home, the love and support of my partner Tammy and my daughter Elona while I obsessed over this series and stressed over the details, continues to make me want to be what I believe Andre wanted to be: *a better man.*

Finally, the last two people to thank are the first two people I reached out to when I conceived of this project: Andre Dubus III and David R. Godine.

David first published Andre Dubus's short stories and novellas more than four decades ago, and for that reason alone, this book simply would not exist if not for his unflagging support of Dubus's work. After every turn, David's enthusiasm and considerable knowledge was invaluable.

Andre III's generosity and big-hearted embrace of this project girded my confidence to proceed. He quickly invited his sister Suzanne Dubus into the process, and both became steady sources of ideas and support. In a world that sometimes seems stymied by a dearth of good men, Andre is one of the very best men I know. *Thank you, brother.*

AUTHOR'S BIOGRAPHY

ANDRE DUBUS (August 11, 1936–February 24, 1999; pronounced da-byüs) was born in Lake Charles, Louisiana to a Cajun-Irish family and educated in Catholic schools. After peacetime service in the U.S. Marine Corps, Dubus attended the University of Iowa Writers' Workshop, where he earned his MFA in 1965. In 1966, he moved north, settling in Haverhill, Massachusetts to teach literature and creative writing at Bradford College until his retirement.

Dubus's short stories and novellas appeared in distinguished literary journals such as *Ploughshares, The Paris Review, The Sewanee Review*, and *The Southern Review*, as well as national magazines such as *Harper's, The New Yorker*, and *Playboy*. In addition to his many short story collections, he published two collections of essays: *Broken Vessels* and *Meditations from a Movable Chair*. The award-winning films *In the Bedroom* and *We Don't Live Here Anymore* were adapted from his stories.

His prose earned him a MacArthur "Genius" Award, the PEN/Malamud Award for Excellence in the Short Story, the Rea Award for the Short Story, the Jean Stein Award from the American Academy of Arts and Letters, and nominations for a National Book Critics Circle Award and Pulitzer Prize.

Andre Dubus published just one novel during his career: *The Lieutenant* (Dial Press, 1967). After falling under the spell of Anton Chekhov, Dubus would consciously devote himself to the short story and novella for the rest of his life. While his stories were revered when they appeared in literary journals and magazines, after the publication of his novel, Dubus received rejection after rejection when it came to publishing a collection of his stories.

Literary agent Philip G. Spitzer became one of Dubus's earliest and most loyal supporters. During a casual lunch in New York City, Spitzer handed David R. Godine a plain manila envelope with the manuscript for *Separate Flights*. Godine called Spitzer the next day and offered to publish the collection. In the end, Dubus waited seven rejection-filled years between the publication of novel and his first short story collection.

In a 1998 interview with *Glimmer Train*, Dubus recalled "The rejections that really hurt during that period after I published *The Lieutenant* were not the rejections slips that said 'I don't like the collection of stories,' but the ones that said, 'We'll publish this collection of stories if you write a novel.' That hurt. I thought I was being told to be somebody else."

Neither Spitzer nor Godine insisted Dubus write a novel but instead supported his devotion to the short story. Godine quickly realized "there was more punch contained in one Dubus short story than in 99.98% of all the novels being published. I still feel that way."

"I'm one of the luckiest short story writers in America because of Godine," Dubus told the *Black Warrior Review* in 1983. "How many publishers would publish four collections of stories by a writer, without *one* novel?" Indeed, the closest Godine ever came to publishing a novel by Dubus was issuing the long novella *Voices from the Moon* as a gorgeously designed standalone book in 1984; the novella appears in full in volume three of this project, *The Cross Country Runner*.

Dubus's devotion to the short story form—the novella bears a much closer relation to a long short story than a short novel—fit him not simply as a prose form, but from a philosophical stance. "I love short stories because I believe they are the way we live," he once wrote. "They are what our friends tell us, in their pain and joy, their passion and rage, their yearning and their cry against injustice."

In 1986, while attempting to aid two motorists on a highway in Massachusetts, Dubus was struck by an oncoming car traveling nearly sixty miles an hour. Dubus stopped at what he thought was a car broken down in the travel lane. The car, it turned out, had become wedged on a motorcycle abandoned in the middle of the highway. As Dubus helped the two motorists—Luis and Luz Santiago, a brother and sister from Puerto Rico—to safety, another car approached. Dubus pushed Luz out of the way. Luis, a young man of only twenty-three, was hit and killed instantly. Dubus was struck, thrown over the car's hood and landed in a crumpled, bleeding mass; a quarter found in Dubus's pocket after the accident had been bent in half by the impact.

While it's startling that Dubus somehow managed to even survive the blow, the accident left him with thirty-four broken bones. He lost his left leg below the knee and his right leg was crushed to the point of uselessness. He would be confined to a wheelchair for the rest of his. After the accident, Dubus was unable to write for some time. He eventually found his way back to writing fiction, in part, by writing a series of powerful essays. In need of money for medical and living expenses, Dubus finally—with the blessing of his longtime publisher, David Godine—accepted an offer from a large New York City publisher. A full decade after Dubus's accident, *Dancing After Hours* appeared in 1996, published by Alfred A. Knopf, and went on to be named a finalist for a National Book Critics Circle Award; the fourteen stories in that collection are his only stories not included in this three volume collection.

On February 24, 1999, at the age of sixty-two, Dubus suffered a fatal heart attack. He was laid to rest in Haverhill, Massachusetts in a simple casket handmade by his sons.

A NOTE ON THE TYPE

THE CROSS COUNTRY RUNNER *has been set in Jonathan Hoefler's Mercury types. Originally created for the New Times newspaper chain and later adapted for general informational typography, the Mercury types were drawn in four grades intended to be used under variable printing conditions—that is, to compensate for less-than-optimal presswork or for regional differences in paper stock and plant conditions. The result was a family of types that were optimized to print well in a vast number of sizes and formats. In books, Mercury makes a no-nonsense impression, crisp and open, direct and highly readable, yet possessed of real style and personality. ♦ ♦ ♦ The display type is Quadraat Sans, a family originally designed in 1996 by Fred Smeijers for FontFont, and subsequently enlarged and expanded into a much larger constellation of types.*